DESOLATION ISLAND

I0630632

Terry L. Vinson

DESOLATION ISLAND

DOUBLE DRAGON

CHAPTER ONE

Desolation Outlaw

The shot glasses smacked the oak bar at precisely the same moment, the retort of which echoed like a shotgun blast within the deafening silence of the otherwise deserted structure.

"Nothin' like a Southern Comfort burn to ignite the soul, am I right, partner?" the larger of the two men asked, his grotesquely oversized hand cupping the shot glass like a child's marble, its contents completely hidden within his massive palm.

The smaller man grinned through a dark crimson cowl, his meticulously toned physique perfectly defined through maroon-shaded tights.

"I'm not the elbow bender I was in our day, Force. Whoops...sorry, I mean, *Desolation Outlaw*. I'm gonna have a hard time calling you anything but Force, Benjamin. *Force* of habit, you might say," he replied with a sly grin, reaching up to push the cowl from his face.

Bending forward, the larger man studied the other for a moment while leaning onto forearms as large as a normal man's thighs.

"Ya don't look too worse for wear, Condor. We've both added a few wrinkles, not to mention scars, over the past.... damn, how long *has* it been, Ray?"

"At least four years, Ben," the Crimson Condor replied, "Haven't laid eyes on your ugly mug since Baton Rouge back in two-thousand...one...or maybe two."

"Baton Rouge. Got'cha...," he agreed with a

nod, reaching over to refill their shot glasses to the brim's edge," ...helluva brawl, as I recall. Lost a tooth to *Slayer's* left hook. Damn thing is probably still lodged in his knuckle. You broke an arm that day, didn't ya? Or was it a leg?"

"Right arm just below the elbow. Tried to glide beneath *Stingray's* electro-cane and never saw *The Brute* coming. Big bastard straight-armed me right through the wall of that bank building. I had migraines for six months afterwards. Closest I ever came to permanent retirement, Force...uh... Ben." Both men paused, then traded winks before downing the shots in twin blurs of frenzied motion. Again, the room filled with the thumping echo of glass against oak.

"I remember droppin' ya off at Doc Wilkes office that evenin', Ray. Grumpy old bastard. The government was payin' him quite a wad to bandage up hero-types. Never could figure out his rabid Doberman personality."

Wiping his mouth with a gloved hand, the Crimson Condor then laughed aloud, glaring at the mostly empty whiskey bottle as if it were a crystal ball.

"He was an ornery SOB, all right. I'll say this, he was an equal-opportunity jackass. Treated everybody like crap, from what I saw. Ben, you'll never guess who I spent some rehab time with at Doc Wilkes' place."

Shrugging his massive shoulders through a snug-fitting black muscle

T-shirt, Ben then pushed away from the bar and stood, various popping noises filling the air as he stretched his colossal frame.

"Old Flag-Face himself, *Captain A. The Red Skull's* cronies had messed him up pretty good. Cracked ribs, concussion; the works."

Now standing behind the waist-high bar, Ben pulled a fresh bottle of Jim Beam Gold from a dust-coated cardboard box and blew a wad of cobwebs free from the cap.

"Hoo-boy, spendin' time with true royalty there, Ray. Livin' legend material. So what was Mister Patriot like up close an' personal? Real ego-maniacal a-hole, I'll bet..."

"Believe it not, Ben, the man was as down to earth as you could imagine. At least, for a guy who's done and seen the things he has through the years. Quiet and reserved, but a real professional in every sense. Least, that's the impression I got."

Ben broke the seal and proceeded to pour two more shots.

"Cap's *old* school, Ray, like us. He's waded into hell and back a few dozen times, no doubt. Only brush with hero greatness I had was a year or two 'fore I hooked up with the *Revenge Squad.*"

As before, they each slammed down the shot and displayed similar grimaces.

"Who was that, Ben?"

"Met up with the *West Coast Avengers* in Phoenix. I was trailin' *The Lost Souls* gang for the CIA at the time, searchin' for stolen payroll money and a kidnapped heiress. Ran into Hawkeye, Vision and the Scarlet Witch smack dab on Main Street, brawling with some radioactive mutie with a head the size of a Mack truck. Got in a few decent swings 'fore he dumped a nearby building on top of our heads. Vision saved our ass with some kinda force-

7

field. Weird dude, that one. Not exactly what you'd call a conversationalist. Ol' Hawkeye was a real hoot, though, and the Witch was drop-dead fine. I've rarely seen spandex stretched over anything so tantalizin', 'cept maybe for *Marvella* a'course."

The Condor laughed heartily as Ben poured them still another refill.

"Hey, I'd heard you and Leah, um, Marvella were an item a few years back. What's up with that, Benji? Never thought of you as the 'steady girl' kinda guy, not unless you've transformed dramatically since our days of running together."

Ben scanned the Jim Beam label as he replied, although his mind's eye was instantly transported to a faraway place and time.

"Ah, Leah. Have to admit, I miss that little Asian firecracker. Special woman, Ray. Not exactly painful on the eyes, either." We grew pretty close after that nightmare in Oklahoma. Spent a few months lyin' low in the Bahamas. Hell, we even tried reformin' the Revenge Squad, but found very few takers. Word is that she…*Marvella,* retired from the business a short time back. Doin' fashion design in Fresno, last I heard. Lately, I've *severely* regretted *not* joinin' her within the ranks of inactive superhero for hire."

Condor studied his old friend closely, mildly surprised at the genuine emotion on display from a man who rarely allowed a crack in his grim, business-like demeanor. As freelance partners taking assignments from both the CIA and FBI, they had shared many a battle and countless brews, but rarely a secret pertaining to each other's personal lives.

8

"That was the…when most of the Squad was…wiped out, right? I recall you never said much about it, other than being set-up by the team leader." Groaning in disgust, Ben took a quick sip from the bottle.

"Oh yeah. Richard Masters. Ass wipe went by the name *Four-Star*. Sold us out for a backhanded payoff from the *former* governor of Texas. Some good people died that day, man. Solid warriors and trusted teammates. One of 'em, *Johnny Reb,* was half owner of this dive when it was still takin' in a profit. Gave me a key and said to contact his Uncle Walt if I ever needed a place to lay low. Found out that Walt passed away a few months back, but still owned the deed. Place is in litigation hell as we speak. I was just glad they hadn't cleared out all the booze. You hungry, Ray? I've mostly been livin' off rameon noodles and Snickers bars the past few weeks, but I do have some Hot Pockets and cold Coors stashed away. Got some semi-fresh jerky that'll put hair on your chest…or at least yer tongue."

Condor waived him off, gently patting his taunt midsection with one gloved hand.

"No thanks, Ben. Had a bite a few hours back. It's getting harder than ever to maintain the washboard abs of my youth. How long you been stashed away in here, anyhow?"

Pouring himself another shot, Ben strolled back around to the front of the bar and took a large chew of beef jerky.

"Couple of weeks. I had been toolin' around Charlotte at a campsite a few miles outta town, but even in civvies I felt like somebody was constantly tailin' me. Just my imagination playin' games more 'n likely, but it was too big of a risk to take. When yer faced with a half-million-dollar bounty, there ain't no shortage of clowns willin' to risk a severe beatin' to bring ya in. Spent a week in Birmingham, then a few days in Biloxi fore coolin' my heels here. What brings you to the Big Easy, Condor?"

"Tracking quarry, what else?" Condor replied with a shrug.

Ben instantly ceased chewing and cocked a decidedly bushy eyebrow. "Somebody other than *yours truly*, I hope."

Folding his arms tightly across the monogrammed 'CC' adorning his chest, Condor stared into the tiled ceiling and frowned in deep thought. "Weeeelllll, of course somebody else, Ben," he smiled, "almost embarrassing to mention, actually. Corporate embezzler skipped bail in Hot' anta and the company President hired me to sniff him out. Supposedly the little geek is guarded by a trio of goons that label themselves 'Ninjas'."

Quickly concealing the grin covering his face with one huge palm, Ben muttered through splayed fingers.

"Don't sweat it, Ray. A check's a check these days, right?" he asked, suppressing a guffaw, "Ninjas, huh? Preppy with unlimited finances rarely goes cheap on protection. Hell, he might have *Inspector Gadget* or *Captain Caveman* on the payroll by now."

Both men broke into hysterics almost simultaneously, slowing only when their lungs had emptied of oxygen and their tear ducts had ran dry.

"It *is* pathetic, old buddy, there is no doubt,"

10

the Condor finally managed, wiping his eyes with a napkin.

"Hey, the big boys only want the marquee names these days. Major leaguers like the *Avengers*, *X-men* and *Fantastic Four* have the rep and clout. Guys like us were always considered second-tier, man. Damn shame. I never backed down from a scrap regardless of the pay they offered."

"I hear you, Ben. They've been slowly fazing us out for years. I'm taking assignments these days I would've laughed at back in the 90's, you know?"

"Same here, my man. Just might'a taken my last one, though. At least, as far as the government's concerned. To the stuffed shirts, I'm nothin' but an out of touch dinosaur gone to seed. Fifteen years of dedicated ass-kickin', and I'm labeled a homicidal fugitive in the single blink of an eye. Ray, it just ain't right."

Condor removed his gloves only after checking the retractable claws built into each, then began massaging the palms of his hands as Ben reached over and poured each of them a fresh refill.

"If you're trying to get me wasted, Ben, your task is better than half complete," he said, merely sipping this time around.

"What did happen between you and Rap-Master XXX, anyhow? I may be prejudice, you and I being former partners and all, but I never could buy into any of the horse manure his camp's been spreading to the media."

Ben gulped down the shot and grimaced only slightly, then quickly poured himself another and smiled as Ray waived off the same.

"Getting smoother with every swallow, Ray.

Lemme know if ya change your mind. Got at least half a dozen fifths stashed away, and at least that many pints, but I loathe drinkin' alone."

Leaning back as he re-fitted his gloves, Condor feigned shock.

"Sure, Benji. Three more shots of that stuff and you'll be hauling me out of here in a wheelbarrow. Those legs of yours are as hollow as ever, pal. You still own that 'little black book' of super-hero groupies? Man, I recall you used to stash that thing away like it was the Holy Grail."

"Man, you're talkin' 'bout decades long removed. Most of those chicks are housewives these days, doin' the 'Leave it to Beaver' bit. Now, what were you askin' me before?"

"Rap-Master XXX and the reason we're presently hunkered down inside a closed bar like cornered rats. You do know they raised the bounty to an even mil, Ben."

"The hell you say!" he replied, his eyes widened dramatically. "Little ol' me rates a cool million? Second string superhero from a small town in North Carolina? Guess I had to go *ultra* bad to hit the big time, huh Ray?"

"NAACP stepped in to back the AASHS. Political pressure, Ben, backed with truckloads of cash. They want your Caucasian rump hung from the highest podium, old buddy."

Shrugging his bulky shoulders, Ben's demeanor and tone remained surprisingly calm. Knowing his old running mate as he did, Condor had expected nothing less than a volcanic rage.

"Yeah, I had a feeling the *African-American Super-Hero Society* would call on a higher power to

12

ensure I end up planted feet up in the nearest bone yard. Ya think they'd at least perform a token investigation on the gutter trash they represent. Rap-Master XXX wasn't worth the skin off my knuckles, Ray. You ever run into any of the *Hip-Hop Militia*?"

Condor nodded to indicate he hadn't, then quickly raised a gloved finger to contradict "Shared a conference room at S. H. E. I. L. D with *Princess Ebo*ny once. We were never formally introduced though. That's about it. Aren't they mostly centered around Detroit, Cleveland, and Chi-town?"

"Started out East Coast and Mid-West, I think, but are pretty much nationwide these days. Rap Master and his hood thugs were the southeastern reps. Scuttlebutt is they've got teams on both coasts and in Miami these days."

Ben paused, eyeing his former partner curiously.

"Ya mean they never offered you a... membership, Ray?"

Groaning in dismay, Condor folded his arms across his chest in mock defiance.

"Benji, are you mental? I'm part Cherokee Indian as well as black, remember? The HH boys don't take kindly to half-breeds. Besides, my rep as one of the government's 'token' blacks for hire in the hero trade is well documented.

"White Dogs', they call us. Your old teammate in the R Squad, *Dark Claw*, was referred to as such."

Once again, Ben's eyes grew instantly distant, his lips pursed tightly. "Helluva warrior, ol' Claw. Surprisingly, it never really bothered me that he was

13

a tad bit 'light in the loafers', if ya catch my drift...." This time, it was Condor's eyes that widened.

"Dark Claw was gay? Never heard that one through the vine."

"Wiser to stay in the closet those days, at least for us hero-types, anyhow. Almost makes ya laugh, don't it? Dime a dozen now. I hear the *Gay Bolt* is next in line for a Hollywood franchise. Pretty boy in pink tights with matchin' earrings to boot with a five film deal probably worth a few hundred mil. Fag groupies shadow 'im like flies on a fresh pile of steamin' crap, I understand. Seriously cracks me up

'til I ponder on it further, then I always wanna start bawlin' my eyes out at the warped universe we inhabit, Raymond. Sure makes hidin' from society an easy task, I tell ya."

Condor laughed lightly, nodding in agreement as his former partner poured himself still another refill of tinted firewater.

"You caught a glimpse of the newest *West Coast Defender*, Benji?"

"Oh cripes, yes. That *Silver Fairy* freak, you mean?" Ben replied, frowning in pure disgust, as if detecting a particularly reeking odor through wildly flaring nostrils, '*The Defenders* actually granted that wimpy lookin' butt-pumper membership? Snooty Som' Bitches turned me down three separate times. Government must've assigned 'em a queer quota, ya think?"

"Possibly. Anyhow, didn't mean to change the subject. I know how you are about homo-. ." Condor began, cut off abruptly by the bellowing rant he had known was inevitable as soon as the subject had been breached.

"Half the gals donnin' tights these days are lezzies, anyhow. Ran into one last fall while workin' the Pentagon Security circuit callin' herself '*BullDyke-Devil*'. Woman had more facial hair than yours truly. Owned a mug that could crack titanium and an ass shaped like a deflated medicine ball. You hear 'bout that sicko rapist outta Washington state that was callin' herself '*Strap-on*?' Rumor has it she had ol' Spidey KO'd and bent over a crate with his tights pulled down around his ankles before The Avengers showed up to rescue 'im. Man, it ain't bad enough we're forced to face down rampagin' muties, power mad lunatics or extraterrestrial baddies. The 21st Century has sure added some seriously scary categories to the

'Super Villain' ledger, pal."

"Um, Benji..."

"Man, I understand this business lends itself to freaks, but these days ya seriously don't know who the baddies are without a name tag. What's with that '*Mystic*' Shrimp? Looks like a walkin' stick in spandex...saw his weak ass on a

Cola commercial a few weeks back..."

"Man's website, *Mystic Realm. com*, supposedly gets a few thousand hits a day, Ben. Mostly teens and young..."

"...looks like a girl scout could wipe up the floor with his bony ass. What was his main power again? Altering airspace? What the *hell* does that mean exactly? Can he fart and then transport the stink across a room?"

Condor raised a finger and extracted a shiny, metallic talon, then waived it back and forth like a

15

parent scolding a young child.

"Earth to *Desolation Outlaw*, come in, Benjamin…"

"Oh…uh…sorry, Ray. Y'know how I get. Once I click into 'rant' mode, its damn near impossible to find the 'off' switch," Ben groaned, lowering his head in mock shame.

Along the back wall, hung between an ancient Budweiser ad and a faded photo of Mike Ditka in his coaching days with the Saints, a 'Jack Daniels' wall clock chimed in weakly, announcing the ten PM hour with a series of muffled rings more suited for a palm-held cellular phone.

Displaying a wide, toothy smile, Condor reached over the bar and gently pushed a full shot glass closer to the other man.

"You are consistently consistent, Benji. The one constant in an otherwise topsy-turvy Universe. Time hasn't altered you a single iota."

After downing the shot in a blur, Ben wiped his mouth with a tree-trunk sized forearm and then eye-balled his former partner suspiciously.

"You just insult me, Ray?"

"Jeez, Ben…am I going to have to wait for the book or *movie* version?" Raising his mammoth hands in defense, Ben paused to inhale deeply. "Ain't too complicated, Ray. I had tracked Shaker Jake and the Cocaine Cowboys to an abandoned sports complex just outside Tulsa. Been trailin' those slippery jackasses for a month and through five states, and you know the legwork involved ain't exactly my strong suit. Jake had been runnin' a crank/crack empire through the Southeast for years, usin' the Coke Cowboys for transport. Lean, mean

16

crew of roughnecks, Ray, with firepower to spare. ATF had originally hired *Power Man* for the job, but he called 'em at the last minute and cancelled. I gotta tell ya, partner, it was one helluva paycheck those boys were offerin'. Best I've seen in years; transportation, meals, per diem, the works. Course, I knew it was far from bein' gravy. Shaker and the Coke Boys were suspected in at least two dozen homicides in the past year, and were well rep'ed as bein' the textbook definition of ruthless. Still, they were just common thugs after all, and we're used to dealin' with a more lethal species of villain. Man, I snatched up that contract before the ink had dried."

"I remember hearing a few years back Shaker Jake McKay was the main distributor in the South and Midwest. Rumor was that he was raking in a few hundred million annually. Supposedly had a two-thousand-acre ranch in Mexico and a fifty-room mansion in Puerto Rico," Condor interjected, now leaning back with his highly polished boots propped atop the bar.

"Those were just the *confirmed* hideaways. He also had a seventy-room castle in Spain and several villas in the Bahamas. Ran prostitution in South America for a sideline, as well as an 'Assassin for Hire' business that was thrivin' in Eastern Europe. Ol' Jake was a true renaissance man, all right. Closest thing to a rattler in human form you'll ever run across."

"What was he doing in Oklahoma? Warehousing?"

"Bingo," Ben answered with a wink, creating a mock gun with the thumb and forefinger of his left hand, then pulling the 'trigger' several times in

17

Condor's direction.

"Had rented a thirty-thousand square foot warehouse buildin' and proceeded to pack it to overflowing'. Som' bitch had enough smack, crank, and weed stuffed away to OD the entire west coast. DDA estimated the street value at over fourteen billion. That's with a 'b', not an 'm'. Heard it took two days of constantly runnin' forklifts to move it all outta there. Said it was like clearin' out a friggin' Super Wal-Mart. 'Course, I didn't get a chance to witness any of this firsthand, bein' the fugitive psycho that I am."

"Double homicide can taint one's reputation, Benji, and you weren't exactly known as a choir boy to begin with," Condor interrupted with a sly smile.

Crossing his grotesquely pumped arms across his chest, Ben winced as if stung by the sad truth of his former partner's words.

"Yeah, I'll admit I cultivated the image of loose cannon in my younger days. An extra edge is always helpful, especially when you're just startin' out in the business, you know that, Ray. That said, I ain't never shattered a rib or jawbone that didn't deserve it, and I sure as hell didn't terminate anyone without ample justification. Rap Master Shit heel and his grille-toothed clones crashed my bust in an obvious attempt to collect the reward. Triple XXX all but admitted he'd tracked me to Shaker's warehouse with a crap-munchin' grin drawn onto his ugly mug. What pissed me off the worst was his crackerjack timin'. They didn't even jump into the fray 'til I had already taken out most of Jake's hired muscle. I'd already caught an M-16 slug in the

18

shoulder and grenade shrapnel in both ass cheeks. Chicken shit jackasses thought I was just gonna step back, bleedin' like a stuck hog and let 'em take both the credit and the cash? Benjamin Thomason's mama didn't raise no chumps, Ray. Least, none I ever *knew* about."

"So the Rap Master was just blatantly jumping your claim or… was he under contract as well?" Condor asked, squinting past Ben momentarily to check the wall clock.

"Claimed the CIA had hired 'em six months earlier to nail Shaker J. I asked the dumb-shit if he'd arrived in Tulsa via Amsterdam, i. e. what the hell had taken so long. That's about the time his steroid-puffed goons jumped me from every friggin' direction. At the time, I had Shaker in a headlock and had pretty much heard him cry 'uncle' in three or four different tongues. In between absorbin' shots to the back, face, and groin from those damn stinger-canes, I saw XXX reach down real casual-like and cut Jake's throat from lobe to lobe, all the while performin' some kinda rap lyric like he was bein' shown on MTV close-circuit. Took me a few well-aimed jabs and sidekicks to break free, but by then my back-up generator had spewed forth quite a load of adrenaline. I hit Rap master XXX one time, Ray…*once*. A single right hook to the upper portion of his afro. And even that punch had ricocheted off one of the goon's shoulders *before* it landed."

Sighing heavily, Ben began vigorously rubbing the knuckles of his left hand, his eyes growing increasingly distant.

"Still, not bein' in the best of moods, what with the gunshot wounds and the bleedin' and all, I'm sure I didn't exactly pull my punch as I normally do when dealin' with cupcakes like XXX. Needless to say, I was still wearin' the majority of his noggin' on my fist when I pulled back. Cracked his skull like a damned eggshell. His body ended up on top of a pile of jagged pallet wood 'bout twenty feet from impact. Looked like somebody had nailed 'im there like a crucifixion. Next thing I know, CIA Storm Troopers raid the place like fire ants on a friggin' banana peel, and I'm bein' accused of excessive force for Shaker's death and flat out murder for the Rapmaster, the gist of which his goons are claimin' as I was bein' hauled off for questionin'. Once I caught wind of the trumped-up charges, I hauled ass. Needless to say, *without* the fed's permission. No doubt they've added assault of federal officers to the previous list of charges. Least I did remember to pull my punches on 'em. Been coolin' my heels ever since."

Condor stood from the barstool and stretched his arms high into the air, setting off a series of low, popping noises.

"What's the plan? You can't hide out forever, my man. Sooner than later, you're going to run out of booze, edible grub, and worst of all, toilet paper. Who's your contact with the feds? Surely they would at least listen to your side."

Nodding vehemently, Ben quickly waived him off.

"Been there, done that. Contacted my assignment rep as soon as I got into Birmingham and settled into a suitable safe haven. Within five minutes of makin' the call, I found myself surrounded by a Swat Team decked out for urban warfare. Don't think they were there to shoot the breeze or compromise in any form or fashion, Ray. My gunshot wounds had just begun to heal and be damned if I didn't catch another slug in my right thigh. They weren't shootin' to wound, ol' buddy, that much I do know for certain. Lucky I got out with my leathery hide intact. If not for my fast-healin' metabolism, I'd be a walkin' advertisement for gangrene."

Strolling stiffly from behind the bar, Ben then pulled up a chair from a nearby table and sat down with a loud, exasperated huff.

"Bottom line seems pretty clear. NAACP and AASHA needed a scapegoat and I filled the boots perfectly. Triple X's goons would collect the reward, pass on a portion to the NAACP boys and I'd take the fall for all the mayhem. The fact their perpetrator is a second-tier mercenary for hire with a penchant for rampagin', not to mention a white man from the Deep South, probably had 'em droolin' with anticipation, ya think?"

Condor walked around to the opposite end of the table, taking another quick peek at the hanging clock before pulling out a chair and straddling it.

"You never were much on conspiracies, Benji. Don't tell me you're buying into the 'Dino Spandex Sweep' theory that's been making the rounds the past year or so."

Wearing a deep scowl, Ben lowered his head, rubbing his hands slowly through his gray-tinted crew cut.

"Truth be told, Ray, I hadn't given it much thought. Now that ya mention it though, the '*Dinosaur Spandex Sweep*' theory does explain why

21

us old-timers have been droppin' like flies the past few years. If the government did set out to purposely rid the world of us older generation of hero-types, it ain't like the younger generation would shed nary a tear. It's a 'flavor of the month' world, Raymond, and I ain't even rated a taste in years. Ol' Rap-Master turd-breath was part of the new wave 'hip-hop' breed that's all the rage these days, along with powder-puff pansies like *Mystic* with his thousand-dollar haircut, silk cape and gold-plated trading cards bein' auctioned off to the highest bidder on E-Bay. Bet my old *Crispy Cream Cereal* trading card ain't worth a friggin' dime on today's market, ya think?"

Reaching back to pull forward and then re-secure his mask, Condor grinned while adjusting the tight-fitting cowl.

"You know, I'd forgotten all about those. I remember the day we posed for them at the Cereal Headquarters in Dayton. *The 'Future of Justice Set'*, they were called. The wife was thrilled beyond words her old man was going to have a trading card all his own. I think my oldest boy still has the entire set tucked away in a closet somewhere. Damn, Benji, hard to fathom that was almost fifteen years back."

"True enough, partner. Hey, maybe yer son outta hang onto those cards after all. I hear memorabilia for murderin' lunatics like myself goes way up in value followin' capture. Almost like makin' the bad guys hall of fame."

Condor stood without replying, swinging a booted foot gracefully over the chair back as he backed away in one fluid movement.

"What's up, Ray? Ya got an appointment somewheres?" Ben asked, flexing his triceps as he also stood.

"The Ninjas await, old friend, as does the monthly payment on my cliff-top condo. Can't possibly pay the latter without kicking the hind end of the former," Condor replied while running in place, the dull thumping of his boots on the wooden floor almost drowning out the badly muted dialogue.

"Got a bottle of Jack Daniels *Premium Gold* I was 'bout to crack open. Have a snort for the road."

Ben quick-walked a few steps and leaped over the four-foot high bar in a single bounce, displaying a sleek, fluid agility that belied his mammoth bulk. Reaching into a lower cabinet, he pulled the bottle free, held it high into the air, and then blew away a layer of dust coating the front label and neck.

"Wish I could join ya, Ray…at least give ya some backup in case the Ninja's turn out to be authentic. I ain't broke a decent sweat in weeks, I..."

The remaining words hung in Ben's throat just as the double-door entrance to the bar blew inward in a rush of shattered oak and twisted, torn metal, sending shards sailing into the glass wall behind him in an explosion of glass, wood, and metal shavings.

"Som…. BITCH!" Ben screamed, ducking his head beneath the bar just as the bottle of whisky blew apart in his hand like a detonated grenade.

Despite the sudden carnage, Ben realized he hadn't heard an explosion to indicate the use of the artillery normally associated with such instantaneous destruction. Duck-walking to the eastern side of the bar, he peeked around the corner justas the small room was bathed in swirling bright light originating from the tattered ruins of the bar entrance. He heard numerous voices permeate the opening, growing clearer as moments passed and the room filled with frantic movement. Crawling backwards a few feet, groaning silently as his knees crunched over jagged glass fragments, Ben reached into a lower shelf and retrieved the burgundy and white cowl he'd worn since adapting the identity of *Desolation Outlaw*, the forehead of which displayed a black-shaded '*skull and crossbones*'.

As he pulled the form-fitted mask and hood snugly into place, scattered bits of conversation became audible through the frenzied commotion.

"Charles Pierce for WJPM TV…New Orleans First News…live report from the…"

"…Williams reporting for Big Easy Live Dot Com,   we…about…from   a possible…confrontation…"

"…Evan Largent… WVIT TV…suspect in the murder…Rap-Master   XXX   has   been…in… bar…formerly   known   as…Head East Bar & Grille…Davidson Street. This reporter is…. advised to don Kavlar in order to avoid possible injury…"

"…hero known as Mystic has…. the suspect, known…Desolation   Outlaw,   but…formerly   as Force…served   in   the   mercenary   Super   Group known as…Revenge Squad… in the late nineties and   early   twenty-first   Century…violent confrontation…is imminent…"

Cupping his hands behind his back, Ben executed a quick succession of stretches while remaining crouched securely behind the thick oak stand.

"Set up like a fuckin' bowlin' pin by one of the few people I still trusted. Un-freakin'-real..." he muttered through teeth gritted as tightly as banded steel.

"Desolation Outlaw, or shall I refer to you using your former entity, *Force*?" the rather shrill voice rang out casually, "...I have been duly licensed by the United States Federal Government to serve a warrant for your immediate arrest and detainment. *Mystic* hereby offers you the opportunity to surrender peacefully, although use of excessive force is a viable option."

A chattering of mingled voices followed the obviously staged, overly dramatic announcement, as the media hordes prepped their perspective audiences for what they hoped was the battle royal to follow, jockeying for position like crazed fans fronting a concert stage.

"You've got thirty seconds to choose a method of detainment, Force. After that, *Mystic* will make that particular decision for you."

"Just love hearin' your own name, don'cha punk?" Ben growled in response, rolling over the bar top and landing in a crouched pose with his oversized fists clinched tightly at his sides. The T-shirt he wore seemed poised to literally rip at the seams from his massively pumped chest and pecs, just as the blue jeans wrapped around his tree-trunk sized thighs looked on the verge of splitting up both sides.

The semi-circle perimeter formed by the media-swarm instantly spread to the far corners of the confined space upon Ben's abrupt arrival, as if distancing themselves somewhat from the impending combat.

"I take it this means you won't go quietly?" the slim young man in

Aqua-marine tinted tights queried, the spit-polished, dark green boots he donned floating several inches above the bar's hardwood floor.

Ben shot him a playful wink, although his steely grimace remained firmly intact.

"Tinkerbelle old son, you have a definite talent for statin' the obvious. Truth be told, all this inactivity of late just ain't me. I have an 'ass-kickin' quota that needs filled something fierce. Looks like you'll have to do 'til a *real* scrap comes along."

The young man smiled beneath his dark green cowl, crossing his slim but well-toned arms across his chest.

"As long as we're clear that a peaceful solution was at least offered." Quickly scanning the smoke-filled structure, Ben was temporarily blinded by a bombardment of camera flashes, backing up a half-step until his heel propped against the lower portion of the bar's solid foundation.

"Play it up for the folks at home, ya little shit. I think we both know what gets ratings, am I right? White flags don't cut it in the world of reality progammin', I hear."

Levitating forward a foot or so, Mystic swept his right arm around as if shooing away a pesky fly.

"I'm paid to provide a service to our government, Force, just as these fine folks are compensated for keeping our world informed through electronic and print media. The viewers at home have not only a need to know, but the *right* to

26

know what's happening around them."

Ben watched as a handful of overeager reporters attempted to move forward, only to be halted in mid-step, their faces awash in a mixture of shock and awe. With a single flick of a wrist, Mystic had apparently created an invisible perimeter; a transparent force field put in place to protect the news crews from possible injury, while also providing them a clear line of site to fully capture the action soon to follow.

"Why don't ya turn up the volume on that little speech a little louder, pecker-head. I'm not sure the guys in the back caught it all. Ya sure don't wanna be misquoted, now do ya?" Ben yelled, attempting in vain to drown out the building wave of wailing sirens emanating from the street. Trying not to be too obvious, he gradually scanned his inner circle for botha workable escape route and possible weaponry to utilize if the need arose.

"Last chance, Force. Lay flat on your chest and place your hands behind your head."

The chorus of sirens was near deafening as Ben poised in mock defiance, his head cocked hard to the left.

"Sounds like an army of reinforcements, son. They must know somethin' you don't," he quipped just before lifting both arms and waving in a mocking, 'come on ahead' gesture.

Mystic sighed heavily, lowering his head in stage play dramatics. When next he spoke, his tone was purposely stern but strangely emotionless.

"Very well. It's your medical bill, or better yet...... that particular burden will, unfortunately, befall the taxpayers of this fine land."

Ben rolled his eyes beneath his own tightly fitting cowl.

"Geez Louise, queer as a three-dollar bill and a friggin' politician to boot," he muttered, then sprang forward as if shot from a cannon's thundering barrel.

Mystic waited until Ben's lead fist was mere inches from his breastbone before sailing straight up in an amber blur of frenzied motion.

Landing hard on his left shoulder, Ben combat-rolled until his right side nailed the force field in a bone-jarring thump, instantly knocking the majority of the air from his lungs.

Jesus... like... runnin' into a titanium wall. So...... why don't the prick just... wrap me up in a body-suit version of the same thing? Punk's playin' with me. Toyin' with... me for the cameras.

Resting on one knee while trying desperately to refill his battered lungs, Ben could hear Mystic speaking in the foreground, although he was unable to comprehend the gist of what was being said. He did hear the Crimson Condor's name spoken more than once, just the mention of which instantly caused his teeth to gnash together ever tighter.

Just as he found the strength to stand upright, a blur of maroon filled his still-bleary eyes. The forearm landed with a muffled thud across his forehead, sending him reeling back until his upper back again made contact with the force field Slumping to the dusty wood floor, Ben could taste his own blood coating the surface of his tongue.

"Truly sorry about this, partner, and I'm not just *saying* that,' Condor groaned in a half-whisper, as if purposely muting his words from nearby microphones, "... but, man, I've got credit problems you just wouldn't believe."

Attempting to shove himself upward, Ben rose only halfway before a series of lightning quick kicks to his abdomen and upper chest drove him into the field like a ricocheting pinball, followed by a hard right hand to the jaw, jarring him to his knees.

"Margie has turned into a real gold-digger, Ben. I've got a least a dozen credit cards maxed to the hilt. Got collection agencies crawling up my rear on the older son's Jaguar. Little shit goes through cash like a Vegas gambler."

Slumped on all fours, Ben shook his head vigorously from side to side. "Fourteen-year-old daughter wants a new Dell set-up for her birthday, along with a laser printer and top of the line scanner. It seems everything I buy is outof date six weeks later," Condor continued, his body language resembling a preacher delivering the ultimate in fire and brimstone sermons to an enraptured parsonage of exactly one.

"This crap keeps up, I'll end up selling the house in Jacksonville and living out of our Explorer. They just don't get it, Ben. The daily pressure, the humiliation...the toll it takes...the shit *I* endure. Just to keep them content. Sad to say, old buddy, but turning you isn't even *close* to the lowest I've sunk in the past year or so. Whore'd myself out in ways you could never comprehend, old pal. All in the name of good old American greed."

Ben lifted his head slowly and spat a mouthful of bloodied saliva onto the Condor's right boot tip, then displayed a wide, malicious grin.

"Yer breakin' my heart, ass wipe," he managed in-between labored huffs, his thighs, forearms and upper back noticeably tensing as if ready to spring forward at a split-second's notice, "... what I'm wonderin' is, how is it that the Green Pickle back there agreed to split his take of the reward stash with a gnarled up old washout such as yourself? Damn, Condor.... don't tell me the *Mys-ti-c*al fairy back there is your personal government assigned *pimp*."

Condor's mouth opened for a quick rebuttal just as Mystic floated by and administered a light tap to his left shoulder, causing him to cringe back in comical shock.

"Cut the chatter and prep him for the fall, Condor," he murmured just inches from Condor's left ear, "... just remember, the decisive blow is *mine*."

Turning to face the smaller man, Condor openly smirked.

"Yassam, boss...whatever you say, massah Mystic Suh," he replied sarcastically, jerking forward a moment later as frenzied movement appeared at the corner of his eye.

Ben leapt forward at blinding speed, plowing his elbows into Condor's upper chest with jackhammer force just as Mystic levitated safely out of range.

Condor sailed into and through a series of stacked bar stools, landing with a resounding crash into a mirrored wall, shattering as if struck by a wrecking ball, shards of glass shrapnel filling the air like handfuls of tossed sand.

Ben reached down and jerked Condor from the

30

rubble, hoisting him airborne with his right hand wrapped tightly around the smaller man's throat. Rearing back with his left, the fist he displayed loomed as large as an over-inflated beach ball.

"Fuckin' traitor. Hate to add to yer financial woes, Ray, but you got one helluva dental bill comin'…"

The fist shot forward and halted less than an inch from the nose tip of

Condor's cowl, his squinting eyes and frozen grimace still awaiting the blow that never landed. Ben felt the tendons in his shoulder catch fire as the punch was forcibly prevented from properly landing or following through. Releasing Condor's throat, he tried to use his free arm to force the other to his side, desperately pulling and tugging on the forearm and biceps like a street mime performing a comedic sketch.

"What…in the… *hell?"* he grunted, watching helplessly as Condor rolled away while grasping at his wounded neck.

"It's referred to as a 'floating pocket of unmovable air', Force. Nothing fancy, mind you, but it serves its purpose in a pinch. I could easily encase your entire head within a similar prism, thus cutting off precious oxygen, but alas, the authorities do frown on my utilizing such grisly techniques," Mystic bellowed while circling Ben's paralyzed form in a green blur of chaotic movement.

"Ya keep playin'…with dynamite…son…your gonna lose…an appendage... or two…" Ben groaned aloud, his face and neck coated in sweat as he continued to strain and struggle to no apparent avail. In the background, mingled voices, some

31

muffled and guarded; others loud and overly boisterous, could be heard analyzing the scene like play-by-play commentators witnessing a historic sporting event.

Pausing in mid-flight, Mystic hung upside down, his dark brown eyes parked mere inches from Ben's own.

"Benjamin, I don't question the brute strength you possess, nor take it lightly. That said, I'm about as intimidated by you as I would be in the presence of a Golden Retriever pup."

Ben threw a vicious uppercut with his free arm, growling in obvious agony as the flesh of his knuckles first flattened, then split open upon contact with the field encasing Mystic's skull.

"Ouch. That must've stung a bit," Mystic beamed while flipping right side up and levitating gently onto the floor, the field encircling his boots crushing chunks of glass into even tinier segments. A few dozen feet away, the voices of the media hordes grew ever louder, as if each were trying to drown the other out. Cameras flashed more rapidly in succession, resembling a grouping of ignited fireworks.

With his bleeding, wounded hand tucked tightly against his chest, Ben wrenched back in a final attempt to free the other, succeeding only in separating the attached shoulder, which popped loudly as he collapsed onto one knee.

"R-release the arm... magic boy... and I'll... c-consider not... pullin' your lungs out through your asshole..." he barked with a snarl, lifting himself back up to alleviate the pressure from his wrecked shoulder.

Shaking his head slowly from side to side, Mystic glanced past his trapped quarry to where the Crimson Condor stood semi-slumped, his gloved hands propped wearily atop his knees.

"I'd always heard what a true charmer you were, Benjamin. I must say, all the stories of unchecked barbarianism and animalistic behavior tied to your legend have indeed done you justice. Pardon me while I check my partner's status, will you?"

Without a single movement other than a brief flip of his right hand, he sailed upward until the tip of his cowl practically scraped the tiled ceiling, hovering like a feather swept along by a mild spring breeze before landing next to where Condor kneeled.

"Condor, are you able to rise?" he practically yelled as the flash bulbs freeze-framed his heroic pose, dramatically leaning over his fallen comrade as their embattled opponent continued his fruitless struggles in the background.

Gradually pushing himself upright, Condor took a few deep breaths before turning on Mystic with an expression of utter disdain.

"Aw, go to hell, camera hog. I'll live. Let's... get this…charade over with before what's left of my conscience makes a surprise appearance and I take a swing at *you* instead."

Mystic leaned over until the two men came dangerously close to butting heads, his voice barely audible over the clatter surrounding them.

"If I were you, fly boy, I'd refrain from spouting such vile dialogue for the remainder of this particular drama, or I just might turn the rabid pit-bull over there loose on your creaky old behind. Oh, I'd step in for the rescue, but only after he's managed to break a handful of bones, cracked your sternum, or ruptured your spleen."

Swallowing hard, Condor refused to meet the other man's gaze as they moved slowly forward.

"Do you read me clearly, Chicken-Man? Just keep your mouth shut and you'll walk away with a third of the reward and at least that much of the credit."

"Under.... I got it. Now, let's just... end this."

Mystic giggled briefly, though shielding it with the back of a gloved hand. "I thought so. Just for the record, Pigeon-Toes, if not for your connection within the AASHS, I'd feed you to that animal for the sheer pleasure of watching you die."

Condor visibly tensed, opened his mouth to reply, then hung his head slightly and fell silent before continuing forward.

As they neared his sweat-soaked, spastically weaving form, Ben twisted around until it looked as though his head was literally sewn onto his back.

The two halted a half-dozen feet from his crookedly hanging frame.

"Jeez, t-talk about... the Odd Couple. How'd you... t-two meet... at a local

Costumed Pricks c-convention?"

Unable to maintain eye-contact with his former partner, Condor instead turned to Mystic, who now floated horizontally with his head in the lead, lying flat as if perched on an invisible ironing board, his chin resting on his folded wrists.

34

"Put the air-cuffs on him, Mystic. He's no threat now. Let's just take him in ..."

Mystic's face turned towards him and away from the camera's intrusive glare, the expression he displayed no longer heroically wholesome but obscenely malevolent.

"Not... just... yet, Wing-Nut. We need just a bit more action to fill in the chinks of tonight's little venture, don't you agree? After all, the news boys have traveled all this way. They deserve more than the mundane, the ordinary. The capture must contain... a suitable filling. Besides, if you're receiving a portion of the reward for this capture, you're going to earn it."

"Kid, you are one seriously cracked egg, you know that?" Condor mumbled beneath a gloved hand, "... you cut that man loose, injuries or no, he *will* find a way to hurt you. Believe me, oh great and mighty master of the mystical arts, the man I knew as Force thrived on inexplicable comebacks. Heed my warning, forget the goddamned cameras for a minute and don't... chance... it."

Mystic tumbled to the debris-strewn floor, falling to his knees as his hands engulfed each side of his cowl at the temples.

"C-can't... h-hold h-him, Condor. He's... t-t-too strong. The p-pressure of.... maintaining separate... f-force fields... h-has d-drained me so." he announced loudly, tossing his head back for additional dramatic effect.

Shaking his head in disbelief, Condor managed to keep his reply in the form of a muffled whisper, despite the overwhelming urge to reveal the charade being played out solely for the media at large.

"Selfish, scrawny little weasel. If we *do* survive this, I swear I'll take you apart myself."

Tumbling down like a puppet with severed strings, Ben landed on his injured shoulder before instantaneously rolling to his feet in one amazingly swift, fluid motion

Condor leaped back several steps and took a quick inventory of the immediate area as Mystic again bowed his head, tucking his upper body into a semi-fetal position.

"Looks like... I ain't the only…one bein' sold out on this particular evenin', huh Condor old com padre?" Ben blurted before spitting another thick wad of bloody saliva onto the dusty floor.

"Give it up, Ben. Kid's a sick pup. He's playing up to the masses, that's all. Don't give him a reason to humiliate and injure you any further," Condor whispered harshly, watching in disgusted dismay as Mystic writhed and wriggled a few feet to his right.

Adjusting his cowl with his mangled right hand, Ben lunged back with one leg and assumed a defensive posture. The assault of clicking flashbulbs seemed to intensify two-fold, as did the manic, chattering dialogue accompanying it.

"Surrenderin' don't exactly come naturally, Ray. The thought of it kinda sickens me, truth be told. Always has.

"Immediate danger and extreme risk, on the other hand, give me a full-throttle boner every time."

"Do your worst, Pigeon-man. Rest assured, I'll step in if the need arises," Mystic murmured from between splayed fingers. He rolled over onto his back, keeping his face covered as his legs kicked out spastically.

Cocking his head to one side, Ben clasped his injured arm at the upper bicep and jerked it roughly towards his body until an audible pop was heard. All the while, he never hinted at the intense pain surely associated with such a reckless procedure.

"Ah, good as gold. I guess it's show time, Condor. By all means, let's give the people what they crave."

Shrugging weakly, Condors' fists uncurled momentarily as he turned his gloved hands palms up.

"Wish it didn't have to be this wa..."

"Cram it, Ray. Yer no better than the green turd over there. Ya might as well be *fartin'* in Russian for all your words mean to me now."

Sailing forward at break-neck speed, Condor's left boot ricocheted off Ben's breastbone, using the blow as a springboard to flip up and over his obviously weakened, groggy opponent. Following a smooth, perfectly executed landing, he followed up with a sidekick to the pit of Ben's lower back, sending the larger man scrambling onto his stomach with a loud groan.

Wiping embedded glass fragments from his abdomen and chest as he sprang to his feet, Ben wore a wry smile.

"Yer still damn quick for an old man, Raymond. Forgot all about yer patented 'tumbleweed kick' maneuver. Wouldn't advise tryin' that again, though..."

"Save yourself any further pain and take a ten-count, Ben. Even if you do manage to get past me, Wizard-boy over there will take great pleasure in bending you like a soggy pretzel before unmercifully ending the festivities."

Lurching forth, Ben threw a succession of short jabs, all of which Condor effortlessly avoided with a simple bob and weave. After tossing a pitifully telegraphed right hook which found nothing but stale, smoke-filled air, Ben fell to one knee and swept the other across Condor's ankles, toppling him over onto his back with a resounding thud. He then landed an elbow into the pit of his former partner's midsection, followed by a solid right to the jaw, spraying a fine, misty mix of blood from his shattered hand, as well as that from Condor's upper lip, onto the facing of a nearby jukebox.

Covering his battered face with both hands, Condor rolled weakly onto his right side as Ben wobbled shakily to his feet.

"Tactical errors can and *will* get ya hurt, Ray. You definitely need a bigger room if ya wanna stand toe to toe with me. Without flyin' space, yer just another half-assed kick boxer wearin' spandex. And, speakin' of flyin'..."

Reaching down with his right hand, which looked as though it had been run through a meat grinder, Ben grabbed Condor's left ankle, braced his feet a full two feet apart, then proceeded to sling the smaller man airborne, spinning his splayed frame overhead like a human lasso.

Upon release, Condor easily cleared a series of stacked bar stools and a trio of ancient pinball machines, a crimson line-drive who eventually soared head-first over the bar and dead center into a shelf half-filled with dust-coated liquor bottles.

Vanishing behind the chest-high bar, he was

subsequently bombarded by whatever bottles he hadn't already shattered upon impact.

Just as the renewed sound of shattered glass began to subside, Mystic quickly pushed himself upright and started to levitate back at a deliberate pace as Ben turned to face him.

"Where ya goin', squirt? Felt a sudden burst of energy, did ya?"

Mystic paused his backward momentum only when the protective force field he'd created for the media was mere inches away. Floating upward, he held his slim arms straight out as if to continue flight by flapping, keeping the palms pointed down as he grew completely still, as if in deep meditation.

Tugging again at his ravaged shoulder, Ben paused to refill his lungs with three quick inhales.

Cheese-dick is playin' it for all it's worth. He ain't about to give me a free shot, and I can't afford another broken hand courtesy' a that body-bubble armor of his. Guess I'll have to play it by ear...or better yet...foot.

"By the power authorized to me by the Federal Government as well as the fine city of New Orleans, I hereby place you, Benjamin Thomason, now known as *Desolation Outlaw*, formerly the man called *Force*, under arrest for the crime of Murder, as well as the additional charge of evasion."

Ben slung his head back and howled.

"Whatever you say, Ace. Don't bother takin' the initiative. I'll gladly do the honors."

His speed increasing with each step, Ben raced forward like a charging bull, covering the twenty-yard space between them in just under four seconds. He leaped feet-first with his arms crossed over his

39

chest, like a pole-vaulter attempting a record height.

Somewhat surprisingly, Mystic held his ground without even the slightest attempt to levitate out of harm's way. As soon as the bottoms of his steel-toed Wolverine's made contact with what should have been the man's upper stomach and chest, Ben unfortunately understood the reason why. Bouncing away like a racquetball from a stone surface, Ben felt as if his knees and ankles had endured a ten-story fall onto a brick sidewalk. Tucking his torso like a platform diver, he landed with a tight roll, ramming still another stack of chairs like a human bowling ball before the far edge of the bar finally halted his forward progress.

Struggling to his feet, he spat a thick mix of dirt and blood onto the nearby bar top, acutely aware of Mystic's slow ascent towards him.

"Yer a real man's man, *Misses-tic*, yes indeed. How's about droppin' that damned bubble for half a sec, what do ya say? De-*pussy*-fy yerself, so to speak."

Ben sidestepped over to a nearby table, which had been flipped over in his tumbling descent.

"You know, prove to yer internet fan club what a real action *he-ro* ya really are?"

"I'm not here to play games, mister. I'm here to enforce the law." Snapping a baseball-bat sized table leg free with frightening ease, Ben casually propped it onto one shoulder while positioning the circular tabletop as a makeshift shield. Resembling a battered, battle worn warrior from two centuries past, he then pointed the club airborne and waived it playfully.

"Then by all means, turdheel, *come on* with yer

40

bad self."

"You know, Benjamin, your blatant recklessness is surpassed only by your innate crudeness," Mystic remarked sourly, floating cautiously ahead, "stereotypical southern white male. It will be a true pleasure shutting you up."

"Better watch it, son…that remark *borders* on politically incorrect. Don't wanna accidentally sabotage your future career as Mayor of Pansy-ville, now do ya?" Ben smirked, rearing back and tossing the thick, jagged-edged chair leg like a javelin while simultaneously charging forward with the shield posed chest-high.

The chair leg struck the field at Mystic's groin, shattering into three separate pieces as it bounced harmlessly away.

As a new barrage of camera flashes doused both men in frenzied, intermediate strobe-light, Mystic began throwing his fists forward in short, precise jabs, as if shadow boxing With every jab tossed, a new chunk of the tabletop shield splintered and sailed away, forcing Ben to back away with the constant jolting of his already tattered shoulder.

What the…? He's usin' pockets of air like ball peen hammers Ben old pal, ya just might be up crap creek without the proverbial paddle here.

Heaving what little remained of the tabletop in Mystic's general direction, Ben turned and bolted back towards the bar, not exactly sure as to why he had chosen to do so, other than the fact that breaking additional bones punching an impenetrable force field seemed the only *other* viable option.

Hell, maybe runnin' ain't such a horrible notion after all. Fightin' the good fight only works if

41

both parties are scrapin' under the same rules. Can't win this one, any way ya look at it. Might as well try to duck away to fight another day.

He got to within six feet of the back entrance when it felt as if the grille of a

Mack truck nailed his upper back at seventy miles per hour, driving him into and *through* the solid maple door, which tore from its hinges while splitting neatly in half at the center.

Remaining airborne until he crashed into a large metal rack containing a half-ton of compacted boxes, Ben drifted in out and of consciousness for what seemed like hours, but in reality was less than a full minute in duration. Stumbling to his feet like a buzzing wino, it became obvious he had become the proud owner of a full-blown concussion. It had been a few years, but all the sure-fire symptoms were present and accounted for.

Jeez...Crow...he shifted...the air... collected it as... a solid object...somehow...then...belted me with it. Kid...might be a...p-pussy, but... that's one helluva party... trick. Got... gotta...get my rear in...gear...and va...vamoose...

As sporadic waves of dizziness momentarily forced him back down to one knee, he heard Mystic's slightly nasal tone barking orders from just outside the dilapidated door.

"Retrieve our quarry, if you will. There's no need to prolong this particular dance any further."

Lowering his chin onto his chest, Ben sucked in a long, labored breath and stood for a second time, allowing an extra moment for his lower extremities to properly adjust.

The back exit was a scant ten to fifteen yards

42

away, through a small kitchen and past acombination office/storage room. Ben stumbled ahead, fighting off pangs of guilt that were at least as powerful as the physical injuries threatening to send him into a lengthy coma.

Som'bitch! Where exactly do I think I'm goin'? How far can I really get...like this? Cops gotta be swarmin' like flies on shit out there. Swat teams, National Guard probably circlin' the whole block. Gonna end up with bullet holes to accent my busted hand, torn shoulder, and cracked skull. Kinda glad I sucked down all the booze now...least I ain't feelin' the full...misery.

"The hell with it. I never was worth a damn at retreat," he muttered, whirling back around just as the blow shattered his left collarbone, catapulting him into a tall, narrow metal filing cabinet that was crushed like an empty beer can.

Rolling away with a muffled groan, Ben peered up through bleary eyes as his attacker stood posed just inside the ruins of the back-room entrance.

Condor held his arms in a blocking stance, his shoulders and upper chest riddled with ragged, seeping slash marks. A hooked shard of glass, presumably from the liquor cabinet he'd been tossed into earlier, protruded from one shoulder like a reptilian claw. Standing a bit shakily, the words he managed were slow and slightly slurred. Clearly, a man as close to complete collapse as his quarry.

"It ends... right here, Ben. You open that back door and there won't be enough left of you to smear on a cracker. Special forces have about a dozen AK-47's pointed dead center at that bad boy. I'd rather see you locked away than shoved inside a body bag.

Just lay down, man. You're racked up... pretty bad as it is. Don't give the Green Jeanie out there another excuse to add to your pains."

Literally crawling to his feet, Ben shrugged his lone working shoulder.

"Yer concern...for my well-bein' is...tuggin' at my heart strings, Ray, it really is, but Louis Thomason's baby boy failed 'coward 101' class...I'm af-afraid...so...bring on the badness...or shut the hell up already."

Lurching forward at an angle, as if favoring his left side, Condor threw a succession of right jabs that were easily swatted away, followed by a vicious side kick aimed at the left side of Ben's ribcage. Twisting away as the heel of Condor's boot tore through his tee-shirt, Ben flung his elbow back at an upward angle, using the momentum of his leaning torso to full use.

He heard Condor's jaw snap upon impact, the sound of gnashed teeth shattering like crushed granite. Flailing back as blood gushed from between his pursed lips in a fine, thin spray, Condor managed to rake his razor-sharp talons across Ben's lower neck and chest as he fell, leaving behind five evenly carved slash marks in their wake.

Bounding forward with a renewed surge of vitality, Ben willingly relented to the pent-up rage fueling his inner combative demons. Keeping a 'cool head' in the midst of battle had never been his forte, nor had he ever been willing to 'pull back the reigns' and control the bombastic temper he was legendary for displaying. As *Force*, the fighting edge he had discovered and skillfully honed through years of confrontations had centered around what others had labeled 'controlled rage'. To Benjamin Thomason, backing down or pulling punches for any reason was a sure sign of weakness and of blatant insubordination to the god or gods responsible for granting one powers above that of mortal man. The individual lying at his feet was a former partner and once trusted friend. He was now nothing more than a treacherous leech; a pathetic, back-stabbing greed-monger who had turned him in for nothing less than rent money. Still, others might see fit to show pity for sentimentality's sake. Others might site the past as something worth preserving regardless of how sour the present. Benjamin Thomason, however, had never been regarded as a follower of what others practiced or preached.

Despite the obvious handicaps; a badly broken hand and collarbone, separated shoulder, concussion, and open gashes that coated his chest, stomach and groin in streams of his own blood, the mission objective was distinctly clear. Kill his former partner and afterwards, despite the implausibility of such, try like hell to do likewise with the gay 'genie'. No holds barred.... no questions left unanswered at a later date. If, indeed, such a date might exist.

Condor had tried to push himself up just as Ben brought a forearm down at the middle of his back, followed by a leg drop across the back of his skull that utilized all two-hundred fifty-five pounds of his body weight. Ever resilient, as Ben had always known him to be, the Crimson Condor continued to struggle, attempting an impromptu 'tuck and roll' to escape further damage. Ben smiled silently as his former comrade backed himself against a far wall

45

and somehow managed to pull himself upright, using his talons as climbing hooks to dig into the stone wall at his back. He could no longer trust the man, true, but he could respect the pure grit he displayed, a determination and mettle born and bred from thousands of similar tussles. Ben stepped forward and planted a size twelve boot into the man's exposed groin, then fired a quick jab that crunched his nose like a dried matchstick. His face a mangled mess of red that was easily a shade darker than his trademark cowl, Condor attempted in vain to claw Ben on the way down, but was unable to forge enough strength for a single swipe.

"Jackass.... I was gonna plant yer ass in the nearest boneyard. Now... I think I'll just *cripple* you instead. That... gorgeous wife'a yours won't stick around with... a rotted veggie to support. Maybe I'll send ya... a get-well card from stir, Ray. Would ya like that, ya turncoat bastard?" Ben snarled spitefully, kneeling down to grasp one of Condor's shoulders as thick trails of blood dripped from his lips onto the fallen man's upper back.

With shocking quickness, Condor flipped over and ripped a two-inch gash just under Ben's chin with a single extended talon.

"Awwww, shiiit!" Ben yelped, easily blocking Condor's weak follow-up left hook.

Pile-driving forward and down, he executed a thundering head-butt that sent Condor into an instantaneous coma, a ferocious blow that could have conceivably decapitated a normal man.

"Yer one fiesty Mo-Fo, Ray. I'll give ya that. Ain't sure any amount'a money is worth such a beatin', though," he muttered wearily, utterly oblivious to the silent observer levitating just to his right.

"Witnessing such barbaric brawling firsthand only serves to remind me how hopelessly outdated warriors such as yourself and your former partner have become, Benjamin."

Lurching hard to one side, Ben practically tripped over Condor's still frame, only regaining his balance when the concrete wall halted any further momentum. His fists shot up in a blocking stance, an instinctive, rather simple maneuver made virtually impossible by the checklist of injuries he'd sustained within the last half-hour.

"Fossils of a different era, and thankfully so."

"Kid, I'm sufficiently pissed off...as it is. It ain't...necessary to keep eggin' me on this way," he grumbled, a fresh trail of blood leaking from his chin and onto his already drenched upper chest.

"Looks to me like... that 'fossil' lyin' right there has...done the dirty work... for ya. I'm fairly...certain that a cub scout could kick my...ass about now. So... I guess it's time you dragged my thoroughly mangled carcass outside...and play hero...for your adorin' public, huh?"

Casually raising his right-hand palms up, Mystic pointed a single finger Ben's way and wriggled it just slightly.

"Not quite yet. In fact, the first item on the agenda doesn't involve you at all, Benjamin. Although he performed admirably as a decoy on this night, I'm afraid the Crimson Condor's share of the federal reward has been ruled unjust, thus I'm hereby canceling his contract...thusly."

"Cancel... his contract? What are you babblin'

abo-..."

Condor's feet and legs began to twitch uncontrollably, as if experiencing a mild electric shock. His right hand moved shakily to his bludgeoned face and began scanning the forehead, nose and mouth, as if performing a semi-conscious inventory of what remained intact.

Ben noticed when the hand fell away a moment later, it was strangely bloodless, despite the fact Condor's nose, mouth and chin were painted red with his own seeping fluids.

He watched as Condor's chest began to heave wildly, his eyes fluttering in spastic ticks.

Bastard's usin' one of those fields to suffocate 'im. Christ, the role model for a new generation of 'hand's off' crime-fighters is nothin' more than a cold-blooded assassin. Question is, how in hell's bell's am I supposed to stop 'im?

"Hey, Twinkle-Toes! Ya might wanna... reconsider croakin' my boy Condor. That is, unless you plan... the same fate for yours truly, 'cause I'm gonna sing like a coked-up parakeet once the feds question me about my former... partner's untimely demise. Death by suffocation ain't exactly inconspicuous to 21st Century forensics, ya know."

Resting his chin on a clinched fist as if in deep meditation, Mystic thoughtfully cocked an eyebrow.

"Let us study the scenario as it currently stands then, Benjamin. Fact number one: former partner turns in federal fugitive and is soon immersed in deadly hand-to-hand combat. Fact number two: Countless media witness said event and have, in fact, taped an ample portion for future viewings on World-Wide cable news networks and websites.

48

Fact number three: Postmortem injuries to the deceased will show numerous broken bones in facial area, as well as several hundred embedded shards of glass, wood, and metal fragments from said battle mentioned above. Fact four: eyewitness to Crimson Condor's death, that being little old me, will state that early efforts to resolve fugitive's capture in a peaceful manner were met with vicious indifference, leading to tragic outcome in regard to a fallen hero.

"*Actual* cause of death will be irrelevant, Benjamin. Besides, who the *fuck* will believe you anyway?"

Growling with newfound rage, Ben took two long strides and leaped into the air with his arms spread wide, his neck, biceps and forearms pumped to hideous proportions.

Mystic visibly tensed, as if temporarily caught off guard by the sudden assault, floating over a few feet as if to simply avoid impact. As Ben sailed by with a loud groan, Mystic's left arm shot out in a straight line, the fingers tucked tightly in a 'karate chop' pose.

The air around Ben's falling form seemed to instantly alter, thickening like an oversized bubble of helium just seconds before he was shot through the adjoining oak wall like a human mortar.

Studying the almost perfectly circular hole his air-shift blast had helped create, Mystic shook his head as if sincerely awed by his own unique capabilities.

"Never been touched. Never *will* be. When will these brutish types *ever* learn?" he mused, turning his attention back to Condor, whose periodic

49

movements had since ceased.

Spitting bits of dust, wood and instillation from between badly cut lips, Ben rolled to one side and away from the pile of rubble that had accompanied him as his body had been forced to play the role of wrecking ball. Coughing harshly as fresh trails of blood spewed forth from both nostrils, he was acutely aware that a rib or two had snapped upon impact with either the wall, the floor, or a combination of both.

Ain't had...an ass-bootin' like this since The Mangler broke my...legs back in...ninety-six...lucky I'm a...fast healer...or my next mode...of transpo might...just be...a friggin' wheelchair...

Propped upon his knees, the jeans he sported torn into blue/red strips up to his groin, Ben could hear the clamor at his back as the media-hounds honed in,but was unsure if the flashes of light and bright white spots coating his vision were media or *beating* related.

Sharks...are...circlin', no doubt. Son...of a bitch. I ain't never felt as...damned...helpless...so damned...useless...

Emerging from the wide opening that his quarry's body had so dramatically opened, the expression Mystic wore was a tangled mix of deep regret and building fury. No longer floating, he walked purposely with clinched fists at either thigh. His face seemed overly gaunt; his lips pursed and visibly trembling.

"Good people of New Orleans, it is my unfortunate duty to announce that an additional death can now be tied to the name of Benjamin Thomason, the fugitive better known as *Force*.

Despite my best efforts to revive his tattered, heroic soul, The Crimson Condor has…. passed on to another realm."

"L-lyin' J-jacka-ass……" Ben blurted between hacking coughs, grimacing in agony as he tucked an arm tightly around his left side.

"The man spent the last two decades of his life making our streets a safer place. He stood for all that was *good* in our business. A business that is less glamorous than cruel; less rewarding than it is extremely unkind. I'd only known the Condor for a scant few days, but it was truly an honor to be tutored by a skilled veteran of the game. What he taught me, the advice he doled out, I will always hold dear."

His sarcastic howl laced with the occasional hacking cough, Ben threw his head back in comic disbelief. He performed a half-bow, wincing as his ribs screamed a hardy disapproval.

"All h-hail…. Mr. fuckin' P-President…s-sir. B-better…k-kill me…. q-quick, shit for… b-brains, 'fore I…find…the e-energy… to spout the… truth…as… the w-whole damned. world…listens…"

Standing no more than two feet from where Ben sat semi-paralyzed, Mystic ignored the comment and raised both arms overhead until his fingertips lightly connected, keeping his elbows bent to form an oval shape.

"As for you, Force, it is taking every fiber of self-control within my being to refrain from inserting an air-bubble into the soft tissue between your brutish ears and imploding what little brain you possess. Instead, I'll display a sense of mercy and humanity you obviously have no inclination

51

of."

Raising his good hand to his chest with a mighty struggle, Ben's middle finger pierced the dusty air just as Mystic's elbows began to descend inward until the forearms connected.

"Go... f-fuck yourself, ya miserable...piece of d-dog shi-... ..."

As if caught in an invisible vice, Ben's entire body bent inward onto itself; a grisly, distorted parody of abstract art, then just as quickly deflated back to normalcy as his limp, lifeless form collapsed face first into a thick mound of mangled instillation.

Lifting the field that had shielded the media since his entrance, Mystic maintained the manufactured visage of concern as the hordes quickly grouped around both himself and his fallen prey.

"My god, Mystic, what did you do to him?" a young reporter asked excitedly as his cameraman jockeyed for position at Mystic's side. Floating upward to allow additional room within the confined space, Mystic shrugged unenthusiastically.

"I simply compressed the air around him, literally squeezing him into submission. It was far less than he deserved, I must say."

After several moments, whereas the attention seemed to divert from himself to the motionless bodies left in the wake of battle, Mystic levitated to the bar's demolished entryway, pausing only to add a final soundbite as an armed task force rushed onto the scene.

"My thoughts are awash with emotion, my friends. I've lost... a mentor and friend. Perhaps...

I'll attempt to express my feelings, better yet…purge my soul…on my website within a few days."

The uniformed task force shoved their way through the circle of humanity entombing the fugitive's body like ravenous vultures, ignoring his obvious injuries as they strapped him to a specially designed gurney, resembling a torture device from centuries past.

Wheeled towards a waiting van fronting the smoking crater that had once served as the bar entrance, the fugitive's eyes fluttered uncontrollably.

The dreamscape he wondered was one he had rarely experienced on reality's embattled plain, littered with scenes both spiritually soothing and physically reenergizing.

He sat atop a grassy hill, the landscape beautifully green and lush, sharing a springtime picnic with a strikingly gorgeous Asian female. He sipped a frosty beer and she a cantor of peach brandy, the aroma of which, when mixed with the heady fragrance she wore, instantly inflamed his heart with primal desire. He told her things; things he never dared utter before in her regal presence in fear of a gradual but inevitable rejection. People in their line of work rarely crossed the taboo of true commitment. Surprisingly, he found such trivialities no longer viable. Worries of old faded like morning fog beneath blazing sunlight.

They laughed. They caressed. Their bodies were one. He felt as though his heart would burst from a contentment and happiness never before achieved within mortal restraints Deep within his

53

fevered subconscious, Benjamin Kyle Thomason prayed for an eternal coma, possibly even for death. Anything to be allowed an extended period residing in his own personal Shangri-La with the woman he loved so dearly. Deeper within the pits of his mind, the section which handed out 'wake up' calls within extended slumber's hazy corridors, stark reality shrieked out the cold, hard truth without mercy.

The message was simple: enjoy it while it lasts, for such a surreal state of mind was far from infinite.

Benjamin's subconscious sighed in relief, albeit temporarily.

CHAPTER TWO

Desolation Island

Fading in and out of consciousness, the running dialogue spoken by those leaning over his prone frame is fractured; only partially comprehendible. Their darting shadows sweep over his senses like scattered bird formations; their movements frantic but strangely controlled. Their tone is laced with anxiety, but also with a stern professionalism that is equally cocky and indifferent.

".... need the monitor... at fifty-six five... won't have an OD...my shift."

"... density scanner reading is...... can't be right...... Healing at.... rate of..... at least ten times faster.... normal human being...."

"Not.... normal human being, Doctor Welch.... he's... almost as though.... mutated metabolism... much greater capacity for unnatural healing..."

"... ribs are almost completely mended.... hand is.... ly bruised but no longer showing break.... any kind...."

"... ready for trail... next week.... keep heavily sedated...... Federal Law states we... him alive... but not necessarily conscious..."

"... word on conviction? ..."

"...... more than likely he's off to... land of Detention..."

"... I'd wager a ... -ble life sentence."

"... Murder on nationwide TV and internet... open and shut...."

The sweet aroma of cinnamon fills his flaring

55

nostrils, the verbal exchange growing increasingly inaudible even as the shadows intertwine with the darkness beneath his eyelids.

"... riddance to... bad trash, I say...... all freaks of nature... in my book."

***

Part I:

TWO WEEKS LATER:
Kangaroo Court

LOCATION: Undisclosed   underground Government facility

"How do you plead, Mister Thomason? Please begin with charge number one."

Battling the urge to scream his reply until it echoed off the thick stone walls like a Supersonic boom, Ben sighed heavily instead and concentrated on the razor-sharp cuffs binding his wrists. He felt the blades open his flesh with the tiniest of adjustments, sticky warmth filling his palms.

"Not guilty, Sir."

Judge McMillian, infamously nicknamed 'Judge Misery' by the media decades earlier, openly smirked.

"Charge two, Mr. Thomason?"

Grinding his teeth until a muffled crunch chipped a partial filling onto his tongue, Ben felt his self-control melt away despite the industrial strength sedative filling his veins.

The armed guards on either side of him seemed

to tense in unison as he barked his reply a bit louder than he'd intended.

"Not... GUILTY...Sir."

The gray haired man sitting behind the large oak podium gently pushed the thin bifocals back onto the bridge of his prominent nose and studied the tiny PC screen sitting before him. Judge Raymond McMillian had tried all 'PWEG' (Persons With Extraordinary Gifts) cases since the early nineties, once the Federal Government had seen the need for a separate branch of justice to handle such 'special' types. He was legendary for his lack of compassion in dealing with 'superheroes gone awry', occasionally dolling out harsher sentences than for what he termed the 'darker side' of heroism; that being the criminal element, or 'super-villains' as the media dubbed them.

The Judge grunted several times as his fingers pecked away at the PC's miniscule keyboard. Ben heard the guard stationed on this left chuckle beneath the metal-plated sun-visor covering his face.

"You're toast, hero. Burnt and cris-pi-fied."

"You a lawyer now too, crap for brains?" Ben grumbled, twisting his head until his searing gaze was just inches from the tip of the guard's face plate, "... how's about keyin' these cuffs for a sec and I'll reach 'tween your ass-cheeks and pull out your diploma?"

"SILENCE, Mr. Thomason, or I'll be forced to order a stun-gun deterrent. Are we clear?" the Judge bellowed, peering over the bifocals even as he reached up to close the PC's cover.

Ben faced forward, forcing the predatory smile

57

from his chapped lips with great effort.

"Yes... Sir, Judge. Won't happen again... Sir."

Folding his arms across his slick black robe, the Judge's tone was similar to a political acceptance speech; calm and appreciative, but with just a hint of self-importance.

"Benjamin Thomason, alias *'Force'*; alias *'Desolation Outlaw'*; I have studied the history of your service to our government over the past decade and a half and must admit the whole of the work you've accomplished merits nothing less than my up-most respect.

"That said, such an upstanding record does little to extinguish the events of the past several months. In fact, such a despicable about-face in terms of honor and good will are sickening in the extreme.

"I do believe that mutual combat resulted in Mr. Shaker's death, as you were in the line of duty and attempting to bring the man to justice. However, in regard to the death of one Clarence 'Jiggy' Wilkes, AKA 'Rapmaster XXX', I hereby find you guilty of murder in the second degree."

Bowing his head until his freshly clean-shaven chin rested atop his massive chest, Ben felt his chest tighten as if suddenly compressed by an enormous weight.

"In the wrongful death of Raymond Jacques, AKA 'Crimson Condor', I hereby find you guilty of murder in the first degree.

"The Condor's list of commendations surpassed even your own, and for his life to be so brutally ended by a man he once referred to as 'partner' simply emphasizes just how dangerous a menace to society you've become."

Raising his head in order to meet the Judge's stern gaze, Ben felt his lips involuntarily curl into an angry sneer he was no longer able to reel in. While the judge paused, the guard on his left softly whispered the word 'toast' just loud enough to be heard beneath the face plate. As the pulse at his temples began to thump and drum like fired pistons, Ben's line of vision grew a light shade of maroon.

"Do you have anything to say in your behalf before sentence is passed, Mr. Thomason?" the Judge finally asked, removing his bifocals while nonchalantly crossing his arms across his chest.

"As a matter of fact, your honor, I most certainly do," he replied, planting his feet as firmly as the steel-reinforced bonds at his ankles would allow, "... on count one; Shaker Jake was a worthless pile of steaming rat shit that deserved to die, and die badly. Regardless that it wasn't by my hand, good fuckin' riddance.

"Ditto for Rapmaster dick-weed. Wasn't worth soil in' my hands, but at least he's finally fillin' that assigned seat in hell contracted for him at birth."

Inhaling deeply, Ben bent his knees ever-so-slightly as he continued, a subtle movement neither guard seemed to notice.

"As for the case of my one-time comrade turned back-stabbing traitor; one of the few in the business I ever completely trusted with my own life, he sold out and paid... period. Mystic never intended to share the reward, and I was the perfect scapegoat, a role I've played many times in many incarnations, it seems I ain't denyin' I wouldn't have put a helluva hurtin' on Ray, but a handful of

59

broken bones is a far cry from cashin' in a man's ticket. I've killed before, many damn times in fact, but *only* in self-defense. It was murder one, no argument, Judge. You just happen to be hangin' the wrong outlaw."

Wringing his liver-spot ravaged hands, the Judge's expression reeked of disinterest.

"So say you, Mr. Thomason. Your comments are duly noted as a matter of record, and are automatically recorded for case file purposes. Now, to the matter of sentencing…"

"Buttered toast, hero…" the guard on the left mumbled gleefully.

With that, Ben realized his inner-rage gauge had just red-lined past the point of no return. It was a feeling equally feared and whole-heartedly welcomed by his battered psyche.

"…Benjamin Kyle Thomason, I sentence you to life plus twenty-five years; time to be served at an undisclosed location. You are *not*, sir, eligible for parole." The Judge raised his gavel just as Ben laughed aloud; a sarcastic howl that coincided perfectly with the onslaught of pure adrenaline coursing through his veins like a crimson tidal wave. The gavel's incessant pounding played in time with the thunderous pulse on either side of his skull.

"Appreciate the fair shake, Judge! Sorry for delayin' your golf game…"

"This court is adjourned. Please remove this murderous bastard from my court."

Before the guards could even attempt to lean towards him, Ben utilized the whole of his stocky, muscular frame, planting his shoulder into the one stationed to his right The man grunted in shocked surprise upon impact, then was sent sailing airborne, landing with a resounding thud as he bounced from the top of an oak table onto the hard marble floor. The guard from the left backed away several steps, reaching for his utility belt, even as Ben fell in the other direction, the metallic restraints keeping his ankles locked mere inches apart. The guard had pulled his stun gun free and had just begun to point it in Ben's direction when his left knee exploded with a sickening crunch. Lying on his right side, Ben had kicked forward and caught the man's upper shin with the heels of both boots. As theman fell back with a shrieking yelp, his shattered leg bent backward at the knee, Ben rolled over onto his back and quickly sat up, wearing a wide, warped grin.

"Maybe it's just me, but that bone snappin' did sound pretty damned 'cris-pi-fied', now didn't it?"

The other guard managed to stand even as the echoes of tripped alarms filled the room. His hands, wrists and forearms now soaked with his own blood, Ben twisted his upper body like a human funnel and rolled into the standing guard, whose own stun gun flew from his gloved hand as he tumbled forward in a clumsy lurch. Halting his forward progress by using his bound legs for leverage, Ben then rolled back in the opposite direction until his head was even with the fallen guards. "Hiya, cupcake. Here's hopin' your government dental plan is a good one." Flinging his head forward in a frenzied blur, Ben ducked until the top of his skull impacted directly onto the center of the guard's faceplate. Metal and fiberglass shattered like splintered kindling into jagged shards, leaving the man screaming in agony as the flesh on his face was instantly shredded.

Ben could hear a virtual herd of boot-steps grow near, as well as the Judge's grizzled tone bellowing for immediate assistance.

He attempted to rise as his right elbow found a sticky puddle of his own blood, forcing him back down just as the initial charge of electricity lit up the back of his neck with a loud snap.

"Oh... hell....", he managed to utter a moment before his entire body seemed to ignite from at least a dozen separate stun gun assaults.

"Gentlemen, kindly remove this freak of nature from my courtroom...," the Judge spat as the room grew mercifully dim around Ben, "...so he may be allowed to join his own kind in earthly purgatory."

Benjamin Kyle Thomason wouldn't be allowed to regain consciousness for another seventy-two hours, wherein he would awaken as the newest addition to a bizarre, alien landscape that could *best* be described as nightmarishly surreal.

***

Part II

76 Hours Later

In-Brief
Location: *Eagle Island Detention Center* (Exact location unspecified)

"Welcome aboard, Benjamin," the man announced in a cheery, wholly insincere tone, the

62

high back leather chair swinging around gradually as if electronically controlled.

"Such formalities are tedious, I know, but are a necessary evil. I'm Charles V. Terry, the warden here at Eagle Isle."

Benjamin felt the rounded end of a shock-stick dig into the pit of his back as he stumbled forward a step.

"Speak when spoken to, mister," the guard stationed at his back whispered as the stick was then jabbed firmly between his shoulder blades.

"Might wanna call off your pet gorilla there, Warden, or you're gonna end up payin' him a shit-heap of disability pay."

The Warden rose from behind the wide, metallic desktop and stood with his hands curled behind his back, displaying a thin smile while shaking his head slowly from side to side.

"You're no longer on a street corner, Benjamin," he said, leaning back onto the edge of the desk while crossing his thickly muscled arms across an equally buffed chest. "I'm afraid carrying out such threats is no longer an option. Such possibilities ended the moment your transport landed. As I'm required to tell all new arrivals, this can either be hard...or it can be even harder. It's completely up to you."

Sighing heavily, Benjamin locked his eyes onto the other man's and allowed his rage to subside through random thoughts not remotely associated with anyone or thing within the room he presently occupied. Scattered images filled his mind's eye as his pulse calmed, the majority involving Leah and the beach home they'd once shared off the

Mississippi coast. If even a portion of saneness was to be spared during the in-processing ritual at Eagle Island Detention Center, the identity of his mental savior was never in doubt. No denying the fact that Leah Chang was back in his life, if only as a static-stream holograph created out of sheer desperation.

"I suggest you drop the bad-ass malcontent persona right here and now, Benjamin. To use the vernacular, it just doesn't fly. Waste of effort…waste of breath…waste of time. Now, let me lay down a few select ground rules."

Ben had, of course, heard of Charles Terry, formerly known as 'The Chief Justice' during his spandex days in the mid-to-late seventies. Unbeknownst to most, the man had been awarded the prestigious position as Eagle Isle's head honcho following a yearlong interview process during which time over two-thousand applicants had been considered. During his hey-day roaming the crime-laden streets of D. C, Terry had wielded a fifty-pound iron 'gavel' to doll out justice to pre- and post-Vietnam era law breakers. One of that rare breed of superhero with no apparent superpowers, he'd been infamous for his gritty 'by the book', 'cut no slack whatsoever' approach to fighting crime, a credo no doubt endeared him to those on the Eagle Isle hiring board. Now a quarter-century older and sporting a balding plate and grayish beard, the man nevertheless carried an air of intimidation with his bulky frame and authoritative demeanor. It was obvious he still spent some serious time in the weight room, and possessed the fierceness of a rabid pit-bull beneath an outwardly cool exterior.

"Go for it, Warden. I'm just tinglin' with

anticipation," Ben whispered, hanging his head slightly as he felt his entire body rev down several notches. Despite the serrated cuffs cutting into his wrists and a similar discomfort at his bound ankles, he managed to manufacture a continuing stream of flash images with Leah at the forefront.

The Warden cleared his throat, ran a hand over his hairless scalp, then returned to the cushioned confines of his throne.

"The medical staff will brief you further during the cleansing phase, but I always make it a point to hit on key issues upon meeting any new arrivals," he said, sitting down with a huff. A PC unit arose with a low hum from the center of the otherwise empty desktop, complete with a flat monitor and adjoined tower, along with a combination fax/printer and scanner unit.

"Let's see here," the Warden mumbled while lightly tapping the keyboard, "You'd think I'd have the speech memorized by now. Then again, you are the first 'new meat' in a month or so, and we've had several recent updates from home base."

Pushing his chair back, the Warden leaned back with a resounding sigh, his eyes darting back and forth from the glowing monitor to Ben. Eventually, his gaze locked on his newest charge even as his expression soured and his tone turned noticeably grim.

"Okay…the Reader's Digest version then. Let's disperse with the most obvious first, what say? Benjamin, there is no escape from Eagle Island Detention Center.

"I'm not saying this to sound cocky or brash, simply stating the cold hard truth. Facts are facts. I take no credit for such an unprecedented, unblemished record. I'm simply minding the store. A multi-billion-dollar store that essentially takes care of itself.

"Since its inception as the Maximum of *all* Maximum-security units, no one has even come close to departing this tiny sand-dune without expressed written consent. I know, it may sound like a cheap line from an old Alcatraz flick, but like I said...facts are facts.

"Not to say it hasn't been from a lack of attempts, you understand. Over the years I've seen everything tried from teleportation to cell alternation to just plain brute force. Take my word for it, Benjamin, Eagle Isle contains over two-hundred separate security measures, each especially designed to effectively offset whatever power our inmates possess or could possibly attain while on these grounds. Eagle Island was built with specially endowed types such as yourself in mind. We've housed and presently house some of the most noted bad asses of the last quarter century. Each individual case is carefully, meticulously studied, analyzed, and outlined before being assigned an applicable security risk.

"For example, you have been assigned as a category 'C' security risk. We rate from A to E, depending on the power and...special endowment rating of each inmate."

Leaning forward, the Warden again assaulted the keyboard with a lightning quick barrage of pounding strokes.

Meanwhile, Ben's expression remained solemn even as he envisioned himself and Leah strolling

66

along a sandy beach with a warm, gentle breeze slapping his face.

"Your personnel file lists you a strength rating of seven out of ten, meaning equal to or greater than twenty average men, plus the added risk those wrecking-ball sized fists of yours create. Thus, without any type of harnessing power, whether by electrical, chemical, or unknown origin, a cell constructed of titanium-based alloy is all that's required. In laymen's terms, we match brute force with brute *resistance*. Attempting to punch your way out will result in nothing more than shattered exo-skeleton and an extended stay in the infirmary. I wouldn't suggest that, Benjamin. I hear the food is pretty lousy."

"Appreciate the tip, Warden," Ben replied, looking up through hazy eyes, as if just awakened from a deep slumber, "Say, ya wouldn't happen to have a shot or three of *Jack Black* handy, would ya? I'm parched."

"Quiet, numb-nuts," the guard growled, reaching up and over to tap Ben's left shoulder with the shock-stick's cool metallic edge.

Again leaning back with his hands propped atop his slick, shiny dome, Warden Terry's robotic monologue continued unabated, as if lecturing a room full of inattentive students.

Meanwhile, Ben pulled Leah close, her sweet scent intoxicating as his hands pressed against the warm, smooth flesh of her lower back.

"The outer perimeter of the island is encased in a multi-layered laser screen created solely with disintegration in mind. The '*flesh-mixer*', as its been dubbed by inmates and staff alike, was designed to

67

effectively scramble human or mutant cell structure on contact, while allowing only the oxygen outside its transparent dome to successfully enter and/or exit. The few unfortunate individuals who failed to heed our warnings, and there've only been two such cases thus far, resembled something akin to 'eggs over easy' by the time the clean-up crew got to them. Not a pretty site, I must say."

The PC unit slid back into the desk as the Warden leaned forward, propping his elbows on the cleared space where the keyboard had sat.

Meanwhile, Ben reached back and ran his fingers through the silky softness of Leah's hair, which flowed over his hands, wrists and forearms in dark, billowy waves.

"Twenty-three hours of each day will be spent inside your assigned cell, while government regulations allow for one hour within the 'Free Zone', a specially designed space containing various exercise equipment, TV screens, and stereo equipment.

"Since inmate movement is frowned upon for obvious security reasons, all personal grooming takes place within the cell sector as well, as specially constructed 'self-cleansing units' are placed in each individual cell. Their use, of course, is optional. One can freely choose to reek if he or she so desires.

"In 'prison terms', Benjamin, all inmates housed on Eagle Isle are placed in permanent Admin Segregation from day one. There is no 'general population' here, due to the obvious conflicts that would assuredly arise between warring factions of inmates. Let's face it; you're libel to come face to face with one of your deadliest former enemies, no doubt instigating a brawl-type scenario I have neither the time nor available staff to properly quell.

"Segregation also eliminates many of the daily issues dealt with on a state and federal level, such as the forming of cliques or the ever-popular rumor mill that serves as a catalyst for fictional hearsay both within the inmate population and the working staff. Communication between inmates is relatively nil, as it should be. That, along with the lack of drug and sexual abuse so commonplace in 21st Century penal units, is the most substantial pro connected to such a special facility as the EIDC. There are cons, as well, but too few to mention without sounding.... well, a bit petty."

"Yeah, I guess not havin' to worry about super-powered rump-humpers is a load off one's mind, at that," Ben responded through glassy eyes, now sharing a toast of sparkling red wine with Leah as a picturesque waterfall cascaded off a jagged mountainside in the background.

"One more time, tough guy, and I'll light you up like a neon sign," the guard whispered harshly.

As before, the Warden seemed oblivious to all other banter save his own. "There is no visitation allowed here, thus eliminating still another security headache. There is no dining hall; no inmate cafeteria to speak of. Three complete meals, for those inmates who *require* regular nourishment, are allowed per day at seven AM, twelve noon, and six PM. These FDA approved dishes are served within the inmate's cell via computerized teleportation. Inmates have exactly fifteen minutes to consume each meal before re-teleportation procedures commence.

"Behavioral problems, the few that do surface now and again, are handled with the overall security of the site in mind, thus such trite issues as political correctness or legal consequences are not an issue. One warning per customer, Ben," he paused, lifting his right hand and extending the forefinger into the air, "Behave yourself. Consider the consequences of your actions *before* you act. Any pain inflicted will be of your own making. As I stated, this is the first and final warning on such childish matters."

The Warden stood up, yawning as he strolled over to a nearby bookshelf, where he casually filled a large brown mug with steaming black coffee.

"Bottom line, Benjamin…this is your home now. The last place you'll ever call home. You'll depart Eagle Island in a sealed casket on whatever date the Good Lord has chosen. Complaining won't change that. Harming yourself or forcing my hand to harm you won't change that. As I tell all new arrivals, whether they be of human or synthetic origin, mutant or extraterrestrial, make the *best* of what you have. And what you have…is time. Embrace meditation. Embrace the power of the written word. Embrace solitude, for it is all you truly have left."

After a series of noisy slurps, the Warden stepped forward until the tips of his black dress boots sit mere inches from the site-issued flip-flops adorning Ben's size thirteen feet.

Although the two men stood approximately the same height, Ben's massive girth dwarfed the other man in decisive fashion.

"One final thing, Benjamin. You won't be seeing me again, at least, not on a one-on-one, face-to-face basis. I'm an administrator, *not* the head bull. The *Guardsman* is my CO in charge. You'll be dealing with him exclusively. Now, I'm required to ask, so please bear with me," he sighed heavily, "Benjamin Thomason, do you understand the policies and procedures as I've explained them to you?"

Cocking his head slightly to the left, Ben displayed a look of comic befuddlement, his eyes blinking rapidly and his mouth hanging agape.

"Oh, sorry, Warden. You say somethin'? Afraid I might'a been driftin'..."

"I'll...take that as a yes then," the Warden replied in a tight-lipped whisper,

"...and a final welcome to Eagle Island, Mr. *Outlaw*, where I'm afraid you will learn the true meaning of *Desolation*."

Feigning shock, Ben shot the other man a playful wink just as the CO reached forward and parked the edge of the shock-stick against the base of his neck.

"Nice play on words, Warden. A real 'solitary confinement' gem, that was. Nice to know the head cheese is such a fun-lovin' card."

"Take him to the infirmary for cleansing," the Warden concluded, turning back towards his desk, "his T-Walled suite is prepped on D-Block."

"You heard the man," the CO growled, pulling Ben along by the thumb-cuffs that pinned his hands to the pit of his back, "its bath-time for bad-ass."

"Nothin' kinky now, pal, not 'til we're o-fficially engaged," Ben replied, turning slowly as to

71

not tangle his feet from the limited movement the leg-irons provided.

The hydraulically powered door closed with a hum just as both men re-entered the narrow, green-painted hallway that served as a back-exit from the site's command center. Moments later, they entered a nearby elevator, where the CO pressed a dark maroon key labeled '*B-Level – Infirmary*'. Blinking yellowish light filled the confined space as they sailed downward at what felt like warped speed. Staring straight ahead at the elevator door, which consisted of at least a dozen rows of Laser beams in lieu of a solid base, Ben felt a gradual reemergence of the anger he'd fought so hard to restrain.

"Bet ya can't wait for the cavity search, huh pal?"

The guard paused full five seconds before responding.

"Better talk it up, tough guy. You're about ten minutes away from one hell of an attitude adjustment."

"Cut it out, bud. You're gonna 'cause my inner child to soil his huggies."

As the ride concluded and the laser beam guardrail vanished like blue flame from an acetylene torch, they stood facing a massive double-door entrance marked '*CLEANSING-OUTER/TUBE BOOTHS 1-3.*'

"We call this the 'purge and re-gurge' room. Here's hoping your last meal was a light one, Outlaw," the CO giggled, shoving Ben roughly forward.

"If I'm allowed a final request, I'll make mine a shot of Wild Turkey with a Coors chaser," Ben chimed in while stumbling ahead and almost directly into a tiny, squared keypad outside the knob-less entrance.

"In your dreams. Pucker up and prep for pain, smart-ass."

With that, the CO stepped up to the keypad and punched in a long series of numbers.

The doors parted inward with a grinding buzz, and Ben instantly felt his midsection tighten.

***

Part III:

Purge, Peel and Reel

As his head submerged from the thick, glutinous gel which reeked of disinfectant, a veritable gusher spewed forth from his parted lips, splashing against the glass tubing just inches from his face and ricocheting back into his eyes and open mouth.

He continued to vomit the blackened bile as his upper body was racked with violent spasms. Clamped at the shoulders, elbows and hips by vice-grip apparatuses that resembled metallic lobster-claws, he was lifted into the upper portion of the glass tube until his feet levitated a few inches from the dark pool's oily surface.

An android-like voice rang out in timed intervals from overhead speakers, repeating coded instructions in triplicate.

INTERNAL   AGENT INGESTED/DIGESTED/EXPUNGED...PURGING

CYCLE COMPLETE AT...THREE MINUTES...EIGHTEEN SECONDS...

The sooty liquid instantly began to empty from the clear glass cylinder, which resembled nothing more elaborate than a giant-sized 'test tube', the stone chamber room filled with loud gurgling noises, as if a tall straw were being used to extract the pudding-thick contents.

INITIATE TANK FLUSH SEQUENCE...INITIATE TANK FLUSH SEQUENCE ...

Within seconds, the tube was filled with a soapy, milky-white substance, instantaneously stripping the glass clean of any residue left over from the previous filler, then re-emptied just as quickly.

INITIATE OUTER PEEL SEQUENCE ...INITIATE OUTER PEEL SEQUENCE...TO PROCEED IN THIRTY SECONDS...TO PROCEED IN THIRTY SECONDS...

The crane device holding him airborne slowly descended even as the tube refilled yet again, this time with a clear substance one might initially identify as water, but that held a stout, chemical-laced scent that filled the room with an antiseptic fog.

He released a guttural, animalistic grunt as his feet, calves and thighs were slowly submerged into the mix.

As the vice-clamps forced him down, coating his groin and lower waist, the grunt transformed into a garbled screech.

Just as the acid-based liquid reached his neck and the bottom portion of his chin, a man who had been on a first name basis with physical pain for nearly two decades, having suffered countless broken bones, concussions, and stress fractures, nonetheless screamed out in unbridled anguish as never before. Mercifully, his cries were muted in seconds, as his mouth and nostrils were subsequently filled with the source of his suffering.

"Amazing, isn't it, Sir? How the old 'peel and shred' turns even the self-proclaimed toughest SOB's on the planet into whimpering six-year olds?" the young technician asked while timing the sequence with a laptop PC balanced atop his knees, his pasty lips frozen in a cruel, sadistic smile.

The masked man next to him stood in a textbook 'parade rest' pose, with his gloved hands clasped tightly at the pit of his muscular back.

After several moments, wherein they bore witness to the bound subject wrestling and squirming in futility within the transparent tube as his lungs filled with liquid, the masked man shot the young techie an angry glance.

"You find this particular task amusing, Mister Barnes?"

The technician, nervously adjusting the wire-rimmed glasses hanging at the tip of his beak-like nose, twitched and shook as his fingers continued to dance atop the keyboard.

"Um... well…uh…well, sir, I don't exactly feel pity, if that's what you're asking."

"Freakish scum is getting what he deserves, correct?"

Coughing into his palm several times, the techie then paused to clear his throat before responding.

"Well, sir, that is…well, yes. They're not exactly here for meritorious service to the country. Just rewards, I say. Let the punishment fit the crime, am I ri-"

"Just buzz me when you finishup here, Mister Barnes. I…feel the need for a breath of fresh air, even if it is laced with solar field particles."

"Ye-yes, Guardsman, sir. Shouldn't be more than twenty minutes tops. Just have to run him through the rollers and clean him off, followed by a quick dip into the Cortizone vat."

The Guardsman, AKA Lucas T. Bradley, departed the viewing room without speaking further, his steel-soled boots clanking loudly off the concrete flooring leading to a nearby walkway.

As he halted midway down a slim glass corridor, breathing deeply while leaning against a metal rail and staring out into a picturesque landscape filled with cloudless skies and cascading blue waves, the throbbing at his temples gradually subsided. In his seven-plus years as head CO at Eagle Island, he'd found little use for the '*intuition*' that had once been such a vital asset in his street crime-fighting days. Rubbing his eyes through the narrow holes of his cowl, he was hapless but to endure the familiar ringing in his ears; the tingling at the back of his skull, just above the nape of his neck. Such symptoms were rarely translated to mean anything other than something nearby being horribly amiss, as in 'extremely rotten in Denmark'.

"Ben, Ben, Ben. What has befallen you, old friend?" he whispered, his upper body slumped as if suddenly beset by complete, utter exhaustion.

He wouldn't find the motivation nor energy to

76

change positions for an additional ten minutes.

***

"I'd say he's around sixty percent healed already, sir. This one's skin rejuvenates like a mutie." The Guardsman nodded without speaking.

"He's ready for the tour anytime you are, um, sir," the techienamed Barnes continued, no longer meeting the masked man's searing gaze, and falling conspicuously silent while scanning a checklist from an electronic clipboard.

"Have him brought up to ground level one while I sign out a hover," the Guardsman muttered weakly, turning to depart but halting abruptly just as the lab door swung open.

"And, Barnes..."

"Sir?"

"Let's make damn sure the man's living quarters are prepped. I really don't want to be sitting on my hands for half an hour like that goat-rope we had last month with *Screaming Eagle*, got it?"

"Yes, sir. I've already coordinated with Rogers up top. Desolation Outlaw's sector is prepped for immediate housing following the tour"

"Good to hear. Nothing worse than being forced to make small talk with cons."

Moving with renewed vigor, The Guardsman strolled briskly into the adjoining hallway.

"Or grumpy CO's with a bug up their rear end, for that matter," Techie Barnes scowled while scooping up a nearby phone.

"Rogers? Barnes. Hey, Mister Outlaw's sector

is good to go, correct? Just checking. King Shit CO was riding my ass again. Later, dude…"

**

With a heavily armed three-man security team posed at his back, Ben was led down a long, circular hall and into a wide, glass-dome breezeway. Though thoroughly flushed and treated with specially medicated drops, his eyes still burned as if coated with kerosene. The thumb-cuffs and leg irons had been replaced by thick, strangely pliable restraints of unknown substance. Though slightly bendable, they were no doubt constructed of an unbreakable material utilized solely within the EIDC. For reasons yet unknown, his hands had been cuffed in the front and not behind his back.

The sun's penetrating rays shining through the glass walls struck his pupils like guided spear-tips, causing him to flinch back and cover his face with upraised arms.

"Better take a good luck, Outlaw," the CO to his right barked beneath a mirrored visor, "you aren't liable to see sunlight again 'til you're lying face up in a coffin."

"Was graduatin' Charm School a prerequisite for this job, pal?" Ben growled through an unusually husky, horse tone, "Professional assholes, the whole lot of ya."

He lowered his bound arms while gradually allowing each eye to adjust to the sudden burst of light.

"Daaaamn. Surf's up," he mumbled without even realizing he'd spoken aloud, turning his head

78

in a deliberate one-eighty even as his vision cleared to at least a semi-normal state.

From their vantage point at the ground floor of Building 'A' (*Cell Sectors*), the entire substructure was encased in non-tinted glass walls and supported by thick steel and concrete beams, allowing a full ocean view from the east side, and panoramic, beachfront views from all others.

"Real scenic. Who chose the location, Don *Freakin'* Ho?"

"As far as you're concerned, Benjamin, we might as well be floating on an ice-burg smack dab in the center of the Antarctic," a bland yet authoritative voice rang out from the opposite walkway, accompanied by loud, clanking footsteps that grew louder as they neared.

As the masked man strolled into view, Ben couldn't help but smile despite the situation.

"Luke T, as I live and barely breath. I hear you're the head bull in these here parts," he managed before being seized by a frantic coughing spell lasting almost a full minute.

"Chief Correctional Officer, to be precise," The Guardsman replied, standing less than a foot away from his newest charge, who was still slightly hunched from the hacking spell.

"Gotta say, Luke, you're lookin' a little flabby in the shanks. Must be hard to get any serious scrap-time when the place pretty well runs itself. Don't they have a gym on this burg?"

"You're not exactly the picture of health yourself, ham-hocks. Almost didn't recognize you without your facial decorations," The Guardsman said, crossing his arms over his chest, "The boys at

79

the infirm shot you up with the best we've got. How you feeling?"

"Hammered crap, truth be told. Why not just peel my hide with a straight razor? That chemical acid even burned all my *pubes* off, man. That shit just *ain't* right, ya know?"

Covering his mouth to suppress a giggle, The Guardsman gave the larger man a quick once-over for no other reason than simple distraction. The mandatory uniform (at least for all 'non-mutant', 'non-intergalactic' types) was a pair of loose-fit cotton coveralls, 'flip-flop' styled rubber sandals, while gym shorts, and a T-shirt. In addition, hard toe boots were allowed within the *Free Zone* for workouts.

Under textbook circumstances, such casual interaction and fraternization with an inmate was not only frowned upon, but in most cases a fineable offense amongst CO's of any rank. None present were privy to the past between the two men, although The Guardsman had no doubt Warden Terry had surely done his homework on such matters.

"The Cleansing is simply a precautionary measure, Benjamin. Everyone, including staff, receive similar treatment upon arrival. Can't be helped, I'm afraid. Besides, I hear you're a fast healer. Within a few days, you'll never even know it transpired."

"Uh-huh. I hear ya talkin', Luke. I can't remember much of it, and that's probably a good thing," he replied with a nod, reaching up with clasped hands to rub a white patch of flesh beneath his nostrils. "Shit, man...I haven't been without my

80

mustache since I was knee high to a Bourbon Street hooker, not to mention lookin' like Kojak's long-lost brother with this cue-ball noggin."

"It'll grow back, Ben. Not that anyone will notice, but it *will* grow back. Looks like the tattoos are permanent enough."

Glancing over and down, Ben performed a brief 'status check' on said body art, which included a spiked mace over his left biceps; a striking cobra with crossed swords over his right, and a flaming skull across his breastbone.

"Take a flame-thrower to dent those beauties. Had 'em done up in Thailand and the Philippines back in the late eighties. Damn ink goes right down to the exo-skeleton bone."

The brief pause that followed seemed to drag on much longer than it actually did, an awkward interlude wherein both men took turns staring at the others feet. It was the low hum of an approaching hovercraft that broke the uncomfortable silence "You ready for the 'one-time only' tour, Mr. Thomason?"

"Do I truly have a choice, Luke?"

The tiny, three-seat craft, which had obviously been auto-piloted from a hanger two buildings over, floated up to the small congregation and stopped, levitating less than afoot from the tiled floor.

"Afraid not. Regulations and all that," The Guardsman said, backing away with a slight bow as to allow the larger man initial entry, "We'll be entering the Cell Sector a floor above."

As he boarded, followed closely by one of the armed CO's, Ben paused to take in the scenic splendor outside the dome glass one final time.

"I take it beach parties ain't part of the rehab program…"

Again, The Guardsman fought off a laugh while taking a seat directly across from the man he was sworn to incarcerate. The hover rose at a snail's pace even as a wide hatch above them parted to allow entry.

"Quiet, EISR dash D-Fourteen. All conversation, save the Chief CO's, ceases upon entering Cell Sector space," the armed CO said without a hint of actual anger, as if simply reiterating a long-rehearsed line of stale dialogue.

Ben glanced back to the CO, then back to the Guardsman, executing a perfectly choreographed double-take.

"Come again, Clyde? E... I... S... R dash D-Fourteen? What's the deal, Luke…. that my new personalized license plate?"

"Stands for *Eagle Island Security Risk D.* You're…you'll be addressed as such from here on out. Once you're assigned a cell, personal monikers no longer pertain to the staff, and are actually forbidden to use. Inmates are referred to by security risk only," The Guardsman replied in a bland, somber tone. He'd come dangerously close to verbally chastising his subordinate for speaking out of turn, until he'd realized the 'inmate gag-order' was indeed a by-the-book reg.

"Swell. Testicle slashin' can't be far behind," Ben scowled as the craft ascended past the hatch opening and into a well-lit circle between twin metal railings.

"Permission to correct inmate, sir?" the CO asked calmly, as if asking for a saltshaker at the family dining table.

The Guardsman waived him off, and the CO instantly dropped the shock-stick he'd posed just the left of Ben's bald, peeling scalp.

"Zip it, Ben, or Myers here has every right to use correctional measures. Although all cell sectors are sealed and supposedly noise-proof, there are other factors involved that require we keep verbal exchanges to a minimum."

The CO reached over and placed a bulky headset over Ben's ears as The Guardsman donned a similar get up to include a tiny speaker device positioned at his lips.

The craft rose until it hovered between separate three-tiered blocks containing rows of squared cubes. Ben couldn't help but think it resembled those used to construct an old 20th Century child's toy known as a 'Rubik's Cube'.

Behold the nucleus of Eagle Island Detention Center echoed The Guardsman's voice inside his headset.

Unbeknownst to all but those housed here either by choice or otherwise, truly the unofficial Eighth Wonder of The World.

***

Part IV:

IN THE ZONE

"Screw me to tears. I'm supposed to spend the remainder of my days rotting away in a high-tech egg-crate. All of the sudden I'm feelin' a sincere pity for all those assholes I sent to stir."

DAMN it, Ben...PUT A SOCK IN IT! No more warnings or Myers is liable to crease your skull with that shock-stick.

Ben shrugged like a scolded grade-schooler as the craft rose to the third level of cells and halted momentarily before sailing slowly forward.

There were a dozen rows of boxed-shaped cells per floor on each side of them, all of equal size and dimension. If not for the spiral designed, cathedral-like ceiling, they might well have resembled medium-sized storage units stacked atop one another. The surrounding walls were painted in the same dark green hue as virtually all the corridors and hallways, the only visible markings being a series of stenciled numbers grooved into the front of each individual cell.

Currently the facility consists of thirty-six cell sectors, although expansion is already in the works that'll call for at least a dozen more by the end of the calendar year. Needless to say, it's a booming business with no end in sight.

Unlike the federal and state pens built for the civilian crime element, all inmates reside in a 'blind cell', thereby not allowed a visual outside the four walls surrounding them. This is due to the obvious animosity created by 'old advisories' being housed in such close proximity to one another. Our 'client list', so to speak, is a guarded secret to all but those we answer to at the highest government level.

The craft descended to ground level and halted, floating a few feet above what looked like a small, circular landing pad outlined in dark red.

Tour of outer cell sectors complete.

Introduction to the 'Free Zone' is next. Proceeding to underground level one.

The padding below separated in pied segments until the opening was just large enough to allow the hovercraft to descend beyond its limited perimeters.

They glided through a dimly lit, tube-shaped passage, engaging several steep curves illuminated by a trail of tiny blue-light strobes.

"Gag order still in effect, Luke?" Ben whispered while leaning forward until his chin rested on his clinched fists.

Removing the headset first from himself and then from his bound guest, The Guardsman then reached back and punched in a multi-digit code on the hover's built-in keypad. An octagon-shaped hatchway marked 'Z-1' opened just to their left, and they sailed through without pause.

"You're free to gab, D-fourte-…um…Ben. Knowing you the way I do, I'm sure the last five minutes of silence have been a living hell."

"Gotta be honest with ya, Luke, I ain't real impressed with the new digs. Outside walls looked like cheap stucco. You seriously tellin' me that some of the world's most powerful baddies are kept at bay in those cardboard lookin' rigs?"

They floated through two similar hatches, marked 'Z-2' and 'Z-3' respectively, until reaching a dead end fronting a slightly inverted wall which glowed bright yellow. Still another keypad hung at its center, complete with two separate ID slots and a voice identifier.

"Like the old saying goes, ham-hocks, it's what's on the *inside* that counts. Just maintaining the cell sectors alone costs the American taxpayer upwards of ten million annually.

"You'll understand better in about a half hour."

Turning towards the keypad, The Guardsman punched in still another code, then proceeded to retrieve two separate line-badges from his utility belt and slide them through the narrow slots.

"Guardsman – six…. one…four…three," he announced, backing away as the entire wall slid silently upward.

As the craft drifted forward, the metallic wall was instantly replaced by a series of pencil-thin, crisscrossing laser beams, soon mutating into a solidified force field that made up the entire perimeter of the room.

The hover levitating just inches from the floor's steely surface, the Guardsman departed the craft with a graceful leap, landing just a few feet to the right of a mammoth Universal squat rack.

"Welcome into the designated *Free Zone*, Ben. For two hours per day, five days a week, this will serve as your personal *'Gold's Gym'*; the place where you can work out all your daily frustrations. An armed escort will, of course, accompany you from your cell and back, but isn't required to remain inside the room."

"Sounds reasonable. Does it come with unlimited booze and strippers on demand?" Ben asked with a shrug, exiting the vehicle with the armed CO close on his heels.

"Not quite," The Guardsman replied with a shake of his head, "Budget restraints, you understand."

"Then you can stow that 'all your daily frustrations' remark, Luke."

"Listen up, D-fourteen," the other CO barked, though again with no real conviction, "the man has a briefing to give."

"Well, excuse me all to hell," Ben shot back, leaning back to address the other man before turning back towards The Guardsman and nodding, "pardon my uncouth soul, Luke. Please continue."

"Um, appreciate it, Ben. We are on a schedule here, after all."

"Yeah, I reckon you might well be. On the other hand, I got *alllll* the time in the world."

The three then strolled casually forward, momentarily pausing at the outer edge of each piece of equipment they encountered.

"No doubt you recognize the majority of the machines featured, but regs do require I give a brief description of each. They've all been specially constructed and designed for Eagle Island users in mind, meaning they are able to withstand massive amounts of weight and are practically unbreakable," The Guardsman began, stepping aside to allow a clear view of the spacious enclosure.

"We have, in order of appearance:

...one Universal squat rack that can safely hold up to one ton...

...a combination weight bench with a weight max of just under eighteen-hundred pounds...

...a Universal combination thigh/calf raise machine with a max weight of one thousand...

...a Universal Incline bench press with max weight of twenty-one-hundred pounds...

...an upright row machine, single or double grip, with a max weight of twelve hundred...

...assorted heavy and curl bars.... weights from

fifty to two-hundred pounds. Heavy bars hold max load of five-hundred pounds per side, one-thousand total. Curl bars hold max of three-fifty per side, seven-hundred total...

"Assorted free weights on three separate racks. Heaviest among the lot is one-hundred fifty-pound plates. Total free weights provided is twelve thousand pounds, or six complete tons.

"On the aerobic/cardiovascular side, we have:

...a Model G-II Electric treadmill with incline capability and six various levels of difficulty and speeds ranging from five to forty miles per hour...two heavy duty hard-bags with outer layers constructed of impenetrable exo-plastic, the first sand-filled with a weight of three-hundred pounds. The second is liquid filled with a weight of five hundred. Each can withstand measured punching force equal to or slightly greater than six-hundred pounds per square inch. I'm sure you'll provide the ultimate test with those oversized mitts of yours, Benjamin.

"...and last but not least, two R-3 Model Stationary bikes with incline capability and seven levels of difficulty.

"Truth be told, there are professional sports teams who don't have access to such equipment, much less the technology involved to build 'em."

"Real impressive, Luke, no question. On the other hand..." Ben paused with a wry smile, stepping over to study the closest of the two hard bags, "...exactly why would I bother to stay pumped at this point? It ain't like I'll be strollin' muscle beach anytime soon. Don't get me wrong", he continued, bumping the bag playfully with one shoulder, "...I've spent a big chunk of my adult life tossin' weights around, but sincerely, why the hell bother? I stayed in shape to survive in my chosen profession, ya know? Well, there ain't an enemy in sight, and I ain't one to take up shadow boxin' as a hobby."

Standing on the other side of the bag, The Guardsman threw a series of light jabs before dancing away in a classic 'Ali' shuffle.

"Believe me, it'll be good for the soul, Ben. You'll need...any distraction you can find, I'm afraid."

"Yeah, ya just might have a valid point there," Ben shrugged, "I ain't exactly the soul-searchin' type, and with alcohol and the ladies outta the picture, somethin' has to take up the slack. By the way, Luke...real sorry to hear 'bout Lynnie. That was one classy chick. Damn shame..."

"Thanks, Ben. Believe it or not, she once told me what a 'gentle brute' you seemed to be. Lynn didn't enjoy the company of many in our...clique. You were indeed one of a very select few."

The two men stood silent for several moments, then nodded in unison and walked slowly back toward the craft, where the CO casually leaned with his back resting on the hover's front end.

"Cell assignment, sir?"

Checking his watch, The Guardsman nodded with a sigh.

"Affirmative, Myers. It's almost noon, and we have that meeting with the Warden at one. Let's do it."

As the three men re-entered the craft and the laser wall behind them gradually faded into a thinly veiled mist, Ben felt his chest tighten as if bound with steel banding.

"Home, James..." he quipped without a hint of the nervousness gripping his soul in a fast-tightening vice.

The hover backed from the space and then accelerated forward, following an upward trajectory while passing countless detours that Ben instantly realized were simply pathways to other cells like the one he would soon call home.

***

Part V:

Cubed

"This is it, Ben," The Guardsman said, pulling a small backpack from the hover's rear compartment, "last stop. For informational purposes, though I doubt you really care, the cell assignment number is D-Fourteen."

Taking a seat on the cell's lone cot, Ben watched with some measure of fascination at the open hatchway they'd entered through, which had held the exact shape of the hovercraft, only several inches larger as a whole. The tubular passageway led into the room from the center portion of the cell floor, the only spot within the twenty by twenty space unoccupied by equipment of some type.

"Well, it ain't the Embassy Suites, but I've sure as hell seen worse. 'Bout five years back I spent a couple'a weeks inside a dungeon in Peru that had maggots coatin' the stone walls like wallpaper,

90

courtesy'a *Stingray* and his aquatic goons.

"Then there was the time that *Mister Hate* chained me up with razor wire in some abandoned warehouse in the Everglades. Dropped thirty pounds in three days in that damn heat and humi-"

Clearing his throat loudly as he removed his protective helmet and attached visor, Officer Myers' tone was no longer placid or calm, but openly annoyed. The man looked to be in his mid-to-late thirties, with marine-cropped brown hair graying at the temples. A long, crooked scar ran from his right ear to the tip of his squared chin. His eyes seemed frozen in a permanent squint, and the smile he displayed was laced in sarcasm.

"Thomason, the duration of your stay isn't four days, four years, or even four decades, you get that? There is *no* comparison you can make that will change that fact. Now please allow my supervisor to brief you one final time so we may depart for more…pressing issues."

Ben refused to return the man's stare, instead continuing to address The Guardsman with a look of comical dismay.

"Damn, Luke…you take away Barney Fife's bullet or what?"

He then turned towards Myers with a drastically altered expression, one that many a lawbreaker had witnessed just moments before a rather savage assault had commenced.

"What crawled up your ass-crack and died, Mac? If it's somethin' personal, by all means feel free to remove these cuffs and we can settle it…. *old*-school style."

Officer Myers reached for the shock-stick

91

hanging from his belt just as The Guardsman instinctively stepped between them.

"Enough. Myers...back off and down. You're supposed to be a professional, damn it. Try and remember that.

"Ben, don't even think about it unless you want those restraints to be permanently assigned for the next thirty days or so," he snarled, though his posture remained relatively relaxed and non-combative.

"Yes, sir," Myers whispered, staring down at the tips of his own spit-polished boots.

In contrast, Ben flashed a toothy smile while standing to inspect the connecting toilet and sink just a few feet to the right of the cot.

"My tool's cool, Luke. Just don't like bein' interrupted when I'm cruisin' down memory lane, that's all."

"Fine. Besides, our suits contain a built-in tracking device that's instantly activated at high levels of blunt trauma, sending a code red alert to the command center. You might well get your jollies, but there's a hell of a price to pay about thirty seconds later.

"Now, I've got a few things to cover. First things first..." he said, gesturing to Myers with one raised hand.

"Lift your arms chest high, Thomason," Myers instructed, stepping forward while pulling a plastic badge roughly the size of a credit card from his uniform's left front pocket.

"I'm going to remove your cuffs. Do me a favor and don't even twitch. You got my back, sir?"

The Guardsman nodded without speaking,

taking up a defensive posture to Ben's right.

"Mac, I won't even pass gas without express written consent."

Myers swiped the card through the narrow slot at the top of the wrist cuffs, and they slid apart with a low click. After pocketing the cuffs, he then knelt onto one knee and grasped the leg restraints at the center of the expandable chain.

"Hands behind your head, and keep them there 'til further instructed."

"Yes, dear," Ben barked sarcastically, staring at the iron-plated ceiling above.

After Myers had backed away several steps, the Guardsman motioned for Ben to lower his hands.

"Take a seat, Ben. Allow me to complete a quick verbal inventory."

Lying sideways onto the cot, Ben's head was propped within the massive space of his left palm, the visual equivalent of a softball balanced within a catcher's mitt.

"Thrill me, big guy."

Retrieving the clipboard from the hovercraft, the Guardsman took up position at the center of the room.

"Genuine leather recliner to your left; to your right, of course, is your combo toilet/sink. The toilets are self-flushing and paper is provided on a weekly basis in six-roll increments.

"Notice the tubular design of the pipes leading from each and into the adjoining wall. This unique design..." he paused, walking over and placing his free hand over the thick metal tubing which held both the toilet and sink airborne before curving slightly upward and vanishing into the nearby wall,

"...haven't done this briefing in a while, so I'm reading this verbatim from the manual...anyway, this unique design essentially eliminates the possibility of vandalism or other inmate-related destruction, as the interior pipes are encased in the same titanium-steel based material as the walls themselves.

"Now, the cot provided is four feet wide by seven-and-a-half feet long, steel reinforced with adjustable padding.

"To your left," he continued, strolling back towards the center of the room while Ben released a series of muted yawns, "is the latest in Eagle Isle innovations, the inmate 'self-cleansing' booth. Measured at thirty-eight inches wide and eighty-four long, it effectively eliminates the need for daily grooming transports from the cell sectors to a designated shower room."

"Looks like a tannin' booth, or an oversized microwave," Ben quipped, suppressing yet another yawn. Miraculously, the effects of the 'flesh purging' had already diminished to the point where his skin was only slightly reddened and color had already returned to his rugged cheeks, along with a light shading of stubble.

"We refer to them as 'flush pods'. Takes only three minutes to effectively clean the skin and flush the pores. Utilizes...let's see..." he again paused while scanning over the clipboard, "...yeah, here it is. Utilizes a mix of cleansing and softening agents, followed by an 'Aloa Vera' coating, to simultaneously cleanse and soften the skin."

Ben got up from the cot and strolled shakily over to the pod, placing a hand atop its slick, metallic surface.

"Load off my mind, Luke. You know the importance I place on skin texture. Seriously man, I'll reek like a week-old turd 'fore you catch me layin' in that horizontal pora-potty."

"Completely up to you, Ben. Now that we've covered grooming and toiletries, let's go over the electronic side of things."

A small oak desk and sliding chair sat in a far-left corner, complete with a flat screen PC and keyboard and several lined notepads and various boxes filled with pens, pencils and text high-lighters.

"Before you even ask," The Guardsman said with one raised hand while fronting the desk, "you don't have internet access. Regulations strictly forbid inmates of Eagle Island access to current events and/or headline news." Moving gingerly and with a slight limp, Ben walked over and took a seat in the chair, which he comically dwarfed.

"Figures. Man, I could'a burnt some serious hours surfin' the web, specifically my fa-vor-ite porn sites. Exactly what good is this contraption without internet capability, Luke?"

Booting up the PC with three quick clicks, the Guardsman pecked away at the keyboard for several moments, backing away as the screen lightened.

"Educational programs galore. The 'Electronic Encyclopedia', 'Earth History' and several others. There's also Excel and Word programs, and…um…at least two-hundred separate…uh… video games have been installed for immediate use."

Pushing the chair back with a loud screech, Ben

threw his scar-ridden head back and howled.

"Hell's *bells*, Luke. You've gotta be shittin' me. No 'net but a lifetime's worth of Pac-Man? What the hell kinda rehab specialist came up with that little gem?"

Clapping the larger man lightly on the right shoulder, The Guardsman first glanced over at Myers, who had leaned down onto his hunches and was shaking his head slowly from side to side.

"Benjamin, this isn't about rehabilitation. There is no such program on Eagle Island. No one is paroled from this unit, remember? I would've thought the Warden covered that in his brie-"

"Yeah, yeah...slipped my mind, what little remains of that deep-fried fucker..." Ben barked angrily, rising in a clumsy lurch and barely avoiding tripping over the overturned chair, "...just get on with this shit, will ya? I'm losin' my patience, bein' that my mind has long since flown the coup."

"Sorry, Ben, I know how you feel, but it's not..."

Scooping up the fallen chair with one hand, Ben reared back and flung it against a far wall, instantly shattering it into at least a half-dozen fractured segments.

Myers leapt up in a blur even as The Guardsman held his ground without a single movement save a 'back off' gesture towards his excitable subordinate.

"Like *hell* you do, pal. 'Til you've been framed, convicted, and tossed away like so much bagged trash, you ain't got a clue. Like I said, get on with this shit and leave me be," he snarled, ripping his shirt away with two quick tugs.

After briefly clearing his throat, The Guardsman continued his verbal inventory without further interruption as Officer Myers took up position at the front of the hovercraft, a thick-barreled stun-blaster gripped tightly in both hands and held snugly against his chest.

"Let's wrap this up, then. The plasma TV is a twenty-seven-inch model. Channels received are restricted by the nature of programming and are controlled by Eagle Island Communications. It comes with built-in DVD. Selected DVD's can be requested on a month to month basis. No more than ten DVD's may be received in a one-week period. Said DVD's are chosen by Eagle Island communications staff after approval by government board. Similarly, select CD's are available for monthly usage. Inmates are allowed a weekly sign-out form to request each. Request forms are in a blue folder next to the PC. They're picked up on a bi-weekly basis, at the same time your toiletry supplies are dropped off.

"The assigned stereo is a combo cassette/CD player with two hundred-watt speakers. Being that the walls are soundproof, inmates are allowed full discretion on desired sound levels. Translation; going deaf is purely a personal choice."

Dropping the clipboard to his side, The Guardsman walked past the hover and faced a far wall while pulling a small circular device from the front of his belt. "Daily meals, via teleportation, are served at seven AM, twelve noon, and six PM," he stated as a boxed section of wall approximately a foot and a half in diameter slid upward and a metal tray protruded outward from the narrow chasm.

"Ensure all dishes and service ware are left atop the metal tray no later than two hours after each meal is provided, otherwise the next scheduled meal will automatically be aborted by the system."

Seconds later, the tray vanished and the wall resumed its former appearance, leaving behind not a single trace such a compartment even existed.

"Ben, there's just one more thing," The Guardsman began, holding his position while motioning in a 'come here' gesture with his free hand, "... if you'll be so kind."

Rolling his eyes wearily, Ben rose from the cot and shuffled over with a noticeably wobbly gait.

"Yeah?"

The Guardsman stepped over as to allow the larger man access to the section of the wall where the portal had appeared.

"Nail it," he said, touching a gloved finger to a specific spot. "Come again?"

The Guardsman gently tapped the spot several times.

Tilting his head to one side, Ben took turns glancing at the wall and then back to The Guardsman.

"Let me get this straight. Ya want me to haul off and punch the wall?"

"No need to wait for a later date or time. You know you're going to, for curiosity's sake if for no other reason. All new arrivals feel a need to 'test' the system, usually within hours of arrival. Go ahead, Ben, give it your best shot.

Take care not to shatter a knuckle in the process."

Stepping forward, Ben eyed the spot while

balancing on the heel of his back foot.

"I ain't exactly feelin' my oats," he continued, rearing back his right arm and balling his massive fist, "but what the hell? I'm pissed enough to *chew* through the damn thing if nothin' else."

His fist shot forward in a grainy blur, and a muffled clanking noise followed, sounding like a hollow pipe hammered from a far distance.

Ben glanced first at his bared knuckles, which had already turned a dark shade of purple, and back to the wall.

"Okay. Got'cha. I get the point. It's hard. Damn hard. Ya want I should h*ead-butt* the son of bitch now or is exam -time over?"

"As I'm sure the Warden mentioned," The Guardsman said, seemingly ignoring the sarcastic query, "it's titanium outer shell and foot-thick stainless base make it impenetrable by anything less than a small nuke detonation. We've even calculated that a man with your brute strength rating, roughly equivalent to twenty normal men, would need approximately si-"

"I get it, man, I *get* it." Ben blurted, holding both hands airborne with the palms facing up, "Geez, Louise...talk about beatin' a dead horse."

"Sir," Myers interrupted, "meeting starts in thirty clicks."

"Okay then. Benjamin, I'll return either later this evening or mid-day tomorrow to wrap up a few minute details that haven't yet been covered. Your noontime meal, somewhat delayed, should arrive a few minutes after our departure."

"Luke, I truly couldn't give a shit," Ben sighed, lying back on the cot with a loud grunt. "Adios, men. Don't let the floor smack yer butt-cheeks on the way out."

"I…um…well, then…let's hit it, Myers. Can't keep the Warden waiting. Man has been a bit edgy of late, as it is."

As both men stepped aboard the hover, The Guardsman turned to address Eagle Island's newest inmate one final time, but saw Ben had lain back onto the cot with his forearms crossed over his forehead, and thought better of it.

Moments later, the hover drifted downward at a snail's pace through the circular part in the cell floor, allowing the highest ranking member of the corrections staff a lingering glance at his one-time comrade.

A one-time comrade who, during the heat of battle, was infamous for uncontrolled rage, unpredictability, and a blatant disdain for authority.

A one-time comrade who, in a career of crime-fighting that spanned over fifteen years, had managed to accumulate an arrest record as long as many of the bad elements he'd help put away.

And more importantly, a one-time comrade who, some eight years earlier atop a frozen mountainside off the coast of Greenland, had saved the hide of a soon-to-be highest ranking Correctional Officer from certain death.

Lucas T. Bradley, AKA *'The Guardsman'*, couldn't help but ponder the surrealistic irony of the situation, being that he was now charged with housing both his savior *and* would-be killer from that faithful night, each of whom were now assigned to the same cell block.

As the hover vanished into the tubular

100

passageway and the floor hatch immediately slid back into place, Lucas Bradley attempted, somewhat in vain, to leave images of the past behind and turn his thoughts to the immediate task at hand.

Meanwhile, the lone occupant of cell sector D-Fourteen dreamed of more tranquil settings, most of which involved himself and a certain Asian female for whom an inner flame would always smolder, no matter how desolate the present realm of reality.

CHAPTER THREE

Desolation Horizon Place: *Uninhabited desert region, eleven miles North of Kingston Springs, Wyoming* **Time:** *The Present*

The three individuals exited the chopper and trudged purposely up a steep, rocky grade infested by gnarled shrubbery and knee-high weeds.

"When you government boys hide something, you *reeeeally* hide it, don't you?" the trailing figure asked, side-stepping a jagged rock formation with the grace of a highly trained dancer. Dressed in faded blue jeans, a Hawaiian-style button-up shirt and brown colored work boots, it was solely the presence of a snugly fitting, dark green cowl that distinguished him from a hopelessly lost tourist.

"They had their reasons, sir," the taller of the other two men replied stiffly, "it'll all be explained in the briefing."

"Doctor Cartwright is being piped-in via satellite. He'll map out the assignment for you both," the second chimed in with in a similarly robotic monotone. Both were dressed in dark blue suits, black dress shoes and matching Raybans; their close-cropped hair and stoic expressions completing the less than conspicuous ensembles that screamed 'government flunky' to even the most casual observer.

The smaller man's stride slowed somewhat just as they crested the hill, his hands pinned to his sides in a decidedly feminine pose.

"Both of us? I wasn't informed of any tag-team

102

partner in this deal." The first man turned and shot the second a grave look. "It…um…Deputy Director Willis will explain the gist, I'm sure," he finally barked as the trio trekked single file through a narrow opening between two man-sized boulders.

The smaller man shrugged, scanning the surrounding plains through the narrow slits of his mask.

"No sweat off my lightly powdered nose, gents, as long as my cut's the same."

"Almost there," the first exclaimed as they entered a wide, flat clearing mysteriously free of vegetation and shrouded on all sides by gnarled, lifeless trees that looked weirdly fossilized.

"I just adore a good mystery," the masked man announced, playfully clapping his hands together.

"What *is* that rancid smell?" he whined, sniffing wildly, "something has definitely turned for the worst."

"More than likely animal carcasses, sir. A common odor for this specific area, I've been told," the second man replied, his face comically contorted.

"Charming. No doubt I'll reek like a decomposing coyote for the rest of the day."

The other two glanced at him indifferently before halting at the base of a large, rectangular rock centered by two small, similarly shaped ones.

One bent down and removed the largest rock while the other stood behind him and pulled a tiny com device from his belt.

"We've arrived at the entry point, Sir. Implementing code."

"Affirmative. You'll have to use the stairwell,

Conners. Freight elevator is out. Be advised we're on generator power down here," a deep, husky voice responded.

"Got it. We're on our way."

Seconds later, the three stood back in an impromptu formation as the ground at their feet split open like a blooming flower built from sand and clay. The trio formed a single line, cautiously descending a dimly lit escalator leading into a squared marble tunnel which was illuminated only by the faint flicker of emergency lighting.

"Oh, this is sooo X-Files," the masked one blurted excitedly, "I simply love this business."

***

Part I:

Entombed

Standing on opposite sides of a lengthy oak conference table, the five individuals remained silent for several moments, as if sizing each other up for an impending political debate.

"Deputy Director Willis, I presume?" the masked man finally asked while focusing on a separate individual altogether.

"Mystic, isn't it?" the man responded, reaching across the table with an outstretched hand. He wore a headset device connected to a flat-screen PC at the center of the otherwise bare table.

"All day long, sir. Nice cave, by the way."

They shook hands briefly before the director, a stoutly built white male in his early to late forties with a shaved head and pencil thin mustache, backed away a step as to introduce the female standing to his right.

Folding his thin, pale arms behind his back, Mystic nodded as the figure drew closer.

"And this must be my erstwhile partner on this little excursion..."

"Mystic, this is Marvella, late of the *Revenge Squad* and currently one of our best freelance ops," the director announced with fatherly pride, "welcome to Base Camp K- Tut, named after the infamous child Pharaoh for its tomb-like qualities."

Donned in full 'working' garb that included a bright yellow spandex body suit riddled with various sized, dark-crimson lightning bolts, a purple-shaded cowl and coal-black, calf-high boots, the figure stepped elegantly from the shadows until her upper thighs rested against the edge of the table.

"The website photos make you look bigger, I must say. Headed to a luau?" she asked, grinning mischievously. Her pitch-black hair hung across her shoulder in a tightly wound ponytail, and her thick, ruby lips seemed set in a permanent pout.

"Ouch. Seems your 'dragon lady' rep indeed does you justice, my dear," he replied with a wink, striking a runway stance with his hands posed lightly on both hips.

"I'll avoid all stereotyping if you will, *honey-buns*," Marvella shot back quickly, placing her hands flat across the table as to openly display her long, spear-like fingernails, each at least two inches long and painted blood-red.

The youngest of the two agents covered his mouth with one hand and released a muffled giggle, clearing his throat noisily in an attempt to regain his composure.

"Okay, let's get down to brass tax, folks," the director barked as the second agent took up position behind the PC and began tapping lightly atop the connecting keyboard.

"While Agent Graham connects us with the Wright-Patt Medical Center, I'll begin the briefing."

As the first agent joined the second at the PC, the remaining trio took seats at the far-left end of the conference table. The room itself, though bathed in shadow from the lack of proper lighting, resembled a 'war room bunker' from another era, with its low roof, slick concrete walls, a pull-down projector screen and matching blackboards shoved into opposite corners.

"Why all the secrecy, Chief?" Mystic inquired, leaning onto the tabletop with his bony elbows pointed outward.

"More a matter of *World* than National security, Mystic."

"I was told this was a simple transport mission that might require a particular skill I happen to possess," Marvella injected, her slanted, hazel green eyes locked on Mystic, who sat directly across from her wearing an expression of bland indifference.

"There is…quite a bit more to it, Leah…um, Marvella," the Director replied, sighing deeply while crossing his arms across his chest, where a blue tie draped over his pale forearms like a soggy dinner napkin.

"This particular site was built over four years ago for…storage purposes. Actually, 'entombing purposes' might be a more apt term.

106

"It consists of only two rooms; the one we now occupy, and another down still another corridor that runs an additional half-mile straight down into God's good earth.

"No doubt the higher echelon had hoped this site would be the permanent home for the object we're prepping to move. As with several previous locations, it just wasn't meant to be."

Stifling a yawn, Mystic leaned back with his hands resting behind his neck. "Chief, I'm simply enthralled. Please continue."

"What exactly is it being entombed, sir?" Marvella asked, her searing gaze never wavering from Mystic's direction.

"A...relic of sorts. A relic unearthed five summers back off the coast of southern Peru, between the cities of Talara and Piura. A strip-mining corporation discovered it while clearing a site, buried two dozen feet beneath a six-ton boulder they'd had to dynamite from the clay. The thing was...*is* perfectly squared, measures twelve feet long and eight wide, and weighs upwards of eleven-hundred pounds.

"It was first thought to be made of fossilized wood of some sort, but its true origin remains a mystery to this day. A real baffler that even 21st century technology hasn't been able to solve.

"That thing's called several locations home since its extraction. It was first shipped to a museum in Mexico City, where it was initially analyzed by a team of archeologists. Less than two weeks later, it was flown via U. S Government transport to Homestead Air Force Base in Florida. Eight weeks later, it found its way to this location for what most

107

figured to be its final destination."

"Hook-up to Wright-Patterson almost complete, Sir," the second agent announced as the first repeated a series of numerical codes into the headset's tiny mouthpiece.

"The good doctor will provide a more in-depth summary. The main point I want to stress to you two is the potential hazard that exists in regard to what on the surface seems like a cakewalk of a transport detail.

"People," he whispered gravely, "believe me when I tell you…it's *anything* but."

"We're set here, sir," the first agent said, removing the headset

The Deputy Director pushed his chair back and stood with a resounding grunt.

"Marvella…Mystic…come introduce yourself to Doctor Stephen J. Cartwright."

***

Part II:

Stone (*Un-*)Hinged

Director Willis took up a standing position behind Mystic and

Marvella, who occupied adjoining chairs facing the fifteen-inch PC monitor. "Doctor, are you hearing me okay?" the director asked, holding the headset mike to his lips even as the earpieces hung limply from his palm.

"Ye-yes. Loud and c-clear," came the reply in a noticeably weak, raspy tone. Leaning up in what was obviously a hospital bed, the man was horribly pale save the underneath of his badly drooping eyes, which held dark, splotchy patches that seemed to stretch the length of his worn, haggard visage.

"Good. We've established audio and visual. Doctor, I have Marvella and

Mystic here with me, and they are prepped for your narrative concerning

Stone-Unhin-...um...the relic in question. Whenever you're ready, doctor." The man nodded weakly, reaching up with a shaky hand riddled with various IV lines to scratch the tip of his balding head.

"Greetings to one and all. I sincerely wish I could be there (coughs)...pardon me... in person to share the information you require, but I'm afraid my present state prohibits anything other than constant care.

"I'm sure the deputy director has provided a prologue (coughs)...excuse me...so allow me to fill in the appropriate blanks. Give me a moment to collect my thoughts."

"Here's hoping he can finish before the mortician arrives to pick *him* up," Mystic mumbled, covering his mouth with one hand as to shield the words.

"Hey, Einstein, he can't hear you," Marvella said, rolling her eyes beneath her dura-plastic cowl," the director has the mike."

As if on cue, Director Willis handed the headset to Mystic, who studied it as if it were some strange alien artifact. He peered up at the director, who gestured towards the headset with a slight nod.

"In case you have questions, as I'm sure both of

you most assuredly *will* as the briefing commences."

Staring directly into the camera lens, Doctor Stephen Cartwright's expression was shockingly blank. His mouth hung slightly open, and a thin line of drool seeped from the left corner onto his stubble-coated chin.

Mystic brought the mike to his lips to speak just as the doctor's eyes widened and his lips curled into a gruesome smile.

"Lord, the man's got…green teeth," Marvella gasped, unaware she'd spoken aloud.

"Ready when you are, doc," Mystic said timidly.

The man's dazed expression gradually faded as he inhaled and exhaled several times as to normalize his breathing.

"Alright. I'll make this as brief as humanly possible (coughs)…although there's little chance the subject matter involves anything remotely human."

The briefing began:

I was first able to view the object a few days after it had been transferred to Wright-Patterson Air Force Base in, I believe, late June or possibly early July of two-thousand one. General Brad Clausan had been tasked (coughs) to assemble a team of evaluators in hopes of identifying its origins. I'd plied my skills as a veteran Petrologist for the government many times through the years, and found it a true honor to be handpicked to work alongside some of the best-known Paleontologists, Geomorphologists, and Anthropologists in the country. My field of study, by the way, deals with

110

the history and identification of rocks. To say the very least, we all (coughs) found the object to be a major challenge to both our professional knowledge, but also to the very sanity we hold dear.

To rewind a bit, just days before the object's arrival via KC-135 transport, we'd all been briefed as to the unusual circumstances surrounding its many travels since the unearthing years earlier in Peru.

To begin, a few hours after the blasting that essentially freed it from beneath a gigantic metamorphic formation, the foreman of that particular work crew was hospitalized, along with a bulldozer operator and two laborers, for what was labeled 'flu-like symptoms'.

All four passed away by nightfall. The following day, after (coughs) the object had been loaded onto a tractor trailer for transport to the Menedez Museum of Spanish Art & Folklore in Mexico City, still another worker inexplicably attacked several other co-workers with a pickaxe, killing three and seriously wounding two others. The man, who was later described by friends and family as mild, polite and soft-spoken, fled the site and was later shot to death by local police after taking a bus loaded with tourists hostage with little more than a pocketknife. Witnesses reported the man (coughs) speaking what they referred to as 'biblical gibberish', frothing profusely about the mouth, and even occasionally invoking self-mutilation techniques by cutting his own forearm and wrists with the pocketknife.

Motives for the man's actions are still unknown, and autopsy results did little in terms of

111

providing solid evidence.

Just days following this tragedy, the object was driven to a local clinic and X-rayed to solve the mystery of its internal contents.

The results were somewhat enigmatic (coughs), as the image that did appear, that of a brick-shaped mass of some type, was far too faint and blurred to properly identify. The museum curator then made the decision to crack the seal and retrieve said mass.

They flew in a veteran Petrolotgist from Miami, whose personal journals would later state that the origin of the object's outer shell and core were 'undefined' in terms of rock formations. In other words, the man didn't have a blessed (coughs) clue.

He'd reportedly drilled no more than a half-inch into the outer perimeter of the object when...well, he was found deceased by museum workers. He'd been slumped in his chair, the victim of an apparent coronary. The man had been forty-two years of age and a lifelong jogger and fitness enthusiast. An autopsy revealed his heart had literally imploded. Needless to say, the piece was returned to the museum and no further drilling expeditions imminent, especially considering the pattern of bad fortune that followed.

Less than a week later, a man who'd worked as a security guard for the Menedez Museum for over a decade was arrested for the triple murders of his wife and two children, a girl of six and a boy of barely four. Just days later, he was found deceased in his jail cell, having apparently ripped out his own throat with his bare hands. Again, acquaintances of the man stated such homicidal and suicidal

112

behavior was completely out of character, and that he'd always come across as a gentle family man; stern but caring.

Point of order, this particular individual had been specifically tasked to guard the object in question since its arrival at the museum.

Just days following that incident, a well-respected (coughs) female anthropologist from a local college entered a restaurant located less than a mile from the museum and attacked several patrons in an unprovoked rampage. After stabbing one man to death with a carving knife taken from the man's plate, she'd wrestled a seventy-year old woman to the ground and proceeded to kick and stomp her to death with hard-soled boots. She was eventually taken down by several staff members, who imprisoned her in a walk-in freezer before calling authorities. One of the workers later stated (coughs) that the woman, listed as barely five-feet tall and weighing less than ninety pounds, had possessed 'supernatural strength'.

By the time police arrived, the woman had died of an apparent brain aneurysm. Again, autopsies divulged nothing that would explain such.... maniacal behavior.

Once the object was placed on display within the museum, listed only as

'Unidentified Stone Relic of Unknown Origin – South America – 2001', it took less than two weeks for several museum employees and even a few patrons to fall victim to a mysterious illness. Symptoms ranged from high fevers, cold chills and night sweats to severe diarrhea, vomiting and, in a few select cases, memory loss and mild dementia.

113

A subsequent investigation by museum officials concluded with a rather strange verdict, that each individual being treated had spent considerable time and within close proximity of the object. Despite strong reservations from top museum officials, a self-proclaimed exorcist was brought in to...evaluate the object from a spiritual (coughs) angle. It took the man, a highly respected shaman originally from Tibet, less than two hours to label the object a 'beacon of evil' he insisted be 'vanquished to the ends of the earth' and as far away from human contact as possible.

That particular nugget of superstitious wisdom was soon born out as cold-hard fact less than twenty-four hours later, when the man's plane crashed over Bolivia with no survivors among the eight- person crew.

Four days following this latest malady, the museum happily turned the object over to government scientists at Wright-Patterson for a small, nominal fee, basically just enough to cover shipping costs. Incidentally, the semi-truck used for said transport crashed upon its return trek, skidding off the highway and into a deep ravine. Needless to say, the cause of the (coughs) crash will forever remain a mystery, as the driver of said vehicle was burned beyond recognition within the truck's cab. Just another tragic coincidence, you say? Possibly, but with a body count of twenty-four in such a relatively short span, that qualifies as 'Monkey's Paw' numbers (coughs), people.

Let me state for the record that I am not (coughs)...repeatedly, NOT, a person who is prone to superstition. Most involved in scientific research believe only in what they can see...what they can prove with cold, hard, analytical facts and rigorously researched numbers. Then again, being that I've lost just under thirty pounds in the past two weeks, along with the majority of my hair and a few select teeth, let me say that my opinions on such matters aren't quite as staunch as they once were.

Since its relocation to Wright-Patterson, the object, which a colleague nicknamed 'Stone Un-hinged', has (coughs) been analyzed and studied by a panel of some of the most revered in (coughs) my field (coughs). Excuse...(coughs)...me for a (coughs) moment, please...

Leaning hard to the left as to retrieve something off-camera, the doctor's complexion had gone from fish-belly white to a deep shade of purple.

Tucking the mike into the palm of his left hand, Mystic turned to address the director, who was sipping steaming black coffee from a Styrofoam cup.

"Hey, I enjoy a haunted rock story as much as the next guy, but is it possible Doc Bones is coming to a point soon? Like maybe within the next week or so? My ears are falling asleep."

Director Willis sipped cautiously before responding in a harsh whisper.

"It's all pertinent to the mission, Mystic. Thus far, the man hasn't wasted a single syllable."

"Twenty-four dead bodies is certainly nothing to sneeze at. Something definitely isn't kosher. I've heard of coincidence, but that's downright eerie," Marvella said, staring at the monitor through tightly squinted eyes, "has anyone brought up the possibility that it could be a meteor?"

115

"And there it is...the alien factor," Mystic blurted in a deliberately mocking tone.

"I was wondering who'd be the first to bring *'little green men'* into the picture."

"Put a sock in it, smart-ass," Marvella replied, pointing at the monitor, where the doctor had swam back into the frame.

I a-apologize for that. I...my throat gets quite d-dry. To continue this rather sordid tale...

It was duly cat-scanned and small samples were taken and broken down in specified chemical equations. The result was less than conclusive, to say the least. We were now officially dealing with a mystery wrapped tightly within an enigma. An overused cliché, I know, but true.

We found trace amounts of mercury and lead within a mix of fossilized marble and granite that made up barely ten percent of the outer shell. The other ninety percentile is utterly unidentifiable as any mineral known to man, be it a metal or plastic alloy... or of rock origin.

Similarly, the scan results for the squared piece of stone melded within the inner core isn't readable as any of the above as well. Further research was to continue unabated, although what direction to take was somewhat in question. That is, until the people tasked to continue said research began to...(coughs) began to expire at an alarming rate.

Four days ago (sighs heavily) Mort Gassner, a highly respected anthropologist and a man I considered both a colleague and friend...passed away from a blood clot to the brain. Much like the petrolotgist from Miami, Mort had been a vocal advocate of physical fitness. The man didn't smoke, drink, or eat red meat, and possessed a demeanor so calm there were times I was compelled to check him for a pulse. Yesterday, a paleontologist named Bill Timmons, whom I'd only met for this assignment...fell into a deep coma from complications from a sudden bout of influenza. I was informed only hours ago that he's been moved to the ICM ward in critical condition, and has since been placed on life support.

As you can plainly (coughs) see, I'm not exactly feeling at the top of my game either. At first they were saying it might be walking pneumonia plus a touch of food poisoning, being that I spent the majority of the last twenty-four hours vomiting in half-hour increments. Once that finally subsided, my fever has gone off the charts, from ninety-nine point five last evening to around one-oh-three this morning I feel...(coughs)...my flesh feels a bit singed, while my chest and midsection have that 'simmering' feeling, as though I were being cooked from the inside (coughs). Excuse the rather graphic descriptions, but it's getting increasingly difficult to play down the symptoms. (coughs) I...um...well, enough of the (pauses to take a series of deep breaths) medical report. Let me get on with what really counts here, that being the mission at hand. The object, 'Stone-Un-hinged' if you prefer, is to be transported to an undisclosed, Top Secret location post haste.

With...what's transpired there in the desert these past few weeks, it's obvious it can no longer remain at its present location.

"Um, pardon me, Doctor. What...uh...exactly has...transpired that makes this transport so…vital?" Marvella inquired after snatching the mike from Mystics bare palm, where he'd been casually twirling the headset cord in a circular motion.

Pardon my ignorance. I would have thought that Director Willis would have…well, never mind. I'm sure he'll provide more in-depth information once we're done here.

Since its (coughs) arrival there at 'Base Camp Tut', several unexplained air disasters have occurred, all within the same general air space. Air space that provides a circular perimeter directly over the underground campsite. I'm sure you took notice that the Director had each of you walk quite a distance to reach the camp (coughs). As you depart, scan the area and you can plainly see the burnt regions of charred ground created by three separate crashes. I understand the black box from one of these aircrafts recovered leaves little doubt of the cause. Again, I'm sure (coughs) that the director will fill provide details of this rather…grisly case history.

From what I understand (coughs, sighs heavily; bows head) a twenty-mile radius has recently been declared a no-fly zone to all private, commercial, and government airlines.

"And they…you think that this…object caused the acciden-…the crashes somehow?" Marvella inquired.

Tilting his head back just slightly, the doctor's eyes seemed a bit glassier than just moments before, his movements jerky and spastic, as if suffering from a severe nervous disorder.

While not exactly a scientific theory, there's

118

(coughs) no denying the object's short but fatal history does indeed mark it as a most probable suspect, however illogical such a possibility may be. At this point, I personally have little doubt. Then again, I might be a tad bias for obvious reasons. It...it's... (coughs, closed eyes, shakes head slowly from side to side) ...as if I've undergone a year's worth of chemotherapy treatments in a matter of hours. I...can't imagine the effects of nuclear fallout being as severe (coughs, gags).

Regardless...of my...fate, the mission that stands before you cannot...must not...be taken lightly. The secret location was chosen not simply due to its remoteness, but rather for the possibility of closure...of unlocking... the mystery (coughs) at hand. There is a team currently being assembled with the...unique skills required to solve the enigmatic code of the stone, while also, hopefully (coughs) possessing the power to permanently terminate its negative effects. As I understand it, the site has been duly prepped for the objects arrival and housing.

Now (pauses; coughs), to avoid still another air disaster while in (pauses; takes several deep breaths) transport, you two will be tasked to create and maintain a continuous force-field around the object until its arrival, and also until it is deemed safely housed on site (coughs, gags). It's...obviously (coughs; pauses for a deep breath; rubs eyes)...imperative that the object arrives without incident...so that it may...be...be studied...analyzed...its o-ori-...origins revealed...(coughs uncontrollably; leans hard to the left and out of camera view).

"Doctor? Are you...you still there?" Marvella asked after a thirty-second pause.

Tapping her softly on the left shoulder, Director Willis then retrieved the mike as the trio continued to lock on the monitor, which remained focused on the pillow the doctor had been leaning onto. The bed's metal-headboard began to noticeably shake as several sets of jumbled voices could be overheard in the background.

"Doc? Is someone there with you? Do you need hel-..."

The man's head shot back into frame, gyrating wildly from side to side like a bobble-head collectable and resembling a snippet of videotape being fast-forwarded at warp speed.

"Jesus, what's the matter with 'im?" Mystic whined, cringing back and away from the monitor as if to avoid impending attack.

"Doctor? Is someone there? Hello?" the director barked, his forehead now slick with fresh sweat.

Within moments, the visual cleared somewhat as three separate sets of hands could be viewed attempting to hold the wriggling form in place.

"Get that damned sedative over here!" one voice bellowed.

"Hold his hands *down*, for Christ's sake!" screamed another, this one obviously female.

"How the...hell can...he be this...s-strong...?" groaned still another in a huffy, strained tone. A syringe shot into view, plunging into the left side of the man's neck just seconds before a second needle sunk into his upper right shoulder.

It took several more moments of intense

120

struggle to steady the man's upper body, neck, and head.

Staring directly into the camera's lens through hollowed-out eye sockets drenched in yellowish gore, Doctor Stephen Cartwright's lips curled, revealing blackened gums and a mostly toothless maw.

"You're all going to die, you know,' he shrieked, spitting a mouthful of bloodied bile onto his already soaked chin, neck, and upper chest, "...just like me...like *ALL* of us! Die like dogs. Die...like...*FUCKING DOGS!*"

A third syringe entered the picture just as his words had become nothing more than incoherent ramblings, puncturing his throat just above the Adam's Apple. A thick white towel was then wrapped around his face and forehead just before the camera was knocked from its tripod perch and onto the hard, tile flooring. A smattering of feet filled the frame from a tilted angle, at least four separate pairs of lab shoes smeared and spattered in blackish fluid.

Moments before the monitor was to fill with jagged waves of static, a hodgepodge of fragmented words rang out in various states of panic.

"Goddamn it...get...fingers away from his eyes!"

"We've...stop the bleeding..."

"Holy *SHIIITTTT!* Get him...oooofffff me!"

"We're all gon-...be infected!"

"Break the motherfuc...neck!"

"Got to...all...quarantine..."

Dropping the headset onto the tabletop, the Director reached down and clicked off the monitor, then walked over to a far corner of the room and stood with his hands clasped at his lower back. The two agents remained seated at the far end of the table, each staring straight ahead without speaking. The pair wore deadpan expressions even as their fingers tapped atop the surface of the table at breakneck speed.

After an additional thirty seconds of silence, Mystic leaned back and yawned.

"I take it this concludes the initial in-brief segment of our program?"

"I'd…say yes," the director replied solemnly, "movement will begin first thing in the morning via military transport. We'll… continue this briefing at the Best Western in Kingston Springs. We've booked rooms for the night. Transport team is scheduled to arrive at 5am. You'll be riding in a CH-54 Sky crane built for extremely heavy loads. Hope you each packed butt-pads. It's a good seventy-two-hour ride from here to…our destination."

Turning back towards them, Director Willis' face was deathly pale save the dark splotches below each eye.

"Right now all I really want to do is get the hell out of his damned cave." Moments later, the five figures ascended from the catacombs of the desert floor and into the searing glare of the mid-afternoon sun, their collective strides quick-paced and purposeful. As the faux grounds behind them re-sealed without leaving a clue to the opening's existence, the director blazed the trail back towards the waiting helicopters.

"What about those local airline crashes the

doctor spoke of? I didn't see any burn sites on the way in," Marvella inquired, shielding her eyes with splayed fingers.

"Swept over as soon as the black boxes were retrieved," the director replied, side-stepping a wide sinkhole.

"The doctor mentioned something about what the black boxes revealed?"

"Incessant babbling mostly."

"Mostly?" Mystic asked, his body motionless as he levitated several inches above the dusty terrain, "So there was something else a bit more…meaningful, then?"

Sighing wearily, the director stopped in his tracks as the others formed a semi-circle around him. They stood atop an oval-shaped ridge overlooking a wide, bare valley where a pair of Huey Helicopters sat idling less than a hundred yards in the distance.

"In each case, a voice identifying himself as the aircraft's pilot was heard…making terrorist threats, seemingly right before impact. Luckily all three instances occurred in rural, unpopulated areas just miles from here."

Assuming the 'lotus' position, Mystic floated several feet higher as to acquire a more panoramic view of the valley.

"Terrorist threats? You mean like suicide bomber type threats in the twin towers mode?"

"Nothing like that. It was more along the lines of… *'we're all going to die now…and the rest of the world will soon follow'*, that type. Strangest thing was, their voices were mechanical, like recorded messages left on an answering machine.

No emotion whatsoever. No sorrow…no rage. Just…inhumanly cold."

"Not sure you can even term that a threat. Sounds more like someone accepting their fate," Marvella muttered almost to herself.

"What exactly are we babysitting here, chief? *Satan's* traveling mausoleum?" Mystic blurted while executing a series of mid-air somersaults.

"Might be closer to the truth than you really want to know," Deputy Director William Paul Willis whispered as they descended the hill, the gist of his words drowned out by the chopper's swirling blades.

***

Part III:

Iron-Box Confessional

"I'd offer ya a drink, Luke, but I'm afraid it's outta the question. How 'bout you offerin' me one? Good stiff shot of Beam would sure hit the spot about now."

Removing his cowl, The Guardsman pulled the office chair over from behind the computer console and took a seat directly across from the larger man, who was sitting on the edge of his cot wearing only a pair of dark brown boxer shorts.

"Wish it was in my power, Ben. I'd probably sit right here and get loaded to the gills with you, and I haven't been tempted in years."

"Don't get me wrong, Luke, but I'm findin' it real difficult to feel sorry for anybody but *myself* right about now. The ol' pity-meter is pegged to the max," Ben replied sourly, reaching up to scratch the thick stubble that had already begun to form on his squared chin." Sorry about the chair incident, bro. Don't think I'll ever hold a degree in Anger Management."

"Completely understandable considering the circumstances, Ben. Now…" Straddling the chair with its back hugging his chest, The Guardsman ran a hand through his thick brown bangs and stared at the larger man through tightly squinted eyes.

"…I know the *official* details of why you're here. What I really want to know now is the truth."

Ben paused, briefly freezing up as if caught badly off-guard by the bluntness of the query.

"What can I say, Luke? I've always been a cold-blooded, murderin' psycho at heart. Least, that was *always* my rep. Guess my vile acts finally caught up with me."

"Cut the BS, Benjamin. I'm a former teammate, remember? Downed quite a few bad guys together, not to mention a small ocean's worth of alcoholic beverages.

"The rep was earned, but only in the heat of battle against some of the worst the criminal element had to offer."

Holding his hands out palms up, The Guardsman's stoic expression never wavered as he cocked his head slightly to the right.

"Talk to me, partner."

"Let's just say there's nothin' original about my story, Bro. No doubt you've heard it a few thousand times in your line of work. Set up like a bowlin' pin, I was. Took the fall for a little green fag named

Mystic. From what I gather, that limp-wristed, pint-sized Doc Strange is the new media darlin'. A real internet sensation, 'specially among the Queer Eye community in Southern Cal-I-forny.

"Well, what the fans and news-hounds don't know is that the little bastard is also one greedy, sadistic son of a bitch who derives obvious pleasure from the act of killin'. Seen it more times than I could count. Kids got that certain sparkle in his eye that only your true lunatics possess, ya know? Saw it up close and personal, Luke. *Too* damn close, truth be told."

"You're right as rain about the media types sucking up to his act. I hear he's got his own reality show coming up this fall. Saw a promo just last week on the WB," The Guardsman replied, resting his chin on the tip of the chair-back's padding.

"I knew the story about you offing Crimson Condor was bogus. What about that other thing involving Shaker Jake McKay and RapMaster XXX? Quite the sordid mess, I heard."

"Real Grade-A goat-rope for sure. Triple X sliced Jake up like Christmas goose, and there I stood, a ready-made-to-order scapegoat if there ever was one. Hid out in Johnny Reb's old stompin' grounds 'tilCondor found me and the really bad shit went down. I just can't get over the fact that the Condor turned traitor, ya know?

"People change over time, Luke, and that ain't always a good thing."

"Don't really know what to say, ham-hocks. Raw deal City, for certain You appealing?"

"Negatory. Not even eligible, screams Uncle Sam. Federal Judge denied the first request 'fore my

126

lawyer had filed the full motion. Some ancient legal stipulation about murderin' former government agents. I guess Condor had been on the payroll several times in the past few years."

Stretching his bulky frame as he stood, Ben smiled wearily and then began flexing his biceps an arm at a time.

"Man, I'm gonna shrink away to flesh and exo-skeletal remains in no time."

"Uh-huh, you're a real shrimp alright," the smaller man grinned, observing the other's tree-trunk thick appendages as they bulged and contracted, "...damn things are bigger than my thighs already. I get the feeling we'll be replacing some gym equipment quicker than originally planned."

"No booze; no chicks. I think ya just might have hit on somethin' there, Luke old bud," Ben replied with a wink.

"Well, I'd better get back on watch," The Guardsman said, pushing the chair back to its original position before refitting his cowl with a gentle tug.

"Don't be a stranger, Luke. I get the feelin' it'll be no time 'fore I'm holdin' summit meetings with the furniture, know what I mean?"

The smaller man stood at the edge of the circular hatch as it slid silently ajar.

"Let you in on a little secret, Benjamin," he said, flashing a wry, mischievous smile that lasted but a split-second as he prepped to descend into the dimly lit tunnel below.

"You just might be surprised at how *little* peace and quiet you're actually gonna get. See you soon.

And by the way, I'm going to mention your case to the Warden and see if I can get the ball rolling on a possible appeal. Perhaps you simply had the wrong lawyer."

Tossing the other man a mock salute that halted in mid-waive, Ben's expression remained comically dumb founded, his mouth hanging partially open, until a few moments after the hatch had re-secured.

"Say...*what?*"

***

Part IV:

The *Mind Sweep* Effect

A few hours following The Guardsman's departure, Ben was still attempting (in utter vain) to solve the riddle his old comrade had uttered upon exiting. He'd tried the stereo and could only receive 'Eagle Isle' radio, which, from what he'd heard thus far, consisted of a non-stop barrage of late twentieth century pop tunes in rather nauseating 'elevator music' renditions. Clicking it off with a disgusted groan, he allowed himself another verbal reminder about filling out a CD 'request' form with Classic Rock headliners from an era long past. The TV was a blank slate other than the 'Eagle Isle test pattern' channel, which he found equally irritating but also strangely hypnotic.

Lying on the cot with his massive hands massaging the cool stone floor, he replayed his old running mate's words over and over in his head until mental and physical exhaustion took their toll.

Once he'd passed over, the misty dreamscape he traveled was mercifully void of all things 'Eagle Island', and again occupied by a dark-haired Asian beauty whose sweet, perfumy scent he could almost taste. Pulling her close, he began suckling the warmth of her neck while reaching around to fondle the perfect curvature of her lower back and tightly muscled, exquisitely shaped rear end. Raising his head as to search out the soft cushion of her ruby lips, he suddenly became aware of an alien voice growing louder and more pronounced as moments passed.

BENJAMIN? BENJAMIN THOMASON? ARE YOU RECEIVING? PLEASE RESPOND IF SO. BENJAMIN THOMASON, PLEASE RESPOND...

"Wha-w-who-who-zat?" he babbled, rolling off the cot and onto the chilled concrete with a resounding huff.

SO SORRY TO WAKE YOU, BENJAMIN, ALTHOUGH I WOULD HAVE THOUGHT YOU'D BEUP BY NOW, BEING THAT IT IS NEARING ELEVEN AM. SOMETIMES I...FORGET THEJETLAG EFFECT SUFFERED BY NEW ARRIVALS. MY APOLOGIES THEN, SIR, FOR THE RATHER RUDE AWAKENING.

Executing a textbook 'combat' roll, Ben's head whirled about frantically as he scanned the room for his yet unseen guest, his colossal fists clinched at his chest in the classic pugilistic pose.

"A-alright, Jackass...show yourself. I ain't in the mood for this transparent bullshit," he growled, blinking rapidly as to literally shake the grogginess from his fogged senses.

AH, THE ADJUSTMENT PERIOD IS ALWAYS THE HARDEST, IT SEEMS. YOU MISUNDERSTAND MY PRESENCE, BENJAMIN. I CANNOT BE FOUND INSIDE YOUR CELL SECTOR, YOU SEE. AT LEAST, NOT IN A PHYSICAL SENSE. ALAS, I AM COMING TO YOU IN METAPHYSICAL FORM ONLY.

Rising from one knee to a flat-footed crouch, Ben felt the tenseness of his upper body drop several notches as his breathing began to normalize.

"Methafor…method…what kinda Pig Latin psychobabble you spoutin', pal?"

Come to think of it, I ain't so much hearin' 'im talk with my ears as inside my head. Hell's bell's, don't tell I'm crackin' up this early in the game…

RELAX, BENJAMIN. CONTRARY TO WHAT YOU MIGHT BE THINKING, WHAT YOU ARE HEARING IS NOT SOME WARPED FIGMENT OF A BADLY FATIGUED, WOEFULLY OVERTAXED IMAGINATION. LET ME FORMALLY INTRODUCE MYSELF AND THEN EXPLAIN MY PRESENCE WITHIN THE RECESSES OF YOUR SUBCONSCIOUS.

"Yeah, you…"

Yeah, you do that, Mac, 'fore I start bangin' my noggin' against the nearest wall just to drown you out…

No longer prepped for an impending attack, Ben sat back down onto the cot with his back propped against a far wall. As he uncurled his right fist, he noticed with some trepidation that it was shaking uncontrollably.

THE TITLE I WAS GIVEN YEARS AGO,

AND NOT OF MY OWN CHOOSING YOU UNDERSTAND, IS MIND SWEEP. I WAS APPREHENDED IN THE YE-...

"Mindsw-...? Hey, didn't the Silver Surfer corral your hide back in the early nine-"

Uh, in the late nineties? Word was you were ET in origin, pal. I heard Mars or Pluto or some similar floatin' rock in a Galaxy far, far away... TRUE, IT WAS THE SILVER SULFER IN DECEMBER OF

NINETEEN-NINETY-NINE TO BE EXACT, AS I WAS ONE OF THE FIRST INCARCERATED UPON EAGLE ISLAND. AN HONOR I HESTITATE TO CHERISH, YOU UNDERSTAND.

Uh, I ain't much at names or dates, Pal. How's about cuttin' to the chase on exactly why you're parked inside my noggin, or more important, why the hell you'd want to be? Last Jackass to attempt a 'mind meld' with yours truly paid a painful price. Ever hear of The Seeker? Girl limped away from the experience with one helluva migraine.

OF COURSE...MY APOLOGIES. I DO HAVE A TENDENCY TO RAMBLE. MY UNANNOUNCED OCCUPANCY WITHIN YOUR 'NOGGIN', AS YOU SO ELOQUENTY PUT IT, IS MERELY A SERVICE I WILLINGLY OFFER TO ALL INMATES WITHIN THIS PARTICULAR CELL SECTOR BLOCK. I SERVE AS THE INNER-GRAPEVINE, SINCE THERE OBVIOUSLY ISN'T AN 'OUTER' ONE TO SPEAK OF. OF COURSE, THIS IS A VOLUNTARY SERVICE A FEW HAVE SHUNNED IN THE PAST SEVERAL YEARS, THOUGH MOST FIND IT A WELCOME

RESPITE FROM THE EVERYDAY HUM-DRUM
THAT DEFINES SOLITARY CONFINEMENT.

*What exactly do ya mean, inner grapevine? I
wouldn't think they'd be a helluva lot of 'juicy'
gossip to pass on, 'ceptmaybe who took the
smelliest crap or whose salt peter wore out the
quickest. I mean, we are cooped up twenty-three
seven in these government-created Charlie Tuna
cans, right?*

ALLOW ME TO ELABORATE FURTHER,
BENJAMIN, THE...

*Cut the 'Benjamin' shit, will ya, Mac?
Nobody's called me that since Mama Thomason.
Let's make it 'Force', for now...leastwise, 'til I get
to know ya better...*

NOT A PROBLEM...FORCE, ALTHOUGH I
WAS UNDER THE ASSUMPTION YOU WENT
BY THE PROFESSIONAL NAME OF
'DESOLATION OUTLAW' THESE DAYS.

*Uh...long story for another time, Sweep. Let's
just say that particular ID just hasn't worked out,
and leave it at that. 'Sides, I prefer Force. Now, you
were sayin'...uh...thinkin'...*

YES, IN REGARD TO WHY I PROVIDE
WHAT SEVERAL OF OUR EAGLE ISLE
INMATES REFER TO AS THE 'TELEPATHY
HOTLINE'... IT IS SIMPLY A LINE OF OPEN
COMMUNICATIONS THAT I ALONE AM
ABLE TO BOTH CREATE AND MODERATE. IF
YOU DO DECIDE TO JOIN OUR LITTLE IN-
HOUSE CHAT GROUP, YOU WILL BECOME
AN ACTIVE PART OF OUR TWICE-DAY
GROUP SESSIONS. IT'S SIMPLY A MATTER
OF BREAKING THE BOREDOM,

BENJA...UH...FORCE. TRUE, THE TOPICS WE COVER AREN'T GROUNDBREAKING IN TERMS OF NEWS FROM THE OUTSIDE WORLD, SINCE WE AREN'T PRIVY TO SUCH INFORMATION. ALAS, I DO PICK UP THE OCCASIONAL TIDBIT OR TWO FROM THE STAFF EVERY SO OFTEN, AND NEVER FAIL TO SHARE WHATEVER I'VE HEARD WITH THE GROUP. MORE OFTEN, WE SPEAK FROM THE DEEP WELL OF THE PAST, AS EACH OF US HAS DONE OUR SHARE OF LIVING. THE HERO AND VILLIAN GAME IS MANY THINGS, I'VE LEARNED, BUT RARELY BORING OR MUNDANE. YOU BEING A FORMER WHITE-HAT, MEANING HERO, WILL NO DOUBT BRING A FRESH PERSPECTIVE TO THE TABLE.

POINT OF NOTE; BESIDES THE AFOREMENTIONED TWICE A DAY CHATS, YOU CAN COMMUNICATE WITH ME PERSONALLY ANY TIME OF THE DAY OR NIGHT. I DO NOT REQUIRE SLEEP, SO THERE IS NO NEED TO HESITATE NO MATTER THE TIME. AS THE OLD SAYING GOES, THOUGH I HAVE ALTERED IT A BIT TO BETTER SUIT OUR PREDICAMENT, MY CELL DOOR IS ALWAYS OPEN.

So the staff don't have a clue about this little 'Ma Bell mind-bender' ya got goin'?

I HAVE THE CAPABILITY TO AVOID DETECTION, TO EFFECTIVELY SHIELD OUR THOUGHTS FROM EVEN THE MOST NOTED OF MENTAL SCANNERS. SEVERAL YEARS AGO, THEY BROUGHT IN SEVERAL

NOTEWORTHY TROUBLESHOOTERS TO RUN A THOROUGH SCAN OF THE ISLE, ONE OF WHICH WAS AN OLD ADVISORY OF MINE YOU MIGHT WELL HAVE HEARD OF IN YOUR TRAVELS. DESPITE HIS BEST EFFORTS, *THE SILVER FAIRY* WAS UNABLE TO DETECT EVEN THE SLIGHTEST OF TELEPATHIC ACTIVITY ON STILL ANOTHER OCCASION, THE LEGENDARY MUTANT KNOWN AS 'VULCANIZE' WAS TASKED WITH THE SAME CHALLENGE. NEEDLESS TO SAY, THE END RESULT WAS THE SAME.

IN TRUTH, HOWEVER, I HAVE THE DISTINCT FEELING THAT THERE ARE THOSE WITHIN THE HIGHER HIERARCHY THAT ARE AWARE OF OUR DAILY CHATS, BUT HAVE INEXPLICABLY MADE THE DECISION NOT TO DISCLOSE OUR LITTLE SECRET TO THE WARDEN.

THE SAD FACT OF THE MATTER REMAINS THAT OUR BEING ABLE TO COMMUNICATE THROUGH THESE INPENETRABLE WALLS PROVIDES NIL IN TERMS OF A TRUE SECURITY RISK. THIS PERSONSIMPLY UNDERSTANDS THIS, AND ALLOWS US THIS MINUTE 'BENEFIT' OUT OF…WELL, FOR WANT OF A BETTER TERM, PITY. EITHER THAT, OR THEY'RE SIMPLY BIDING THEIR TIME FOR SOME UNKNOWN REASON BEFORE OUR SECRET IS DISCLOSED FOR POLITICAL GAIN OR SOMETHING SIMILAR. PERSONALLY, I CHOOSE TO BELIEVE THE FORMER.

There was a full minute pause, during which

time Ben had leapt from the cot and began pacing the room like an expectant father.

I get the feelin' you're waitin' on some kinda answer then...

DON'T FEEL PRESSURED, BENJAM...UM, SORRY AGAIN...FORCE. YOU MAY CONTACT ME AT A LATER TIME WITH YOUR DECISION. IN FACT, YOU CAN DECLINE FOR NOW AND THEN JOIN US WHENEVER YOU DECIDE. SIMPLY CONCENTRATE AND SILENTLY REPEAT MY NAME SEVERAL TIMES. I HAVE NO BUILT-IN ANSWERING MACHINE TO IGNORE THE CALLS THAT COME MY WAY, SO A RESPONSE IS USUALLY IMMEDIATE.

Tell ya what, Sweep. It ain't that I don't trust ya, but I ain't exactly feelin' warm 'n cozy bout the set-up as a whole. Don't wanna come off as some 'do-gooder' snob, but I gotta know exactly who I'm dealin' with 'fore I sign on to somethin' this wacky. Shit just don't feel right...

FORCE, PLEASE REFRAIN FROM FURTHER USE OF SUCH BLATANT.... OBSCENITIES, IF YOU DON'T MIND. IT'S A...PERSONAL REQUEST I MAKE OF ALL WITHIN THE BLOCK. I APOLOGIZE IF IT'S AN INCONVENIENCE, BUT I DO CONSIDER IT A MATTER OF COUTH.

Uh, yeah, tell ya what, Mac, you're askin' a lot for somebody that's trespassin' as it is. (pause). Alright, damn it...uh... I'll give it the old college try, but it ain't gonna be easy. Anyhow, about my fellow sardines...

I DO APPRECIATE THE EFFORT, GOOD

SIR. NOW, TO THE ISSUE OF YOUR FELLOW BLOCK-MATES. SOME OF THE NAMES MIGHT WELL BE FAMILIAR. IN FACT, DON'T BE AT ALL SURPRISED IF YOU'VE GOTTEN...UP CLOSE AND PERSONAL...WITH MORE THAN ONE OF THE INDIVIDUALS LISTED.

I'LL BEGIN WITH THEIR NAMES, PHYSICAL DESCRIPTIONS, AND A BRIEF HISTORY, ALONG WITH ANY INFORMATION CONCERNING ORIGIN THAT I MAY BE PRIVY TO.

FIRST UP, HAVING SO FAR SERVED FOUR AND A HALF YEARS OF A MANDATORY LIFE SENTENCE IS:

Name: **ANVIL**

Race: White Male

Age: 35-40 (approximate)

Height: Seven Feet, three inches

Weight: Four-sixty to four-seventy

Personality Evaluation (three words or less): Headstrong; temperamental; unrelenting

Super Powers: Super Strength (equal to twenty men); also donned anvil-shaped titanium-based helmet used as a battering ram Origin: Canadian government '*Super Soldier*' Project of the late '80's

Group Affiliations, and/or frequent enemy: Defenders (on several occasions from late 90's to early 21st Century). Captured by: *The Incredible Hulk*, June 2002, inside an underground Missile silo, Lincoln, Nebraska Territory: Eastern and Mid-Eastern U. S/Southern Canada

I've heard of this one. Real bad-ass brawler

136

from Ottawa. Also heard it took a dozen of ol'
Green & Uglies best haymakers to put 'im away.

NEXT, SERVING YEAR SIX OF A
MANDATORY LIFE SENTENCE, IS:
Name: **SCREAMING EAGLE**
Race: White Male
Age: 40-45 (approximate)
Height: Six-Three
Weight: Two-thirty (approximate)
Personality evaluation: Dedicated; devoted;
disciplined.
Super Powers: Super-Strength (equal to five
men); flight (gliding only); utilizes razor-sharp
talons made from unknown metal alloy
Former Group Affiliations and/or frequent
enemy: Long-time nemesis of *Daredevil*. Also
reported run-ins with *Captain America* and the *Gay
Bolt*, then lead man of the San Francisco based
Super group *'Gay Defenders of The Universe'*
Origin: Unknown, although reported by sources as
being 'mutant' in nature Captured by: The *Gay
Defenders of The Universe* while attempting to
kidnap a federal official's daughter outside a Fort
Worth Courthouse
Territory: West/Southwest United States

NEXT, HAVING SERVED FOUR YEARS OF
A TWENTY TO TWENTY-FIVE YEAR
SENTENCE IS:
Name: **OBLITERATION**
Race: Native American (Choctow Tribe)
Age: 34 (confirmed)
Height: Six-four

137

Weight: Two-fifty-five

Personality evaluation: Stoic; stubborn; determined

Super Powers: Limited super strength (equal to 3-4 men). Emits ultra-powerful 'shock wave' blasts from either hand Origin: Reported in some circles as being extraterrestrial in nature; never confirmed.

Former Group Affiliation and/or frequent enemies: Founding member of 'Native Savages' Super group of the late '80's which officially disbanded in 1994. Turned to crime soon thereafter.

Captured by: Captured By: *The Revenge Squad* in November 2002 on the outskirts of Wichita, Kansas, along with '*Shetah*' following a failed attempt at hijacking a government shipment of a newly developed, Top Secret laser-guided missile system.

Territory: Southern and Mid-Western U. S.

You gotta be shittin' me, Mac…whoops…sorry, slip of the tongue. It's just…man, I put this guy away. I get the feelin' he's gonna be less than thrilled to be sharin' sector space with yours truly.

ALONG THE SAME LINES, WE NEXT SHOWCASE, ALSO SERVING OUT YEAR FOUR OF A TWENTY-FIVE YEAR SENTENCE:

Name: **SHETAH**

Race: Female of unknown origin (possibly human/feline mix)

Age: 28-32 (approximate)

Height: Five-two

Weight: One-hundred five to one-hundred ten

Personality evaluation: ill-tempered; mischievous; unstable

138

Superpowers: Limited super strength (equal to 2-3 men) agility, flexibility; vertical leap measured at up to eight feet; horizontal leap up to 84 inches. Utilizes sharpened claws and teeth to render and tear. Has ability to 'sense' impending danger.

Origin: Reportedly raised by African mystics with bloodline mix of human and feline (unconfirmed)

Former Group Affiliation: Part-time member in good standing of both Defenders (1998-2000) and East Coast Avengers (2001-2002), until arrested with *OBLITERATION* in aforementioned clash with Revenge Squad in November 2003. On-going feud with *Bull-Dyke Devil* included several noted skirmishes in various cities

ALL... FORCE, ANYTHING TO ADD? I MEAN, YOU WERE THERE...AFTER

Can't recall who took her down that day. Might'a been Johnny Reb with those tranquilizer bullets he always toted around in his cartridge belt. Sexy little vixen, but a tad too furry for my taste. Nice ass for a mutie, though. Whoa...my fault again. Warned ya it wouldn't be easy.

(AHEM) AT LEAST YOU SEEM TO BE PUTTING FORTH A REASONABLE EFFORT. I CANNOT ASK MORE OF YOU AT THIS EARLY STAGE.

THE NEXT MEMBER OF OUR LITTLE 'TELEPATHIC' COMMUNITY IS THE SELF-PROCLAIMED 'PROBLEM CHILD', NOW SERVING HIS NINTH YEAR IN A THIRTY TO THIRTY-FIVE YEAR SENTENCE; THE ONE,

AND HOPEFULLY ONLY:

NAME: **THE MASS**

Race: Asian Male of Japanese descent

Age: unknown (presumed in the thirty-to forty range)

Height: Six-six

Varies ('stable' weight of five-eighty)

Personality evaluation: Vicious; unpredictable; of low intelligence

Power: Can expand his glutinous girth to upwards of one ton while retaining normal speed and agility of a two-hundred-pound man. When fully 'expanded', has strength of twenty to thirty men. Seemingly impervious to physical assault, can only be brought down (and thereby controlled) by electrical charges of at least twenty thousand volts.

Origin: Unknown (rumored to be a former Japanese 'super-soldier'; a 'cellular structure' lab experiment gone horribly awry).

Former group affiliation and/or frequent enemy: The X-Men, Storm, Stars & Bars Super group (defunct since summer of 2000)

Captured in December of 1997 by Stars & Bars Group. RING ANY BELLS, BENJA- FORCE?

Oh yeah…I've heard of the walkin' blob. Old teammate of mine in the Revenge Squad, Dark Claw, rest his soul, had a scrap or two with 'im. Said it was like punchin' a bowl of half-settled Jell-O (laughing). Claw also said the man stunk like rotten Sushi and un-wiped ass. Shit…my fault again, Mac. Geez, this is harder than I thought.

I UNDERSTAND, FORCE. NOT TO WORRY, IT WILL BECOME SECOND NATURE OVER TIME.

LAST BUT NOT LEAST IN OUR LESS THAN ILLUSTRIOUS LINE-UP, SERVING ONLY HIS SECOND YEAR OF A MANDATORY LIFE SENTENCE IS:

Name: **BLACK PLAGUE**

Race: White Male

Age: Thirty-three

Height: Six-two

Weight: Two-fifteen

Personality evaluation: Intelligent; wily; ruthless.

Power: Able to transmit non-fatal as well as fatal diseases and toxic poisons via touch or by contamination of air space.

Origin: Powers were reportedly 'installed' as a deterrent to terrorism following the 9/11/2001 Twin Tower bombings.

Group affiliations and/or frequent enemies: None listed. Apparently turned rogue agent following an assassination attempt on a noted Middle Eastern dictator.

Captured by: *Mystic* in September of 2005 while reportedly just moments away from attacking the Presidential Motorcade in Washington D. C.

Didn't hear anything about it. Guess I was already in hidin'. BP is supposedly one nasty mo-fo. Hard to believe the green fairy took 'em down.

IS IT TRULY, FORCE? ISN'T MYSTIC RESPONSIBLE FOR YOUR PRESENT STATE OF INCARCERATION? *true enough, but I ain't nowhere near BP's league. I'm basically just an old-school brawler with oversized toilet grabbers. And before ya ask, I ain't no mutie.*

141

NO NEED TO ELABORATE FURTHER, FORCE. YOUR HISTORY, OR AT LEAST A BRIEF SYNOPSIS OF SAME, HAS ALREADY BEEN MADE AVAILABLE. ALLOW ME TO EXPLAIN. FEEL FREE TO CORRECT ANY AND ALL INACCURACIES:

Name: **FORCE** (known as *'Desolation Outlaw'* beginning in late 2003)
Race: White Male
Age: 35-40 (approximate)
Height: Six-Three
Weight: Two-forty-five to two-sixty
Personality evaluation: Undisciplined; unpredictable; (loose) canon
Powers: Super Strength (equal to twenty average men); possesses hands twice the size of a normal man, thus the legendary punching power that can reportedly penetrate steel barriers up to six inches thick. Skeleton is reportedly exo-alloy based, thus virtually unbreakable Origin: Reported to be offspring of man and *'Wendigo'* (unconfirmed). Most believe this to be blatant mythology.

Former group affiliations and/or frequent enemies: Full-time member of *'Revenge Squad'* from 1999-2003
Territory: Southern and Western U. S.
Captured by: Mystic while a fugitive from the US Government. Convicted in wrongful deaths of *'Shaker'* Jake *'King Snake'* McKay and the *Crimson Condor* ANYTHING TO AMEND?

For the record, Hoss, I'm thirty-eight and wasn't hatched from the hairy loins of no Bigfoot

142

wanna-be. Plus which, while it is true I witnessed both Shaker Jake and The Condor bite the bullet, it wasn't this man pullin' the trigger. Guess only the good Lord and myself will know that to be stone-cold fact.

DULY NOTED, ALTHOUGH YOU UNDERSTAND THE OBVIOUS IRONY IN PROCLAIMING ONE'S INNOCENCE BEHIND TITANIUM-CONSTRUCTED WALLS.

Yeah, yeah...I know. Never been a guilty man behind bars, right? Anyhow, where you getting your data, Mac? You that good at readin' minds?

YOU VASTLY OVERRATE MY TALENT, GOOD SIR. I'M SIMPLY UTILIZING EAGLE ISLAND'S VERY OWN PERSONNEL FILES FROM THE HUMAN RESOURCES SECTION OF THE MAINFRAME HARD DRIVE.

Bein' able to 'read' files off a computer chip ain't exactly commonplace, Mac. Overrated my a-...uh, rear end.

POINT TAKEN. I SOMETIMES FORGET THE LIMITATIONS OF YOUR SPECIES. NOW, IN THE INTEREST OF GOOD SHOWMANSHIP, ALLOW ME TO SHARE THE SELF-SAME FILE ON MYSELF. I AM CURRENTLY AROUND THE MID-POINT OF YEAR SIX IN A THIRTY-YEAR SENTENCE, THOUGH PAROLE SEEMS QUITE UNLIKELY UNDER THE PRESENT REGIME. IT STATES:

Name: **Mind Sweep,** AKA *'The Overseer'*, AKA *'Brain Melt'*
Race: Male of unknown origin
Age: Unknown

Height: Five-ten

Weight: One-sixty-five

Personality: (Extremely) intelligent; (cool) Collective under pressure; (Unyieldingly) stubborn

Powers: Telepathy; mind-control; hypnotism

Origins: Unknown. Rumored to be extraterrestrial in nature

Former group affiliations and/or frequent enemies: *The Fantastic Four, Doc Strange, the East Coast Avengers*

Captured by: *The Silver Surfer* in December of 2000 following a series of Middle Eastern leaders falling victim to his patented '*Mind Sweeps*', wherein each were left in a comatose, vegetable-like state utterly void of brain wave activity I CAN ONLY STATE THAT THE INFORMATION PROVIDED IS SURPRISINGLY ACCURATE, THOUGH FAR FROM COMPLETE IN PAINTING THE FULL PICTURE.

Hey...seems I do remember a couple of towel-heads havin' their brains turned to pudding back in the late nineties.

Extraterrestrial, huh? You an' ET frequent the same stompin' grounds? No wonder ya talk like the Professor from Gilligan's Island.

AS YOU YOURSELF STATED EARLIER, IT'S A LENGTHY STORY FOR ANOTHER TIME. FOR NOW, I WILL ONLY SAY THAT, REGARDLESS OF THE ENTITY RESPONSIBLE, JUSTICE WAS DULY SERVED FOR ASTROCITIES COMMITTED.

Uh...got'cha. Leastways, I think I do. Not my business, anyhow. Are we done yet, Mac? I mean, this is a real gas an' all, but I'm startin' to feel like

you really are trompin' around in my skull wearin' steel-toed boots.

I'M AFRAID THERE IS A SLIGHT HANGOVER EFFECT THE FIRST FEW SESSIONS. WE ARE INDEED DONE FOR NOW, FORCE. YOU'VE BEEN INTRODUCED TO EACH OF YOUR NEIGHBORS, SO TO SPEAK. WHEN YOU'VE MADE THE DECISION ON WHETHER OR NOT TO JOIN OUR LITTLE IMPROMPTU CHAT LINE, LET ME KNOW. AGAIN, YOU'RE FREE TO CHANGE YOUR MIND EITHER WAY. SUCH FREEDOM OF CHOICE IS RARE ON EAGLE ISLAND, AND IT'S MY DISTINCT PLEASURE TO BE IN A POSITION TO MAKE THE OFFER.

What times the first jawin'...uh...mind meld session anyhow?

YOU'LL FIND TIME INDEED HAS NO MEANING HERE, FORCE. LET'S JUST SAY IT SHALL COMMENCE FOLLOWING THE EVENING MEAL. DOES THIS MEAN...YOU'RE GAME AFTER All?

Why the hell not, Mac? After all, the old appointment book is a blank slate from page one.

VERY WELL, THEN. GLAD TO HAVE YOU ABOARD. THE VINE IS NOTHING IF NOT A WELCOME RESPITE FROM THE EVERYDAY MUNDANE BEHIND THESE CURSED WALLS. TRUTHFULLY, I LOOK FORWARD TO THE INITIAL EXCHANGE BETWEEN YOURSELF AND OBLITERATION WITH THE UNBRIDLED GLEE OF A SEXUALLY AROUSED TEENAGED MALE.

Hey, whatever gets your rocks off, Hoss.

145

Speakin' of which, I take it there ain't no porno flicks listed on the ol' movie request list, huh?

MY UNDERSTANDING OF THE HUMAN LIBIDO IS SEVERELY LIMITED, FORCE, BUT WITHIN THE RULES GOVERNING SUCH MATTERS, I'M FAIRLY CERTAIN SUCH FILMS AREN'T ALLOWED WITHIN THE ACCESSIBLE STOCK, NO.

Figures. I just hope the salt peter kicks in soon. Say goodnight, Sweep... GOODNIG...GOOD DAY, FORCE. MIND SWEEP...SIGNING OUT... Lying back on the cot with his massive hands draped over the whole of his face, Ben felt a faint throbbing at his temples that seemed only to increase in intensity as moments passed.

"Geez, Benji, exactly what kinda circus sideshow *freak* exhibit have you hooked up with?"

Falling into a fitful snooze, he was unable to re-conger Leah's heavenly image no matter how stringent the effort, instead bombarded by pictures of a much more malevolent nature, along with a feeling of deep-seeded dread filling his midsection like molten lead.

***

Part V:

Sleeping Dogs Lain to Rest

"Bad news, troops. Looks like our ETD is still a good forty-eight hours away. Just got off the line with the Warden. Construction delays no doubt caused by security issues. Damned place is off the map as it is. I've heard you've gotta be carrying a level six badge just to avoid being shot on site."

Director Willis paced a small circle at the center of the already less than spacious motel room, having already lit his third cigarette in the previous ten minutes.

"One question, Chief," Mystic blurted, holding a gloved hand airborne and waiving it about in frantic haste.

"You know I can't divulge the actual location, Mystic…at least, not yet."

"Oh, it's not that. What in the name of Morris the Cat is an ETD?"

Sitting a few feet away on the edge of a badly sagging mattress, Marvella rolled her eyes in genuine disgust.

"Estimated Time of Departure," Willis answered without a hitch, pivoting his left foot and executing a textbook 'about face' just as he'd gotten to within a half-step of the front door.

"Oh…what a relief. For a sec, I thought it was some new sexually transmitted disease."

"Sorry for the inconvenience, people," Willis prattled unabated, never breaking stride while wearing a deeper path into the already well-worn shag carpet, "of course additional meals and down time will be added to your per diem."

Rising from the bed, the springs of which creaked their disapproval, Marvella studied the tips of her inch-long fingernails with a frown.

"Great. Officially stranded dead center in the middle of *absolute* nowhere with two days to kill. I've been needing to redo my nails, but we're talking serious overkill here."

"Aw, curb your bitching, girl," Mystic replied, peering out from the second-floor balcony onto a badly cracked two-lane blacktop that served as Kingston

Springs' main street, "it's not *that* bad. Check out the view! Why, to our west stands the legendary Golden Arches of Mickey D's, and to the east there's a Seven-Eleven with not one, but two gas pumps! Big Mac's and Slurpees all within walking distance. What more could you possibly ask for?"

Marvella pulled a small nail file from her handbag and began casually sanding away at her left index finger.

"A leather bar or two, perhaps? Or how about a surprise '*Chippendales*' review in the hotel lobby?"

"Oh, you're so... vile...but *deliciously* so." Mystic sang, backing from the wooden ledge in an impromptu break dance.

"I can already tell these next two days are going to be heaven on earth." The director finally halted his incessant pacing, walking over to slide the balcony's glass doors shut with a forceful grunt.

"Stay out of open view, both of you, at least while you're in costume," he barked through gritted teeth while drawing the thick, dirt-brown curtains closed until the room was cloaked in shadow. "The last thing we need is a bevy of media hounds filling the parking lot."

"Relax Chief. Don't blow a vessel. Besides, it'd take CNN three or four days to reach us in this godforsaken burg," Mystic said, taking a seat next to Marvella and placing a slim arm around her well-toned shoulders.

Willis took a long draw off his cigarette, which

148

hung from his lower lip as if super-glued into place.

"Don't bet on it. It's a damn wonder someone didn't spot you both levitating onto the motel roof or climbing down the fire escape. Wouldn't it just be easier to ditch the spandex and walk around in civvies?" he concluded, exhaling thick smoke streams from each nostril.

Mystic leaned over and placed his chin on Marvella's shoulder, seemingly entranced by her nail-filing technique.

"Sorry, Chief, but the code of secrecy we 'specially endowed' types live by prohibits such reckless behavior, isn't that correct, my Asian queen?"

Sighing wearily, she shrugged just enough to force him to back away.

"Sad but true, I'm afraid. Personally, I'm tempted to strip down to *nudist colony* standards to escape this rat trap."

"Fine, *whatever,*" Willis huffed, mashing the cigarette butt into a tin ashtray. "Just keep out of sight. Meals will be delivered to you starting with dinner in a few hours. If you need anything, call me directly on my cell."

"How about a can of RAID, chief?" Mystic whined, scanning the thick carpeted floor with obvious disdain. "Although I'd hate to cause further structural damage by killing off the roach-foundation holding this place upright."

"I'll…see what I can do."

"Chief?" Marvella asked, finally looking up.

Willis had already started for the door, and turned about with his fist wrapped around the doorknob.

149

"Yes, ma'am?"

"What's your take on this...thing we're transporting? I mean, purely off the record."

"Ma'am, I can't even begin to speculate without coming offas a second-rate *Fox Mulder*. If some of the sharpest scientific minds in the business don't have a clue, I'm certainly left scratching this bald plate of mine in total confusion."

"Besides," he summed up, smiling weakly while pulling the door slightly ajar, "you two have spent your entire adult lives rubbing elbows with the weird and fantastic. Probably by the time the chopper lands, you'll have that particular quandary all but solved."

Closing the door gently behind him, director Willis strolled the deserted hallway like a man literally walking atop eggshells, his eyes nervously scanning every corner.

"And I'm the Queen of *Freaking* England..." he whispered, wearing a hideous grin while repeatedly beating his left fist against his upper thigh. His upper left shoulder burned and throbbed from the barrage of inoculations he'd been subjected to just days earlier. Reaching up to wipe the building sweat from his forehead, he felt the heat radiating from his flesh, which stung like a fresh cut upon contact.

"Better you than me, assholes."

***

"The Chief look a bit piqued to you? I mean, even more than usual?" Mystic was lying atop the second of the room's twin beds, casually flipping

150

channels on the nearby television while keeping the sound muted.

"Could be that damn rock slowly turning him into a pumpkin. Might eventually affect us in similarly strange ways," Marvella replied between blowing softly onto her sparkling wet nails. "You're not feeling horny in my presence, are you?"

"Heaven forbid…certainly *not*."

"So far then, we're clean."

"Seriously, Leah, he was stalking about the room like he was about to birth a kitty litter…or is that litter of kittens?"

"Well, people have died after all. Quite a few of them, in fact. Can't blame the man in charge for being a bit edgy. Quite natural, considering…"

"Possibly. Still, I feel strangely ill at ease, and believe me when I tell you, that's a rare sensation indeed."

Glancing over the tips of her spear-sharpened nails, which she placed side by side as to compare their evenness, Marvella's eyes were squinted so tightly one would have assumed they were completely shut.

"Are you hinting that the self-proclaimed '*King of the Mystical Realm*' is…dare I say it…*apprehensive* over the coming mission? Say it isn't so. Why, I know for a fact one of your fan-club websites deemed you 'the mystic without fear'. Kind of a blatant rip-off of *Daredevil* territory, but hey, I'm sure you have little control over such matters."

Dropping the remote onto the mattress, Mystic crossed his arms over his chest and floated slowly upward without shifting his horizontal pose, then drifted over several feet until he was positioned directly over Marvella, who feigned ignorance while continuing to fan her nails.

"Correct me if I'm wrong, dear lady, which is *indeed* a rare occurrence, but do I detect a note of bitterness in your tone with each and every remark pointed my way?"

"Don't take it personal. That is, unless you feel an overwhelming need. Can't say I'll lose any sleep regardless."

With undeniable grace and agility, he twisted about until his head hung upside down and directly across from her own, sticking his lips out in a hurtful pout.

"Wouldn't have anything to do with my part in the capture of a former flame, now would it?"

"And who, pray tell, might that be?"

"Don't play innocent with me, Miss Leah. Let's clear the air right here and now. As much as I despise utilizing a cliché of such cornball magnitude...I was just doing my job."

"I don't doubt it for a minute," she said, hovering several inches from the top of the mattress before floating gradually over and lowering herself onto the other bed, all without benefit of even the most minute gesture. "Whatever you say, Ace. Um, what is it you were hinting at again?"

Descending onto the mattress below, the childish pout had transformed into a tight-lipped scowl.

"Goddamn it, woman, stow the sarcasm and talk to me. It's no secret among our kind that you and Ben Thomason were an item."

Scooping up the remote, though palming as not

152

to smear her nails, Marvella flipped channels in silence for several moments, her stoic expression unchanged. "Key word there is *'were'*. Ancient history is just that, Mystic. Unlike many, I'm the type who doesn't waste time dwelling on past events. Once I pass a signpost, I don't rewind to re-read, dig?"

Throwing both arms airborne in a mock 'surrender' gesture, he found it utterly impossible not to smile.

"Sooooo-rry. I sincerely apologize for bringing it up. Just wanted to get it out of the way, formality wise. Couldn't help but assume it was the reason you were breaking my testicles at every turn. Got to tell you, I didn't shed a single tear when the man's sentence came down, not after witnessing what he did to the Crimson Condor. Wasn't the least bit pretty, girl. I'm sure you know all about the man's rather…infamous temper."

"Let me explain something to you, pal, once and only once," she replied with a twisted snarl, turning on him like a hissing feline, "I don't like you. In fact, you grate my last nerve with every gesture, every movement, every flowery word that spews forth from those glossed-over lips of yours. But…" she raised her left forefinger into the air as to emphasize the coming point even as her demeanor calmed somewhat, "…that only places you in the majority of ninety-nine percent of *every* person I come into even casual contact with these days. Pretty much all of society irritates me to no end, *especially* those who deem themselves 'specially endowed'. Other than a select few I worked with while a member of the *Revenge Squad,*

153

I find most so-called hero-types arrogant, pompous, and surprisingly ignorant of their own flaws, most of which are glaringly obvious in terms of personality. In other words, don't take it personally, Mystic. Though I *do* find you a royal pain in the posterior, don't label yourself the proverbial 'red-headed stepchild.' It's a mighty big class...you're just another student. On the other hand, don't expect an apology. That's just me."

After a brief pause, Mystic fell back onto the pillow with his mouth frozen ajar.

"Leah, if for some reason I don't survive this mission, please...*please* don't allow anyone to talk you into performing my eulogy, okay?"

"Not a problem, pal," she responded with a wink, "now go pluck your eyebrows or shave your legs and allow me at least a half-hour's peace and quiet."

Staring up at the badly stained tiled ceiling as the TV's volume blared loudly in the foreground, Mystic wore a wry grin that was the very definition of smarmy.

"Dig? Did she really say *dig?* Where am I, the TV Land version of hell?"

CHAPTER FOUR

Desolation Destination

"Just got off the line with Deputy Director Willis. He was none too pleased, understandably."

"From what the foreman told me, it's all about the specs, Warden. Guy said his crew has cracked the glass at least three times trying to secure it into place. Have you seen this stuff, sir?"

"Only a sample about the size of a tea saucer," Warden Terry responded, leaning back with his highly glossed work boots balanced on the far-left edge of his desktop, "never saw or felt anything like it. From what I gather, it's some type of modified Plexiglas/clear metal substance similar in makeup to Mind Sweep's cell walls, only they've added something new to the mix that upgrades it to almost 'stabilized black hole' status. Heard it took a team of chemists, biologists and physicists holed up twenty-four seven over two months to perfect the formula."

Leaning against a far wall, just below a black and white framed photo of Warden Terry in his 'Chief Justice' days, The Guardsman stifled a yawn with great effort.

"Ours is not to fully comprehend, I guess. What's the updated ETA, sir?"

"They won't fly out of Wyoming until day after tomorrow, so we won't see them for at least another ninety-six to one-hundred ten hours. Is Danley and his crew sure they'll have that damn glass dungeon prepped by then?"

"Man insured me no later than noon tomorrow, sir. Marble framework is long since done, just a matter of completely drying. The problem's that glass coffin. Stuff cracks if someone farts within ten feet of it. Blows my mind how something that brittle is going to serve to house such a potentially grave threat."

Leaning onto his haunches, The Guardsman placed his hands on each side of his cowl and began twisting his upper body, stopping only after several loud pops reverberated from his upper back and both shoulders.

"Ah, much better. Confidentially sir, what is this…thing they assigned us to baby-sit?"

"Your guess is as good as mine, Luke. I was told an in-depth in-brief won't occur until after its arrival and safe storage," the Warden shrugged, "Tell you what though, the whole mess reminds me of that damn ruby crystal we stored back in two thousand. Nobody was happier than this man once they finally shot that sucker off into space on a one-way ride to Jupiter and beyond."

"Oh yeah, that was one of *Mysterio's* toys, right? The one that would literally turn you inside out once it drew a bead on your thought patterns?"

"That's the one. Don't think I got a good night's sleep for two years with that cursed thing pulsating away just a few dozen feet underground."

"Makes one wonder why they'd ever want to store anything so potentially hazardous. Hard enough keeping the live ones in line, much less their demonic playthings."

Whipping his chair hard to the right, the Warden hopped up and walked to a far corner, where a steaming pot of coffee awaited.

"Obviously there's a matter of usefulness there. Someone of a lofty rank wants it studied, dissected and analyzed, more than likely for future use as a weapon, possibly a terrorist deterrent or something similar. Come to think of it, they tried the same moves on that glowing crystal, and only threw in the towel once four or five scientists got fried into piles of smoking gristle for their efforts. Took weeks for that damn smell to fade, as I recall. Like burnt beef and heated copper."

No longer able to fight it off, The Guardsman released a lengthy yawn, then stood and shook his head vigorously from side to side.

"Sounds like you could use a cup or three yourself. Nice 'n stout," the Warden said between sips, reclaiming his earlier position behind the desk.

"Could never hack coffee, sir. Does really nasty things to the old digestive track. By the way, who's providing escort? Anybody we know?"

"Know *of,* possibly, though you might have met them in your earlier travels. According to Willis, a...*Marvella* and *Mystic* have the duty."

"Marvel-..." the larger man gasped, the single word hanging at the center of his throat like parched toast. "Old friends of yours?"

"We've...we bumped each other on a few battlefields, you might say. Talk about your galaxies far, far away...we were both practically kids then. Wet-behind-the ears rookies, both of us."

"I hear she's a real looker of the Asian persuasion. Korean, right?"

"Affirmative. And unless there've been some dramatic changes through the years, she's every bit as stubborn and ornery as she is beautiful."

Slurping noisily, the Warden then laid the cup aside and positioned himself directly behind the computer screen, tapping the keyboard's exposed keys at light speed.

"What about this Mystic guy? Word has it he's the gay movement's newest and brightest star."

"Never met him," The Guardsman replied, executing a series of deep knee bends, "... but he's all over the 'net, for certain. Can't click on any website without his face popping up. Since the *Silver Fairy* got caught in that kiddie porn scandal a few months back, Mystic is the new *alternative lifestyle* spokesman of the moment. He has to be raking it in on endorsements alone."

"I'm sure. Big money in being the most popular queer these days. Hell of a statement on modern society is all I can say," the Warden huffed, studying the monitor's greenish glow with unblinking eyes.

"Oh, by the way, did you get Benjamin T. squared away in his new digs?" Halting in mid-squat, The Guardsman hesitated before responding, though he wasn't at all sure why.

"Yes, sir. He's all set. Not really sure how much really sunk in, though. He was predictably drained."

"I'm sure. The *peel* and *reel* gets 'em all, no matter how strong. You knew the guy pretty well back in the day, correct?"

"We…occupied the same worn trail on occasion, yes, sir."

"Straight up then; he gonna make it or flake it?" the Warden asked, no longer typing but still watching the monitor.

"He'll make it. They don't come much tougher, mentally or physically," the larger man answered, resuming his stretching reps at a much quicker pace.

"Good to hear it. After the past few months of putting up with *The Mass's* BS, it'll be a welcome change of pace."

"No argument there, sir. That boy's crazy as a rabid bed bug. Ultra-warped. Not of sound mind, but of bloated body."

The Warden openly winced, his gaze finally departing the monitor for a far wall, which he stared at, seemingly entranced.

"I hear he keeps 'demanding' a meeting with me to discuss the availability of porn in the DVD listings. Be a chilly day in the Mojave before I share a room with that fat perv."

"Sir," The Guardsman responded with a shrug, "this must be why you garner the big bucks."

"Oh, you're a laugh-riot, Luke. Chris Rock in spandex, you are," the Warden quipped, turning his concentration back to the keyboard and monitor.

"Appreciate that, Warden Terry Sir, though I prefer Richard Pryor *or* Bill Cosby. Old school all the way, baby."

The Warden released a loud, cackling snort just as the Guardsman exited. Moments later, the dour expression he'd worn vanished in wake of a worrisome scowl. As if transported through some unseen time machine, the man seemed to age a decade in a matter of seconds.

"I get the feeling *no* amount of money is gonna be worth the next few days," he mumbled through bleary, rapidly reddening eyes.

***

Part I:

FIVE-Party Line

His stomach groaning its vehement disapproval, Ben took a half step from the wall and watched the metal tray slide smoothly back into position with a low hum.

"Well, that was predictably nasty," he blurted, rubbing his midsection with both hands while walking back to the cot with a wobbly gait.

Following several loud belches, he collapsed onto the leather recliner like an over-sized puppet with severed strings.

Staring at his own reflection provided by the plasma TV's wide, blank screen, he reached up to scratch the stubble sprouting rapidly forth along his jaw line and chin.

In studying his forearms and chest, he noticed a dark infestation of the same bursting forth in thick waves. Similarly, his scalp was riddled with a quarter inch of fresh growth less than twenty–four hours since the 'strip' treatment.

"King Kong lives," he whispered, "Great to know the old family genes can take a chemical peel lickin' 'and keep on tickin''."

He'd played the role of POW countless times over the past decade-plus, the lengthiest term to date being a seventy-three day marathon in late two-thousand, pinned to a stone wall by razor-wire straps as a 'guest' of the *Black Vulture* and the long-disbanded *'Birds of Prey'* gang. Beaten to a pulp and left for dead in a stony catacomb two miles below the Earth's surface, he'd ended up losing sixty pounds all told, with no logical explanation for survival other than the inhuman metabolism he'd been handed at birth. A metabolism that steadfastly refused to allow starvation while self-healing a broken jaw, nose, and two cracked ribs and still somehow able to feed on its own meager enzymes.

Then there had been the eight-day sabbatical he'd spent in an abandoned warehouse outside of Tuscon, hanging by his ankles while various members of the Mexican Mafia took turns pelting him with aluminum baseball bats and burning his testicles with heated coil wire. Fun times all, for certain; knee-slapping laugh riots for the masochist set.

Still, through all the torture sessions he'd endured while playing thepart of 'hero', both mental and physical, none could even scrape the surface in terms of utter hopelessness and bitter despair as compared to the past twenty-four hours. Consequently, it felt like years of indenture had *already* passed since he'd begun playing the role of fugitive following the 'Shaker' Jake incident.

Glancing back and over toward the oak desk and PC set-up, he briefly considered filling out a DVD/CD request form for at least the third time in as many hours. As before, he simply couldn't force himself to perform even the most menial of tasks, instead gripping the recliner's adjustable handle and giving it a gentle tug, stretching out in a prone position as the chair creaked and whined from the strain of his bulk.

His lips curled into a tight smirk as he squeezed his eyelids shut and initiated an inner chant, all the while unconscious of the fact that he was silently mouthing every word.

ALL RIGHT, BRAIN MINER...I'M READY TO CHAT WHEN YOU ARE...COME IN, BRAIN MELT...

...ARE YA THERE, MIND BENDER?

"Geez, just what I thought,' he muttered, folding his arms across his chest and feeling every fiber of his being ease towards a gradual meltdown, "No doubt a dope induced hallucination brought on by those damn chemicals they bathed me in. Should'a known. Gotta admit though, I got one hell of an imagination. Had a real meltin' pot cast of characters runnin' around 'tween my ears. Must'a pulled a few 'em straight outta my ass cheeks, 'specially that *Mind-Reader* dude.

Scaaaary shit, Mac...

"Oh well, guess it's time for an afternoon nap. Could be the start of a twice-daily trend, in fact..."

PARDON THE DELAY, FORCE. I WAS...PREOCCUPIED, I'M AFRAID. CERTAINLY, NOT A RARE OCCURANCE.

HOW CAN I BE OF ASSISTANCE?

"Shit on a shingle!" Ben blurted, jerking himself into a sitting position despite the recliner's steep incline.

Damn, son...I'd already given you up as a brain-fart figment of my imagination. Gotta say...I ain't quite sure ya ain't even now.

(PAUSE)

SUCH DOUBT IS NORMAL AT THIS EARLY JUNCTURE, BEN...FORCE. REST

162

ASSURED, MY PRESENCE IS REAL (PAUSE). I TAKE IT YOU'D COME TO A MORE…PERMANENT DECISION CONCERNING THE CELL SECTOR

GRAPEVINE, AS IT WERE…

Uh, y-yeah, I guess…I mean, for now anyways. You did say I was free to… discontinue service anytime, right?

AFFIRMATIVE, FORCE. AS I STATED BEFORE, NO ONE'S UNDER CONTRACT HERE.

Then count me in, Mac. Beats the hell outta PC video games or watchin' my body hair sprout…

YOUR TIMING COULDN'T BE BETTER, BENJA-…FORCE. THE AFTER-DINNER SESSION IS JUST MOMENTS AWAY (PAUSE). SPEAKING OF WHICH, WHAT WAS YOUR INITIAL IMPRESSION OF THE PROVIDED NOURISHMENT IN QUESTION?

Can't really say. Ain't much for chowin' down just yet. Took a couple'a bites and thought I was gonna repaint the walls. Main dish looked kinda like a hairy pork chop. Mashed potatoes were kinda green to boot. Can't make a fair judgment 'til I get my appetite back, which should be around this time next year the way my gut's rockin' and rollin'…

IT GETS BETTER. AT LEAST, THAT'S THE CONSENSUS OF THOSE WHO REQUIRE SUCH DAILY NUTRIENTS. FORTUNATELY, MY SYSTEM IS SELF-SUFFICIENT IN TERMS OF RECHARGING MY INNER BATTER--

(NEW VOICE, FEMALE IN ORIGIN, INJECTS) Enough with the scientific banalities, Sweep. Let's get this gab show on the road…

OF COURSE I DO HAVE THE TENDENCY TO RAMBLE. FORCE, ALLOW ME TO INTRODUCE SHETAH, SELF-PROCLAIMED 'QUEEN OF THE CONCRETE JUNGLE'...

BEN: *No intro's necessary, pal. Me and Morris the Cat go waaaaay back. So how is my favorite slice of pussycat?*

SHETAH: Ah, always the gentleman. Sweep, don't you count such double-entendres as profanity violations?

MIND SWEEP: ONLY IF I'M ABLE TO COMPREHEND BOTH POSSIBLE MEANINGS. IN MOST CASES, I'M WOEFULLY UNDEREDUCATED IN SUCH MATTERS.

BEN: *Seems your SOL, fur-ball.*

SHETAH: Perrr-fect. No surprise there, Force. One of Sweep's biggest weaknesses as a mental mediator is his lack of ignorance in matters of 'crude speak'. My pussies fine, by the way. How's your *Johnson*? Feeling a bit...heavy *handed*? Wishing someone *would 'grease your palm?'* about now? Well, buck up, tough guy. You ain't seen nothing yet.

BEN: *Ah, as sassy as ever, I see. Must be going without those monthly 'Frontline Plus' treatments.*

MIND SWEEP: SOMEONE ELSE ON THE LINE FOR YOU, FORCE. HE STATES YOU AND HE WERE BRIEFLY TAG-TEAM PARTNERS IN A FARAWAY LAND...

(LONG PAUSE)

OBLITERATION: Why, howdy there, shat-heel...let me be the first to extend to you a Laurel ...and Hardy handshake...brain-wave version, of course...

BEN: *Oh, Christ.... talk about your dis-fuck-tional families. Bet you're as thrilled to hear my voice as I am that foghorn'a yours, man.*

OBLITERATION: Sure bet, *Arse*-hole. I've got to admit, just hearing you'd be joining us here on 'Isolation Isle' has added years to my life. Not really sure that's a positive, considering the big picture. And to think, the very person to whom I owe this life to luxury is now but a hop, skip, and titanium wall away. To paraphrase my noble ancestors, '*white man now find himself sitting in heaping pile of steaming buffalo dung*'...

BEN: *Swell...Chief Flapping jaws lives on. Can't blame no one but myself. Many's the time I could'a sent his red ass packin' to the happy huntin' grounds only to capture 'im instead...*

MIND SWEEP: BEN...UNLIKE THE EARTHLY GAME OF BASEBALL, I ONLY ALLOW TWO STRIKES PER SESSION IN THE PROFANITY DEPARTMENT BEFORE I PULL THE PLUG. NOW, FOR THE NEXT CONTESTANT:

(LONG PAUSE)

THE MASS: Som of Bitch! Why you can't wait another few second, huh? I not done choking the monkey!

MIND SWEEP: STRIKE ONE, MASS. NOT EXACTLY AN AUSPICIOUS BEGINNING...

THE MASS:...... swollen like a po-lock sausage... that's what all the ladies used to love about *Mass*...I can make the one-eyed trouser (pronounced *towel-ser*) whatever size they desired! In Tokyo, they used to line up by the dozen just to take a peek at my pride and joy.

165

BEN: *Uh, Sweep...I could really do without Mr. Yak-A-Moto's play by play concernin' his mutating wiener...*

OBLITERATION: Pipe down, pinhead. The Mass-ster is just getting warmed up. Just sit back and enjoy the filth...

THE MASS: ...goes off like Mount Sakira-Kima...all I got to watch is old episode of '*Charlie's Angels*' and the magic *bloat* begins...it really, really (pronounced '*willy*') amazing site...

SHETAH: Oh, for cripe's sake, Sweep, cut him off before he *goes* off...

BEN: *I second the motion......*

THE MASS: ...you first-class asshole to interrupt my pole-vault massage, Brain-fucker...

MIND SWEEP: STRIKES TWO AND THREE...YOU'RE OUT. END OF TRANSMISSION...

BEN: *Did he say...pole-vault massage?*

OBLITERATION: Another fine triple-X rant wasted...

MIND SWEEP: PARDON THE RATHER CRUDE INTERLUDE, FORCE. I'M AFRAID THE MASS RARELY FALLS OUT OF CHARACTER. NORMALLY, HE WILL LAST AT LEAST A MOMENT OR TWO LONGER...

BEN: *No great loss, Hoss. Don't think I could ever get bored or lonely enough to wanna hear some fat Jap's masturbation techniques. So tell me guys, when are we bustin' outta here? Who's hoggin' the nail file?*

SHETAH: Simply hilarious. How perrrrrrfectly droll you are, Mister Hero turned murdering, cold-blooded bad guy. Saw the tendencies in you many times...looks like you finally acted on what came natural.

OBLITERATION: Ah, give the jack-arse a break, cat-girl. He's trying to fit into a new clique, after all. Really makes me yearn for general population status soI could take the young man under my wing.

BEN: *I hear ya talkin', Obie. I'll just bet you and Fritz the Cat there are yearnin' for some face time.*

OBLITERATION: You read me incorrectly, ye of the *shovel*-sized hands. Revenge is only wasted rage, especially considering our present situation. Besides, the way I figure it, if you hadn't busted me, someone else would've. It was destiny, plain and simple. Then again, I can only speak for myself...cat-girl?

SHETAH: Personally, Force (pause), I'd love nothing better than to gouge your fucking eyes out and cook the severed eyeballs over an open flame. (pause) Hey, a girl's gotta have a dream...

MIND SWEEP: NOW, SHETAH...YOU KNOW BETTER...

OBLITERATION: As I was about to say, to each his own...sorry about that, backhoe mitts.

BEN: *No sweat, Chief. There's a reason I've always considered myself a 'dog person'...*

OBLITERATION: Oh, by the way Forcy... you must recall my personal profile does state 'compulsive liar' as one of my...less than savory traits. In other words, eat my shorts...

BEN: *That's better...me an' you as buddies would'a never worked out...*

SHETAH: Glad to have you with us, tough

guy. Only thing sweeter would be if *Johnny Reb* could join the chat. Heard he got his southern-fried, cornpone ass deep-sixed a few years back, by a teammate no less. Four Star, I heard. Gotta be honest, big fella, these reflective orbs of mine shed nary a tear.

MIND SWEEP: YOU'RE TRYING MY PATIENCE, WOMAN...

BEN: *So it was Reb who put the leash on ya that day. Kinda thought so. Didn't know felines were so apt to hold a grudge. After all, the man was just doin' his job.*

SHETAH: Is that right? Oh, yeah, a true professional he was. Then why did that red neck mother fuc-...(pause) why did he feel the need to cop a feel or three after paralyzing me with that tranquilizer dart? Sick son of a bi-...pretty sad that the last touch I'm gonna feel in this lifetime was his groping hands.

MIND SWEEP: UM...FOLKS, I'M AFRIAD I'M GOING TO HAVE TO CUT THIS SESSION SHORT. I'M...UH...I...THERE'S A DISTURBANCE OF SOME SORT...JUST DOESN'T FEEL QUITE RIGHT...I...WE'LL CONTINUE A BIT AFTER LUNCH TOMORROW...

OBLITERATION: What's up, doc? Electrical interference or what? I didn't know anything from the outside could affect you...

MIND SWEEP: I'M NOT...REALLY SURE. JUST...I APOLOGIZE FOR THE ABRUPTNESS OF MY EXIT. BESIDES, MAYBE IT'S A POSITIVE. THE EXCHANGES WERE GETTING A BIT...HEATED. MORE THAN LIKELY

WOULD HAVE BEEN CALLED FOR
PROFANITY INFRACTIONS...

SHETAH: Lay down and rest that noggin,
Sweep. Don't want you burning out on us now. And
Force?

BEN: *Yeah, Fur-ball?*

SHETAH: Welcome to our little corner of hell,
asshole. Sweet dreams...

OBLITERATION: Night, Benji...I'll do my
best to leave you a stale fart or two in the workout
wing...

MIND SWEEP: GOOD DAY, ALL...BY
THE WAY, SHETAH, YOU'RE HEREBY
PLACED ON PROBATION FOR THE REST OF
THE WEEK. SIGNING OUT...

Ben awoke with a start, a loud gasp escaping
his parched lips. Blinking rapidly, it took several
moments for his blurred vision to clear. Wiping a
thick trail of drool from his chin, he pondered how
long he'd been out since the 'chat session'.

*Talk about your kick-ass side effects. Usually
takes a fifth of JB or better to produce this kinda
buzz. Make that, used to take.*

Rising from the recliner with all the speed of a
heavily sedated sloth, he took in several deep
breaths, releasing each in timed intervals.

Lying on his chest atop the cool stone floor, he
leaned a bit to his right and began a slow, deliberate
series of one-armed push-ups, alternating arms
every ten reps until both were noticeably pumped.

*Damn, I can't wait for my first gym session.
Whatever else, I ain't gonna allow myself to shrivel
to skin 'n bones in this joint.*

After a cumulative total of seventy-five reps

169

with each arm, he flipped over and began a furious set of crunches.

Finally feelin' my second wind. 'Bout damn time.

Collapsing with a huff following the three-minute set of two-hundred reps, he rewound the chat session in his mind while flashing the tiniest of smiles.

What're the odds? Serving life in stir with two jackasses I help put away. Hell, if nothin' else, this psychedelic ride ain't liable to be borin'.

Moments later, he began to shadow box; first with a flurry of short jabs, then gradually building to a series of sweeping hooks and brutal uppercuts.

Roughly four minutes later, with his neck and upper body bathed in fresh sweat, he knelt onto one knee, panting heavily as his chin rested atop his upper chest.

Barely day two and I'm already crackin' at the seams. Funny, I feel an urgent need to prep for somethin', but what in Sam Hill'sname could somethin' be? Never gonna make it at this rate, Benji. Liable to be makin' shadow animals on the nearest wall by the end of the week.

Lifting his right arm airborne, he could smell his own sourness. Turning about as he rose to stand, he eyeballed the 'personal cleansing unit' cautiously before shrugging in apparent resignation.

"Oh, why the hell *not*? Guess it's better'n smellin' like boiled buttermilk..." he muttered, stepping over to the domed unit while peeling off his government issued boxer shorts.

***

Part II:

Midnight Confession

"So...how close were you two, if you don't mind my asking?"

Donned solely in beige colored Dockers, parachute shorts and a sleeveless white T-shirt, Mystic floated several feet off the carpeted floor in a lotus-style pose.

The television provided the only illumination within the tiny room, although the sound was duly muted.

Marvella, still regaled in full costume other than the calf-high black boots she'd removed an hour earlier, was lying atop her bed with a sheet half-draped across her chest and midsection.

"You certainly are the curious one, aren't you *girl*-friend?"

"Have to pass the time, correct? Stilted silence only serves to prolong the wait, I've found."

"I've already told you I'd rather not discuss personal matters best left in the past," she sighed, leaning up onto one elbow.

Facing her as he floated up a bit until they were eye-level with one another, his broad smile revealed teeth that gleamed and sparkled with an almost unearthly glow.

"I'll show you mine if you'll show me yours..."

"Now there's a nauseating thought."

"Come on L, talk to me. I'd recall hearing that you and Ben Thomason were close to marriage at

171

one point, even going so far as getting officially engaged," he chided, tilting his head dramatically to one side as his corn-rolled brown bangs hung over his forehead and eyes like uncoiled snakes.

"A guilty conscience is a powerful thing, isn't it, *Madam* Butterfly?"

Turning an impromptu flip while remaining airborne, he hung upside down with the thick rolls of hair barely scraping the carpet's dingy surface.

"Big swing and a miss, Leah. When bad guys do bad things, Mystic brings them down. Heroic past or not, *Desolation Outlaw* was a wanted man.

"It's just that…I find it fascinating that a woman of your obvious beauty and grace would ever…*could* ever…find romance with such a brutish…uncouth… dinosaur. I mean, I understand the 'bad boy' appeal and all that, but lawdy lawdy me, the man had hands the size of manhole covers and a face that could launch a thousand cruise ships …"

"Wasn't just his *hands* that were oversized, M," she replied with a playful wink just before reaching up with both gloved hands to remove her cowl.

Mystic's mouth unhinged in comic shock.

"Suffered from *groin-us Elephantiasis*, did he? Well, that certainly solves some of the mystery."

"Seriously, Ben was…woefully misunderstood, as are many in our business," she said, seemingly ignoring his last comment while casually discarding each of her dark red gloves, "He's been…hardened by mistrust and the sudden death of teammates he'd just begun to take a shine to.

"Not an easy man to get to know…he puts up one hell of a thick wall, so his loyalty is *legend* to

172

those few who do make the cut. We fought side by side and back to back on many occasions, and believe me, there is…was no one you'd rather have watching your back."

"I can only report what I witnessed, Leah. That man beat the Crimson Condor to a bloody pulp, and was in the process of finishing the poor man off just as I'd arrived. I saw the look in the *Outlaw's* face, girl. He'd have happily done the same to me without hesitation."

"Well, I can't say I knew Desolation Outlaw, but I knew *Force*. Yes, Force had a ferocious temper. Yes, Force displayed a raw rage in combat that was almost uncontrollable at times. Did I ever see him kill? Yes, but only when forced to save his own life or the lives of his teammates," she responded, although less defensively than Mystic had expected, "The man I knew would never have committed such vile acts save in self-defense. Maybe…well, it's possible he isn't the same man I knew. Personally, I have my doubts."

Mystic spun about until he was upright once again, waiving the corn-roles from his field of vision.

"You were lovers, Leah. You can't help but doubt. I just…simply want a partner I can fully trust. So we are on the same page, yes?"

Marvella paused thoughtfully while vigorously massaging her scalp through the thickness of her pitch-black hair.

"Buddy-boy, you haven't known me long enough to question my professionalism."

"That's *not* an answer, sweets," he needled with obvious glee, waiving a raised forefinger back and

173

forth.

"How about this then; *fuck* off, needle nose," she replied curtly, pushing herself from the bed and walking towards the opened bathroom door, "by the way…

…does the *Marley* family know you stole their patriarch's hair-do?" Shrieking loudly, Mystic studied the shapely curvature of her rear end as she passed by.

"Whooa boy, J-Lo's got nothing on you, girl. Let looooose the cabooose!" he sang, reaching for the remote just as an episode of '*Will & Grace*' flashed across the screen.

Part III:

Fever(ed) Pitch

"So where's the end of the line?"

"Wheeling…West Virginia, eventually. No big hurry though. Figured I'd see as many of the sites along the way as I could fit in. You know, like, historical shit... uh, stuff. Places and things I've seen on TV or read about on the net."

"Sounds like a plan. Better do it while you're young and unattached. Too late to enjoy such freedoms once you get my age."

Pulling a cigarette from her handbag, the girl eyed him curiously. The heavy, pancake make-up smeared onto her face and eyes did little to hide her youthful appearance. The man figured her to be no more than nineteen at the outside.

"Aw, you don't look *that* old."

A light rain began to pelt the windshield, just as

174

the bright lights of an approachingbig rig illuminated the sedan's interior like a stage spotlight.

"Probably old enough to scold you for hitchhiking," the man replied sternly, squinting as he leaned forward to obtain a clearer visual through the semi's glaring intrusion. "Your parents approve of such recklessness, or are they simply oblivious?"

Thewoman/girl giggled before taking a long drag from the cigarette. The truck passed, and the man leaned back with an audible sigh of relief.

"Honesty, sir, I'm sure they couldn't care less, being that I haven't seen or spoken to either of them in over two years. Black sheep gypsy of the family, that's me. Besides, I'm plenty old enough to do what I damn well please…sir. You…um…don't mind my smoking, do you?"

Without responding, the man removed his left hand from the top of the steering wheel and pressed a button that instantly lowered the passenger window a few inches.

"Guess not. Thanks a load… uh… sir. Like, I gotta have my smokes. Does wonders for the nerves."

"You can drop the *sir,* missy. I'm not your dad," he growled through tightly gritted teeth, "or your goddamn parole officer for that matter."

The girl's winsome smile froze into a twitching grimace, her eyes widening even as her hands began to shake involuntarily.

"I…uh…like, I was just being, you know…polite. S-sorry…" she mumbled, instinctively cradling the handbag to her narrow bosom.

175

At just past midnight, the interstate traffic was sporadic at best, with semi's and ton and a half's making up the majority of moving vehicles.

"What's with that? When did such blatant ignorance become acceptable...applauded even?" he muttered in a noticeably calmer tone while passing a white delivery truck with the words '*BETTER BREADS, INC*' painted on the side panel.

Reaching tentatively to mash out her cigarette in the tiny dashboard ashtray, the girl exhaled one final puff of smoke.

"Um... what...do you mean?"

Slowing, he veered off onto an exit ramp that read '*CHARLESTOWN* – 6

Miles – *LAST CHANCE TO FUEL-UP FOR NEXT 56 MILES*!'

"The younger generation's version of the English language. It's...inane. More than that...it's irritating as hell. Where do you pick up such garbled gibberish?"

Feeling her throat begin to hitch, the girl clutched the handbag ever tighter as the vehicle neared a darkened intersection lit only by a single blinking red light. "I...um...not really sure. I...never was, like...well, my grades were never, you know, too good."

The man paused only briefly before swerving hard to the right, causing the vehicle's rear tires to squeal their disapproval.

"THAT'S exactly what I'm talking about!" he bellowed, spattering the windshield with white, foamy spittle. The narrow, curvy two-lane was riddled with potholes and provided little shoulder space on either side. Pinning herself ever tighter

176

against the passenger door, the woman/girl released a muffled shriek as the vehicle thrust forward at a rapidly increasing rate.

"S-slow down, m-man...you're gonna kill..."

"Don't you mean...slow down man, *like*, you're gonna kill us?" he spat, hunched forward with his squared chin practically resting atop the steering wheel, "...or possibly...*like,* slow down,man...you're, *you know*, gonna kill us?"

Shoving herself as far over as the door handle would allow, the woman/girl noted the yellow glint of the man's bared teeth; the shocking paleness of his cheekbones...the dilated eyes with maroon-shaded pupils.

"What the fuck are y-you t-talking about, man? St-stop the c-car..."

"Stop the car, *like*, now? Is that what, *you know*, you want me to do?" he mocked as the vehicle sailed airborne for a brief moment before landing with a resounding thud.

Resting the handbag onto her bony thighs, the girl dug in with both hands even as the vehicle lurched hard to the right and onto a wide, paved shoulder.

"Wh-what are...y-you...?" she blurted just as the vehicle screeched to an abrupt halt, sending her upper body lurching forward towards the dash. Jerking the purse up and out, she managed to halt her progress by using it as a buffer, spilling the majority of the contents all over the dash and floorboard.

"It's sad, you know? *Like*, I've got a fourteen-year-old daughter I can't even have a normal conversation with," the man growled, shoving the

177

gear shift into park, then whirling about to face his mortified passenger, "It's, *like*, talking to a goddamned alien. Know what I mean?"

Reaching back with her right hand, the girl fumbled for the door handle while discarding the now-emptied purse, all the while cradling a yet unseen object in her left.

"S-stay away from m-me, man...just stay the hell away..."

Tumbling from the vehicle onto the moist pavement, she'd been both shocked and relieved to find the door unlocked. Rolling into the nearby grass, she gripped the object in both hands before rising onto one knee.

The vehicle sat less than a dozen feet away, both doors standing ajar. Whirling about in a spastic jig, she was oblivious to the steady stream of gurgling noises escaping her own severely parched throat.

She continued to scan the darkness while backing into a weed-infested field, her face and forehead moist with fresh sweat.

"What we have here..." whispered the voice, seemingly mere inches from the girl's right ear, "is a failure to communicate."

Lurching forward, the girl then toppled over onto her left side, shrieking wildly until the impact of the hard clay ground cut her off.

The man loomed over her with his legs spread in a wide blocking stance. The girl stared into the twin barrels balanced less than a foot away from the center of her face, holding the tiny twenty-two revolver airborne as her arms and hands shook and gyrated uncontrollably.

"Do-don't ma...don't make me sho...shoot your ass, man...I...I'll do it...I..."

"Young lady, there's a hard lesson to be learned here," he said calmly, the whole of his face doused in shadow, "The difference between our generations is a broad one, I'm afraid. You see, folks my age will not only brandish weapons such as the one you're holding there...they also have the balls to use them."

The thundering retort of a government issued, sawed-off thirty-gauge was only partially drowned out by a mini-convoy of passing semi's on the nearby interstate.

***

Part IV:

Vibes Of A Decidedly Negative Nature
Eagle Island Detention Center Incarceration
- Day Three

"Sure ya don't wanna join in, Luke? I could use a spotter, least 'til I get good 'n warmed up."

"Afraid I'll have to pass, Ben. Got a meeting in less than fifteen minutes. Besides, I hit the home gym every morning at five AM sharp."

Lying back on the cushioned bench, which was set at a slight incline, Ben reached up and wrapped his gloved fingers securely around the chrome-coated iron weight bar before pausing to eye the other man curiously. Within the workout room's static-filled, temperature-controlled confines, even the most gradual of movements appeared weirdly

179

segmented and unnaturally sped-up; almost robotic in nature.

"Damn, does this vertigo shit ever let up? Feel like I'm workin' out under a hundred strobe lights."

"It's the static from the lasers. You'll get used to it."

"Says the head screw with a butt-load of indifference," Ben said, grinning, "Hey, speakin' of the home gym, where exactly is the ol' homestead located, Luke? Own a deserted isle nearby or what?"

The Guardsman shrugged, leaning over as to check the amount of weight on each side of the bar.

"No comment."

Ben groaned briefly while hoisting the bar, then proceeded to execute ten lightning quick reps without so much as a grunt.

"Don't tell me they force you to bed down on this damned rock every night. Hell, Luke…you're as much an inmate as I am."

"It has its perks, believe it or not," The Guardsman replied with a wink, "Lord, Ben…you were tossing that half-ton of steel around like the weights were hollowed out. How do you come off a month of total inactively and manage that?

You sure there's no mutant blood sprinkled somewhere down the Thomason family tree?"

Leaning up, Ben studied each of his biceps, which had already begun to visibly swell and bloat.

"Nope. Just kick-ass genes, old buddy. Slide another hundred on each end, will ya, Luke? I'm just startin' to feel the burn. What's with all the pow-wow's, anyhow? Is that just SOP or is somethin' big brewin'?"

180

"SSDD, Benji," the other man said, straining a bit as he slapped on the first of two circular plates, "seems I spend half my shift sitting at a conference table discussing such pressing issues as insulation regulations and plumbing repairs. You're all set, big guy. Twelve-hundred pounds worth."

Following a more deliberate set of five reps, Ben sat up and took a series of deep breaths before leaning forward with his elbows propped atop his knees.

"Gotta tell ya, Luke, I'm feelin' a weird vibe. A dangerously weird vibe. A real scalp-tingler, man. Might be that I'm just not used to bein' couped up...I dunno...but somethin' just don't feel right."

"That's a natural vibe, Ben, especially at this early stage. Such...disorientation is magnified about ten-fold in this joint. Don't sweat it, you'll get with the program by default before you know it," the Guardsman responded, although without sustaining eye contact with the larger man. "In the end, it's all about repetition and habit. I've had some tell me it took them months before they fell into a comfortable groove."

"Guess you're right, boss-man. I ain't never been one for premonitions," Ben responded, though studying his former teammate for an additional moment before laying back into position for another set.

"Make 'er an even fourteen hundred if you will, good sir."

The Guardsman added the requested plates to each side, then turned abruptly and headed towards the laser-bar exit.

"Well, I'm off to the roundtable. Be back in an

hour or so to escort you back. Don't overdo it, Ben, or you'll be one hurting pup in the morning. We're not the spring chicks we used to be, remember?"

"Speak for yourself, pal. This boy's just hittin' his prime."

Ben dropped the bar at almost the precise moment his former cohort and present keeper vanished behind a wall of tubular laser beams.

Standing to perform a series of upper and lower back stretches, he huffed in frustration, his lips curled in a sardonic smirk.

"Disorientation my *ass*. Luke ain't one to spook easy, and that man's as nervous as an alley-cat in a room full of rockin' chairs. Somethin' rotten is brewin', and it ain't just my armpits."

Forty minutes and at least a dozen increasingly strenuous sets of arm, chest, and leg routines later, Ben hopped aboard the larger of the two treadmills and began a deliberate progression from brisk walk to fast-paced jog. All the while, he continued to ponder the mysterious feeling of dread filling his gut. While The Guardsman's theory was certainly plausible, being that the simple act of being incarcerated might well be the culprit, he couldn't help but dismiss such a solution as far too simplistic and pat. Despite the machismo and outward bluster of his act, Ben Thomason had indeed spent some serious face time with the emotion known as fear. This was different. There were other elements; less recognizable but not wholly alien in nature. He couldn't help but dwell on the remote possibility perhaps others were experiencing the same enigmatic brain-klaxon, but were equally hesitant to broach the subject in mixed company.

YES, BENJAMIN...YOU RANG?

"Holy sh-" he stammered, lurching awkwardly to the left and forced to stumble from the treadmill and almost directly into a nearby weight rack.

Damn, son...what the hell, over? How's about a knock first? Just try a light tap on the side of my skull 'fore the yellin' begins, what say?

MY...APOLOGIES, BENJAMIN. I'M AFRAID I'M EXPERIENCING RANDOM WIRE-CROSSINGS THE PAST FEW DAYS. I THOUGHT YOU'D CHIMED IN WITH A REQUEST.

You'll find I ain't much for jawin', Pal, mentally or otherwise. In fact, after that last brain-twistin' conference call, I'm damn close to pullin' the plug permanently. Still feelin' some kick-ass jetlag, man. Doin' my damndest to sweat it out.

(A new voice intrudes, obviously agitated) Damn it, Sweep...what now? I was just getting into a *Green Acres* rerun...season three is just chock full of classics.

What the fu--? Oblit? Who the hell gave permission for this little three-party line?

MIND SWEEP: I...CAN'T EXPLAIN EXACTLY...THAT IS, I DIDN'T PURPOSELY CONNECT...GIVE ME A MOMENT PLEASE...

BEN: *You blowin' a fuse, Hoss? Can't say much for this phone company's customer service procedures...*

OBLITERATION: Aw, clam up, you jackass. This might be serious...

BEN: *Ask me if I give a hairy rat's rear, Injun-Joe. By all means, disconnect away, 'cause I ain't*

183

plannin' on payin' my bill anytime soon.

OBLITERATION (sighs heavily): Jeez, once a prick…always a prick.

BEN: *Eat my briefs, numb-nuts.*

MIND SWEEP: I…I'M SURE BOTH OF YOU ARE…ARE VIOLATING PROFANITY GUIDELINES…I…UH…UM…GETTING HARDER TO HOLD THE LINE, GUYS. SOR-SORRY FOR THE UNPLANNED INTERRUPTION…I…WE'LL TALK TOMORROW AT SIX…THE... UM... REGULARLY SCHEDULED CHAT…FADING OUT…

OBLITERATION: Take a sabbatical, Sweep. Sounds like you need it. Oh…and Force?

BEN: *Yeah, Anus-ville?*

OBLITERATION: Blow me.

BEN: *Far as I know, they have yet to invent a straw that narrow, Mac.*

OBLITERATION: Oh, that rapier wit. Honed to X-rated perfection as usual, I see (pauses). Uh…Forcy? You still receiving?

BEN: *Unfortunately, yeah. Somethin' to add, Professor Dink-less?"*

OBLITERATION: Hmm. That's a first. Sweep signed off and the vine's still hot…

BEN: *Ya mean, normally it…cuts the line automatically when he…uh…*

OBLITERATION: Yep. Just like a phone jack pulled right out of the wall. That is, unless he forgot to put up that personal firewall he uses. Then again, I can't recall that ever happening either. Man hasn't been too stable lately. Come to think of it, he started losing it the day you checked in.

BEN (laughs): *That's it...blame the new con on the block.*

OBLITERATION: Must be the thickness of your skull...or possibly all that blank space between the ears (laughs). Whatever, it's throwing that poor boy into quite the quandary.

BEN: *Cut the BS for a sec, bud. Let me ask you somethin' straight up before the line goes dead...*

OBLITERATION: You helped place me here, asshole, remember? Not exactly an easy detail to forget...

BEN: *Your feelin' it too, right?*

OBLITERATION (pauses): Feeling what? You going fag on me, Force? Guess those rumors about you and Marvella were just that...

BEN: *Goddamn it, you know what I'm talkin' about, man. Don't you hear that hum? ...that damn static buzz? Wasn't there last night...that much I know for a fact.*

OBLITERATION: What exactly are you trying to say, Thomason? Been here two fucking days and already created a conspiracy theory? No sense in playing the part of *instigator of Eagle Isle.*

You're cracked, buddy-boy...severely fractured.

BEN: *Only if I'm the only one hearin' it, or the only one with a ball of dread the size of Coney Island rollin' around inside his gut (pauses). Talk to me, Obie. Tell me I'm nuts, and I'll just go away. Otherwise...Houston...we might have a big problem.*

OBLITERATION (long pause): The buzzing *is* new. I was gonna ask Sweep about it just before he bugged out. As for the dread thing, I can't really say. In your case, it's more than likely just 'first week' blues.

BEN: *So everything feels kosher to you? No different from any other day? Just SSDD...same today as it was before, right?*

OBLITERATION (pause) Weellll, I didn't say that. Routine's the same...but the air's thickened a bit, no doubt. Who knows, maybe they put something in our salt peter.

BEN: *Appreciate the honesty, blockhead. Least now I know it ain't just me. I wonder if any of the others are fee-... (loud static buzz, followed by a low clicking noise) ...Obie? Hey lunk-head...you still on the line?*

"Damn it. Cut off at the knees," he muttered angrily, flipping a one-hundred twenty-five-pound barbell into a far corner with a casual flick of his left wrist.

Mind Sweep...you there, bud? Come in master control...ground control to Major Tom...ground control to Major Tom...

"Aw, geez," he groaned, rolling his eyes and holding both hands out with the palms facing up, "mama, look what they've done to me. Enough of this horseshit...back to something real...somethin' I can feel and relate to...like pain."

Fifteen minutes and three sets of squats later, the last of which consisted of five reps of an even two-thousand pounds, he strolled over and began a slow paced but ferocious assault on the larger of two hard bags. A wicked combination had sent the bag spinning away like a roulette wheel as he turned to acknowledge The Guardsman's re-entry into the workout room.

186

"Nice hook, Benji. Isn't that the one you used to call the 'decapitator?'"

"Back in the day, yeah, before all the pin-headed bureaucrats with their politically correct agendas startin' suckin' all the fun outta the heroin' business.

How'd your pow-wow go?"

"Same old, same old. There's always a solution waiting on a crisis, and vice versa. It isn't easy housing the 'baddest' of the bad on a daily basis. You about done?" The Guardsman asked, stifling a yawn with one gloved hand.

"One more set of arm-blasters and I'll call it a day."

"You always were a glutton for punishment."

"Hey, it's a time *and* frustration killer, if nothin' else. One of the few hobbies of my old life that wasn't considered self-destructive, ya know?"

The smaller man nodded without response, studying the massive bloat of the other man's biceps and forearms.

After placing two one-hundred-pound plates on each side of a 'blaster' curl bar, he then scooped it up without a hint of strain and began a set that would culminate at an even dozen reps.

"Let me ask ya somethin', Luke...confidentially of course," he said after dropping the bar roughly to the floor.

"I'll answer if I can, Ben. Shoot."

"Been havin'...um...seein' any weird behavior lately? I mean, from the other inmates or your staff?"

"Weird behavior?" The Guardsman replied, cocking his head slightly to one side. "Ben, this *is* a

187

penal colony, remember? Strange behavior is both expected, and to some degree, accepted as the norm. Specifics, please."

"I dunno. More than usual, then. It's…well, it ain't easy to explain somethin' ya don't quite understand yourself."

"Still fretting over that *vibe* you were talking about earlier? Ben, it's natural to feel out of sorts when your whole world just collapsed and you're tossed into this *Rubber-Mate* universe of ours."

Leaning against the squat rack's main frame, Ben dabbed his face, chest and arms with a small white towel.

"It ain't just that. Somehow, I know better. Don't ask me how. I ain't…you know I don't shake too easy, right?"

Again, the smaller man nodded without a verbal response.

"These kinda Willies are a new, *untried* breed, man, and one of the few names I ain't never been called in this life is 'chicken-shit'. You know what a hard-headed bastard Obliteration is, and even he mentioned that…um…that is…ah…awwww shhiiit…" Ben stuttered, hanging his head as his shoulders instantly drooped.

Despite an ardent attempt, the smaller man was unable to keep a straight face, laughing aloud while side-stepping over to take a seat on a nearby incline bench.

"Not to worry, Benji. You're not exactly leaking trade secrets. I've known about the '*Sweep-vine*' for years."

"It's gotta be a violation, right?"

"Not really. I figure anything that cuts into the

frustration factor has to be a positive. Besides, it isn't like it poses a security risk. Talk is definitely cheap behind *these* cell walls."

Facing his former teammate while lying back on a cushioned mat, Ben began a furious set of crunches.

"Ya mean the warden gives it his okay? Man, what a softy," he remarked afterwards, showing only the faintest signs of being winded.

"Well, actually, therein lies the rub," The Guardsman commented with a thin smile.

The larger man returned the grin, reaching up to scratch the darkened outline of facial hair he'd already begun to cultivate since the 'peel and reel' treatment just days earlier.

"Keepin' secrets from the boss can get your ass in a sling, Luke."

"That man has enough on his mind. I'm just saving him from an additional migraine he doesn't need. Besides, there isn't a hell of a lot we could do about it anyway. Only logical solution would be to find Mind Sweep his own private island, and that would call for some serious government funds. In other words, ain't... gonna... happen."

"Got'cha. Tell ya the truth, Luke, I ain't real comfortable with the whole *inner-mind conference call* thing anyhow. Creepy as hell, I'm tellin' ya. Not that I got many deep thoughts I mind sharin', but you get my meanin'."

"Understood. Now, you were saying about Obliteration sharing the same...uneasy vibe as yourself?"

Ben worked in another quick set of crunches before responding.

"Yeah, no shit. Ol' rock-head pretty much confirmed his own personal case of *heebie-jeebies*. You sure they ain't nothin' you wanna let me in on, Luke? Last time I felt this queasy was that day in West Texas when I watched *Johnny Reb* and *Dark Claw* die not three feet from where I stood."

The Guardsman stood, raising his left hand with three fingers pointed upward.

"Scouts honor, Benji."

"And you couldn't spill even if there was, right?" Ben scowled, leaping to his feet in a fluid, graceful movement that belied his considerable bulk.

"Affirmative. Ready?"

"Let's shag. Startin' to get homesick anyhow."

As they departed, the smaller man reached over and clipped his former cohort lightly on the shoulder.

"You order any movies or books yet? Does wonders for the boredom factor."

"Nah. Started my DVD list, though. *Debbie Does Dallas* in stock?"

"Only if it's the Disney version."

"How 'bout a quart of Schnapps? I warnin' ya, I feel the first wave of DT's comin'… won't be a pretty sight, Luke."

Stepping into the tubular walkway as the laser wall reemerged behind them, the one-time allies strolled side by side in a gesture of mutual respect.

"I'm sure your liver will adapt to H2O and orange juice, Benji. Just gonna take a while."

"That's what I keep hearin', Luke. Wish I could make myself buy into it."

190

***

Part V:

Shake, Rattle & Roll

Despite the relatively calm winds and mostly cloudless sky, the Sky crane transport shook and shimmed as if trapped within a pocket of turbulence exclusively its own.

Peering out from one of only three portholes provided from the spacious cargo hold, Marvella felt the tightness at her chest gradually decrease as her breathing eased a shade. Just moments earlier, she'd been on the verge of hyperventilating, as if the cabin itself had been repeatedly decompressing at varied intervals.

"Penny for your thoughts, Leah," Mystic bellowed, as was mandatory in order to be heard over the mix of humming engines and metallic grinding.

"You really want to know?" she managed after several hard swallows to empty the bile that had filled her throat.

"Chill out, girl. It'll pass. Just sit there and try to recharge. I've got this bad-boy well in hand."

"Give me a couple of minutes," she replied between coughs, "...to shake it off. I'm...almost there."

"No strain. I can handle a double-shift if necessary. Just wish the ride would smooth out a tad."

Sitting between them, Deputy Director Willis' complexion was the textbook definition of pasty,

191

like partially dried caulk. He spoke with his head tilted back and his eyes tightly closed.

"Afraid it isn't going away anytime soon, people. Being that it isn't mechanical or weather related, I think we all know the source, whether we want to admit it or not."

Marvella turned from the porthole, where she'd become temporarily hypnotized by the ocean blue landscape below, and stared at the assigned cargo while reaching up to massage her temples with both hands.

"Doesn't the damn thing realize that if we go down, it goes down with us?"

Keeping the oblong object locked within a steely, unblinking gaze, Mystic's shrill cackle was forcefully restrained.

"If one chooses to believe the *Pandora's Box* theory you two have so easily fallen prey to, I seriously doubt the prospect of a watery grave worries it in the least, Leah. Just another place to homestead 'til some Jacque Cousteau wanna-be digs it up."

"All I know is," she confessed with a weary shrug while tightening the waist and shoulder harness presently holding her upright, "fourteen more hours of this roller-coaster ride and I'm gonna need a colon transplant."

"You take the Dramamine I gave you?" Director Willis asked, turning to face in Marvella's direction without ever opening his eyes.

"Right before…takeoff," she said, reaching to cover her mouth as her gag reflex kicked in, "…might as well…have eaten a couple of M&M's for all the…good it's doing me."

192

"Pop another one before you go on shift. Might not help, but it can't hurt." The chopper shook and bounced like a train car riding on horribly uneven rails as the co-pilot stepped gingerly through the tiny opening into the hold, whacking his protective helmet against both sides of the narrow doorframe.

"What's the good news, Left-tenant?" Mystic shouted gleefully, though he'd never broken eye contact with the object of his concentration, "…still trying to find us a way out of this mobile blender?"

Ignoring both the query and its source, the young officer instead stumbled ahead until he leaned down onto one knee directly in front of Director Willis.

"Sir?"

"Something amiss, Lieutenant? Other than my own bruised kidneys, that is?" Willis barked in reply, cracking his left eye for just an instant before re-closing it.

"Sir, Captain Ryan wanted me to…uh…that is…he wants to know…ah…"

"Spit it out, son. I promise not to bite unless this maddening crap continues for another hour or so."

"Well, that's kind of what the Captain was…wondering," the Lieutenant continued, his boyish face having already turned a light shade of red. "Go on…"

"Well, is there any way to…if not stop completely…at least slow whatever's causing the turbulence? It's…playing hell with the instruments, and the Captain is afraid that the eventual strain on motor function might cause internal damage to the co-"

193

"Jesus, son, you think we're sitting back here enjoying the ride?" Willis barked angrily, though still not bothering to make eye contact or even sit completely upright, "To state the obvious, this wasn't an expected dilemma. Correct me if I'm wrong, but I don't believe the DOD checklist exists that covers 'How to Control Effects of Powerful Entity of Unknown Origin while Airborne'."

The Lieutenant started to reply, but instead turned about to study the object more intently.

"We're open... to suggestions, Officer," Marvella chimed in, the color slowly returning to her cheeks, "...obviously the force-fields can only block out a percentage of whatever poisonous fog that damned thing emits."

"So it's definitely *not* a whirly-bird problem, Left-tenant Honey?" Mystic asked, levitating a few inches from his seat as the attached harness fell away.

"Negative. All systems were checked and double-checked before we left Vandenberg, and again as the cargo was loaded in Wyoming. Engine and electrical system readings are right on the money."

"Well then, looks like the one and only suspect is indeed this fossilized b*ooger* with an attitude. Maybe it just has gas. Motion sickness, perhaps..." The Lieutenant eyed him briefly before returning his sights to the object. "So, there's nothing more that can be done, then?"

Director Willis leaned forward with a loud grunt just as the craft seemed to stabilize for a few moments before falling back into a steady rhythm of shakes and spasms.

"Other than jettisoning the damned thing into Mother Ocean, no. Have you radioed Warden Terry on our progress, Lieutenant?"

"Um...yes, sir. Every hour on the hour. My god..." he exclaimed in dumbstruck awe, "what's in that thing, sir?"

"I'm guessing *Pet Rock* from hell," Mystic quipped, floating a few inches higher as to avoid the constant shifting of the craft's interior.

"They've got a team of multi-degreed eggheads headed to our future destination to answer that very question, Lieutenant Bagwell. At this point, I'm beyond caring," the director replied in apparent exhaustion, his head lowered into the palms of his hands. "It's nothing more than a dump and discard from our standpoint. Right now, surviving the ride seems to be priority one."

"Yes...sir. I'll inform the Captain." Following the young officer's less-than-graceful departure, the remaining trio fell silent for the next several hours; Director Willis with his slumped pose and fish-belly white complexion; Marvella with her strained breathing and building nausea; Mystic with his blasé attitude and brazen cockiness. Every few moments, as the transport would rattle and creak from the latest series of mysterious tremors, each would address the object before them with a quick glance or wary stare.

Although triple-sealed for transport, there was little doubt of the vital role the applied force-fields played from a security standpoint. The man-made housing consisted of a foot-thick rubber sealant compound, then by a hard plastic lining that had literally been melded to the rubber layer, followed by a three-inch thick metallic shell that was equal parts lead, magnesium and titanium. Air and watertight, as the shell had been welded on site before being loaded onto the transport, the casual observer might have logically concluded nothing short of highly radioactive and/or toxic materials were enclosed.

The four corners of the box had been secured from the bottom by oversized metal brackets and by the top from solid steel poles hooked directly into the transports frame, thereby ensuring stability no matter the level of movement. Despite its relatively compact length and width (eight feet long; three and a half wide), the object weighed in at an inexplicably hefty eleven hundred fifty pounds, creating much speculation amongst those in the know within the scientific community as to both its true origin and content.

Fast asleep with her face and cowl pressed firmly against the glass portal, Marvella dreamed uneasily...

...*frenzied images of grisly death and dismemberment dominated a grayish/black landscape where only a single face ringed familiar. With his scarred, squared chin, bushy Fu Manchu mustache and bared teeth, he stood posed like a granite statue come to life, battering and bludgeoning everyone or thing in their path. Despite the warrior blood raging in her veins, she nonetheless succumbed to and willingly accepted her role as frail, hapless potential victim to his of fearless protector. Somewhat surprisingly, she discovered that allowing the feminine side of her persona to overwhelm the soldier within wasn't at*

196

all difficult (She welcomed the rush, in fact, with an orgasmic shudder causing her to moan aloud while grinding her hips within the cramped confines of the hard plastic seat).

As he utilized his oversized, seemingly indestructible fists to hammer and pound through wall after wall of shadowy enemies that seemed hellishly infinite in number, she leaned forward and practically glued herself to his massively muscled upper back, which flexed and bulged with each punch thrown.

Eventually, the enemies vanished and they entered a room flooded with bright rays of sunlight. She stood with her lover atop a sandy dune, staring into the clearest, bluest seawater she'd ever seen. She found herself hypnotized by the perfectly synchronized waves as the faint echoes of a sea gull's shriek filled her ears. She was squeezed firmly to his still-heaving chest, his flesh slightly moist and his scent pleasantly husky. He was saying something, but she was beyond comprehending the actual words. The waves had entranced her, as had his very presence. A presence she'd yearned for so strongly but had denied through pride and self-loathing. She felt him press his lips against her forehead, the edges of his mustache tickling the flesh just above her left eyebrow. She leaned forward and was in the process of glancing up towards his rugged visage when they were...

...spun around as if riding atop a child's merry-go-round. They now faced a large, domed structure roughly the size of a resort hotel. The main building centered two smaller ones, all windowless and seemingly constructed of marble,

the outer walls having a slick, moistened look. A crimson-colored, circular roof protruded from the main building, and a transport chopper, possibly a CH-54 or similar model, descended through a wide portal and quickly vanished within the red-shaded dome as if it had simply landed on the opposite side of the building. Once again, she leaned back and tilted her head to address him, and was instantly blinded...

...by a series of lightning strikes occurring directly above the main structure. The sky above had turned black and ominous. She whirled about and noted the tranquil sea of just seconds before had mutated into a raging inferno with tidal waves that looked multi-stories high. Returning face front, she saw her lover's arm pointed straight ahead, his voice relaying a message in booming tones that remained frustratingly incomprehensible. The lower portion of the main building seemed to implode from within, sending boulder-sized chunks of marble and steel whizzing by them in a barrage of smoking shrapnel. Her lover pulled her down by the shoulders, using his considerable bulk as a human shield. Peering over his left shoulder, she noticed the previously tumulus scene had metamorphasized yet again. Feeling a frigid chill cloak her flesh like an invisible blanket sewn from crystals of ice, she instantly lost the power to speak, move...even twitch (while visibly stiffening within the chair, the waist and shoulder strap stretched to the snapping point).

Her lover continued to bark out even as his grip on her intensified. She reached around him, attempting to obtain a solid handhold on his torso. His mid-section and lower back were coated in

198

sweat and sand as her bare hands floundered about in search of an anchor. Try as she might, she found it impossible to force her gaze from the horrors drifting ever closer to the very grounds they crouched upon.

The sea was again calm...surreally so. Like stagnated lake water, not a single ripple appeared other than that formed from the mass of humanity floating within. It was no longer blue nor black, but a hideous mix of yellowish crimson, much like bloodied pus from a long-festering wound.

A virtual army of detached heads, arms, legs, and torsos bobbed and gyrated, filling the infinite space as far as the eye could see. Several of the severed skulls contained faces she thought vaguely familiar, though each time a positive ID seemed mere seconds away, the head would either sink or twist away into another direction. Many of the disembodied faces wore cowls, just as an occasional flash of insignia was evident on torn sections of spandex that adorned an arm, thigh or calf.

Old teammates or advisories, perhaps? Perhaps old acquaintances that had long since passed, like Dark Claw or Johnny Reb, both of whom had died horrible deaths in her presence. What did it all mean? Was this nightmare real or some type of elaborate warning? Her mind overflowed in a speculative mishmash, halting abruptly once her lover arose to lift her airborne like a dry leaf in a wind tunnel. Wrapping her arms ever tighter around his steely, slick midsection, she bear-hugged him like a small child within a parent's protective embrace.

They turned as one, just in time to witness the Thing emerge from the shattered wreckage of the main building, The Thing they had obviously been brought to see. To greet. To be sacrificed to. Just like the torn, shredded remains filling the sea at their backs. In her bleary, sand-filled eyes, the Thing was nothing more than a hulking shadow; a colossal phantom constructed of shadows and fog. Regardless of its visual anonymity, she felt the malevolent aura surrounding it, emitted from its very being like the most aromatic of deadly chemical toxins.

As the whole of the Thing enveloped the space above and around them like an approaching sandstorm, her lover pushed her away and subsequently fronted her like the guardian angel he'd always been. As the Thing hovered overhead like the mouth of a great, monstrous cave, she heard five words spoken from her lover's mouth. Five simple words spoken so clearly as if whispered gently inside both ears. The Thing surged forward from every possible angle.

'Love you, Leah...always have' he'd said...as the blackness swallowed them whole.

***

"Leah...Leah? Hey! You got a pulse over there, woman?" a voice echoed as though from the pit of a faraway tunnel.

Her head literally snapped to attention, a tiny smear of drool left on the portal glass.

"Y-yeah...hold you...hold your water. Be right...w-with you."

200

Shrugging wearily, Mystic's tone had lost its trademark 'sassiness'. He no longer levitated, but had slumped into his seat with the harness holding him upright. The Deputy Director's seat was conspicuously empty, as he'd departed for the cockpit an hour or so earlier.

"Not to be rude, Leah, but I'm entering hour six of operation 'bubble' and my eyes are beginning to cross."

"Give me a sec or two. Just have to…clear away the fog," she replied, stifling a yawn before reaching over to unhook the harness, "…is it just me or have the shakes calmed a fraction?"

"Comes and goes. Not as consistent, though. Maybe 'rock monster' is wearing down."

Mystic snapped his own harness free and stood, his thin frame slumped over like a man thirty years his senior. A moment later, Leah strolled gingerly over, blinking rapidly as to force the sleepiness from her eyes.

"Perchance to dream?" he asked, side-stepping over to allow her access to the seat just as a fresh set of shakes and spasms racked the chopper. Both gripped the chair for support as the assault ended just as quickly.

"Excuse me?"

"You were all over the map. Moaning, groaning, whining. Even a bit of very provocative pelvic *grinding*, if I may be so bold to mention. Having anybody I know?"

Fearing an impending aftershock, Marvella practically leapt into the seat and strapped in.

"No comment, girly-boy. All right, let's do the transfer thing. On what count?"

"You know, I was thinking at first it was just an act, but you're truly no fun," Mystic snarled, his feet suspended several inches from the cargo hold's cold steel flooring, "...let's do it on three."

"Got it. Three..." she began, her upper body growing visibly gaunt as she focused on the iron box with tunnel-vision intensity.

"Two..." Mystic injected, folding his legs beneath him as he floated casually towards the seat Marvella had just vacated.

"On---ohhhhh...shhhhiiiit" they groaned in unison as a violent shudder struck the craft with Level Five force, jerking violently to the left before reversing direction in a single, vicious thrust.

"Did you...are y-you still maintaining the...field?" Marvella managed, gritting her teeth and hanging on to the underside of the seat as a nearby metal locker flung open with a loud crack, sending various emergency gear flying about the hold like debris from a funnel cloud.

"I...no...I mean...don't *you* have it? Son of a... do I have to do everythi-" Mystic spat in apparent disgust just before a utility helmet ricocheted off the left side of his skull with a loud crack.

"Mystic? Damn it, let's double layer it until it settles or this bird's going down. Are you listening to me, asshole?"

Glancing over for only an instant as the chopper spun hard to the left before tilting dramatically forward, Marvella saw Mystic had literally pinned himself to the hold's ceiling with insect-like precision. He wore a pained grimace as a wide smear of blood appeared below the surface of his cowl where the helmet had impacted.

"Ca...can't concentrate," he mumbled, descending slowly downward while cradling the wound with the palm of his left hand.

"Get over it, Mystic... just shake it off, man! It's gonna take both of us to...regain control..."

Marvella began losing her grip on the chair as the transport tilted ever further towards the cockpit end, and the first of the metal poles used to secure the iron box bent with a resounding screech.

"Afrai-...afraid it's...all yours...girl. I'm...not feel...to...to...gawed...gooood"

His arms hanging limp by his sides, Mystic floated only a moment longer before collapsing onto the deck like a puppet with severed strings.

As the front end of the transport continued its gradual descent, Marvella sucked in several deep breaths and focused solely on the iron box sitting less than six feet away from her booted feet. Under normal circumstances, she could construct a working field with a split-second's concentration; a transparent, near impenetrable aura with an impact limit of just under ten-thousand pounds per square inch. There were, of course, variables that determined the level of difficulty when creating, and maintaining such a multi-layered entity, such as desired dimensions, airtight capability (mandatory in this specific case) and time constraints. Having utilized this specific 'gift' since its discovery within her personal arsenal at around age eleven, Marvella was considered a technical master, not quite on par with such luminaries as *Vision, The Seeker* or even *Mystic* for that matter, but far from a novice in terms of 'hands-on' experience.

Ignoring the varied distractions around her, the foremost of which being Mystic's limp form rolling past, his arms and legs flopping about in doll-like fashion, she felt the familiar burning at her chest and an electrified tingling at the tips of each finger.

The second of the two metal securing poles collapsed an instant before all movement ceased and the chopper's front end straightened with a final lurch, settling upright as if invisible binds had snapped.

Marvella maintained the level of trance-like concentration for an additional thirty seconds before allowing for the briefest of respites. Keeping the iron box securely in sight, she was preparing to call out when Director Willis shambled into the hold like a man escaping a cave-in.

"Marv-? You two still in one peace? Wha-
...where's Mystic?"

She gestured towards the sprawled form lying in a far corner, a torn section of supply netting blanketing the majority of his upper body.

Kneelling to check Mystic's condition, he looked back to Marvella while checking Mystic's right wrist for a pulse. What other man? Mystic? If so, then delete 'the other man's' and just place his name instead "He's still kicking...just cold-cocked. What the hell happened anyway?

We came within a hair's whisker of becoming shark chum. I think the co-pilot has a concussion, and Captain Wainwright might've fractured a wrist."

"I'm...not sure. We were...about to transfer fields and...it turned nasty in the blink of an eye, almost like...it..."

"In other words, that was just a taste of the hell that thing can raise when in an uncontrolled environment," Willis concluded, eyeing the box with a disdainful glare while pulling Mystic into a sitting position.

"If that *is* the case, Director Willis," she added, her upper shoulders and arms relaxing an iota, "This chopper wouldn't have made it past takeoff without the fields."

The director propped Mystic into the nearest seat, holding him upright with one arm while unscrewing the top of a small metal canteen with his teeth. He then pushed back and stood, pouring the clear contents onto Mystic's head and through his cowl's eyeholes. Several thin lines of blood had spilled from beneath his cowl and dried onto his jawline and chin. Again you've placed 'other man's—use his name better for a clearer picture to the reader Within seconds, Mystic came to with a jolt, spitting forth the minute amount of water that had creased his parted lips.

"Sh…shi…whaaa…ga…dad…dam…"

"Ah, baby's first words…how utterly revolting," Marvella quipped. While still plenty shaken, she could feel her ultra-sensitive defense system begin to lock into auto-mode.

"Snap out of it, man. Come to, come to," Willis barked, shaking the man's narrow shoulders.

"Wah…wha…-at? What happened?"

"Believe you took a chunk of FOD off the noggin. Might've been a fire extinguisher. Can't let that guard down for second on this ride, son."

"Wow. I…remember…taking one hell of a jolt. Was…I'd just dropped the field when this joint started rocking and rolling…big time," Mystic said weakly, rubbing the side of his head, where a large, oval knot had appeared beneath his mask.

The director stood with a groan, sighing heavily while surveying the metal box and the horribly bent upper struts holding it in place.

"You two need to work out a more streamlined transfer procedure. This bird can't take another shock that high on the Richter scale 'least we all end up shark bait."

"What's our ETA, Director Willis?" Marvella asked casually enough, though her hands and feet still visibly trembled.

"We've got tanker refuel in…" he paused, glancing at his wristwatch, "…less than two hours. Scheduled arrival at seventeen-thirty hours Pacific time. Just under twelve hours total duration."

"Damn. I was hoping, *praying* actually, that you'd say something more along the lines of …forty-five minutes to an hour…tops."

"We'll get there, Leah. I'm…back in the saddle. A little shaky but wiser for the experience. Not to worry, girl, its smooth sailing from here on out," Mystic injected with a more familiar sliver of cockiness.

"So said Gilligan to the Skipper," Marvella quipped, prompting a barely muffled cackle from the director, who walked back towards the hold exit with a comically stiffened gait, as if half-expecting the floor beneath his feet to split and peel away.

"I'll go update our battered navigators. Bring you a wet towel to clean your face, Mystic. Back in a few, Troops. Just maintain, you two…*please*…maintain. I'm all outta clean under

206

shorts."

Levitating from the seat in a lotus-pose, Mystic eyed the iron box through tightly squinted eyes.

"I won't underestimate that bastard again. That's a promise."

Leah nodded in acknowledgement, allowing herself the luxury of blinking for the first time since placing the field.

"Let's hope you never get the chance."

Mystic's lips parted to respond, but instead fell shut in silent agreement.

***

Part VI:

Jitters

"What's the latest word, boss?"

"Twelve hours or thereabouts for the cargo. Six to eight for the study group."

"You don't mind me saying, you look like hammered excrement."

"Trust me, Luke, that's no coincidence. Comforting to know my outward appearance matches my overall mental health."

Staring out from a wide, domed walkway connecting the main building to the supply wing, Warden Terry lit his fourth smoke in the last half-hour, a fact that wasn't lost on his second in command.

"It's been a rear bear, hasn't it?"

"From the word go. Damned engineers went two weeks over schedule and at least a hundred grand over budget. Just got that outside freight elevator finished up late last night. Had to threaten to fire that Jackass foreman just to prevent entry through the main landing pad. No way that thing gets handled like routine transport. Radioed Director Willis the offload instructions just this morning. Seriously, you'd think we were prepping a holding cell for Satan himself."

Leaning against the cool dome glass, The Guardsman stared trance-like into the vast, seemingly infinite blue horizon beyond.

"From what you've told me of this thing's background, you might not be far off. Seems just about everyone exposed to it for any prolonged period has met with quite the grisly fate."

"It does have that '*Monkey's Paw*' element, doesn't it?" the Warden replied, exhaling thick tendrils of smoke from both nostrils.

"Weird, wild stuff, boss. Let's hope the weirdness ends once Eagle Isle becomes its permanent address."

"I hate to say it, Luke, but that may just be the beginning. Fact is, that's my main worry. Those damned government eggheads are liable to unleash something we're not adequately prepped to handle."

"Speaking of which, VIP rooms are good to go. Booked 'em all a suite directly below us."

"Good deal. From what I gather, these are some of the tops in their respective fields."

Leering, The Guardsman pushed himself from the glass and stepped slowly towards the supply wing entrance.

"In other words, egotistical assholes, one and all."

208

"You certainly know your beans, Lucas," the Warden quipped before taking another lengthy drag, "by the way...how's Benjamin holding up these days?"

Halting in mid-step, the Guardsman turned about in intentionally segmented movements, flashing a broad, exaggerated smile.

"You don't miss a beat, do you?"

"It's a warden's business to know things, Luke. Checking daily escort logs is part of my morning ritual, right after my first smoke and second cup of Joe."

"Hey, the man's a friend, Charlie. Can't deny I feel a certain obligation to make sure he survives orientation without blowing a fuse. Ben's a...different sort. The word 'loner' isn't just a label. He's the genuine article. Doesn't open up very often, so it's hard to gauge the man's state of mind."

"Understood. Just ragging you."

"He'll adjust to the grind eventually."

The Warden took a final drag before flicking the remains into a nearby butt-can.

"Well, keep me updated," he concluded, headed in the opposite direction, "I feel for the man. Can't be anything harder for a former white-hat to be tossed in with some of the bad apples he helped put away."

Resuming his purposeful stride, The Guardsman gave the relatively calm waters that made up Eagle Island's sole perimeter a final glance.

"By the way, heard over the wire there's a storm brewing. Could be a level-five on the way by mid-week...Thursday at the latest."

"So what else is new?" the Warden answered with a beleaguered moan, "When it rains on Eagle Island, it most certainly pours."

***

Eagle Island Detention Center Incarceration – Day Four

"Can't beat this with a stick, Bubba," Ben muttered aloud, shifting the recliner into a steep incline with one arm while operating a tiny remote with the other. Within his comically oversized mitt, the device seemed doubly small, like an adult hand engulfing a child's toy.

"I do believe I've found me a hobby. A time-*killin'* mind-*numbin'* pastime guaranteed to leave me happily catatonic."

The large screen glowed to life in the surrounding darkness, and the opening credits to '*Baywatch* – Season one' flared to life.

"Nothin' like some late twentieth Century 'jiggle TV' to ease the mind and purge the cells."

BENJAMIN? ARE YOU RECEIVING? BEN?

Witha loud moan, Ben muted the set's sound as an incessant buzzing, much like electrically charged static waves, filled his ears.

Hell, Sweep...do I have a choice?

IT'S A FEW MINUTES BEFORE SIX PM. JUST WANTED TO SEE IF YOU WANTED TO JOIN THE NIGHTLY CHAT SESSION. YOU HAD EXPRESSED SOME...HESITANCE EARLIER.

Think I'll pass, Hoss. Got Pam Anderson's

210

greatest tits...um...hits...waitin' in the wings. You...feelin' any better, Sweep? You were sure spazzin' out yesterday.

I'M FINE, BENJAMIN. APPRECIATE THE CONCERN. BY THE WAY, PLEASE REFRAIN FROM FURTHER...UM...ANATOMY REMARKS. MUST HAVE BEEN SHORT WAVE INTERFERENCE OF SOME TYPE. I'M BACK AND RUNNING ON ALL CYLINDERS.

Short wave, huh? I tell ya, Mac, somethin' is definitely in the water other than salt peter. I've been weirdin' out myself, and it's a feelin' I ain't too comfortable with.

IN YOUR CASE, BENJAMIN, I'D VENTURE TO SAY ITS MORE SIMPLE SHOCK THAN SHOCK WAVE. THIS IS NOT AN EASY ENVIRONMENT WITH WHICH TO ADAPT. GIVE IT TIME. YOU'LL...SETTLE IN, AS IT WERE.

So they tell me, Sweep. Let's just say I ain't brimmin' over with confidence. I get the feelin' I croaked and went to hell, but I'm the last one in on the joke, ya know?

(A new, albeit familiar voice chimes in) Man, it's like listening to a girl-scout whine about a skinned knee. Tell me, Ben-*ni-fer*, where and when did you have the sex change operation? All of America is just dying to know...

Geez, Sweep...ya wanna hurry up and disconnect me? I've had my fill of jabber-jaws there.

OBLITERATION: Now now, don't leave angry, Ben-Janey...justleave.

SHETAH: What's up, gang? What scintillating

211

subject we covering tonight? Projectile diarrhea? Group masturbation possibly?

THE MASS (breathless): Oh, *yes*. By all means, you first, Cat-woman. Can you really (pronounced 'wil-ly') lick yourself (pronounced 'yo-self') (not sure about having these 'pronounced' parts within the story. Wondering if a glossary of terminology and slang shouldn't be had in the beginning on its own? Tell us every detail, you furry little vixen you...

BEN: *Hell's belles, Sweep...pull my plug, will ya?*

(An unfamiliar voice, at least to Ben, then joins the fray)

Welcome to Romper Room Isle, Force. Despite the juvenile banter on display the majority of the time, you'll find these brain-stem storming sessions a necessity as time crawls by as only it can on Eagle Island *Anal-Retention Center*.

OBLITERATION: Eagle? What brings you out of your hole, dude? Been a month of Sunday's since you've graced us with your ever-scentless excremental presence.

SCREAMING EAGLE: Proud to be back. Seventy-hours away from my fellow inmate's wisdom and foresight has left my IQ at least fifty points *higher*. What better way to eliminate unnecessary brain-cells...

THE MASS (exasperated): Quiet, Tonto! Cat-girl is about to tell us what really makes her purr! Ahhhh, I feel my groin (pronounced 'groan') swelling already.

SHETAH: Get a grip, Samurai blob. Whoops, wrong choice of words...

212

BEN: *Sweep, are you hearin' me, man? Cut the cord, damn it...*

MIND SWEEP: NO NEED TO CURSE, BENJAMIN. I'M...JUST HAVING SOME...UH...TECHNICAL DIFFICULTIES...GIVE ME A MOMENT...

(Once again, Ben is subjected to still another new arrival)

ANVIL: What the? What's the deal, Captain Eavesdrop? I didn't give permission to be skull-fucked. Who said this? If Ben, then italics are needed along with his name or whoever said this.

MIND SWEEP: PLEASE REFRAIN FROM SUCH VULGARITY, ANVIL. I...IT WASN'T PURPOSEFUL I'M...EXPERIENCING SOME...UM...

ANVIL: No excuses interest me, Colonel *Spyware*, just count me out, got it?

OBLITERATION: Aww, come on, locomotive breath, join the party. Shetah's about to explain feline self-gratification in juicy detail, um, so to speak...

THE MASS: Would everyone please (pronounced 'pleweeze') clam up! Go ahead, Tigress. I got both hands wrapped firmly around my whopper, and it's lubed up and ready for action...

BEN: *Sweep, damn it...get me outta here...I'm warnin' you man...you ain't heard profanity like this man can dish out. I'm talkin' Atom bomb material, Hoss...*

MIND SWEEP: FORCE, PLEASE. I'M...ALMOST THERE.

ANVIL: Sorry, Force...gonna have to beat you to the punch. Hey Sweep...*FUCK OFF,*

COCKSUCKER! EAT SHIT AND DIE, FUCK-FACE! LICK MY BA-

MIND SWEEP: ONE DOWN...

THE MASS (moaning): Don't even...think about it, you son of bitch! I not done yet...talk to me, Shetah...talk to meeeeeeee...yes! Yes! Yeaaaahhhhhhh-

MIND SWEEP: TWO DOWN...

SHETAH: Appreciate that, Sweep. Now that Emperor *Chicken-Choker* is out of the picture, I do believe I have a tidbit of inside info you guys might find veerrry interesting...

MIND SWEEP: STILL WORKING ON IT, BEN. MY APOLOGIES...

OBLITERATION: What's up, Fuzz-ball?

SHETAH: Buzz is that there's new meat on the way, gents...

BEN: *Hold up, Sweep. Go ahead, Whiskers. This I'm bound to hear.*

OBLITERATION: Go ahead and cut the bastard off, Sweep. Man doesn't want to be in the loop, so be it...

BEN: *Tell ya what, Mac, if you're talkin' useable info, I'm all ears. It's the toilet habit BS I can live without.*

MIND SWEEP: VERY WELL, FORCE. PROCEED, SHETAH.

SHETAH (excitedly): Well, that perverted new CO that's only been on station for a few weeks, Masters or Masterson or whatever, spilled a few precious beans the other day after I allowed him to...pet me for a few minutes. Seems tha-

OBLITERATION (laughing): Whoa, sweet thang. Back up a sec...he petted you? Please

214

define...and feel free to be as graphic as you'd like...

BEN: *Cut the crap, Jackass. Go on, Shetah...*

SCEAMING EAGLE: Bravo, Force, bravo.

SHETAH: Whoever it is, it took the powers that be over a month to prep his cell. A cell budgeted at upwards of fifteen mil. The perv said there's some kind of airtight domed glass; chemically treated walls, and even some kind of laser. We're talking one major league bad-ass, guys.

OBLITERATION: Man might've been feeding you a line just to get more 'hand time', Miss Kitty. Any major capture news on CNN before you got boxed in with us, Forcy?

BEN: *Not a clue. I'd been keepin' the lowest of low profiles. Hadn't exactly been keepin' tabs on the outside world, if ya get my drift.*

SCREAMING EAGLE: Come to think of it, I have noted a twinge of tension in the air of late amongst the staff. Must be some real villainous royalty...the *King Charles* of the bad guy set, no less.

OBLITERATION: Ah, bologna. Remember all the hoopla when Black Plague was being shipped in, Eagle? Man, you would've thought they'd nabbed *Dr. Doom* and *Magneto* in the same Mega-Villain dragnet. Only one who kept his cool was Guardsman, and even he had his moments.

SCREAMING EAGLE: True enough. Haven't heard much from old BP since. They definitely found a way to neuter that boy.

BEN: *Speakin' of old toxie, he is a mental 'mute' or what? I take it he ain't much of a 'joiner'?*

MIND SWEEP: NO IDEA REALLY. IN MY TIME HERE, BLACK PLAGUE IS THE ONLY INDIVIDUAL I'VE FOUND TO BE...UNREACHABLE FROM A TELEPATHIC STANDPOINT. TRULY AN ENIGMATIC SOUL, THAT ONE.

OBLITERATION: Believe me, we're not missing anything. Tangled with the ornery SOB once. Tried to spit some kinda flesh-eating acid in my face. I managed to duck in time, but the poor slob behind me got turned into a vat of pus puree. As I recall, BP wasn't much for dialogue. He saw you...he offed you...period.

SHETAH: Regardless, this must be one seriously big fish. I noticed even Captain Cool himself acting a little antsy the past few weeks.

BEN: *Who ya mean, Felix, the Warden?*

SCREAMING EAGLE: She means The Guardsman. The Warden stays completely out of sight, out of mind after the initial in-brief. Personally, I haven't laid eyes on that pompous prick since.

OBLITERATION: Damn, that reminds me. Guardsman and ol' Forcy there are former tag team buddies with the Revenge Squard. So how bout it, Ben-ja-*mung*? Cap'n Stiffy acting a bit ap-pre-hen-sive in your opinion?

BEN: *Son, you are one irritatin' butt-boil of an individual. Yeah, Lu-...uh...Guardsman and me rode the same trails for a while, but that was years ago. Far as I can tell, he ain't changed a single iota. Always was a man of few words. Kind of a second tier Cap America in a lotta ways.*

OBLITERATION (laughing): *Captain Ameri-*

216

? How's that, man? Those are some big damn shoes to fi-

BEN: *Just let me finish, motor mouth. Like Cap, the man ain't reallygot no superpowers to speak of, but gets more outta his lack of same than anybody in the business save ol' flag-face himself.*

SCREAMING EAGLE: I'm with you there, Force. Guardsman is one guy you'd rather have on your side than the opposite team. Got to respect the man for the heights he's reached with such limited firepower.

OBLITERATION: Enough already. I think I'm falling in love.

BEN: *Punk.*

OBLITERATION: Cram it, shovel-hands.

MIND SWEEP: CAN WE POSSIBLY CONTINUE WITHOUT THE GRADE-SCHOOL TAUNTS, YOU TWO?

BEN: *Sorry, dad...but he started it...*

OBLITERATION: My sincere apologies, old great picker of brains...

MIND SWEEP: SHETAH, YOU WERE ABOUT TO INQUIRE?

SHETAH: Um...yeah. I was just gonna ask if you had a 'guesstimated' ETA for our newest cellmate?

MIND SWEEP: WELL, ALL INDICATIONS POINT TOWARDS THE NEXT FIVE TO SIX HOURS, DEPENDING ON WEATHER CONDITIONS. SPEAKING OF WHICH, THERE'S THE DEFINITE POSSIBILITY OF A STRONG TROPICAL STORM SWEEPING THE AREA WITHIN THE NEXT THREE TO FOUR DAYS. THE READINGS I'M RECEIVING

217

INDICATE TH-

BEN: *Man's part psychic, part satellite, and part freakin' Doppler Radar, already.*

SCREAMING EAGLE: Welcome to the Zoo, Force.

MIND SWEEP: ...AS I WAS SAYING...A TROPICAL DISTURBANCE OF SOME MAGNITUDE IS GATHERING STRENGTH BETWEEN FORTY-EIGHT AND SEVENTY-HOURS AWAY FROM EAGLE ISE.

OBLITERATION: Doesn't mean squat to us, pal. We're permanently 'domed' as it is.

MIND SWEEP: JUST A FOREWARNING, AS SUCH...NATURAL OCCURANCES SOMETIMES EFFECT MY ABILITY TO MODERATE OUR DAILY CHAT SESSIONS. UPDATES TO FOLLOW, PEOPLE.

SHETAH: Make sure to send me b-mail when the new meat arrives, Sweep.

BEN: *B-mail? What the hell kinda wacky stir jargon is that?*

OBLITERATION: Brain-mail, Benji. Get it? Instead of email? Course, in your specific case Sweep might be forced to install an 'upgrade' of sorts...

BEN: *Tell ya what, Mac, if he ever develops the power of teleportation, yours will be the first ass I plant my size twelve firmly into.*

OBLITERATION: Size twelve? You flirting with me, big boy? I do believe you're getting the hang of this *prison* thing.

MIND SWEEP: PLEASE, PLEASE...ENOUGH, YOU TWO. ARE THERE ANY OTHER MATTERS...OF A MORE

MEANINGFUL NATURE...ANYONE WOULD LIKE TO DISCUSS?

OBLITERATION: Yeah, as a matter of fact. Anybody seen the last 'X-Men' sequel? I swear they've got a new chick playing Storm. I mean, she's alright, but definitely no Halle Berry. Met the real Storm once...that's one *ultra*-hot tamale, baby...

(long silence)

BEN: *Uh...meetin' adjourned?*

MIND SWEEP: GOOD CALL, BENJAMIN. SHETAH, I'LL INFORM ONE AND ALL AS SOON AS THE NEW ARRIVAL IS OFFICIALLY ON SITE. CLOSING REMARKS?

OBLITERATION: Yeah, bite me Benjamin.

BEN: *Suck a fat one, queer-bait...*

MIND SWEEP: I'LL TAKE THAT AS A NO. GOOD DAY, PEOPLE...THE GRAPEVINE IS OFFICIALLY CLOSED...SIGNING OFF...

Feeling the faint lightheadedness that normally followed such sessions, Ben leaned down to retrieve the TV remote and froze in mid-reach.

"Talk about your mood breakers," he whispered, staring at the blank screen with a deeply furled brow, "...guess the beach and boobs are gonna have to wait. Got some serious ponderin' to do."

Pacing from wall to wall, it suddenly hit him (for at least the hundredth time in the past few days) how badly he missed Leah, and in ways that genuinely surprised him. It wasn't just the physical aspect of their relationship, active as that had been, but the sharing of ideas and opinions. She'd been the sharpest he'd ever known, man or woman, in

219

terms of troubleshooting, and had possessed the uncanny ability to breath workable logic into any situation. As was normally the case, his chest burned at the mere thought of her.

"Wish you were here, gorgeous. Sure like to bounce a few ideas off ya, not to mention my body as a whole," he said loudly, slowly becoming accustomed to the fact that no one or thing was within earshot.

He began shadow boxing if for no other reason than to quell the incessant restlessness and daily energy build-up that had progressed into a cruel form of physical illness.

Minutes later and bathed in fresh sweat, he dropped for the first in what would become five separate sets of one-armed push-ups, all the while dwelling on a two-part question that had shoved its way into the forefront of his mind and steadfastly refused to be ignored.

Where ya at these days, babe, and how're ya doin'?

For the first time in days, the aching in his chest and abdomen had nothing to do with a mysterious dread or the living hell of being permanently incarcerated. No doubt he still loved her, despite their less than touching parting of the ways all those months before. The mystery of whether she still felt the same was a painfully moot one given his present situation. Still, as he rolled onto his back and executed a furious set of crunches, Benjamin Jake Thomason came to the brutal yet sincere realization the answer to that very question was literally the *only* thing in what remained of his tattered life that truly mattered.

220

CHAPTER FIVE

Desolation Dawn

"Holy naptime, Batgirl...how long was I out?" Mystic asked, a dampened, bloodstained towel draped around his skull like a makeshift turban.

Turning gradually towards him, Marvella yawned twice in succession before responding.

"Couldn't tell you for sure, Boy Wonder. I swear it...feels like I just woke up myself. Lord, talk about your self-induced comas."

"You do look a shade pale, my dear, and I must say that yellowish pale is quite the horrific color scheme, unless you're thinking of changing your name to *Jaundice Girl.*"

"Can't say I feel much better than I look, either," she replied, reaching back to message the back of her neck with both hands, "Guess it's the effects of maintaining the field for this long. Before now I can't ever recall sustaining one for longer than a half-hour."

"I'm with you, girl. I haven't been this drained in years. I can only imagine how wiped someone of your...limited resources would feel."

She turned and shot him a disdainful glance, cocking her left eyebrow beneath the skin-tight cowl.

"No doubt you're the undisputed expert on *wipes.*"

"Ah, Leah my pet, regardless the level of fatigue, you never seem to lose that rapier wit," he replied curtly, "Ready for me to take the reins?"

221

Moving about as if heavily drugged, she shrugged weakly before bowing her head in apparent fatigue.

"Be my guest. The rock of evil must've finally worn itself out. Hasn't been a single shimmy or shake since that one major quake. I'm just wondering how close we're getting to the mystery location. Haven't seen the director in a while. At least, I don't…think I have. Now I understand the true meaning of the word 'discombobulated'."

"Allow me, my dear," he spat gleefully, levitating upward while reaching up to gently touch each temple with an outstretched forefinger, "…Director Willis, report to cargo hold. Director Willis, your presence is requested in the cargo hold…post haste if you will, good sir."

"You forgot to twitch your nose, Samantha," Marvella cracked, loosening her harness and standing gingerly.

Mere moments later, Director Willis re-entered the hold clutching a burning cigarette in one hand and a folded pocket PC in the other. His pale visage was scrunched in obvious anger as he stumbled forward, eventually balancing himself by leaning against a set of small supply lockers.

"Why, hello Director Sir…what brings you to the neighborhood?" Mystic queried, floating upside down just a few feet to the director's left.

"Would you mind *not* doing that unless absolutely necessary? Feels like someone was peeling my scalp from the inside," The Director growled, his flushed cheeks in drastic contrast to his otherwise bone-white complexion.

"Whoops, sorry Chief. They really do need to

install an intercom of some sort in this overpriced sardine can."

"What do you need, Mystic?" The Director asked sourly, obviously ignoring the comment.

"Just a status update, General. We sort of…lost track of time back here, right Leah?"

"That's it exactly, sir. Have to admit I'm far from the top of my game at this point," Marvella said, her eyes closed as she tilted her head slightly forward.

Kneeling onto one knee with the cigarette hanging off his bottom lip, Director Willis opened the PC after balancing it on his lap.

"If you'd waited another five to ten minutes before setting my noggin on fire, I was on my way to inform you both that we'll be approaching our destination in approximately twenty to twenty-five minutes. There's the matter of a mandatory in-brief before actual landing commences.

"Okay…just let me find the right page," he said, typing with both hands as the cigarette jiggled wildly between his lips.

"I get the feeling we're in for a lecture every time we have to use the john," Mystic complained, levitating up and over the Director's prone form until he was peering directly over the other man's left shoulder.

"There she is. All right, listen up lady and gentleman. The object in our care is to be off-loaded and permanently housed on the installation known as *the Eagle Island Detention Center*. A Top-Secret clearance with no less than a Presidential endorsement is required to enter the installation, while its exact location is known only to those within its everyday employment. Upon departure, all visitors will be subjected to a memor-..."

"Eagle Is-...Eagle Island Detention Center? Forgive my crudeness, Chief, but you are shitting us, correct?" Mystic interrupted in a shrill, high-pitched tone comically feminine.

"It...that place actually exists? The prison site part we'd pretty well predicted, and the confidentiality of the site certainly isn't a shock, but..." Marvella chimed in excitedly, suddenly wide-eyed and alert, "...my God, I've heard stories about Eagle Island for years, but...it was like hearing about Mount Olympus or the lost city of Atlantis, you know?"

Mystic began to flip and spin in mid-air, his curled form resembling a green-shaded pinwheel.

"Mythology and legend come to life, girl, and we're gonna get the full tour, up close and personal."

"Best to curb the enthusiasm, you two. Allow me to finish what I'd begun," the Director continued after a short pause as he studied Mystic's acrobatic moves with a look of utter bemusement, "...Upon departure of said installation, all visitors will be subjected to a memory-erasing treatment by assigned medical staff. This procedure is officially known as a '*matter swipe*', its sole purpose to effectively eliminate any and all memories of the visit. As it has been utilized on countless individuals since the island's inception, the procedure has been deemed completely safe and without a single known side effect. Needless to say, this includes everyone present and involved on this current mission."

Halting in mid-spin, Mystic's mouth hung agape even as his eyes narrowed to fine slits.

"Matter swipe? Let me repeat, are you *shitting* us? Surely you jest, General. You're saying we won't recall a single detail of this potentially gargantuan adventure?"

"Precisely. You won't...I won't...the pilots won't. *No one* does. The security of Eagle Island is priority one, for reasons that should be blatantly obvious."

"But...I'd planned on posting a written journal of this whole experience on my website, despite figuring it would be a rather banal experience. This...procedure is not only cheating me, but also my entire fan-base as a whole."

"Personally, I'd be tempted to file criminal charges," Marvella quipped, rolling her eyes in dismay, "although I believe Aggravated *Ego* Assault is only a class C Misdemeanor."

"Not funny, Leah. I'm serious. Without that posted report, I'm looking at losing out on at least two planned endorsements. Entertainment Tonight was gonna interview me on the speci-...Damn! And there goes that cameo in the latest James Bond sequel," he raved, descending downward and into a sitting position in what had been Marvella's seat.

"My heart bleeds," Director Willis blurted, all the while staring down the iron box as if it were a rival gunslinger, "Strap yourselves in, people, if you deem fit. We'll be arriving on the eastern edge of Eagle Isle within the half-hour."

Moments after the Director's departure back towards the cockpit, Marvella couldn't help but feel devilishly amused at her mission partner's pouting expression, complete with puffed lips, slumped posture, and squinting eyes.

"Need a hankie, magic man?" she taunted playfully following several minutes of stilted silence.

"Not now, Leah. I'm no longer in the mood. Man gets the opportunity of a lifetime and is forced to piss it away after the fact. Unadulterated bullshit."

"Chill *out*, Mystic. What's the big deal? Just make something up for your web journal. Sure won't be the first work of true fiction sailing about the 'net, right?

Use your imagination...spice it up Hollywood style."

The pout slowly transformed into a gleeful grin that could have easily been defined as slightly demented in nature.

"Yeah... yeah! Why not, right? It's not like anyone will know the diff, including yours truly for that matter. You know, Leah, you're much smarter than you look. I owe you one, girl."

"Forget it. Just leave me out of whatever twisted story-line that perverted mind of yours dreams up and we'll call it even."

Mystic nodded without a verbal response, his face already contorted in deep thought.

The transport tilted several degrees to the left before straightening, then began a gradual descent noticeable only from the standpoint of an overly alert witness to the minute change in flight pattern.

Both Mystic and Marvella had visibly stiffened during each movement, only to ease down once it became apparent they'd been pilot-initiated.

226

Once the chopper seemed to have settled back into a set pattern, Marvella allowed her thoughts to drift back and settle comfortably onto the potential soap opera scenario ahead. Sharp twinges of pity carved deep grooves into her soul at the image of Benjamin Thomason possibly being caged up on some Top-Secret Fortress of *Lost Souls;* permanently exiled alongside only the most powerful of evils and subsequently tossed into the mix as nothing more than a homicidal psychopath. Try as she might, Leah couldn't convince herself that a man she once loved like none before belonged in such a desolate place, isolated from the whole of society and forever banned from dolling out the brutal form of justice that was his only reason for being. Within the throngs of passion the two had so often shared, Ben once told her she alone had possessed a keen insight to who he truly was, beyond the enraged brute with the hair-trigger temper, a temper second only to *Wolverine* in terms of legendary status. The talent to reel in such rage with a simple touch, gesture, or nod was exclusively hers. As teammates, they had taunted and teased one another unmercifully, building a natural camaraderie while simultaneously forging a deep friendship that eventually became something more.

Following the loss of three cherished teammates in a bloody massacre engineering by their former team leader, the couple had gone into a self-imposed retirement phase in order to replenish their battered souls while also contemplating an uncertain future They'd rented a beachfront bungalow on a tiny, sparsely populated Caribbean island and spent their days wading the warm sea water, sipping cool beverages, and sharing each other's bodies. Looking back with perfect twenty-twenty hindsight, Leah deduced it had been the closest she'd ever experienced in regard to a Shangri-La-type existence. But, as with all things defined as such, it had been as painfully brief in duration as it had been long on happiness. Eventually, the warrior within pulled and tugged at her lover's inner workings until the yearning simply became too strong. The thirst for action had parched his throat like a lit flame; the combative nature that fueled his very being slowly, meticulously overpowering all other emotions, including whatever love he'd felt for her.

It wasn't until he'd announced his intention to rejoin the fray as crime-fighter for hire three and a half months later that a solid rift emerged between them. A full eight months since Ben's rather abrupt departure from her life, Leah could sit back with a clearer mind unclouded by her own selfish needs and better understand the choice her man had made. Understand, and at least on some remote level, accept the fact the reason for his departure hadn't been a loss of feeling for her, but a call to arms that was simply beyond the man's control. At that particular moment in time, she had yet to receive the same inner voicemail. Fear and self-doubt had clutched her gut in a steely vice, and it had taken another two months to garner the courage required to re-don both costume and cowl, thus reclaiming the title of *Marvella, Mistress of Magical Mayhem*.

The day she'd heard of Benjamin's capture by a man she presently called partner, the level of depression that followed wasn't unexpected. The day his conviction and subsequent sentence came down, it was as though a dark cloud swollen to overflowing with misery and despair had entered her subconscious mind like a malignant tumor. She cried long and hard, then cried some more. Following a two-week personal mourning period, she'd thrown herself back into the lion's den at full bore, accepting each and every assignment tossed her way in hopes of a constant distraction to brush away the blackened fog of depression shadowing her every move. Surprisingly, the 'workaholic method' had served as the perfect therapy, at least until the current assignment drudged up a tidal wave's worth of memories placing her on an emotional roller-coaster ride seemingly without end.

Staring past the portal into the cloudless blue skies and matching ocean beyond, Marvella could do little to quell the trembling of her hands and midsection. True, though the odds of a face to face meeting with her former mate was astronomical at best, just the thought such a chance encounter could later be wiped clean from her memory was almost too horrific an irony to contemplate without truly going insane.

"Let it go, damn it," she murmured to herself, "he's not there anyway. What are the odds? No way. God couldn't...*wouldn't* be so cruel." She could only hope and then pray to the same aforementioned entity that such was true.

***

Part I:

The Arrival

"Just got word from the C-Post, boss. Radar shows the chopper thirty miles out and closing."

"Almost show-time, Luke. Damn, don't recall being this jittery since the day they off-loaded Black Plague from that fiberglass cylinder and almost dropped 'im onto the dock."

"No sweat, Charlie. Everything's been triple-checked. Crane's in place with the motor warming as we speak."

Sailing down the brightly lit hallway at breakneck speed, Warden Charles V. Terry felt an overwhelming need to find the nearest toilet stall and anoint it his permanent safe haven for the remainder of the day.

"Egghead brigade all fed and packed away?"

"As of two hours ago. They're in the holding area now, checking out the equipment. Four of the stiffest individuals I've come across in a while, boss. Pretty sure they're all at least half *Vulcan*," The Guardsman replied, forced to take unusually long strides just to keep pace with his immediate supervisor.

"Too much brain for their skull caps, my man. God must feel the need to even the score for rewarding 'em those sky-high IQ's. Personality *and* smarts don't normally share the same package, y'know?"

"Quite the elaborate set-up down there, boss. Heard one of the Vulcan clan say it resembled the inside of a nuke-housing unit. Not taking any chances with this thing, are they?"

"Not at all. From its track history, I can't say I

230

blame 'em."

They rounded a final curve and stopped at the base of a single metal panel withthe words '*NO ENTRY ALLOWED WITHOUT A-1 CLEARANCE*' stenciled across its wide center in bold black letters. A code-key entry box protruded from the wall just to their left, and the Warden quickly reached over without looking and tapped out a five-digit number, then backed away a step as the panel slid open with a low hum.

Both men entered a squared space no larger than a service elevator and stood before still another panel and matching keypad. The Warden turned to the larger man and nodded, and the Guardsman stepped forward and typed in a lengthier numerical code than the first. The compartment they'd entered began to descend almost as soon as the panel door had resealed, sliding to a smooth stop approximately fifteen seconds later.

"How many levels we just cover, boss?"

"I was told one-hundred thirty-two feet below ground level."

"Reminds me of the time I took the family to Mammoth Caves. Got the same symptoms; light-headedness, moist sinuses, tingling scalp."

"Damn, Luke..." the Warden quipped just before the panel opened with a whooshing sound "... guess we could rule out ever calling you the '*Mole*'."

"Why do you think I took this gig, boss? Claustrophobic superheroes have severe limitations, you know," the larger man replied while following the other's lead into a wide opening bathed in bright fluorescent lighting.

Spreading his arms wide with the palms of his hands facing the high concrete ceiling above, Warden Terry resembled a circus barker from another era preparing to announce the main attraction of an ancient freak show exhibit.

"Behold twenty-first century penal technology, Luke. A holding cell built specifically for a non-human inhabitant of possible alien origin. I don't know about you, but I'm instantly reminded of every *Outer Limits* episode I ever saw."

Standing directly behind his boss, whose stocky stature allowed him an unobstructed view nonetheless, The Guardsman felt the hair on his neck instantly stand on end even as a rash of chill bumps coated his exposed arms. A glass window measuring at least six feet high and twenty across fronted the interior, while a curved walkway to their left led to a separate enclosure marked '*ENTRY PROHIBITED WITHOUT FULL PROTECTIVE GEAR*'.

"Wow. They've added a few features since I was down here yesterday, Chief," he replied with awestruck wonder, pointing through the glass exterior towards a slim, metallic cylinder manned with several robotic arms, at least one of which resembled a tank barrel.

"What in the name of *Buck Rogers* is that thing?"

"That's the laser cannon procured for the egghead brigade. One expensive puppy, I understand. Has military nomenclature, but the markings are definitely not 'Made in USA' brand. Russia or Czech, I do believe."

"Sounds like a little selective surgery is on the

232

schedule, huh?"

"Guess so, Luke. Obviously they're taking no chances. Check it out…" They stepped gingerly into an adjoining room approximately the size of a large walk-in freezer unit, where at least a dozen Chemical suits with matching helmets hung inside tubular glass cylinders.

"Unreal," The Guardsman whispered, placing a gloved hand on the nearest cylinder while leaning forward to better study its contents. "Boss, are we certain they're not sneaking nukes in on us?"

The other man shrugged, leaning over a multi-task console consisting of three separate computers, each with its own printer, a speaker mike and numerous hand controls of various sizes and shapes.

"I get the distinct feeling we're not the only ones in the dark concerning the new arrival. These…joysticks must allow 'em to use the laser from here."

The Guardsman stepped over and gave the makeshift console a thorough once-over before glancing up at his own weak reflection in the glass wall ahead.

"Then why the Chemical suits?"

"Plan must be to dissect the thing from here and study whatever readings they get before entering the same space."

"Well," the larger man sighed, his steely glare focusing on the large metallic cylinder centered in the room like a slick, round coffin, "We can only hope they have a workable plan in case of meltdown."

Having been lowered inside a stone base measured at precisely thirteen feet in length and five feet in width, it resembled a futuristic MRI Unit, complete with an inner housing unit that would presumably slide into the outer shell. The barrel of the laser hovered mere inches from the surface of the outer shell, centered at a narrow, horizontal split spanning the length of the cylinder.

"Agreed. No doubt we'll be the first to know if they don't," the Warden replied seconds before the panel door slid open behind them.

"Warden...Guardsman. Checking out the new digs, I see," the first man said with a casual nod as two others filled in behind him. All three wore white lab coats and carried hand-held PC units, their expressions similarly grim and business-like.

"Doctor...James, I presume?" the Warden inquired, backing away from the console as the trio stepped closer.

The first man, a slim, gray-haired man most likely in his low to mid-fifties, responded without looking up as he leaned down to power up the largest of the three computer units.

"Correct, Warden. My cohorts in this rather fascinating venture are Doctors Weems and Sullivan, respectively. I understand our special guest is less than ten minutes away."

"Headed up to the pad now, as a matter of fact. Off-load and transport shouldn't take more than a half-hour to forty-five minutes. Do you...uh...gentlemen have a set itinerary on the task at hand or are you simply flying by the seat of your pants on this one?"

The second man (sporting a laminated line-badge identifying him as 'Dr. Weems'), a balding, rotund individual of apparent Middle Eastern

234

descent wearing a perpetual frown, shot the warden a hateful glance before turning his attention back to a yellow legal pad he'd been scribbling on.

"We don't…fly by the seat of our pants as a rule, Warden," the first man replied after a brief pause, "although I will admit my colleagues and I are equally perplexed on an exact checklist of action to follow in this particular case."

The third (badge reading 'Sullivan'), and easily the youngest of the trio, a thick-bodied black male sporting a lengthy goatee tied with braids at the tip, began the process of powering up the laser via a remote device pulled from his lab coat.

"Understood, doctor. This is new to *all* of us, and believe me when I say, I'm not an easy man to surprise after a decade on this burg."

"Ready to fly, boss?" The Guardsman asked, already taking a step towards the exit panel, "Cargo should be entering Eagle Isle airspace anytime now."

"Yeah, let's hit it. See you gents within the hour, barring some catastrophic turn of events, that is."

Once inside the elevator, the Guardsman leaned over and administered a playful nudge to his supervisor's left shoulder.

"Can't say much for that closing statement, Charlie. *Catastrophic turn of events*? Famous last words, perhaps?"

"Tell me about it, Luke," the Warden replied, smiling sheepishly asthe elevator ascended at a gradually increasing rate, "…felt like a horse's ass as soon as I said it."

Approximately five minutes later, the pair

235

strolled briskly down a separate walkway; a winding stretch of dimly lit corridor leading to a recently constructed heli-pad built specifically for the mystery guest they've come to meet. Despite a heroic, combat-leaden background that spanned close to fifteen years, The Guardsman felt a tightening around his midsection he could only equate to a single emotion. He recalled a recent conversation with a trusted friend and former battle-mate, now tucked away in a nearby titanium cell, concerning strong feelings of unease and troublesome premonitions of events to come. At the time, it had been logical to assume such remarks were tied to nothing more complicated than simple disorientation. Feeling a wave of stark fear clamp his torso in a full-body vise as the entry point to the heli-pad swam slowly into view, The Guardsman couldn't help but ponder Benjamin Thomason's words in an altogether different light.

Something bad was coming, he thought. He...*knew*. Something big; colossal; unstoppable. Something on the grandest of scales. A large-scale drama played out on the most desolate of stages in front of an audience of once-powerful entities who might well find themselves playing the role of hapless victim in the face of something with abilities beyond all imagination.

Stepping onto a mobile landing pad as it began its short trek from the main building out into the salty air beyond, both men visibly stiffened as the transport neared their location from the East.

"Damn...haven't been this shaken since President Powell visited the site last spring," the Warden moaned in obvious apprehension.

236

"Yeah, or the day that Blackhawk Special carted Black Plague's nasty rear onto the island," his subordinate added, attempting with very minimal success to quell the nervous tick developing at the corner of his left eye.

**

Part II:

Homing In

FOR-... UM...DESOLATION OUTLAW...? ARE YOU TH-... BENJAMIN...?

I hear ya, Sweep. I hear ya. Lower the volume a decibel or two, will ya? It's like havin' a bullhorn goin' off between my ears. What's up?

AS PROMISED, I WANTED TO MAKE EVERYONE ON THE VINE AWARE OF THE ARRIVAL OF OUR MYSTERY GUEST. HE...IT'S BEING OFFLOADED AS WE SPEAK FROM A LOCATION ON THE ISLE I CANNOT QUITE PIN DOWN. NEWLY CONSTRUCTED, I'D VENTURE TO SAY. OH, SO MUCH IS ENIGMATIC CONCERNING THIS...ADDITION. I FIND IT EQUALLY WORRISOME AND...STRANGELY...TANTILIZING.

Try to control those synthetic hormones, Sweep.

MY APOLOGIES, FORCE...ALTHOUGH I AM NOT A SYNTHETIC. COMMON MISTAKE DUE TO MY RATHER.... STILTED PERSONALITY, I'M AFRAID.

I was just yankin' your chain, big guy. Anywho,

237

what did ya mean, you can't pin down the offload location? I figured you owned an internal blueprint downloaded in that IBM noggin of yours.

NORMALLY, SUCH COMPLICATIONS ARE MINIMAL IN QUANTITY AND TEMPORARY IN NATURE. SOMETHING...UNUSUAL ABOUT THIS...RATHER BIZARRE. EACH ATTEMPT TO HONE IN IS MET BY A...BLOCKING...MUCH LIKE A COMPUTER FIREWALL, I'D PRESUME.

Guess this mean's whoever Bobby-Joe-Badass is, he ain't sharin' cell block space with the rest of the gang. Guess Shetah's contact wasn't lyin' about this one getting his own private space.

SAFE BET, BENJAMIN. THERE IS A DEFINITE POSSIBILITY THAT A SPECIALLY DESIGNED WING HAS BEEN CONSTRUCTED. I'D FELT A FLURRY OF ACTIVITY ON THE EASTERN EDGE OF THE MAIN BUILDING IN THESE LAST FEW MONTHS, BUT SHRUGGED IT OFF AS ROUTINE MAINTENANCE.

Hey, lemme know if you obtain any additional info on this bird, Sweep. I don't know about the others, but the vibes I'm receivin' are downright disturbin', and I'm talkin' in a haunted house from hell sorta way.

WILL DO, BENJAMIN, AND YOU'RE NOT ALONE WITH SUCH...VIBES. BOTH SHETAH AND OBLITERATION HAVE EXPRESSED SIMILAR FEELINGS QUITE VOCALLY, WHILE ANVIL ALSO HINTS AT SUCH, BUT WITHOUT THE SAME CONVICTION.

Hard-headed ass wipe to the very end.

NOW, NOW, NONE OF THAT. I'LL RE-CONTACT YOU AS SOON AS ANY PERTINENT INFORMATION BECOMES AVAILABLE. MIND SWEEP SIGNING OUT…

Yeah…over an' out…Roger Wilco, Hoss.

Clamping his tightly taped hands to the weight bar hovering above his head and chest, Ben eyed the stacked plates on each side wearing an expression of casual aplomb. The dizziness and brief disorientation, once a regular side effect of the cell grapevine, had digressed into nothing more than a dull headache since the first few sessions. Hoisting the bar with a low grunt, he pumped out five quick reps and replaced the bar with a loud clang as REO Speedwagon's *"Riding The Storm Out"* blared loudly from nearby stereo speakers.

Finally startin' to get the ol' wind back. Still, a twelve-hundred-pound bench ain't shit. Won't be all the way back 'til I heave at least two tons without strainin' a gonad.

Rising from the bench, he pulled two additional hundred-pound discs from a nearby weight rack and was in the process of sliding the first onto the weight bar when he reeled back as if physically shoved.

"Wha-the hell?" he blurted, tossing the weights to one side and barely avoiding tripping into a nautilus squat rack.

Regaining his balance, he felt the flesh of his arms, neck and face begin to sting as the temperature within the workout room seemed to plummet into single digits.

Bracing his feet in a combat pose, his breath escaped from between both his nostrils and lips in a frosty mist.

"Ice-m-man?" he shouted crazily, reaching up to wipe the building frost from his eyelids. Faint patches of frozen sweat stood out from the thick growth of body hair on his chest and arms like icy quills, while his mustache and goatee held the pasty, freezer burned look of someone who'd just stepped inside from a raging blizzard.

Alllllllll…

Willllllll…

*Die…*came the faint whisper, causing Ben to shake his head from side to side as if shooing off a pesky insect.

"Wha-…Sweep…is…is that you, man?" he spat through chattering teeth.

Die…

Froooommmmm…

Withinnnnnnn… it concluded, followed by a loud rustling noise, not unlike brittle leaves blown onto a stone walkway.

"Say…say what? Sweep, is that…y- you, damn it? Not funny, man…not at all…"

Speak up, shithead…what kinda grade-school prank you playin', man? What's with the human Popsicle bit?

Leaning down to one knee, he paused for several labored breaths. The temperature had already warmed to its previous reading, as if the sudden tundra-like conditions had never actually transpired. In the background echoed the initial guitar chords of Nazareth's *'Hair of The Dog'*.

His body re-drenched in defrosted perspiration, Ben sat on the edge of the weight bench and continued to scan the room as if expecting some

240

form of aftershock.

Funny thing...it sure as hell didn't sound like Sweep. Never...heard those golden tones on the vine. Spoooo-ky. Maybe I am crackin' up. Definitely losin' my nerve. Cabin fever in less than five days. Real good, Benji...damned impressive.

Having already decided to forgo the remainder of his workout, he eventually stood and began a series of calf and back stretches, all the while deep in meditative thought as to the origin of the message. He'd just begun to completely recoup his senses when a more familiar tone shattered his thought process like a high-voltage charge directly into the brain.

...Shetah calling anybody...Shetah calling any...damn...body...come in, whoever...

Hold your tender vittles...I'm right here, furball. Just gimme a minute to uncross my eyes...and turn the volume down while you're at it.

Force? (sighed) Not exactly my first choice, but beggars can't be choosers.

Believe me, darlin'...the nauseatin' feelin' is mutual. Looks like Sweeps runnin' the show without a net again...

Did you just...I mean...a few minutes ago...hear something? I mean, something that wasn't associated with the vine?

Weeellll...I did fart a second ago (paused). Be specific, whiskers.

Details...

Smart-ass. It was a...voice. A voice I'd never...it was eerie. Like a...phantom whisper...and the inside of my cell...

Turned colder than a witch's tit on a December

241

night in North Dakota...got'cha. (paused...sighed wearily)

Ya know, I'm really beginnin' to think the powers that be injected my ass with some kinda schizophrenia serum so I can keep myself amused with multiple personalities...most of 'em assholes at that...

Dream on, Bud. So you did receive the same...warped transmission? *Yeah...along with a nasty case of blue balls from a sixty-degree temperature drop that lasted all of a minute and a half. Any chance Mind Sweep is behind it? I mean, poor dude ain't exactly what I'd term stable to begin with.*

No way. Sweep isn't wired for jokes, practical or otherwise. Nor does he possess the power to turn my cell into a *Tastee Freeze*. What...did you hear the voice say? It was...kind of garbled on my end.

Some kinda Helter Skelter shit about... everybody will die or die from within...somethin' similar.

Ditto...thought I caught the word 'within'.

OBLITERATION: Hey, is this a private sex chat or can any qualified pervert join the orgy?

SHETAH: Oblit?

BEN: *Ah geez...man, how can your breath smell like ass even telepathically?*

OBLITERATION: Just wash off that upper lip, pal. Hey, where's the moderator? I've been listening to you two flap your gums for the last few minutes, but I couldn't break in.

SHETAH: No idea. This is all new to me, man. Oblit, did you experience the same pheno-

OBLITERATION: Yep. Complete with low

temps and high-pitched moan. Maybe Sweep was having a nightmare and decided to spread the joy...we were just innocent bystanders that happened to be on the same cosmic wavelength...

SHETAH: Damn, Chief *Toe-Cheese*, do I have to keep repeating myself?

The man isn't capable of that deep freeze maneuver...at least, I don't think he is. Besides, what would be the point of the '*Mr Freeze*' imitation or the death threat?

BEN: *Who says it was a threat? Might'a been a warnin'.*

SHETAH: Good point. Guess it depends on how you take it. Regardless, it was damn weird...

OBLIT: Welcome to haunted isle, no less...

BEN: *Yeah, somethin's goin' haywire. Has been ever since I stepped foot onto this burg. Gotta have somethin' to do with the new arrival.*

OBLITERATION: Seems to me you're the only new arrival that's o-fficially on site, shovel-hands. Ever consider the possibility that all the wacky bullshit going on just might be related directly to your former '*good guy turned bad*' ass?

SHETAH: Oh, stick a sock in it, Oblit. We've covered this ground already. I just can't get over the fact were sitting here swapping thoughts without Sweep playing moderator. Hard as I concentrate, he *won't* answer.

OBLIT: Maybe it isn't that he won't, but *can't*. Whatever's causing this has Sweep's wires all crossed.

BEN: *Ain't the first time either. Been a common occurrence the past few days. Gotta be a strain on a normal day to keep Ma 'Prison Bell'* *runnin' smoothly, much less with all the horseshit of la-...*

I'M...I'M HERE PEOPLE. APOLOGIES FOR THE DELAY

SHETAH: Sweep! Great to hear your voi-...uh...thoughts again. You...okay, man?

MIND SWEEP: I'VE HAD BETTER DAYS, SHETAH. I CAN ONLY EQUATE THE TECHNICAL DIFFICULTIES OF THE PAST SEVERAL DAYS TO ELECTRICAL INTERFERENCE, ALTHOUGH THAT'S STRICTLY AN EXAMPLE TO USE. STILL NOT SURE OF THE ACTUAL ORIGIN. I'VE BEEN ATTEMPTING TO NAIL IT DOWN. TO UTILIZE THE VERNACULAR... 'NO DICE' THUS FAR...

BEN: *Ya been able to get a fix on the cell location?*

MIND SWEEP: EASTERN SIDE OF THE MAIN BUILDING, AT LEAST TWO TO THREE FLOORS DOWN FROM THE GROUND FLOOR, POSSIBLY MORE.

BEN: *So they did build this bird his very own underground tomb.*

OBLIT: King Tut's younger brother, take a bow.

MIND SWEEP: OFFLOAD WAS COMPLETED ABOUT TWENTY MINUTES TO A HALF-HOUR AGO. FROM THE READING I'M NOW GETTING...WHICH IS SPORADIC AT BEST...THE OBJECT BEING TRANSPORTED IS SOLID YET...UNMOVING, AND SEALED SOMEHOW...ALSO...THERE ARE MULTIPLE FORCE FIELDS BEING

244

ADMINISTERED FOR...APPARENTLY...EXTRA SECURITY.

SHETAH: So this thing's strapped down *and* cloaked in fields. Must besomeone new on the scene. Can't think of anyone outside of The *Celestial Slayer* who'd require that much baby-sitting, and the FF supposedly offed him a decade back.

OBLIT: Well, maybe they did and maybe they didn't. You know us super-baddies, Catnip. We've all been presumed dead more than once.

BEN: *Wonder who's providin' the fields. Can ya work up a vision, Sweep?* **MIND SWEEP**: TWO DISTINCTLY DIFFERENT SOURCES...ONE A BIT STRONGER THAN THE OTHER. UNABLE TO OBTAIN...PRECISE READINGS OR BRAINWAVES AT THIS JUNCTURE. NEED A...BRIEF RESPITE. LETS CUT THIS SHORT FOR NOW, PEOPLE. FOLLOWING A QUICK RECHARGE, I'LL REINSTATE THE VINE WITH UPDATED INFORMATION...

OBLIT: Take five...hell, take ten. It isn't as if we're going anywhere, and neither is our new bunkmate.

SHETAH: Yeah, by all means, Sweep. But...don't take too long, huh? You know what they say about curiosity and my kind...

MIND SWEEP: NOT TO WORRY. SHOULDN'T TAKE MORE THAN AN HOUR OR S...

(long pause)

BEN: *Uh...Sweep? Anybody still on the line?*

"Cut off at the knees once again," he mumbled

245

to himself, shaking off the cobwebs with a shrug while stepping over to the massive free-weight rack and scooping up a pair of one-hundred-fifty-pound barbells as the opening cords of Blue Oyster Cult's '*Don't Fear the Reaper*' filled the surrounding air.

When his CO escort arrived to accompany him back to the cellblock some ten minutes later, he'd been standing in front of a wide mirror with a blank expression, curling the barbells in a stiff, mechanical fashion.

"Time's up, D-Fourteen. Let's get you back to the cage before the noonday feeding," the officer barked through a dark-tinted black visor, gesturing with his short-barreled weapon for Ben to take the lead.

"You're the boss, Officer Myers...long as ya got that pop-shooter pointed my way, anyhow."

Dropping the barbells to the padded floor, Ben stepped wearily ahead while massaging each of his massively bloated biceps.

"Really enjoy the zoo references, meathead. Ya missed your true callin' down at the Comedy Store," he continued, shooting the CO a playful wink.

As was usually the case when anyone *other* than The Guardsman performed escort duties, the remainder of the trek passed in utter silence save the constant hum of laser tubing or the occasional muffled rattle of a nearby pipe.

Following a five-minute cleansing session inside the '*flush pod*', Ben remained completely nude while laying sprawled across the couch, peering downward to study the wide growth of soot-black body hair coating virtually every inch of his

246

body.

Who says there ain't livin' proof of the theory'a evolution? Hormones are back to normal, at least.

After activating the combination TV/DVD, he arose and began digging through a pile of requested discs obviously delivered during his session in the *Free Zone*.

"Oh hell yeah...'*Lost*' seasons one *and* two...annnnnd...'*Oz*' season one. Hot Damn! Yeah, buddy...instant therapy. Deserted island *and* maximum-security prison drama at its very best," he exclaimed with boyhood exuberance. "Kinda sums up my current quality of life in a nutshell. Looks like I finally get the chance to catch up on all the boob tube clap trap I've missed out on the last two decades."

He eyed the discs for a few moments more before tossing them back onto the tabletop, his grin, wholly manufactured and void of an ounce of sincerity, gradually fading.

Who you tryin' to kid, Hoss? It ain't like you're ever gonna get the chance to actually watch 'em. There's one Tsunami-sized shitstorm just over the horizon, and no doubt I'll be one of the first to wade chest-high into that mother's swirlin' eye.

Feeling a rush of fresh adrenaline, he spent the next ten minutes shadow boxing in-between sets of one-armed push-ups and crunches.

Within moments of taking a seat on the edge of his rumpled cot, he fell into a deep, dreamless slumber. It would be just over two hours later that he would awaken with a startled jolt to the sound of jumbled voices at varied stages of panic, his body, mind, and soul consumed by mysterious waves of

247

fatigue. As it was, the impromptu 'power nap' he'd so easily collapsed into would be the final restful interlude Benjamin Thomason would ever spend atop Eagle Island Detention Center.

***

Part III:

Ill-Timed Reunion(s)

"Mission accomplished, chief! Looks like the big-bad rock is officially set in stone," Mystic blurted loudly, causing the majority of those packed within the relatively small confines to involuntarily cringe back.

The huddled group stood before the glass window in a military-style formation, less than a foot separating one from the other. Viewed from an under-informed point of view, they might well have resembled a circus troop from another era.

"Are we indeed good to go, Doctor James?" The Warden asked, striking a statuesque pose as the centerpiece of the seven witnesses present.

Leaning over the largest of the three computers, the doctor's eyes scanned the monitor even as his fingers danced across the keyboard at warp speed.

"Readings, to include both inner atmospheric and all three layers of cylinder housing indicate condition yellow across the board, Warden."

The Warden shot Director Willis a bemused glance.

"The light just turned green, Warden," Willis said with a slight nod.

Without warning, Mystic ascended a few inches from the floor and danced a wild jig, his spindly appendages waving and gyrating in a hysterically exaggerated break dance.

"Coooool beans, doc. Sooo…I take it our services are no longer needed then, Mister Director?"

"Lord son…could you be any *gayer*?" Willis needled, executing a comic double-take at the Warden's wondrous, open-mouthed expression.

"Gay-*er*? You mean he's…that is…uh…um…not that there's anything wrong…um…"

"No need to swallow a shoe, Warden Terry. Yes, indeed he is…as the proverbial three-dollar bill," Marvella injected blandly, her eyes never wavering from the circular cylinder where their cargo lay stashed.

The Warden quickly returned his own gaze to the same area, his cheeks and forehead having grown beet red.

"Well…it's just that…you didn't see…much of that in my day."

"Don't be so sure, *Chief Justice* Warden Terry Sir," Mystic chided, floating over until his round, narrow shoulder sat only a few inches from the Warden's own, "our…kind were simply too timid to endure the snide remarks and ridicule in your…time. I'll bet even a few of the legends of the business are closet queens by night. Open your mind, Warden, and your libido might well follow."

"Don't…bet on it, son," the Warden replied sternly, slip-sliding to the left. Marvella snickered despite herself.

"Um, back to the issue at hand, sirs. Are we cleared to drop the fields? I've got to admit to being a bit winded."

"Doc?" Director Willis asked wearily, having strolled over to study the hanging chemical suits through their tubular glass covering.

The doctor responded in a tone slightly less mechanical while continuing to hover over the computer console like a lab-coated ghoul over a freshly dug grave.

"Affirmative, Director. The molecular scrambler is in place and humming along quite nicely."

"Molecular scram-...?"

"More commonly referred to as the 'egg scrambler', Director. It's an electronically powered demarcation line that essentially and effectively disassembles cell structure upon contact, whether of human, alien or synthetically engineered.

"That, coupled with the room's built-in laser and ultra-sonic shields, form an impenetrable perimeter the likes of which man has never seen."

The Director nodded amiably before turning back towards Marvella. "Drop 'em."

Both Marvella and Mystic tensed in unison, then slumped in obvious relief. Each then released a heavy sigh, as if an enormous weight had been lifted.

Descending onto his tiptoes, Mystic struck a Ballerina's pose while staring directly at the director, whose own attention seemed divided between the entombed cargo and Warden Terry.

"Simply *wonder-bra*. Now to more vital matters...when's the next shuttle due out,

Director?"

"Uh…Warden Terry, should I do the honors or would you prefer…?" The Warden turned away from the glass dome and fronted the two costumed figures, although he found he could only maintain prolonged eye contact with the heroine.

"Afraid you two are gonna be with us a bit longer than originally planned."

"Explanation please," Mystic groaned through pursed, pouting lips.

"We've got a high-level storm headed this way, and it's gaining strength the closer it nears."

Allowing her head to droop until she stared down at her own glimmering boots, Marvella started to speak but found she'd simply lost the motivation needed to create a suitable knee-jerk response. Besides, she realized any bitching she might do would likely pale in comparison to the incoming barrage from her erstwhile partner.

"We saw nothing but clear blue on the way in, Warden," Mystic grumbled, waving his hands in a counterclockwise spin, "Surely we could make it out of here *long* before it arrives."

"Surely we could, Mystic, but the impending storm is coming from that same direction. We'd fly right into the damn thing. Not all of us have the power of flight, you know," the Director interrupted sourly.

"*Damn* it! I've got an on-line chat with *Shining Stars of America dot com* tomorrow morning in Chi town, and a personal appearance scheduled at the Rock and Roll Hall of Fame ceremonies in Cleveland the day after that," Mystic whined, his hands perched atop his hips in full 'sassy' mode.

"Someone is going to pay dearly for this boy's time, I can promise you that, Director Willis."

"Mystic, I won't apologize for the weather. It's really beyond anyone's control..."

"An unplanned layover on *Convict Island* is not my idea of spending my time constructively."

"Never fear, you'll receive a full share plus-"

"...and by God, there'll be hide peeled and hell to pay if I'm not off this godforsaken sand dune in time for more important obligations."

"Mystic...you'll get a full share plus double-time. Your agent has been contacted and has rescheduled the aforementioned appointments..."

"...because this man's time is precious, goddamn it...and he doesn't enjoy being trifled wi-...uh...(paused).... *double* time? Well, why didn't you say so before, Director Willis? It is always Mystic's sworn duty to see each and every assignment through to my client's full satisfaction," he concluded with a fabricated smile birthed from the highest possible level of hypocrisy.

"Show me to my quarters, Warden."

"Oh, fuck a duck," Marvella grumbled aloud, covering her eyes with a gloved hand.

"The bridge is officially yours, Doctor James," the Warden said, giving the metallic cocoon housing their newest guest a final, worrisome glance.

The doctor nodded without a verbal reply, continuing to peck away at the keyboard while his two cohorts stood on either side of him, all three studying the main monitor as if deeply entranced as the screen filled with rapidly changing numerical codes.

"Forget it, Warden," Mystic quipped, "...the only way to get the attention of *their* kind is to turn on an old classic episode of *Star Trek*."

The foursome then quietly departed what had earlier been dubbed '*Sector E*' by official Pentagon memorandum, the Warden providing the necessary exit codes; codes which were purposely different than the access codes which allowed entry. For reasons of what had been termed '*Worldwide* Security', the access and exit codes would be changed on a daily basis, and issued solely to the Warden and Doctor James. No other personnel assigned to Eagle Island would be given free access, including the Chief Correctional Officer. As for outside authorization, the list was extremely short but esteemed and included the United States Chief of Staff; the Surgeon General, and the President himself. Rounding out the exclusive list of VIP's were the President of the UN and the Prime Minister of Great Britain.

Just hours before the chopper's arrival, Warden Charles V. Terry had felt his gut tighten an additional notch while being briefed via satellite concerning the extra security measures. Leaning back in his padded leather chair just moments after the briefing had concluded, he'd removed a framed photograph from his middle desk drawer. A photo taken just weeks earlier and showcasing his wife of seventeen years, she of the still-girlish figure and radiant, toothy smile, and their young teenaged son, he of the recently acquired braces and thin, gawky build. Less than a year earlier, he'd been offered the job as Warden at a newly built maximum-security unit just outside Portland, Oregon. Despite a slight

253

raise in salary and the draw of a substantially less stressful situation, he'd declined, much to the chagrin of his wife.

"You have to understand, honey," he'd told her over coffeeat their kitchen table just hours after his decision had been made final, "...being the head man at Eagle Island is special...a one-of-a-kind position. It's a title no one else on the planet can claim. Not an easy title to relinquish. Not ashamed to say, I'm damn proud of it. Besides, I'm...more comfortable with my own kind, whether it be the bad or good element."

Replacing the photo a few moments later, Warden Terry found himself doubting the wisdom of that fateful decision for only the second time in his lengthy tenure.

The Guardsman greeted the group as they exited the domed walkway leading into the main building's second floor, standing in an 'at ease' pose with his meticulously chiseled features showcased ever more dramatically beneath the piercing glare of the fluorescent lighting flooding the narrow hallway.

"Boss."

Stepping to the side as to allow his chief CO a clear visual of the trio who'd been following his lead, the Warden nodded and gestured with a thumb towards Director Willis.

"Guardsman, this is Deputy Director Willis of the FBI Special Ops Branch Director, this is my head security officer and chief CO."

"Sir."

"Guardsman. I've read your file. Very impressive resume, I must say."

As they exchanged niceties, neither man was privy to a barely audible gasp originating from just a few feet beyond the director's position. Unseen by all but Mystic, who whirled about and shot her a curious glance, Marvella coughed lightly into one gloved hand and then nervously cleared her throat.

"And the two individuals who played escort for our new arrival...," the Warden began before being cut off in mid-pause.

"Well, well, well...tall, dark, handsome *and* wearing body tight spandex. Honored to make your acquaintance, Captain of the Guards-man Sir," Mystic chirped, practically shoving the director to one side as he sprinted forward with an outstretched hand.

"Um...this is Mystic. Mystic, my...uh...chief CO," the Warden babbled, red-faced.

Reaching out, the larger man more slapped than actually shook the smaller one's hand.

"I've seen...snippets of the...um...your television program. Very...interesting."

"Thanks loads. Everyone says I'm better looking in person though. My god, how do you stay so...cut? You're like a comic book panel sketch come to life!"

"Let's just say I could legally be charged rent in several gyms."

"I don't doubt it. Im-pres-sive..."

Just as the Guardsman started to step back from Mystic's gradual invasion of his personal space, he caught his first clear glimpse of the costumed form standing between the Warden and Director Willis. As it was, he took a single long stride forward instead, all but pinning Mystic to the nearby wall.

"Marvella. I…I'd heard rumors of your retirement from the business," he said warmly, smiling as his hand wrapped around her own. Dwarfed by at least a half-foot in height, she was forced to tilt her head back in order to meet his gaze, while desperately fighting the urge to collapse onto his tightly muscled chest in a fit of wrenching sobs.

"Let's just say I found inactivity a true bitch, G-man. So you're the head screw in this joint?"

"Well, you know…pays the bills."

"I'm sure, and then some, but don't tell me you don't miss the thrill of cruising the concrete jungle for bad guys."

"Be my guest. *You* catch 'em…*I'll* lock 'em away."

Sauntering forward with his head cocked quizzically, Mystic rotated his gaze from one to the other several times before locking on Marvella's dreamy expression.

"Oh, you two know one another?"

The Guardsman paused, answering only after it was evident Marvella had ignored the query altogether.

"Blazed the same trail together on occasion, you might say. It's a small world, spandex-wise."

"Director, my office is just down the hall," the Warden injected while again taking the lead, "The Guardsman will see you two get bedded down for the duration of the storm. I'll keep everyone abreast of its progress."

Once the Warden and Director Willis had made their way past, The Guardsman gestured towards a nearby door marked 'STAIRS'. "This way, my lady…and uh…Mystic."

"No need to differentiate between the two, G-Man. Old greenie tights over there is just one of the gals…" Marvella said, still clasping to The Guardsman's hand as they neared the exit.

"Isn't she simply the bitchiest?" Mystic asked cheerily, bringing up the rear while ogling the tightly clinched butt-cheeks of Eagle Island's head correctional officer.

***

"Really, really good to see you, Luke. Nothing like a familiar face in a strange place."

Removing his cowl, The Guardsman took a seat on the guestroom's lone recliner as Marvella dug into the small satchel she'd brought along, removing personal items and placing them onto a small oak dresser.

"Got to admit, Leah, I almost jumped out of my boots when the Warden named you as an escort. Don't the powers that be realize…I mean, didn't they check your background and connect the dots?"

"He's *here*, isn't he?" she whimpered, her voice briefly cracking with emotion.

The Guardsman paused for several moments, as if to avoid the question outright.

"Arrived less than a week ago."

"Damn…I had a feeling. Hoped like *hell* I was wrong," she sighed, unfolding a matching tee shirt and shorts and placing them inside the dresser's top drawer, "Nope, the fact Ben and I were once teammates was never mentioned. Evidently, they foresaw no potential conflict of interest mission-wise…'cause here I stand."

"Guess they weren't privy to the fact you and

257

he were…more than simply teammates," he injected rather timidly, carefully studying her response as she'd reached up to remove her own mask.

"In truth, why would it matter? It isn't like there's a snowball's chance in hell he and I will 'rekindle' the flame under these circumstances."

"True enough. No such animal as visitation on Eagle Island."

"We were briefed ad nauseam. This place makes Rikers Island look like Epcot."

"No denials. Can't afford a crack in the armor. Not even a hairline fracture. These aren't petty thieves, crackheads, or even your commonplace homicidal maniacs. Big, bad hombres, one and all."

"You…live here twenty-four-seven? I mean, all the time or…"

"Trade secrets I can and must not reveal in fear of a possible security breach," he responded with a single digit raised airborne.

"Got'cha," she paused, "…teleportation pods?"

"Leah…" he scolded, waiving the finger back and forth "Sorry. This deuced female curiosity, you know."

"We…have our methods. Change of subject, please."

"So…how is he, Luke?" she asked after a short pause, keeping her back turned to him while refolding the same shirt for the third time.

"He's holding up. You know our Benji. Same old ornery, pissed-off psycho with the heart of gold."

"Have you talked to him about…you know, why he's here?"

The Guardsman arose and stood behind her,

258

watching her reflection in the dresser's wide mirror while gently placing a hand atop her right shoulder. As had been the case when they'd been teammates some four years earlier, he found himself pleasantly entranced by her exotic beauty and icy cool charms. He doubted the heterosexual male existed with a built-in immunity to either.

"Don't go there, Leah. It serves no purpose, believe me, except grief." She reached back and touched his hand, tapping it lightly.

"I know you're right. It's just that...being partnered with Mystic...and now to be walking on the same ground with both of them. It's...just beyond weird.

"Still," she concluded, whirling about with a smile that did little to mask the misery behind her moistened eyes, "...it's dam good to see you, G-Man. I'm usually not very keen on reminiscing, but you were one of the few within the RS ranks whose company I actually enjoyed. Just you and...Ben, really, though I have to admit that *Johnny Reb* could send me into involuntary hysterics on occasion."

Laughing heartily, he backed away and fell back into the recliner.

"J-Reb was a hoot alright. It was like bunking with the *Three Stooges* whenever that cornpone cracker was teamed with Benji and Dark Claw. Don't believe I've ever laughed harder."

"Made a hell of a team on the battlefield. We had a scrappy bunch back in the day, G-man. Put 'em up against any second-tier group on the globe."

"You and me both, kiddo. Ah, the good times can never last, especially in this business."

Stepping over to the recliner, Marvella kneeled

down and placed a hand on his forearm.

"I was really sorry to hear about your wife, Luke. I…was on assignment in South America at the time. You know I would've made the services if I'd only known where and wh-…."

"Not a problem, Leah. We… held a private service, just the families. Appreciate the thought."

"This hero crap isn't what it's cracked up to be sometimes," she replied wearily, turning back towards the dresser, "…seems it ends up taking away a hell of a lot more than it gives in the long run."

Tilting his head back, The Guardsman closed his eyes before stifling a sneeze with a raised finger.

"Substantially more cons than pros most days, for certain, but hey…it's what we do, Leah. Better yet, it's what we were *chosen* to do. Lynn knew what she was getting into when we married, just as I realized the danger I was placing her in. It's just that…you never truly believe the two worlds will collide. We took the chance and… paid the price."

"Is that why you took the position here?"

"It played a part. The timing was right, the money was good. I needed to reflect. What better place for isolation, right?"

She nodded without reply, running her fingers through the length of her wavy black locks.

"So…" she asked after a short pause, "…where can a girl find a hot meal on this little beach resort?"

"Allow me to escort you to the staff mess hall, my dear," he announced, leaping to his feet and bowing dramatically, "emphasis on the word 'mess'. Translation: don't over-expect in terms of actual flavor. Budget restraints, you understand."

"Not a problem. Right now a bag of soggy M& M's would be the culinary equivalent to a rib-eye steak and baked potato."

"Now there's a request I can fulfill. Vending machines are located on floor number one."

As they made their way down the hall towards the closest elevator, Marvella leaned in and gently planted a shoulder into her former teammate's midsection, who in turn reached out and lightly jabbed her with an elbow.

Some twenty yards beyond, Mystic had exited his own quarters and witnessed their playful antics. He heard Marvella giggle as they'd turned a far corner, waiting until he was certain the pair had entered the unseen elevator before stepping away from his assigned sleeping quarters.

"Buddies reunited. Isn't that just precious?" he whispered with a scowl, rearing his head back and sniffing the air as if detecting a rather unpleasant odor, "...oh well, there are times it is indeed preferable to be the bridesmaid instead of the bride."

Curling his legs beneath him, he then floated down the hall in his trademark lotus pose, a twenty-first century genie seemingly in search of a suitable master with which to ply his trade.

***

Part V:

Calm Before The Storm

"Now that's one nasty looking cell. These

261

images up to date, Warden?" Warden Terry leaned back and took several sips of coffee before responding. The director hovered over his desk like a feeding vulture, the man's pasty features illuminated ever further by the monitor's bright glow.

"NWS updates every ten seconds."

"How far would you say?"

"Between four and six hours, max. Things rolling along at…," he leaned forward and squinted, "…forty-five to fifty MPH."

"I take it there's a ND checklist you adhere to?"

"ND?"

"Natural Disaster, Warden," Director Willis said with just a hint of sarcasm. "Um, there's really no need for a checklist, being there'd be only a single item listed."

The director turned about with a perplexed expression.

"Retractable dome," the Warden continued, spreading his arms to indicate a wide berth, "…covers the entire island. Air and watertight."

Shaking his head slightly from side to side, the director's contorted features only seemed to intensify.

"The entire isla-…not a cheap feature, I'd imagine."

"Staggering, from what I understand, but undeniably justifiable. There's a high price to pay for maintaining a safe distance between the general population and the element of evil we store on this dune."

The other man maintained his silent scowl, as if listening to a particularly bad lie being told.

"Spent many years in this chair, Director Willis, and believe me when I say, the dome effect isn't just some fancy technical frill. Taxpayers money very, *very* well spent, yes sir."

"Well, you know better than I, Warden. Just seems…a bit extreme is all. I mean, the entire place is constructed in concrete blocks. I wouldn't think a funnel cloud would loosen a single pebble."

Rising from the chair with coffee cup in hand, the warden gestured for the other man to take the seat.

"You misunderstand the most vital of the dome's uses, director," he continued, walking over to refill his cup, "…that of deterrent. Having that impenetrable bad boy in place is the ultimate lock-down measure. It's every correctional officer's wet dream come to life."

"I didn't consider that angle," the director replied, leaning back in the leather recliner with his eyes again peeled on the swirling, multi-colored Doppler image filling the monitor. "Pardon my ignorance, Warden. Guess I just wasn't thinking from a security standpoint."

"Don't sweat it, director. Paranoia is *my* business."

"So there have been escape attempts, then?"

"Director Willis," the warden said after stirring several packs of sugar into the steaming black liquid, "…we've housed mutants, synthetic/human hybrids…even an extraterrestrial or two. With such a…variety of guests and the…special endowments each brings to the table, such incidents are rare but do flare up occasionally."

"So the dome is the last line of defense?"

"Pretty much, although I have a standing order to retract at the first sign of breech at any level. Hell of a weapon to have at my disposal…a real burden buffer, you might say."

The director continued to monitor the computer screen as the other man took a seat in one of the adjoining chairs opposite the desk.

"Although, there is the double-edged sword aspect of having such a convenient crunch at one's disposal."

Cocking an eyebrow, the warden sipped his coffee before responding. "Double-edged sword?"

"Well, once you implement the dome, not only are the inmates locked down, but so is the staff…including yourself."

"In terms of inmate uprisings and subsequent takeovers, let's just say there's a built-in failsafe securely in place. I'm… not at liberty to discuss it further," the Warden said with a sly grin just as the hotline lit up to the right of the computer monitor.

"Excuse me, director…that definitely isn't a tele-marketer calling," he said, walking over to re-take his chair as the other man quickly hopped up and side-stepped over. In one fluid, graceful movement, the warden scooped the phone from the octagon-shaped console while simultaneously leaning back and propping his highly polished dress shoes atop the squared edge of the desktop.

"Terry here…yes, sir. Safe and sound. No problems. Director Willis and his charges did an outstanding job (pausing to shoot the director a wink) …

"Yes, sir. Offloaded and secured…Doctor James and his team are in control as of about a half-

264

hour ago.

"Yes, sir…it looks like a real foundation-shaker. Right now it looks to be about eighty or so miles from our Eastern shore. I'm planning on doming her up within the hour.

"Yes, sir…I'll keep you informed. Thank you, sir."

Departing the chair with a pained grunt, the warden clamped his hands together and curled them inward, then stretched out with both arms, cracking his knuckles noisily.

"Headed to the command center to institute *Condition Yellow,* which is basically a notice to all CO's to insure all inmates are tucked safely away in their cells 'til further notice. Just a formality until we go into *Blue* and raise the dome. "You're more than welcome to remain here if you'd like, director, or take a sabbatical in your assigned room. You'll find Dish TV and internet access. Might even be a stocked wet bar if I remember correct-…"

"Actually, would it be okay if I tagged along, Warden Terry?"

"Sure, if you'd like. Don't expect anything along the lines of excitement, though. Pretty mundane stuff."

The director leaned in and shot the monitor a final glance before following the other man outside.

"Definitely going to be the mother of all tidal waves."

"Not to worry, Director Willis, as far as we're concerned, it might as well be a spattering of wind-blown bird shit landing on the side of a Carrier Destroyer."

Several hundred feet of hallway, one brief

elevator ride and two separate entry codes later, they stood inside a spacious conference room inundated with computers, TV monitors, and electronic visual aids containing blueprints and maps of the island from every possible viewpoint.

A trio of uniformed personnel manned assigned stations, two male and one female. The female, a petite strawberry blonde sporting a deep-creased scar on her left cheekbone, sat behind what looked to be the main console and observed the storm from a large screen monitor. She turned and acknowledged the men's presence with a stiff, robotic nod while simultaneously typing onto an ergonomic keyboard and speaking into a headset mike.

After a moment, she removed the headset and turned towards them. "Storms within thirty-five clicks, sir. About that time?"

"Just about. Officer Mays, this is Deputy Director Willis, FBI."

She repeated the same mechanical nod as before, her stoic expression unchanged.

"Bring up the cell sensors, Mays. Let's get a quick head count."

The officer whirled back around and flicked a series of switches from a nearby code pad, then tilted the chair back a bit as a separate monitor lowered itself from a sealed cubicle within the ceiling.

Addressing the director, the warden gestured towards the monitor flashing on in purplish segments before settling onto a series of blocked images, each containing a single red dot.

"It's much like infrared, though on a much

266

more technical scale Each block represents a cell; each dot the inmate contained within. Since the...*unusual* DNA structures of some of our inmates eliminate the use of body heat as a scanning tool, this particular device utilizes chemical substance and mass equations to pinpoint their location within the block. In other words, they can neither run nor hide from the ever-roving eye of Big Brother...that's me."

"All present and accounted for, Sir," the young CO announced sternly. "Confirm with The Guardsman and then get on the internal horn and let the staff know we're now in Condition Yellow status."

"Yes, sir."

"Just wanted to make sure no one was in the free zone before we locked 'er down."

"Free zone?" the director asked, still scanning the monitor through squinted eyes.

"The workout room. We call it the free zone simply because it's the only area the inmates are allowed access to other than their individual cells."

"Must make it easier on you and your staff."

Resting his chin atop a propped fist, the Warden had positioned himself behind a separate drop-down screen displaying the approaching storm.

"How's that?"

"Well, I would think having each inmate assigned to permanent administrative segregation status eliminates a wide range of possible...incidents."

"True, although you have to understand, Eagle Island is hardly your run-of-the-mill correctional

267

facility. No way we could afford to give the inmates free run of the place. There isn't a max security site on the planet that could successfully hold these bad apples in place. Many tried...all failed, and failed miserably."

"I see," the director replied, stepping over to join the other man in studying the mutated bright orange mass dominating the screen. "Have to admit, I'd always thought Eagle Island to be nothing more than urban legend. Just about fell out of my chair when I read the specifics of this assignment. Thought somebody was seriously yanking my chain."

"We have our reasons for anonymity, director. If our existence was ever verified or our exact location ever divulged to the outside world, there'd be daily...possibly *hourly* attempts to bust these folks out."

Turning to face the other man, the Warden began digging in his left pants pocket, eventually retrieving a small pill bottle.

"You...were briefed on the *matter sweep* procedure, I presume?" Director Willis nodded, switching his focus to the young female CO, who was speaking into her head set while tapping out a series of numerical codes on a tiny keypad to the left of her computer terminal.

"Um...yes. We were told all memories of our visit would be magically voided upon our departure."

"*Chemically* eradicated might be a better choice of words, but you get the gist."

"The ultimate security measure. What about you...your staff? Surely they don't subject you to

268

the same treatment."

"Permanent staff, no. Let's just say our clearances are on the highest of government levels, meaning any breech of site info results in the harshest of judicial punishments."

"Sir?" the female CO interrupted, covering her headset mike with one hand.

Warden Terry turned toward her and nodded. "Condition Yellow instigated, Officer Mays?"

"Affirmative, sir. The Guardsman has been notified, as well as the remainder of on-site *and* off-site personnel."

"Good. Have the Guardsman meet me at my office pronto. After which, I'll contact you with the dome activation code and we'll proceed with closure."

"Yes, sir, right away."

"My god," the director chimed in just as the warden had walked by and towards the command center's lone entrance/exit door, "that thing's growing more ominous by the minute."

The warden paused just long enough to give the monitor a final once-over, his expression one of casual concern, his tone the epitome of cool. The swirling mass churned and spun, its base appearing substantially wider than just moments earlier.

"Not to worry, director, you can leave your umbrella at home. Let's get back to my digs. Have to pow-wow with my Chief CO before we officially lock this burg down for the duration."

"Lead the way, warden," the director said a bit nervously, trailing the other man out of the room by less than a full step. "Color me your shadow 'til this mess blows over."

***

At almost precisely the moment Deputy Director W. Paul Willis and Warden Charles V. Terry had exited the Eagle Island Command Center, the inhabitants of Cell Block D each experienced a momentary surge of euphoria; a mysterious wave of exhilaration that lasted but the briefest of moments.

At the time, each had been engulfed in various forms of tedium while blissfully oblivious to the level-five winds of change that were mere moments away.

In chronological order, cell assignment wise, the chart of inactivity had mapped out thusly:

Cell D-1:

Lying on her side while casually self-cleaning her privates with several well-placed licks, *Shetah* kept a roving eye centered on one of her favorite films, Paul Schrader's 1982 remake of the classic horror flick *'Cat People'*. With a spastic shudder, she could only relate the sensation to the finest orgasm she'd ever experienced. As the tingling at her groin and breasts receded to a dull numbness, she resumed her cleaning session beneath the cloak of a severe depression that was at least the equal of its pleasure-driven predecessor.

Cell D-2:

Sprawled lazily on his couch reading a horror collection entitled *'Reality Check'*, *Obliteration* dropped the novel onto his naked chest and sat wide-eyed as the surge shook his body like a high-

270

voltage charge, then departed just as quickly. Wearing a crooked grin that refused to fade for several moments, his only cohesive thought was of that fateful day when he'd experience the unparalleled elation only permanent liberation would bring.

Cell D-3:

Having just entered his cleansing unit, *Anvil* had groaned aloud as a bolt of viral proportions had caused his entire body to shimmy and shake in an epileptic-like spasm. After the joyous jolt had subsided, he'd been forced to wipe away thin layers of drool from both the right corner of his mouth and the tip of his chin.

Cell D-4:

While performing a series of stretches that had become a nightly routine, *Screaming Eagle* had practically collapsed into a curled heap, arching his back into a u-shape just as the unexpected rush had begun to abate. For just an instant, he'd hearkened back to a better time; a time when so much had been fresh and new and lain out in front of him. A time of innocence when both conscience and law enforcement blotters were unblemished by the horrid decisions of the future.

Cell D-5:

While masturbating to an episode from season one of *Twin Peaks* (Chinese actress Joan Chen the catalyst of his never ending lust), *The Mass* had released his grotesquely bloated manhood (having been altered to a full foot in length and near four inches in girth) and sat frozen with his mouth agape, his eyes having rolled back into his head. Upon culmination of his self-gratification efforts some moments later, the term 'anti-climactic' had rarely been more appropriate.

Cell D-7:

In stark contrast to his fellow inmates, the lethal entity known as *Black Plague* crumbled weakly onto the lead/mercury/fiberglass-based flooring of his cell, gripping his throat with one hand and the center of his chest with the other. Unlike the others, the mysterious wave bombarding his senses was neither pleasurable in context nor temporary in nature.

Never an air breather, the spreader of all things poisonous commonly referred to as the '*Toxic Shadow,*' nonetheless gagged and spat asif choking from lack of oxygen, his pupil-less eyes bugging as if on the verge of ejecting themselves from their narrow, deep set sockets. As seconds passed and the building pressure within his chest and skull only seemed to intensify, a being whose true origin would forever remain a mystery collapsed into a deep coma, or at least the equivalent in human terms.

Cell D-8:

Standing at the center of the cell with his arms

spread wide and his feet shoulder-length apart, *Mind Sweep* tilted his head back and spewed forth a silent, anguish-fueled scream. Falling forward onto his hands and knees, the bland, stoic expression that was his trademark had melted away like a mask sewn from liquefied tar, replaced by a contorted grimace normally associated with someone on the verge of a hysterical crying jag. Purple-shaded tears flowed from the corners of both eyes as he bowed his head and began to sob. It would be a full three minutes before Mind Sweep's head would slowly arise, his chapped, peeling lips curled into a malicious sneer as his torso stiffened and flexed with a newfound reinvigoration. He felt an inner pilot light burst into red-hot embers; his veins bulging and his temples throbbing with a pent-up energy he hadn't felt since that day some six years earlier when The Silver Surfer had so unceremoniously stripped him of both his dignity and birthright. As shock waves of electrified air popped and cracked all around him, the new and seemingly improved Mind Sweep decided to put his newfound powers to the test.

With nothing more elaborate than the twitch of one eye, said experiment was executed to complete success with frightening precision. Like a haggard parent reunited with a long-lost child, the fresh flow of tears that followed were birthed from a heightened level of bliss heretofore untested within human limitations.

CELLS D-9 - D-13:

Undisclosed

273

Cell D-14:

Dozing in and out from a fitful series of nightmares, the majority of which had rerun the deaths of comrades and enemies alike in both slow and fast, frenzied motion, Ben's tattered subconscious eventually settled upon a more peaceful landscape mercifully void of death cries and shredded viscera.

Sharing a soft, netted hammock with the warmth of Leah's naked torso pressed against his own, he first felt then glanced down to view his own budding erection. Responding in kind, Leah had reached to stroke him, at first gently and then with increased firmness and speed. He tasted the sweetness of her as their tongues met, clamping his massive right hand over both her breasts simultaneously and slowly working his way beneath the tight spandex halter she wore.

As their passion level increased, Leah reached with her free hand and planted it at the base of his neck, shoving his head forward. Unable to breathe as he felt her tongue seem to thicken and elongate inside his mouth, Ben noticed the taste of her saliva had turned instantly bitter, almost acidic. Consequently, the tender yet firm texture of her breasts had grown inexplicably hard and scaly, like sun-worn leather.

His groin throbbed and ached from the increased pressure being applied, and a sticky warmth trailed between his shoulder blades and to the pit of his back from deep puncture wounds she'd dug into his neck. As her bloated, slug-like tongue

274

filled his throat like a squirming larva sac, he was finally able to pull her clawed hand from his throat. He heard her animalistic growls while separating her head and torso from his own with several forceful shoves. Struggling for a sense of balance as the hammock threatened to flip sideways, his forearms, neck and upper chest began to burn and throb as if from a thousand bee stings. Leah wrestled and fought his grip, her face and upper body a frenzied blur of spastic movement, kicking forth with both feet while slapping and clawing with curved, razor-sharp talons that better resembled those of a bird of prey. He became aware of a thick fog engulfing them, effectively erasing the landscape beyond the hammock in a cool, ivory mist.

Finally able to still her upper body by wrapping the whole of his left hand around her narrow throat, Ben felt his chest instantly tighten as if steel banding had been wound around his rib cage. Despite the decade-plus passing since their last face-to-face and the countless battlefields he'd occupied since, identification was instantaneous. With her taunt, wiry frame, elongated appendages and a hairless, oval shaped skull complete with bony, spiked quills styled in Mohawk fashion, the mutant female shapeshifter known as 'Shemeleon' was hardly a forgettable character within one's subconscious. Holding her at bay with the palm of one hand cupping her forehead and a clinched fist pressed against her breastbone, Ben first noticed the dozens of horizontal slash marks decorating his hands, wrists, and forearms. As she raked a claw across his cheekbone, he felt the skin flay apart in

275

shredded flaps.

"You're fucked, pal.... don't you get it?" she growled through gnashed, bloodied teeth filed to a fine, sharpened point, like carpenter's nails, "though it's true dreams won't kill ya, there's something waiting on the outside that most assuredly will."

He removed his fist from her chest just long enough to toss a forceful jab towards the center of her snarling face. A crisp snapping sound ensued and he pulled his hand away to see several of her spear-shaped choppers embedded into his knuckles like bulletin board tacks.

"Dead as a hammer, buddy-boy...ya just don't know it yet..." she garbled, spitting a mouthful of blood and acidic bile into his eyes. Reeling back as the hammock tilted hard to the right before flipping upside down, the discomfort at his groin increased ten-fold even as his eyes and face were lit ablaze as if doused with toxic waste.

Landing atop what felt like a mound of moistened sand, his vision still badly blurred, Ben instinctively reached to soothe the source of his pain, his oversized fingers acting as insect 'feelers'; groping, fumbling and dancing in and around his groin.

"Something amiss, big boy? Feel as though you've lost a little weight south of the border?" he heard the Shemeleon quip in true comedic Freddy Krueger fashion, though she was no longer visible through the soupy murk.

"My...m-my...s-son...of a b-bitch...motherfu...sh-shiiiit..." he cursed, lifting both his hands toward his face and studying the

276

shocking results through magically cleared orbs.

Looking through splayed fingers soaked in dark, dripping crimson, he watched her reappear from the mist like a vengeful spirit from an open grave, gripping his severed manhood in one claw while the other pointed up and outward, seemingly gesturing towards someone or something directly behind him.

Cupping his ravaged groin with both hands, Ben was whirled about as if riding atop a mobile platform. The grayish mass loomed overhead like a massive tidal wave, somehow halted in mid-break, its curled tip resembling a giant pendulum blade poised to strike a fatal blow.

"I so wish it could've been different, lover...but I'm afraid everyone's fate is equally sealed..." he heard Leah's voice sob just a split-second before the mass shot forward and descended with deadly speed, cutting into his exposed thighs like a butcher's cleaver into thawed pork. As he was being swept away like a feather in a funnel cloud, Ben watched his severed legs float away like cordwood. Flailing his arms through the glutinous gel, he attempted to swim but found it an impossibility, especially without the benefit of lower legs to propel himself forward. He managed a single desperate gasp just as his head was yanked below the surface by a violent undertow.

Waking with the left side of his face partially submerged in a mound of steaming sand, he pushed himself up onto his knees with true Herculean effort.

He found himself decked out in full Force garb, complete with the dark black combat boots that had been a part of his original costume some fifteen

277

years earlier.

After taking a quick, panic-laced inventory to ensure his genitals and legs were indeed still intact, he shaded his eyes from the sun and stared straight ahead. The detention center buildings stood erect yet strangely at an angle, as if the structures themselves were gradually sinking into the belly of the island itself.

Standing shakily, he took a half step back and heard a muffled crunch beneath his boot. Turning about as he lifted the foot, he stared down at the shattered fragments of fossilized bone for only a moment before lifting his head and scanning the beachhead.

Where once the open sea had dominated, a barren desert now lay. A desert filled with an assortment of dried, bleached bones lain out in a neat, orderly fashion as far as the eyes could see. As Ben trekked forward, careful to sidestep as many of the scattered human remains as possible, he heard a horrid series of banshee-like wails originate from the detention center's main building. It wasn't until he leaned down to inspect a cowl-covered skull, soon realizing it was his own, that the source of the never-ending screams became apparent. He whirled about, protectively tucking the Desolation Outlaw skull tightly to his chest, and saw his own nude, leg-less body floating overhead at warped speed, carried forward by a grayish blob, swallowing the landscape beyond like a recently painted mural.

Tossing his own skull aside like discarded trash, he sprinted forward in a crimson rage, pumping his fists madly while prepping to leap directly into the heart of the beast.

As he sailed airborne and twisted his body to allow his fists to make first contact, the faint outline of a face appeared within the mass; a grinning entity with soulless eyes and baring teeth as wide as a tracker-trailer. Just before all went mercifully dark, Ben realized with crystal clear clarity this was the face of whatever evil lurked within the walls of Eagle Island Detention Center, and the face of the one who meant to collect all of their souls.

"Som' bitch…," he grumbled, messaging his neck while rising from the cot's crumpled outline. Stumbling over to splash hisface with cool sink water, he felt a vague soreness in his arms and thighs he could only relate to battle fatigue. "Gotta find a way to cut the power cord to whatever's fueling these damned nightmares. Drainin' the fire outta me."

Taking a seat on the toilet's cold metallic surface, he had just begun to ponder the origin of his many pains when a mental shock wave seized his senses in a vise, causing him to roll to the floor even as his bladder continued to empty.

*…unnnnnddddeeerrrrrrr ggggggrrrrooooooouuuunnnnnddddddddd…leeeevvvv vvveeelllllllllll…toooooppppppp ……
seeeeeeeeeeee……crrrrrrrrreeeeeettttttttt…*

…the voice muttered in a drawn-out stutter eerily familiar from just days before…

…sallllllllllvvvvvvvaaaaaaaatioooooonnnnn…oo onnnnnnnlllllllly…sallllllllllvvvv aaaaaaatiooooooooooonnnnnn…

As it slowly petered out, the final two words spoken had been less stilted and more easily

279

comprehended, as if a different voice altogether had intervened to assist in clarifying the original text. As he rolled onto his back, coated in his own urine but temporarily unable to find enough strength to rise, Ben reran those final words in his mind until he actually began unconsciously speaking them aloud.

"*Level X*", he muttered weakly before passing out once again.

***

"How's the grub, my lady?"

"Luke, after a day and a half of MRE's, I'm hardly in a position to complain. In fact, I can honestly state this is the best damn tuna on rye I've ever tasted."

Sipping a packaged fruit beverage through a straw, The Guardsman regarded his former teammate with a barely hidden curiosity. Having removed their respective cowls, they sat alone at the center of the relatively spacious dining hall with the faint sound of Musac playing overhead.

"Coffee's pretty damn fine, as well. Might make me re-think turning to a life of crime."

"Really? Guess I just take the outstanding cuisine for granted," he grinned, briefly turning his attention to the small porthole window on the wall to their left.

"Growing dark out there. You'd think it was dusk instead of a quarter past noon."

"Can't believe our timing," Marvella commented between bites, "then again, *Murphy's Law* seems to be laying the groundwork on this particular mission."

They sipped and chewed in silence for several moments, the first echoes of distant thunderclaps filling the void.

"Wouldn't serve a purpose, anyway, would it?" Marvella asked, pushing her plate to a far corner of the table.

"Come again?"

"Level with me, G-Man...they really wipe our memories before we leave?"

"Blank Slate City. The last thing you'll recall is loading the chopper that brought you here," he replied, holding up three fingers in a 'scouts honor' gesture, "I shit you not."

"So...kind of makes a moot point out of...what I was thinking of asking you." After a short pause, The Guardsman reached over and placed a hand on top of hers.

"Not only would you not recall a single word of the conversation, but even that you saw him at all."

"I just..." she shrugged, blushing like a girl fifteen years her junior, "...well, you know. I can't help but wonder. It's just that...it's obvious I'll never have another...chance to...see or speak to him."

"I understand the temptation, Leah. If I were in your shoes, I might well be hatching a breakout plan. All that aside, such a reckless, borderline insane act would not only get me fired, but toss both our asses in a sling with the feds, big time."

Pulling her hand free, Leah pushed away from the table and stood up, then stepped over to the portal and stared out into the looming darkness.

"Damn. Talk about fooling yourself. I thought I could handle this without...*damn*."

281

Going against natural instinct, The Guardsman fought the urge to rise and console her with a touch or gentle hug.

"Give yourself a break, Leah. You loved the man," he replied after a short, awkward pause, during which time the occasional thunderclap grew noticeably louder.

"Yeah, well...such is the price one pays, Luke," she sighed, wearing a grim smile as she turned back around to face him. "Why couldn't I have fallen for an accountant or a UPS Driver? If you asked me, Cupid is one demented little a-hole."

"Not exactly our choice."

"I'd argue that point if I had the energy," she said, reclaiming her seat and taking another quick sip of coffee, "You know, I lectured myself long and hard about staying strong. I knew what accepting this mission meant. Sure, I needed the money. Another notation on the ol' government resume doesn't hurt either. The pentagon bigwigs always remember a job well done when a similar situation arises. But now...well, I question my motives and... the artificial logic I'd used to talk myself into coming here."

"You had no clue you'd end up here, Leah, much less that Ben was a resident. It's *done*. Beating yourself to a pulp serves no purpose."

Nodding solemnly, Marvella stared into her coffee mug while tapping the tabletop with meticulously manicured fingernails.

"Ben Thomason didn't murder anyone, Luke, and you damn well know it," she finally commented, looking up and into her former teammate's eyes with a steely intensity he'd forgotten she possessed.

"I'd be hard pressed to disagree. But you'll have to admit, you and I are undoubtedly prejudiced," he replied sternly while maintaining eye contact.

"Maybe so, but past history should account for something. He's been one of the good guys for far too long to be tossed onto this concrete and steel shit-heap on nothing but circumstantial evidence."

"I get the feeling you don't place much confidence in your newfound partner."

"Mystic is *all* about Mystic. Cares more about his media and public rep than human lives," she said with a deep frown, "...person like that can't be trusted. They'll eliminate or *terminate* whoever or whatever opposes their personal agenda. You've met the type."

"Yeah, but he seems pretty damn harmless."

"Don't let the *queer eye for the spandex guy* act fool you. That's one seriously dangerous closet queen, G-Man."

"Thanks for the warning, my lady. I'll keep an eye on the little butt-bandit from here on out, but not too close an eye...if you get my meaning. Don't want to give the indication that I'm flirting," he said with a smile in an obvious attempt to lighten the mood. Marvella emptied her cup and leaned back without responding as the first indications of a nearby lightning storm illuminated the room.

"You about had your fill?"

"Yeah. One more cup of Joe and I might not be able to sleep through the storm."

"I'd be happy to give you the tour, though guests are obviously restricted from certain areas.

283

Command Center is a laugh a minute. That is…if you're up to it."

Marvella nodded wearily as she stood, and each re-fitted their cowls as they stepped towards the exit.

"Think I'll take a rain-check for now. Still dizzy from the ride in, I guess."

"Not too smooth, huh?"

"Heavy duty blender set on puree, old buddy, courtesy of *the rock from hell*. Good luck with that one, whatever it turns out to be."

The door hummed ajar, and The Guardsman stepped to the side to allow her initial departure into the dimly lit corridor.

"Here's hoping the worst is over," he replied, shrugging after she'd shot him a knowing glance.

"I know, I know…Murphy's Law is large and in charge."

As they made their way down the lengthy hall towards still another set of elevators, the thick stone walls around them would periodically vibrate as if besieged by mild aftershocks of a recent earthquake.

"What's causing that?" Marvella asked, steadying herself by stiff-arming the nearest section of wall.

Staring into the tiled ceiling, The Guardsman looked mildly bewildered. "Dome's closing already. Chief sure isn't taking any chances with this one."

"Aw, damn. And here I was hoping to fall asleep with the sound of heavy raindrops pounding the roof."

"Only the third or fourth time in my tenure we've closed her. Gonna be quiet as a Catholic Church on Saturday night for the next few days.

Can't say I mind the downtime."

"Amen to that, brother G," Marvella added with a heavy sigh. They entered the elevator wearing identical smiles, though each experienced similar twinges in their respective midsections that neither felt obligated to share.

**

Once the initiation sequence had commenced, it took less than four minutes for the dome sequence to complete. Designed by electrical engineers, along with a *heaping* helping hand from such luminaries as Professor Charles Xavier and the Fantastic Four's Reed Richards, the dome was instantly hailed as the ultimate in security/safety measures; a quarter-mile long, one and a half mile wide miracle of science deemed virtually impenetrable following literally thousands of tests to prove otherwise.

Almost a full decade in the making, the specifics of the field's elemental breakdown, along with the gist of the creative process, had been known to bewilder the most scholarly of scientists, but could at least be simplified somewhat in laymen's terms. It was basically the equivalent of the strongest shatterproof glass magnified roughly half a billion times, with a tensile strength literally off the charts in scientific terms. Once the creative sequence began, the field built itself in brick-sized segmented squares until the entire island, both above and below sea level, were essentially domed in an air-tight environment. The duration of the field was as limited or infinite as desired, since it wasn't at all dependent on man-made power sources. Since its inception, the attempt to construct a workable model built to house increased amounts of acreage had consistently failed, dashing hopes of similar fields being used to protect whole regions from either Mother Nature's wrath or possible enemy attacks.

Gnawing on an unlit cigar and sipping a glass of ice coffee as he continued to monitorthe approaching storm on his personal PC, Warden Charles Terry seemed the picture of contentment. While one floor below and three rooms to the right...

...Deputy Director W. Paul Willis lay sprawled on his back in a state of semi-slumbering bliss, his bare feet hanging from the edges of the VIP room's spacious King-Sized bed. Just two doors to the left on the same exact floor...

...the man referred to by a mostly adoring public as the '*Master of the Mystic Realm*' floated several feet from his own room's thick carpeted floor, peering out of a circular porthole into a raging blue tide bounding into the clear force field in twenty to thirty foot swells. Just a single door down to the right...

...Marvella stared out of a similar overlook from her own assigned abode, but instead focusing her attention on the black mass of cumulonimbus fury engulfing the landscape like a CGI movie effect gone mad. A floor down and two clicks to the right...

...The Guardsman studied a monitor mounted in his main bedroom, biting his nails as his left knee shimmied and shook nervously. He scanned the inmate's cells and quickly found himself transfixed on a flurry of bizarre movement in several sectors, but mainly one cell in particular.

He had initially performed the scan out of simple boredom in lieu of wasting time watching a storm that now meant little in terms of danger. Tilting his head quizzically as the subject in question continued a bizarre one-man show/ritual that might or might not have substantial meaning, the Chief Correctional Officer of Eagle Island Detention Center then reached for the hotline headsete sitting just to the left of his headboard, hesitating for only an instant before following through with the call.

After less than two full buzzes, his supervisor answered in a weary but upbeat tone "What's up, Lucas? Your toilet back up again?"

"Something isn't right, boss," came the utterly humorless, foreboding reply, "Maybe it's just the storm, but something isn't a *damn* bit right."

CHAPTER SIX

Desolation Rising

"Almost there, Weems?"

"Just…about…another quarter inch or so and the incision…is… complete." Leaning back with a resounding sigh of relief, Doctor Ismael Weems came dangerously close to head-butting his superior, who'd been looming over him like a predatory insect. The laser canon's outer section contained a lightly padded, adjustable chair, much like a barber's chair from another era, along with a built-in PC connected to twin 'joy sticks' used to operate the laser from a distance.

"You are indeed the best rock surgeon on the planet, Ismael. I cannot tell you how thankful I am to the *University* for sparing you."

"Wouldn't have missed this for the world, Doctor James," Weems replied through a tight-lipped smile, resembling the stereotypical 'mad scientist' of Sci-Fi movie fame as the hair on both sides of his head puffed out in true cow-lick fashion, "Sincerely, it's an honor. Have to admit the Noble Prize possibilities tied to this little jewel helped to um…spice the soup…so to speak."

James returned the grin, reaching over to pat the other man's shoulder.

"I see we think along the same lines, doctor. Sincerely Ismael, I haven't a clue how to operate this monstrosity. Afraid my certification on such matters ends at the textbook stage. Out of date textbooks at that."

"Not to worry, doctor. That's what they pay *me* for."

Working the laser device via the joy sticks, Weems hunched forward and rested the sides of his head onto a padded headset, tucking his eyelids against a makeshift microscope that from a layman's point of view resembled a pair of mini binoculars.

Stationed a few yards to the left, Doctor Sullivan mumbled quietly to himself while scanning an X-rayed image of the object being dissected.

"Incision's almost complete, Sully. See anything remotely identifiable?" James asked, stepping over to study the image while peaking over the wire-rimmed spectacles propped at the tip of his pointy nose.

"I believe the storm is affecting the readouts. All the earlier images, the ones we'd considered might be skeletal fragments, have vanished completely. See here," Sullivan said, pointing at a single blurred image with a rubber pointer, "this...squared blot is all I'm getting, and it seems...larger than before. Earlier images, and I'm talking only a few minutes ago, show it as...much smaller in diameter as it is now. Weird, wild stuff."

The senior scientist reached over and made a circle around the square object with his forefinger, then straightened up with a frustrated sigh.

"Reading from this thing's history, Sully, I'd say such an occurrence is simply par course."

The younger man stroked the ends of his braided goatee with one hand while scratching his head with the other.

"You're the historian, doc. I've just never seen

anything like it. A real mind-bender."

"Gentlemen, the slice and dice portion of our mission is officially in the books," Weems announced, rubbing both eyes vigorously as he stood from the helm of the laser canon's outer section.

Doctor James strolled up to the glass barrier and massaged the glass with both palms.

"Well then, by all means let's pull this baby apart and peek into its dark…" he paused to shudder dramatically, "…*mysterious* core."

***

Part I:

Q & A

MindBender, you readin' me, man? Come in, Mindtwiser… (long pause) …

"Dammit…nothin'. Pyschic phone lines must be down for the count," Ben muttered angrily, pacing the cell floor like an expectant father.

Man, could I use a shot of somethin' stouter than water. Benge ol' buddy, I'm beginnin' to think you were a borderline alchie after all. All the symptoms are present and/or accounted for, no denyin' it. Shaky hands, cold sweats, and weaker than a cub scout after a ten-mile hike. Maybe the assholes put somethin' in the meatloaf, or loaded the tap water with sedatives.

He paused in mid-stride for a brief moment, cocking his head to one side, then resumed the previous pace with a loud groan.

"Thought I felt a brain twinge for a sec," he snarled, "fuckin' stir has already driven me over the edge."

Hilarious shit anyhow. Lockin' down a prison where you're pretty much locked down twenty-four seven as it is. Hurricane my ass. Probably some kinda virus or contaminant. That would at least explain why I feel like a walkin' pile of steamin' crap since that last power nap.

Steaming pile of crap, huh? Pretty accurate self-description there, Brainiac.

"Who th-...Obliteration?"

You don't have to move your lips, Einstein, remember? Oh, I get it...thinking must really pain that swollen coconut of yours...

Stow the comedy central BS, pal. There's somethin' extremely rotten goin' down in this fucker.

Obviously...by my count this is the third time in three days we're able to run the grapevine without Mr. Mediator. Might be the storm, but I can't help but wonder why this never happened before your rancid ass showed up. I still say it's got someth- ...

Listen, ya whiny bastard, it ain't got shit to do with me. What say we dig up another theory? (long pause) ...Oblit? Hey, numbnuts...

"Sonuvabit..."

Force? Can you hear me? Force?

Yeah, catgirl...you're comin' in loud and crystal clear. 'Course, so was Big Chief Bonehead a second ago...

I was picking up portions of what you two were saying...but it keeps fading in and out. This is starting to remind me of a bad cellular connection.

I'm just wonderin' where Mind Sweep is durin' all this, or if he's even playin' a part in all the weird shit goin' on. Before we get disconnected, lemme ask you somethin'.

Yes, I received that stuttering mess saying something about a '*level X*'. Been trying to bring up Mind Sweep ever since.

Same creepshow-styled voice as the other day, right?

Affirmative. The one we figured was either a warning or a threat.

Or a warped practical joke. Hey, one more thing...

Fire away, Mr. Prosecutor...can't promise you anything...

Do ya happen to know if a female baddie, circa late eighties, named Shelmeleon has a room booked here at the Y? I know she ain't been part of the vine, but...

(short pause)

Shetah? Shiiiiiittttt...

"Well, I'll be double damned...not again," he spat, sporting a wry expression while standing at the center of the cell with his hands propped at his sides.

BENJAMIN...BENJAMIN, ARE YOU RECIEV-

Sweep? ...Damn son, where ya been? What the hell is goin'-...

I'M NOT...SURE HOW MUCH LONG...I CAN CONTIN...TRANSMIS...SOM...ING IS...JAMMING...TH...WAVES...ATTEMPT TO...BACK TO YOU...AS POSSIBLE...I'M

AFRAID...VINE WILL BE DOWN...FURTHER NOTICE...

Sweep goddammit...don't even...we need to know who's sendin' us the warnin's or the threats...or whatever the hell they are...not to mention this Level X bullshit...

(long pause)

Throwing his arms into the air, Ben threw back his head and growled before slumping to one knee with his head bowed.

"Game over, Benge. Hurry up and toss in the towel 'fore you lose what little marbles ya have left."

You'll always be my hero, Forcy, demented or not.

Holee SHIT...who zat? ...

Man, Oblit's got you all wrong, Forcy. You are one polished, eloquent Joe.

Anvil?

The one and only, though I haven't the foggiest what I'm doing on your wavelength.

It's a cross-wired goat—rope, no doubt. Lemme ask YOU before it's too late...ever heard of the Shemeleon?

Heard of her? Well, being that she's stationed exactly one cell sector away to my right...I'd have to say yes.

I knew...son of a...BITCH! I knew that damn nightmare had a purpose! There's gotta be a connection to all the other wacky shit goin' down...in...Anvil? You still hangin'...?

"But operator, I ain't got another quarter..." Ben quipped, falling onto the couch with a groan.

Scooping up the TV remote, he punched the

power button only to be greeted by static. A subsequent check of the stereo system achieved a similar result, as did the PC a few moments later.

"Might just be the storm. Hell, that would make sense."

He paused another few seconds, standing directly above the circular point in the cell floor used as a transport exit.

"Then again, since when does logical thinkin' fit into this fucking place?" For the next several minutes, he concentrated his efforts on picking up a fellow grapevine member, despite the sinking feeling such connections were, perhaps permanently, a thing of the past.

***

Part II:

The Unraveling "Rewind it just a bit more, Myers," The Guardsman commanded, positioned directly behind the seated CO, "Right…there. Lock it."

"You seeing what I'm seeing, boss?" he asked, turning towards the Warden, who stared at the monitor through a tight squint.

"He was dancing quite the jig. Well, whatever caused it, the feeling must've been fleeting. He's back to his normal statuesque self. Safe bet it had something to do with our new guest. From what I've been told, that damn rock effects everything around it in some form or fashion."

"What about the other inmates, boss? From what I saw, all of them were experiencing some

294

type of…physical reaction at the same exact time. Might be a good idea to inspect the cells just to make su-…"

"Calm down, Chief," The Warden assured, firmly patting the larger man between the shoulder blades. "All readings are back to normal. No need for a full-scale shakedown. Myers, monitor those cells and call us immediately if you detect any abnormal readings."

"Yes, sir," the CO acknowledged with a brief nod.

"C'mon, Chief. What say you and I check up on the egghead brigade? Maybe grab a soda and a bag of munchies for the trip? I'm buying."

"I'm with you, boss," The Guardsman responded with barely a half-hearted effort to disguise the weariness of his tone.

"Where's your old bud and former teammate, by the way?"

"Leah's taking a nap…or at least trying to. I got the feeling she wasn't quite satisfied the dome-field would hold Mister level-five at bay."

"Same with the Deputy Director. Can't blame 'em really. If I hadn't seen the dome in action, I'd probably feel a bit jittery myself."

"Gotta admit, Charlie, nobody's gonna mistake me for Iceman about now," the larger man said once they'd entered the first available elevator just outside the command center exit.

Reaching to press the button marked 'G' for ground floor, Warden Terry leaned against a near wall and turned to face his Chief CO, who had fallen to one knee in an impromptu football stance.

"Talk to me, Luke."

295

"Well, it certainly isn't the storm that's got me onedge. Been *here*, done t*hat*. Might be the mystery rock, though I don't sense any immediate danger there either."

"Then?"

"Possibly just Leah's presence. That, and the history between herself and Ben…um, Force. It's just damn uncomfortable. Kicker is, I think *I'm* more upset about it than she is."

"Don't tell me. She was asking you to arrange a…secret meeting of some type."

They exited together, strolling up to a series of vending machines and pausing to check the contents of each.

"Well, there was the tiniest of hints tossed my way. I had to remind her that the memory sweep would pretty well eliminate all reasons for doing so."

"Must be hell at that. Love can truly suck in this business. From what you've told me, she's one tough cookie."

"Yeah, she can handle it. Besides, another six to eight hours and she'll be transported out without a single inkling she'd ever visited to begin with."

Reaching forward, The Warden pushed a series of buttons before retrieving several small bags of chips.

"True enough, McDuff. Sour Cream *Ruffles*, anyone?"

"Damn, Chuck. You eat like this when you were in costume?"

"Not quite," the smaller man grinned, patting his own slightly bulging but still taunt midsection, "but hey, only person I've gotta impress these days is the old lady, and she's carrying quite the bay window herself. The hell with public opinion. I've waited all my life to cultivate a pet gut of my own."

"My hero." The Guardsman retorted, popping the top on a frosty cool Diet Seven-Up, "someday I hope to be just…like…you, boss."

Just as they'd re-entered the same elevator a moment before, both men leapt back a step as the Beepers hooked to their respective belts sounded off at precisely the same time.

"Warden Terry, please contact the Command Center …" Blared the buildings PA system a split-second later, the voice undoubtedly that of CO Myers.

It was immediately followed by a similar request: *"Guardsman, please contact the Command Center…"*

"Warden Terry and Chief CO Guardsman, please contact the command center as soon as possible…"

"Damn," the Warden blurted, holding the elevator doors ajar with one hand and a well-placed foot, "that was quick."

For at least the third time in the past seventy-two hours, The Guardsman felt something flutter deep within the confines of his well-toned midsection.

***

INSIDE CELL D-5, APPROXIMATELY SIX MINUTES EARLIER:

Leaning over a narrow TV tray propped atop

297

his tubby knees, The Mass's nostrils flared wildly.

"Uggggh...something bad rotten here. Meat smell like raw ass," he mumbled, his purplish lips roughly the size of mutated slugs, "eat this...and I be shitting colored water for days. No, sir...no thank you."

Shifting his massive bulk as he pushed the tray forward, he proceeded to reach for the TV remote and froze in mid-stretch as a loud crashing sound echoed just to his left.

"Whoa...that not right...not right what...so...ever..."

Shoving aside the middle portion of the sectional couch until he was able to step back through the opening, his eyes and mouth grew similarly wide. The TV tray had toppled over, the contents of the plate having splattered onto the floor and nearby coffee table. All, that is, save one particular portion. The main course, a brownish, heavily breaded pork chop that had reeked of spoilage, flip-flopped about the cell floor like a beached fish atop scolding hot rocks, eventually sailing airborne a final time before landing with a moist plop mere inches from The Mass's bare feet. Scrambling back several steps, The Mass eyed the suddenly stilled hunk of charred tissue with intense scrutiny, as if sizing up the most dangerous of foes. As if to justify a sense of imminent danger, the putrid slab suddenly shook and gyrated as if lying atop an idling engine.

"Somebody definitely not kill it before they grill it." hebabbled, already in the process of expounding his chest, arms and midsection to twice their original size with a casually executed series of short, huffed breaths.

The meat grew still once more as a barely audible whistling noise filled the air.

"A possessed (pronounced '*Poe-sessed*') pork chop…this is new…"

The low whistle gradually built until it reached a shrieking crescendo roughly the equal to an ambulance siren set at full bore, causing The Mass to back against a far wall with his hands clamped tightly over both ears. Moments later, it faded back to an eerie silence, leaving The Mass's labored breathing as the lone detectable sound.

"HEY!' he screamed, whirling about as though scanning the surrounding walls for a hidden camera, his monstrously swollen arms held out with the palms of each hand turned upward, "Is anybody see this crazy shit other than me? HEELLLOOOOO UP THERE! THIS SOME KIND OF TEST? YOU SOME SICK MOTHERS…"

After several moments, he took a cautious step forward, peeking from between his tree-trunk sized forearms, which had formed a V-shaped tunnel between pasty, sagging blobs of flesh.

"Who need you then? I check it out myself. The pork (pronounced '*poke*') chop hasn't been cooked I cannot handle…ha ha…"

With a sharp popping noise not unlike small arms fire, the piece of meat began to bubble and contract, bending almost entirely in half before exploding outward as if a tiny explosive device had been detonated at its center.

Spreading like a net formed of solid black mucus, it stretched from floor to ceiling, essentially sealing off roughly half the cell in a pulsating web that stunk of charred flesh and punctured intestine.

Striking a defensive pose, The Mass clinched his massive fists while loosening his neck with several violent jerks.

"Well…well. Me thinks it do mean to harm my person," he spat angrily, crouching slightly as his torso, thighs and calves began to swell and bloat to mammoth proportions.

Tilting his head back in a 'come hither' gesture, his face a mask of inhuman rage, The Mask growled through teeth literally cracking from the strain of his clinching jaws.

"Come on with it then, you ugly *fuck* you…I not have a good scrap in years…"

As if on cue, the thing shot forward like in a bleary flash, resembling a blanket sewn from solid sewage.

Bellowing a warrior's cry, The Mass leapt forward like a charging bull, his newly constructed eight-hundred-pound plus frame pounding temporary dents in the cell floor that almost instantaneously repaired themselves.

Upon contact, the alien blockade shattered like a wall of mist, collapsing like a fallen shower curtain while coating The Mass's flesh in a gritty, brownish hue.

"Wha…that all you got? That real funny…ha ha…a waterfallmade from dog shit…" he giggled, flapping his arms and hands as to shake off at least a portion of the residue, "…maybe this is some kind of test…"

Whirling about, he again addressed the ceiling and walls even as his body began to slowly deflate at will.

"About as funny as a case of claps, that was. I just hope everyone receive same treatment! I think you just pick on me because I'm Japanese! You always repay for Pearl Harbor! Racists fucks!"

Peering down, he noticed not only had his body almost completely dried, but the cell floor showed no evidence of the dark liquid which had spattered it just moments before.

"Huh! That really queer. How this dry so fast?" he muttered, his nostrils flaring wildly, "I still smell dog doo…"

Flailing back suddenly, as if he'd stepped on live wires, his entire body began to shudder uncontrollably.

Falling to one knee while simultaneously reaching with both hands to clutch his midsection, The Mass's mouth fell open and his eyes bulged.

"OH…this…not…g-gooddddd…"

Falling forward onto his elbows and knees, he tilted his head upward and managed a single, pathetic cry just seconds before his entire body literally came unhinged.

A loud tearing sound ensued as his back ripped directly between the shoulder blades, spewing forth a fountain of bile, blood and splintered bone. As if being carved askew by some invisible scalpel, the base of his neck and the back of his skull soon followed suit. With a series of muffled snapping sounds, his skull, rib cage, and spine were shoved free from their skewered host like ancient skeletal remains from a shifting mountainside.

Within moments, The Mass's outer shell had essentially been peeled like an overripe grape, the flesh, muscle and sinew flayed apart and laying in piles of shredded pulp, while the frame itself remained mostly intact in upper and lower halves.

The being that had freed itself so viciously from its core stood at the center of the cell, utilizing a forked, elongated tongue to clean itself of the various bodily fluids and stringy shreds of gore coating its entire frame.

In scanning its grisly handy work, the being leaned down on its chubby haunches to better survey the slaughter, sniffing like a predatory beast over a mangled carcass.

Thick streams of drool dripped from its bloated, purplish lips, and its eyes grew wide with hunger lust.

It took the being less than a full minute to devour the gist of the remains, to include all bone fragments and every visible drop of fluid, which it sucked from the cell floor with the power of an industrial vacuum.

Breathing heavily as it arose, it wiped its mouth with the inside of both elbows before strolling casually over to the mirrored sink.

"Oh, you handsome devil you," it croaked, its vocal cords obviously still in the developmental stage, "You going to be real killer with the ladies."

Wearing the perpetually warped grin that had been one of his facial trademarks, the being stared into the mirror with a cocked eyebrow and began to howl.

"Oh yes…you the man. You definitely the man!"

Rubbing its overstuffed belly, the being immediately began testing the limits of its newfound host as its chest, shoulders and arms instantly began to inflate as to match the bulk of its midsection.

As its head began to swell and contract to keep pace, the being shot itself a playful wink and giggled.

"I think this gonna work like a charm. Oh yes...just like a charm."

***

"What...was that? Looked like...a damned oil spill...or a shadow of some kind," The Guardsman exclaimed with a barely disguised awe, leaning towards the monitor until the tip of his cowl was less than six inches from the screen.

"Rewind it again, Myers."

Standing off to one side, Warden Terry studied a trio of monitors simultaneously.

"But you're saying current readings are back to normal?"

CO Myers shrugged as he pecked away on two separate keyboards.

"Yes, sir, Warden. The...unknown subject or...*whatever* it was...was only shown to be inside D-5 for approximately six to seven minutes. The chemical and biological readings had gone off the chart during that time, but have digressed back to acceptable numbers since."

Nodding in disbelief, The Guardsman broke away from the monitor long enough to address The Warden.

"Patrol should be checking in any minute, boss. What's your take on this?" he asked, pointing at the blurred image now frozen on screen.

"Hard to say. Maybe some sort of electrical interference caused by the storm. Radar shows the eye to be less than a half-mile to our starboard side."

"But...the thing appeared to be...aggressive. I mean, it seemed to be going after The Mass with a vengeance, and if you read the big man's body language, the feeling was mutual. If the thing hadn't blinked out when it did..."

"Chief, you know as well as I do that in the case of *Samurai Psycho* there, looks can truly be deceiving. Besides, these bleared images are virtually impossible to pinpoint as anything other than heat or chemical blocks. That 'cane is creating gusts of up to one-hundred ten MPH, and would've swallowed us whole by now if not for the field," The Warden grinned, turning his focus to the storm, which continued to pelt the invisible barrier encircling Eagle Island with level-five intensity.

Resting his chin inside a gloved palm, The Guardsman backed away several steps, then began to pace the narrow isle that separated the trio from the middle sector of the command center.

"Most technologically advanced penitentiary on the planet, and they can't figure out a way to install cameras inside each cell. Go figure."

"Now, now, Chief. They tried that a few years back, remember? That damned Mutant-X reject called 'Short Circuit' kept frying the inner workings. Cost the taxpayers about fifty grand every time he farted and cooked the wiring. The powers that be figured the imaging system would work just as well, and without the constant rewiring costs."

"Oh yeah, forgot about that. I spent the better part of a month escorting electricians through the flow ducts. But...*damn* it, boss, if we only had a clear picture..." The Guardsman paused a moment before raising a finger airborne, "Heeeey, Teleportator maybe? No, forget it. Those cells are teleportation proof...unless someone's evolving and kept it hush-hush."

Myer's hands temporarily departed the keyboards as he reached up to secure his headset.

"Sir?"

"What's up, Myers?" The Warden replied absently.

"CO's Richardson and Colby report normal conditions inside cell D-5. Inmate present and accounted for," Myers relayed before pausing to snort brief laugher.

"Continue, Officer," The Guardsman spat impatiently. Known to his lower ranking charges as a relatively good-natured individual but with little tolerance for job related incompetence, the Chief CO's tone was noticeably edgy.

"Oh, um...sorry, Chief. CO Colby reports that when asked about any strange phenomenon or occurrence within his cell sector, The Mass responded, and I quote, '*just the three-foot erection I sport before you two queers rushed in.*

'...um...sir. Nothing further to report."

"Hmm, that's our boy alright," The Warden said, failing miserably to conceal a bludgeoning grin.

The Guardsman gave the monitor's fuzzy imagery a final glance before tapping the CO lightly on one shoulder.

"Damned weird. But…everything seems kosher enough. Readings don't lie. Maybe it's just the storm after all.

Good job, Myers. Keep us posted."

"Yes, sir."

Giving his large subordinate a playful nudge as he stepped by, The Warden gestured towards the exit.

"Well, let's get moving, Chief. I want to check in with those eggheads before they blow up the lab."

Following closely behind, the larger man felt the tenseness on his neck and shoulders ease a notch or two.

"You want to radio ahead to let them know we're on our way, boss?" The Warden paused to respond until they were alone in the hallway.

"No way. *We* run this damn island, after all. They should be reporting to us, not the other way around."

"Right as rain, boss-man. Besides, I'd be lying if I said I wasn't curious as hell about the mystery stone. Now more than ever."

The smaller man nodded as they entered the elevator and stood side by side like mismatched bookends.

"You and me both, Luke. Let's go see if the mystery's any closer to being solved."

***

Part III:

The Very *Core* of Evil

"You say The Guardsman instructed you to meet him here, sir?" the young CO queried, posed like an old west gunslinger with his back facing the tightly sealed, double-door entrance marked '*CELL BLOCK D –RESTRICTED*'.

"Yes, indeed. Here for the grand tour, as it were. I would have thought such a man would be nothing if not punctual."

"Allow me to get on the com with him, sir, and…um…find out his ETA."

"Peachy."

The CO dropped his left hand from the thick-handled stun gun he'd been cradling and pulled a palm-sized, oval-shaped device from his utility belt.

"Pardon me, sir. This will only take a moment," he said, turning slightly to the left as his dark-tinted faceplate slid upward with a low hum.

Just as he'd positioned the device just inches from his lips, the faceplate inexplicably slid back down at warp speed, snapping into place with a loud crack.

The shaken CO instantly backed himself against the center portion of the door, tossing the com device aside while instinctively pulling his weapon chest high.

As a pained, desperate whine filled the hall, the guard began whipping the weapon back and forth, as if attempting to lock on an 'as of yet' unseen target.

His body abruptly stiffened, the stun gun bouncing onto the floor at his feet just as the first of several hairline cracks shattered the outer layer of his protective helmet. Much like a splintered windshield, the helmet began to rapidly 'spider-web', sending tiny fragments sailing airborne like shards from a broken mirror.

"This may sound pathetically cliché, officer, but such struggles are futile. Just relax and…let it end."

Within seconds, the officer collapsed to his knees, gripping the damaged headgear with both hands.

The guard groaned weakly just as a series of sickening crunching sounds ensued. Imploding from within, the helmet creased sharply at the sides. The guard initially lunged back, leaving a circular red splotch at the center of the entrance door, then fell forward in a clumsy lurch.

"Sorry I couldn't be more…gentle, officer. Unfortunately, time is of the essence," the other man said, careful to avoid the rapidly spreading crimson pool at his feet as he stepped near the entrance doors.

He sized up the entrance like an approaching enemy, crouching down and striking a wide pose, unwilling to alter his stance even as the sounds of approaching footsteps became obvious.

"Just in time, it seems," the mystery man quipped, halting less than two feet away from the other's statuesque form.

"You have the prize, I take it."

"Obviously. Failure is not an option, you know."

"You got that straight, cupcake. Let's do this while the timing is still dead-letter perfect."

Clutching the squared object to his chest like a protective talisman, the other man inhaled deeply, his forehead, face and neck drenched in a thick layer of fop sweat.

"By all means…after you, magic man."

Less than thirty seconds later, the door entrance stood partially agape, the left portion horribly bent, providing a space just large enough for an average sized man to walk through. Ignoring the ear-splitting klaxon buzzers left in their wake, the two figures ambled forward as though taking a casual stroll down a narrow park trail.

"Third door to the right," announced the first.

"Affirmative. Get ready for phase II", replied the second as the object clutched to his torso began to glow bright between his outstretched fingers.

***

"This…can't be good, boss. *Damn* it…not good at all."

The two men stood at the center of the confined space, scanning the surrounding carnage while displaying identical expressions of shell-shocked dismay.

"Get on the horn, Luke…" The Warden barked in a raspy tone, unable to pry his eyes from the sprawled body lying a few feet to his right, "… get with Myers or whoever's at the CC helm. Have 'em scan the building and account for everyone locked inside this burg."

Kneeling, The Warden reached out to retrieve the narrow metallic object protruding from victim number one's neck before thinking better of it and pulling his hand back.

"I'm on it," The Guardsman replied, reaching

for his utility belt just as the lights suddenly dimmed and then blinked out altogether, "...shit. Let's hope this is all just a coincidence, boss."

"Myers, this is CO one, over," he practically yelled as a set of emergency lights clicked on and began to gradually re-illuminate the room.

"This is CO one to command center. Controller, are you there?"

After several loud squelches, a barely audible, panic-stricken voice broke through the static in fractured segments.

"...here, chief...outage in all sectors...ver..."

"Listen up, Myers.... you're breaking up. Repeat, you're breaking up. Have you completed the emergency grid checklist? Repeat, have you completed the grid checklist?"

"...Grid...list...generator...short-cir- ...type...we're on backup...blems of its own...back with you...over..."

"Myers, please repeat last message. Please repeat last message."

"...problems, Chief. Grid's down...up's running on the lowest poss...ebb...dome-shield is...menting...Repeat...shield   is fragmenting...over."

"Oh shit...," The Warden blurted, "...the goddamn shield is fragmenting.

Back-up generator must've screwed the pooch."

Inhaling deeply, The Guardsman held his breath while pausing to respond. Once he spoke, it was with the cool, calm demeanor of a true leader; a man born to excel under even the most dire of circumstances.

"I read you, Myers. Institute a power shift and send all the juice we've got left into the shield's power source. I repeat, point the mother lode to the shield's power source. Do you read? Over."

"...derstood. Shifting pow...to shield source. Chief...no longer able...monitor the cell sectors...some...dividual security measures...disabled...over."

"Nothing we can do at this point, Myers. We'll have to rely on the cell's built-in designs to hold 'em at bay. Listen, we've got two dead and one missing from the science team. All signs point to foul play on a Major League level, so keep your weapons close. Attempt to notify all security teams. I repeat; everyone needs to be locked, loaded, and ready for anything. The warden and I are headed back your way now."

"Check...send a runner...all teams. Do me...favor and hustle your big butt...here...Chief...over an...out."

"On our way, Myers. Just hold on, troop. Over and out."

"Lord, Luke... how exactly is it that everything possible can go straight to hell in a hand-basket in less than three minutes flat? Murphy's Law lives and breathes."

Having already reached the exit door with two lengthy strides, The Guardsman paused to bend down and inspect victim number two, whose neck had been twisted at an impossible angle, his eyes bulging and his mouth twisted in an expression of eternal anguish.

"Only if it were planned that way, sir. Planned, plotted, and carried out with perfect execution. You

311

ready?"

Rising from his crouched position, Warden Terry glanced towards the sealed room containing their newest assigned guest.

"Y-yeah, let's go. Gotta tell you, though, if the back-up genny goes, we're gonna be flat out of workable options real qui-…"

Rambling slowly forward like a man entranced, The Warden pointed straight ahead with both hands, having temporarily lost the power of speech.

"Warden? Boss, what is it? We've got to go now."

"Check it…out, Luke. Check…*that* out."

Joining his superior at the wide glass window, The Guardsman cupped his hands and peered through to get a clearer view into the dimly lit space.

"Well, I'll be damned…they sure managed to dissect that sucker in a hurry."

"I'll say," The Warden replied after a loud, choking swallow, "seems they found what they were looking for."

The fossilized shell lay splayed apart like a butchered frog on a lab table, sectioned neatly into two halves with its crusty interior bathed in a single ray of light shining down from just beyond the laser canon's pointed barrel.

"Looks like. All that for something the size of a masonry brick," The Guardsman remarked sourly, gesturing towards a squared crater wedged at the center of both pieces.

Nodding solemnly, Warden Terry pushed himself away from the glass with both hands.

"Well, whatever it was…*is*…I can't help but

312

think it just might be the *catalyst* of this World of Shit we find ourselves wading through."

Turning about in unison, the two men exchanged a worrisome glance before heading towards the exit in a frantic sprint.

***

"Awww, what the hell now?" Ben groaned, blinking rapidly as he crawled on all fours from his cot onto the cell floor. The lone emergency light, located in the far-left hand corner of the cell, flickered on and off like a tiny flashlight bulb with severely weakened batteries.

"There goes my four-star ratin'," he moaned, shuffling towards the center of the room on his hands and knees, "Not exactly one of my shinier moments…crawlin' around like a three-hundred-pound roach."

The TV, which he'd left on while dozing, flicked on and off several dozen times before shutting down, while intermittent waves of loud static shot from the stereo's speakers for several moments before falling silent.

"Can't even keep the joint properly juiced, for shit's sake," he grumbled, reaching the edge of the couch and pulling himself up.

After a moment's silence, wherein he had just enough time to suck in a deep, tension-filled breath, the outer hallway filled with the echoes of a blaring klaxon horn.

"Whazzat…fire alarm? Probably just the storm raisin' cane with the power lines. Either that, or somebody's torched the place. Swell! Not exactly

313

the way I envisioned myself goin' out. Either goin' down with a sinkin' island or fried and cris-pi-fied inside a glorified tin can.

"HEY, Mind-broom, if you're getting this, allow me a single question; what the fuck, OVER?" he bellowed, though mostly drowned out by the wailing sirens, "Anybody in the chat room? Hell-ooooooo, out there…"

Welllll, shit. Guess the psycho hotlines are permanently blown, after all. Ain't even heard a mental fart break through since me, Anvil and Oblit were jawin' ju-…

Tumbling from the couch like a human wrecking ball, Ben rolled into the base of the entertainment center, toppling it like a deck of cards struck by a bowling ball. He continued to tightly clasp both ears while passing out with an internal choir of screaming, screeching voices echoing inside his skull.

Though the sensation had lasted less than three full seconds, he drifted in and out of consciousness several times in the aftermath, eventually waking to the scent of smoldering electrical wires.

"Geez Louise…talk about… havin' your dick knocked squarely in the dirt, think I'd prefer another peel an' reel," he mumbled wearily, pushing a large section of the shattered entertainment center free from his upper back and thighs before struggling to his feet.

"Wonder…what triggered that…particular mind melt. Didn't…couldn't recognize the voices or a single word bein' screamed. Some old story…ask and ya definitely…receive…more than ya ever bargain for."

314

Taking a moment to massage the sides and back of his head, which felt strangely numb, he stood for several moments with a hand on each knee, sucking in several deep breathes. Straightening up with an exhaustive groan, he glanced over at the shattered remains of the large screen TV/DVD/Stereo, from which assorted wires still crackled and smoked.

"Well, it ain't like they can garnish my paycheck."

Scanning the room as best he could through the murky fog, he peered to the right and froze. A wide circle of oil-slick blackness lay just a few feet from the far-right edge of the sectional couch. Side-stepping over, Ben first leaned over the chasm, then knelt onto one knee and submerged both hands into its dark recesses before running both palms over its slick-smooth edges.

"You gotta be kiddin'...talk about your major breeches of security." Looking back up, he gave the flittering emergency light and mishmash of ruined electronics a final glance.

"What the hell, if they nab me, I'll just say I was headed to the gym for a quick workout. Besides, I get the feelin' that sittin' inside that cell waitin' for something positive to happen ain't a viable option."

The emergency light dimmed to a barely visible flicker as his arms, legs and midsection tensed.

"Then again, this shit has trap written allll over it," he sighed apprehensively before leaping into the gloomy abyss feet first.

***

"I take there is a set contingency for such a crisis," Director Willis asked with a 'what now?' gesture, standing across from Warden Terry with the Guardsman and Marvella positioned just to the left of the long conference table.

"*Several*, Director Willis. None of which you'd actually want to know and/or be a part of," The Warden responded bitterly, turning about to face the female CO stationed at the main sector helm.

"Officer Grimes, I need those numbers now, not *five minutes* from now."

"Looks like…" she paused while pecking frantically atop the keyboard balanced atop her lap, "…extreme top portion of the dome is…now thirty-percent fragmented."

"That's bad, right?" Marvella injected nervously.

"I'd say yeah," The Guardsman countered, watching the storm rage from a nearby monitor, "…the dome was designed to disengage from top to bottom. Sounds like we still have a forty to forty-five-minute window before it sinks below the wave line. After that, we're floatation devices."

Crossing his arms defiantly, Director Willis shook his head in apparent disbelief.

"There's no way to get it…back online then? I mean, this *is* a command center."

Facing the other man wearing a fearsome sneer, The Warden's fists were clinched and pinned to his thighs.

"Sir, to state the obvious, this is a scenario that wasn't *supposed* to be possible. Translation, we're presently experiencing the 'adlib phase' of this little *contingency.* In other words, flying by the seat of our fucking pants."

Following several intense moments, Director Willis broke eye contact with the larger man, instead focusing on the same monitor The Guardsman had been watching.

"So you and Warden Terry found two of the science team murdered right outside the holding tank?" Marvella said, leaning towards The Guardsman as to be out of earshot.

"Yep. Dead as hammers, complete with sizeable wounds, and Doc James is still among the missing."

"Lu-...Chief, any word from your search team on either Doctor James or the status of the inmates?" The Warden asked abruptly, as if he'd somehow overheard Marvella's query over the surrounding commotion.

"Nothing yet, boss. I'll give them a buzz."

"Tell 'em to double-time it, Chief. The window's closing, and closing damn fast."

Gearing up a headset, The Guardsman stepped away to find a semi-tranquil corner with which to transmit.

"Marvella, where's your partner?" Director Willis asked off-handedly while still eyeing the monitor.

"Mys-? I'm...no idea, Director. Haven't seen him since we checked into our rooms."

"Wonderful. How can so many bodies go AWOL on a domed island?" he replied angrily, though careful to avoid The Warden's searing glare. "The way things stand, we sure could've used his...special skills. Might help us all to avoid

317

getting very wet…*very* soon."

"Probably just snoring away in his room. The trip over wasn't exactly relaxing," Marvella injected before walking away to join The Guardsman in a nearby cubicle, only to stop in her tracks as he practically leapt from the confined space back out into the open.

Reading the urgency in his subordinates frenzied movement, Warden Terry brushed by both the deputy director and Marvella with surprising fluidity and grace.

"Talk to me, Chief."

"No dice, boss. Nothing but static from two of the search teams. Dead silence from the third."

"Damn…fifteen heavily armed CO's. Alright, give me…just a moment here…"

Reaching up to massage his temples with a thumb and forefinger, the Warden paused with tightly closed eyes, as if proofreading some internal checklist for just the right solution.

"Check D level first. Marvella, you mind accompanying my Chief CO? There's a definite possibility of getting your hands dirty down there."

Cocking her head to one side, Marvella shot the Warden a mischievous grin.

"Warden Sir, I wouldn't have it any other way."

Gesturing wildly, Director Willis took up a comically stiff posture within the trio while failing miserably to mask an expression of doomed dread.

"Um, hate playing the role of doubting Thomas here, Warden, but we…*you* already have a large majority of your staff among the missing. I mean, we only have a handful of CO's remaining

318

for…personal security. Just pondering how wise it is to sacrific…um…to ship off all the remaining firepower into the unknown."

"Here's the deal then, *Thomas*…" The Warden replied in a placid tone that nevertheless reeked of biting sarcasm, "…there's a very good chance that a dozen of this Planet's moredangerous organisms have been liberated or are currently being liberated from indenture as we speak. Thus, as the Warden of this facility, I am obligated to insure these organisms are, at the very *least*, recaptured and again secured, or terminated with extreme prejudice. What this means to you and I is simple; personal security of high-ranking staff and island VIP's is secondary in terms of set priorities. Doesn't mean squat. These entities either get recaptured…," he paused, leaning in until his lips were mere inches from the other man's right ear, "… or this burg transforms into a million separate sand dunes by way of a last-ditch failsafe procedure, that being thermo-nuclear explosion."

"Thermo-…?"

Sticking a finger to his own pursed lips in a 'shushing' gesture, The Warden's eyes gleamed roguishly.

"Now, now, Director…*Top Secret*, you know. I figured you had a need to know…just so you'd fully grasp where we stand."

"Taking a few extra radios, boss…fully charged," The Guardsman blurted, handing over a similar device to Marvella, who immediately stuck it in the front of her utility belt.

The Warden turned away from the director, whose face had grown horribly pale, and stood toe to toe with his Chief CO and number one confidant. From a distance, one would have never assumed that such an odd-looking pair to be the higher echelon of a top secret detention center with a pentagon rating of five in terms of similar locations deemed vital to National Security (only four other locations ranked higher among UN sites under United States control:

Wright-Patterson Air Force Base (*Air Force Logistics Command Headquarters*); Offutt Air Force Base (*Strategic Air Command HQ*); the White House, and the Pentagon). Warden Terry with his clip-on tie, badly rumpled button-up dress shirt and thick-bodied appearance, more resembled a former athlete gone slightly to pot turned copier repair man. On the flip side, The Guardsman with his meticulously toned torso and equally immaculate ensemble, with every available crease honed razor sharp and not a single square inch of spandex out of place, and whose ultra-professional persona screamed 'ultimate soldier'.

"Listen up, Luke. You just might be walking into one hell of a hornet's nest down there. Then again, it might well just be a com problem."

"I think we both know better than *that,* Charlie. We'll give the cells first priority, then move to find Doc James and our missing troops."

"Check. If the natives are running free, at least you'll have Marvella's force-field capability for defensive purposes."

"Yep," The Guardsman replied with a quick wink Marvella's way, "...gonna be just like old home week."

"More like *reform* school week. Lead the way,

320

Lucas," she replied while stretching her neck from side to side as if prepping for an intense workout.

The Warden reached up and over and gave his Chief CO a firm slap on the shoulder.

"Keep in touch, you two…and be damned careful. We'll continue manning this joint 'til the waves come over the bow, at least another half-hour or so. After that…"

The larger man returned the gesture with a light tap of his own. "Got'cha, boss. If we can't find you here, we'll find you there."

"We're ready or you two gonna swap spit?" Marvella said, smiling despite herself.

"Let's hit it. Need to make a quick stop at the armory on floor one."

"Armory?"

The Guardsman nodded briefly before jogging toward the exit. "You'll understand."

A few moments after their departure, the emergency power blinked on and off several times before stabilizing again.

"Readings, Grimes?" Warden Terry inquired wearily, propping clinched fists against the oak tabletop.

"Holding steady at thirty-four percent fragmented, sir," came the exasperated reply, "…prepare evacuation checklist, sir?"

"Not yet, officer. Not until I get a clearer picture of what's going on below. We got at least thirty clicks before successful reinstatement of the dome is a permanent no-go. Go ahead and deactivate the laser screen. That should buy us a minute or five. Besides, the 'flesh eater' can't hold a candle to fifty-foot waves and ninety-mile an hour

321

winds."

"Disengage laser screen...y-yes, sir...right...right away."

Stepping forward, Warden Terry placed a gentle, soothing palm atop the CO's visibly trembling left shoulder.

"Breath deep, Grimes. This is precisely *why* you suffered through all those years of intense training; all the boorish instructors and cocky classmates who couldn't quite cut it when you did. This is precisely *why* you were chosen to serve on Eagle Island. Everyone here is the best of the best; the elite I've seen no exceptions. You're gonna make it through just fine. All of us will."

"Yes, sir. We most assuredly will. Thank you, sir."

Whirling about to retake his position at the head of the conference table, Warden Charles Terry's somber expression wasn't lost on a certain FBI Deputy Director, who had recently become aware of a sharp, burning sensation deep within his own chest cavity.

***

Submerged in pitch blackness yet undefined in mortal terms as its long-dormant life-source pulsed and throbbed with renewed vigor, it slithered from the shattered remnants of the test-tube shaped container that had served as its host for centuries untold.

Tunneling through walls of stone, metal and wood as if they were liquid-based, the unknown power source continually fed its insatiable appetite

322

until its rapid physical growth eventually peaked to gargantuan heights. As a being, it knew only one mission; one reason for being. Conflict was its purpose, mass destruction its lone goal. As it trekked forward at a deliberate yet consistent pace, leaving a wide slug-trail of annihilation in its slime-coated wake, it locked on several potential prey simultaneously.

Although not equipped with neither the emotion nor physical attributes that would allow anything resembling a human smile, the creature nonetheless felt that very equivalent as shock waves of joyous glee shot through its toxic veins like a rampaging virus.

***

Part IV:

Old Friends (and Foes) in New Places...

Creeping up the narrow, tubular corridor in a slight crouch, Ben allowed his anvil-sized fists to cut a path through the murk.

Whether by design or electrical malfunction, only one of every five emergency lights shone, with each operational bulb positioned at least thirty to forty feet apart.

Upon covering a distance of approximately one-hundred yards, he neared a crosswalk in which four separate tunnels intersected.

"My kingdom for a compass...or better yet, a blueprint. Hell, even a *Yahoo* map would serve," he growled, scratching his chin through thick stubble while eyeing each tunnel with a bemused smirk.

After several false starts, during which time he'd jokingly muttered several refrains of 'inny, minny, miny, moe,' he finally decided on the nearest tunnel, which veered sharply to the left.

He'd barely gotten a full five paces in before the corridor inclined steeply to a ten to twenty-foot stretch before veering hard to the right and eventually leveling out.

"Follow the dimly lit road," he whispered, slowing as the tunnel filled with a distant thumping noise; a reverberating echo familiar to that of several sets of heavy boots pounding pavement.

"Looks like companies comin'. 'Bout damn time."

He'd taken only a half stride forward before being viciously chop-blocked at the knees.

Rolling quickly to his feet, he struck a blocking pose with his forearms crossed across his face in an 'X' shape.

He had just enough time to note the pitch darkness leading further down the corridor before enduring a solid blow across his breastbone, followed closely by a similar shot to the forehead. Reeling back, he bounced off the oval shaped wall onto the floor, the mixture of his own bodyweight and forward momentum sending him into a twenty to thirty-foot slide wherein his face, chest and knees suffered the majority of the impact.

"Motherfuc-…" he started to groan just as the left side of his rib cage was pummeled by a frenzied series of blows, the last of which lifted him airborne and again into a far wall.

Coming to a less than graceful landing with the

center of his face acting as buffer, he lay sprawled in a heap, struggling to regain his breath while his chest and midsection burned from the effort.

"Who the hell is that?" he heard a voice, decidedly feminine and strangely familiar.

"Just another tomato can to me, darling," another chimed in, this one decidedly male.

"Damn it, blockhead, I told you knocking all those lights out was a bad idea. What if we need to head back in the same direction we came, ever think of that?"

"Nag, nag, nag. The woman possesses built-in night vision but *still* proceeds to bitch…"

As his inner workings went into overtime to heal the temporary effects of the blunt trauma to his upper body and midsection, Ben allowed himself an additional moment to zone in on the exact positioning of the voices.

"Let's go, then. Whatever that thing is behind us sure ain't getting any further away," the male voice continued as Ben fought the urge to spit out the glut of blood filling his mouth and instead began the still, gradual process of tensing his upper body from the calf muscles on up.

"What about…?"

"Just leave the big slug laying here. Maybe he can serve as an appetizer for whatever's on its way…"

Performing an impromptu push-up propelling him to his feet in a turbulent blur, Ben then executed a combination sidekick (right leg) and backhand (right arm) within the same frenzied movement, each performed with deadly accuracy and withthe quickness of a striking cobra.

The kick caught the male in the chest, though Ben had blindly gauged the height as being that of an average male's head, while his fist narrowly missed connecting with something that had ducked away in the nick of time.

"Just for the record, asshole…this big slug ain't nobodies appetizer," he growled, timing his opponents ricochet from a far wall before throwing a left hook that sent the massive form careening down the corridor like a guided missile.

"Ben…*Force*…is that you?" the feminine voice asked, seemingly from several feet above Ben's head.

"Uh…Yeah," he replied cautiously, instinctively falling to one knee while scanning the blackness above for any sign of movement, "…cat-girl?"

"Affirmative. Cool your jets, man…"

A moment later, Ben felt a warm, furry hand caress his left biceps. "Damn woman…need to borrow a razor?"

"It is you," she sighed in obvious relief, "Big man, if you ever retire from the business, you ought to seriously consider renting those mitts of yours out as battering rams."

"Never heard that one before," he moaned. "Who's the Jolly Green Giant that tried to puree my ass? Felt like I was punchin' Mount Rushmore."

"Oh, that's Anvil. Let's go find him and get the hell out of this damned toothpaste tube."

They turned in unison, though Ben found himself forced to utilize his small-framed ally in true 'seeing eye dog' fashion, gripping her left wrist as they strolled slowly forward.

"Couldn't see the Queen Mary if she was parked two inches from my face."

"Just hang on, Brutis. I see him," she replied curtly, increasing their speed a bit, "Hey blockhead, you still in one piece?"

"Right here, mittens. Oh, my aching everything."

Halting abruptly, Ben felt Shetah shift her position as to reach forward with her free hand.

"Aw, shake it off, big fella. You don't look any worse for wear, except maybe that square noggin of yours seems a bit warped."

"Right. How's about we step into some light we Homo sapiens can use to regain the power of sight?"

"Speak for yourself, hoss," Ben grumbled, "... I like girls."

After a moment's silence, Shetah laughed aloud; a low giggle integrated with a seductive purring sound.

"Priceless. Okay, each of you two macho guys take an arm and I'll lead us to a new enlightenment, so to speak."

As they proceeded up the blackened corridor in a bizarre take on 'The Wizard of Oz'; a petite female form book-ended on each side by separate behemoths, the heavy thumping sound seemed to grow in intensity from the opposite direction.

"Where exactly we headed again, Miss Kitty?" Anvil asked between labored breaths.

"Anywhere but here, box-head," she replied, meowing softly in the aftermath.

***

"Any chance some of them are still… breathing?"

The Guardsman only nodded and continued to stare into the makeshift monkey-pile of mangled bodies. The bodies of at least a dozen CO's he'd gotten to know very well over the past year. Men and women with families; commitments; lives outside the stifling confines of Eagle Island.

After a short pause, he reached to adjust the thermo-blaster rifle hanging from his shoulder.

"This is…all three teams. All three search units. I see…Jackson, Childers, Myers. Those were the team leaders.

Which means…somebody took the time to drag them in here after…" he muttered grimly, shaking his head slowly from side to side.

"We'd…better go, Luke. Only about a half-hour of useable time left, according to my watch."

They'd entered the cell block sector less than five minutes after departing the armory, where they'd each obtained thermo-blasters and exo-skeleton chest shields, finding all cell's vacated save one; that being D-8, formerly the permanent holding area for the entity known as Mind Sweep. It had also been the lone cell whose underground access hatch had remained mysteriously unopened.

The bodies had been stacked, cordwood style, in the center of the room. The CO's had been stripped of their collective weapons, the gist of which had beenleaned in a neat line against a far cell wall. Their face shields had been shattered, as to purposely display the expressions of stark anguish and indescribable pain each had endured before succumbing.

"This shit isn't supposed to happen, Leah. Goddamn it...it just isn't." Approaching him in a short sprint, Marvella fronted her former teammate until there were mere inches separating the two.

"What say we go find the son of a bitch responsible?" she snarled, forced to tilt her head just to read the expression through his tight-fitting cowl.

After a long pause, he glanced down through shiny, moistened eyes. His arms trembled with newfound rage even as he pulled the rifle forward and forcefully cocked its pump-action handle.

"Lets..."

***

Part V:

A Change in Command

"Not to seem overly... curious or pushy, Warden, but... exactly where the...hell are you...taking me?" Deputy Willis spouted in-between labored huffs. Gripping his upper chest with tightly clinched fingers, he could feel the blood course through his veins like molten lava even as his legs grew increasingly heavy. Similarly, he felt a healthy dose of pent-up fury well-up about chest level, and surrendered to its seductive pull without pause.

"You'll know when we get there, Director Willis," Warden Terry replied curtly, barely out of breath despite the lengthy sprint they'd endured since departing the command center some ten

329

minutes earlier. "You okay back there? You sound a bit winded."

What do you care, you pompous fuck? It's all about saving your own ass, anyhow. Am I right or am I right?

"I'm…I'm…fine, d-damn it. Let's just…just get there…already."

Meanwhile, I'll think up a way to smoke your carcass once we do. Self-important prick. We'll see who's in charge then, now won't we?

Despite his best efforts to keep up, the director soon dropped a full dozen steps behind both the Warden and the two armed guards who blazed their trail. The slim hallway resembled a disco room from another era as the corridor lights flickered on and off sporadically. Watching the three men ahead of him build their lead, Director Willis could hear his temples thundering as a wave of primordial rage swept over him. At that moment, he wished for nothing more than to have the speed and agility to catch one of the guards and relinquish them of their weapon, then slowly and meticulously blowing the Warden into a half-dozen moistened chunks. He giggled uncontrollably as a fine line of drool coated his lips in a soapy froth.

The hall abruptly dead-ended as they'd cleared a final curve, forcing the two guards to shoulder the wall following a less-than-graceful, though perfectly synchronized, forward slide. Quick stepping to a much less dramatic halt, the Warden pulled a multi-layered keyring from his left pants pocket.

"Dead-end, sir. Don't we need to turn ba-…" the first guard began, the closed faceplate unable to

330

mask the anxiety in his voice.

The Warden nodded while pointing what resembled a tiny pen-lite towards the center of the beige-shaded wall.

"Nope...believe it or not, we're in the right place."

While the hallway lights continued to sputter, he began whipping the light's narrow blue beam all about the eight by twelve wall.

"Stand back, men. I just happen to have a key. Just have to find...the keyhole it belongs to."

A moment later, the blue beam transformed to a greenish hue as a dark, horizontal square faded clearly into view.

"Got'cha. Now, I just have to train this bad boy and avoid the shakes."

The warden held the miniscule light in a steely, two-handed grip, posing like a marble statue with his legs spread and his head held slightly back as the light remained trained on a two-inch wide, half-inch high square located roughly half-way up the wall on the far-left side. Behind him, the two guards instinctively took a step back while keeping their rifles pulled tightly to their chests.

"C'mon, baby...be a good girl and open up for Warden Terry," the Warden whispered through pursed, purple-shaded lips as the pen-lite's greenish hue soon faded into a swirling mist of purple, yellow, and brown. Exactly three seconds later, it evolved into a solid back line that appeared almost tangible, as if it had been drawn from the tip of the lite to the wall itself.

"That's my girl," he sighed, dropping the lite to his side as the entire wall slid upward with a low, grinding hum, revealing a sizeable freight elevator constructed in solid steel beaming.

"I'm clear troops," he continued, stepping forward while re-pocketing the keyring, "head back to the command center and await further orders."

"Sir?" he heard the second guard query timidly. "What it is, Daniels?"

"Sir, um, where's the director?"

Having just entered the elevator's wide maw, the Warden practically leaped back into the hall just a split-second before everything went dark.

"Jesus…even the emergency lighting is fubared," he grumbled. "It just keeps getting better and better."

Three sets of flashlight beams lit up the slim passageway a few moments later, sweeping in all directions like a trio of rotating spotlights.

"Well, let's backtrack, troops," the Warden finally said, "though it beats the hell out of me how the man could've gotten lost."

Making their way slowly back up the consistently curving hall, the Warden couldn't help but be reminded of 'Dark Vadar' while listening to the guard's heavy breathing beneath their faceplates.

"Maybe he collapsed, sir," the first one said indifferently, "the man seemed to be in pretty bad shape. Huffing and puffing like a freight train."

"He looked sick to me, sir. Pale as a ghost," the second chimed in, taking the point in a slow jog.

The Warden remained silent as they neared the steepest of the curves they'd previously passed. The troopers dashed ahead, gaining a ten to fifteen-yard head start.

"Something tells me I should've loaded into that damn elevator and departed Dodge while I had the chance," he mumbled to himself as a combination of solid body shots punched his mid-section with deadly accuracy. Body shots birthed from an inner dread which sounded off within his subconscious like a blaring Klaxon horn.

***

Whipping the light upward in a frenzied blur even as he fell to one knee, Director Willis could only watch haplessly as the hand gripping the flashlight was then torn free at the wrist.

"SHIT! S-son of a..." he gasped, rolling away while tucking the wounded, leaking appendage to his chest.

"Oh my, my...that had to hurt something *fierce*," the mysterious voice croaked with glee. Rising shakily to his feet, the director immediately began to blur as blood soaked his shirt and pants.

"W-where are y-you, chicken-shit?" he blurted into the pitch darkness. "Why don't...you...face m-me like you've got a pair?"

Spotting the only source of light laying several feet up the hall, still gripped by the permanently curled fingers of his detached hand, he then shambled towards it in a wobbly sprint. A split-second later, he toppled face-first onto the hard tile after feeling a sharp, searing sensation just below his left knee.

"My dear director, you mad, *mad* hatter you...I'm afraid soon you won't have a single *leg* to stand on..." the voice bellowed between high-pitched cackles, "at least, if I have anything to say about it."

Having rolled over onto his back, the director reached down with his lone remaining hand and felt nothing but air where his left shin should have been.

"S-s-son of a...b-b-..." he babbled hysterically as his vision grew increasingly spotty, "...s-show your...self, damn...it..."

As if to magically, or perhaps *tragically*, adhere to Director Willis' dying request, the hallways lights suddenly flickered to life, their inert brightness temporarily blinding his already unfocused eyesight.

"Tsk tsk, it is indeed a shame. I do wish there was a way to harness the unbridled madness you've fallen victim to, Director Willis, "a blurred form croaked from just to the fallen man's right, "You have been quite the good soldier thus far. As it is, I'm afraid this rather sad scene equates to nothing more than a hopelessly rabid dog being forcefully euphonized."

Raising his surviving appendage in a pathetic gesture of surrender, Deputy Director W. Paul Willis could only manage a series of incoherent babbling as the blurred figure clutched his right ankle and gently tugged, pulling him toward a small, squared air vent several feet down the hall.

"Buck up, Director," the creature spewed gleefully, "this is liable to be a rather tight fit."

Just as the lights began to dim and flicker once more, the narrow hallway was briefly filled with a series of crunching noises not unlike dried kindling being snapped beneath heavy work boots.

334

***

Picking up his own pace as his light bobbled wildly in his grip, it was mere seconds before the Warden heard the first of two distinctly delivered shrieks fill the confined space.

"Ohhh...SHIT!" went the first.

"What the...hell is it?" came the second.

"Warden?" he heard the first trooper mumble just as he turned the corner and his own light's wide beam concentrated on a small wall vent less than ten feet to their north.

"Could that be the director?"

The metal air vent, perhaps eight inches high and a foot wide, had been ripped free and laid bent almost in half against the opposite wall. Spread around the squared opening where the vent had been was a shredded pile of still-smoking viscera that seemed to literally ooze with life within the trio of white light trained at its reddish center. A single shoe, brown dress, lay a foot or so up the hall; a blood-splattered ivory stump pointed towards the ceiling like a tattered flag of surrender.

Stepping ever-so-cautiously past the carnage, the Warden bypassed the troopers, who stood frozen in place on either side of the hall.

"Jesus, it looks like..." he whispered, eyeing a crimson-coated 'Visitors' badge that lay crumpled just past the damaged vent, "...it looks like the poor bastard got...pulled through the opening."

"B-but...how...how could he have...fit? It's...it's only..." the second trooper babbled, an audible gag cutting off the rest of his statement.

"Well, in checking out the remains...," The

Warden replied, sweeping his light over the pureed mess of pulsating tissue one final time, "I'd say he didn't fit…very well anyhow. Poor bastard."

Momentarily dropping the light to the tiled floor, The Warden sucked in a long, laborious breath before again speaking.

"Looks as though we have a slight escapee problem, troops. Only logical explanation. Whoever or whatever sucked Willis into that airshaft might still be close by. Keep those eyes peeled and your blasters locked and loaded while I radio The Guardsman. We could have some uninvited company any sec now."

Pulling a palm-sized com device to his horribly chapped lips, The Warden paused as the flashlight slipped free from his other hand, bounding away to a far corner. Stepping over, he kept the transmitter tucked to his mouth even as he bent down to retrieve the light, which continued to roll back and forth in a semi-circular wave.

Gripping the light's hard plastic handle, the Warden's knees popped like twin compound fractures as he arose, the loud snapping all but drowning out a sudden flurry of muffled activity to his immediate right.

"What the-…troops?" he mumbled, his words partially drowned out by a noise vaguely familiar but weirdly out of place; the sound of spilled liquid slapping the tile flooring; much like water leaking from a cracked pipe.

Whirling the light about in a circular arc, The Warden gasped aloud before instinctively leaping back, his shoulder blades pinned snugly against a far wall.

"Oh land…this isn't good. Not good…at all."

The lower body of guard number one stood erect, the knees partially buckled but seemingly locked into place. The upper body, strangely absent from the gruesome imagery on display, had been torn away just above the naval, leaving behind a pair of still-wriggling, shredded intestine overlapping the evenly sliced mid-section.

Guard number two lay slumped further up the hall, minus the majority of his head and the whole of his right arm. As the Warden's light rotated from one grisly scene to the other and back several times, an occasional spurt of blood would shoot from guard one's severed lower abdomen like a geyser from a hot spring. Side- stepping further up the hall as to distance himself from the overwhelming stench of perforated gut and wet pennies, The Warden, nonetheless, kept the light trained on the far end of the hall, past a virtual river of expanding crimson now coating the hall floor.

"CO-one, come in. CO-one, this is the Big Chief, do you read?" he whispered into the com device, which had grown slick from his palm sweat. *"Damn* it, Luke, are you there? I just might be in one hell of a pickle on floor three…"

"There ain't no might about it, Sherlock…" groaned a gravelly voice from above, "…your wide ass is undoubtedly grass…"

Warden Terry had time only to wince while attempting to duck away in clumsily executed move that was, unfortunately, a textbook example of 'too little, too late'."

***

Facing an apparent dead-end, the trio began scanning the surrounding walls for anything resembling a hidden panel or trip-switch.

"I still say it's some kind of experiment, and we're the fucking bait," Anvil growled, utilizing his seven-foot plus height to place both palms on the corridors circular top while feeling around for a crack in the surface.

Crawling about the walls by digging the claws of her feet and hands into the semi-pliable outer layer, Shetah shifted quickly from one section to the other, sniffing and purring as if on a feeding expedition.

"No way. They'd be risking too much."

Growling between a series of hard rights and lefts that had no apparent effect on the wall's outer housing, Ben paused briefly to step over and pick a new target area before resuming his efforts.

"I'm with fur-ball. No way we're runnin' around scot-free on purpose." Turning towards the horizontally shaped dead end, Anvil bent at a forty-five-degree angle and shot forward at full force before bouncing back with a pained grunt.

"Dammit, I'm telling you, they've created some newfangled bad-ass security measure, and we're its first test," he grumbled, leaning back and massaging the top portion of his squared skull.

"Stir's made ya paranoid, Mac. This has technical difficulties writtin' all over it."

"Cut the shit, both of you. Number one, it really doesn't matter how *or* why.

Number two, quit wasting your time and energy trying to poke holes. This tube was constructed with

338

our strengths in mind."

"Guess we head back the way we came then," Anvil conceded, slumping his massive shoulders.

Dropping from the top of the ceiling without a hint of sound, Shetah landed on all fours and cocked her head to the left.

"Damn. I was hoping whatever it was would have taken a different fork in the road," she whispered, centering the trio as all three stood silent for several moments and listened to the thundering commotion that seemed to grow closer by the second.

"The hell with this avoidin' conflict bullshit," Ben snarled, flexing his massively bloated biceps. "Never was much for runnin' or hidin', anyhow. We're supposed to be the worst the planet has to offer in terms of badness. Might as well prove 'em all right."

Anvil took a long stride forward, essentially taking the point.

price."

"I'm with you, meatball mitts. Nobody serves me up as bait without paying a

Both then turned towards Shetah, as if awaiting a verbal seal of approval. "Lead the way then, you big, tough male specimens you."

As if to acknowledge the implications of their decision, the rumbling noises only seemed to intensify further.

"This corridor's pretty damn slim, Anvil. However big the som' bitch is, you nail it with that tracker trailer-sized noggin' of yours smack dab in the midsection and I'll go for the headshot," Ben said, keeping pace less than a step behind the larger man while being careful not to lock ankles.

"Reckon I'll just hang back here and make the coffee," Shetah quipped, "...maybe ensure your *beers* are nice and chilled before the ballgame starts."

"My bad, whiskers. Didn't mean to stiff ya," Ben replied, the trio slowing a bit as they re-entered a dimly lit stretch of corridor which would eventually lead into total darkness, "...incidentally, make mine a *Bud Light*, will ya? Gotta monitor those carbs, ya know."

Nearing the four-way intersection, the trio slid forward on their collective heels just as the wide circle positioned at the crossroads opened like the jaws of a snapdragon and swallowed them whole.

***

Tumbling onto a cushioned platform like giant tumbleweeds, the three scrambled to their feet as one cohesive unit, each facing separate directions while striking distinctively different fighting stances.

They stood at the center of a spacious, oval-shaped room that broke off into four separate walkways leading to just as many wide-panel doors.

"Some kinda transport depot. Like I said, my kingdom for a bluepr-..." Ben muttered, freezing in mid-word as the figure posed to his immediate left swam clearly into view. A figure he initially thought to be nothing more than a cruel illusion; a superbly formed hallucination created from the deepest recesses of his fractured psyche. It wasn't until moments later, when the imaginary shape refused to fade or simply fragment into a fine mist that Benjamin Thomason felt his very soul, which he'd long given up for dead, take flight in a surge of emotion that was almost electrical.

Altering his aim while swaying the thick-barreled blaster towards each potential target, The Guardsman finally locked on the larger of the trio.

"Back up a step, Ben. Leah, if Anvil so much as passes gas, blow his ugly ass through the nearest wall. Shetah, you just tuck in that tail and hug the floor like it was an empty milk bowl."

"Well, well, well…if it ain't the head screw his bad-ass self," Anvil bellowed, practically elbowing Ben to the side with acrane-sized forearm, "Whoooo-weee, who's the dragon lady, Chief? Think I'll taste me a sample of her charms right off. I always did prefer *ori-en-tal* cuisine."

"Anvil, I'd seriously reconsider…" The Guardsman warned, his close-range aim towards the center of Ben's face never waiving.

"For the record, Chief ass-lick, I couldn't give a shit less about your advice…"

Lurching forward with the top of his skull leading the charge, Anvil'sforward advancement never made it past the first step before he was battered airborne by a flurry of punches, the most effective of which a brutal uppercut that had caught him square in the throat. He spun to the floor a full dozen feet from where his four-hundred-pound frame had been so unceremoniously hoisted, rolling into the wall with a resounding thump that seemed to shake the entire structure to its foundations.

Lowering the thermo-blaster just a hair, The Guardsman paused for several tension-filled

341

moments while studying the man responsible.

"Nice shot, Ben. Seems incarceration hasn't affected your punching power."

"It's all about the timin', Luke," Ben replied, his bulging chest heaving from the effort.

"Goddamned traitorous asshole," Shetah spat, still posed on the floor like the predatory cat that bore her origin.

Twisting his head about to address her, Ben shrugged his shoulders in a 'what did I do?' gesture.

"If ya asked me, I did the big lunk-head a favor by clockin' him. You ever seen what one of those nuke-powered popguns can do to a man, cat-girl? Believe you me, it ain't pretty."

He paused to shoot The Guardsman a quick wink.

"Sides, push comes to shove…afraid I'm still one of the *good* guys."

Shetah released a growling hiss, the hair on her back and neck standing on end.

"Sorry, Catnip. Nothin' personal," he concluded, turning his sight away from her and onto Marvella, whose stiff, combat-ready pose belied the plethora of mixed emotions bubbling behind her rapidly blinking eyes.

"Leah," Ben said, nodding shakily and barely avoiding choking on the single word. A word he'd given up hope in every using in the actual presence of the woman it addressed, "fancy meetin' you here."

"I'll say," she replied with a nervous giggle, "then again, you never were what most folks would call predictable. Nice beard by the way. The Unibomber could sue for identity theft."

342

"Misplaced my razor, darlin', I was-"

Unconsciously taking a half-step forward, Ben halted in mid-step as the gun barrel was pressed tightly to his upper chest. His smile quickly faded into a tight-lipped grimace while alternating glances between the weapon and its possessor.

"Just hold your position, Ben."

"Kinda figured we were still on the same team, Luke."

"Not... from a technical standpoint. I'm...only following regulations." Strolling purposely forward, Marvella placed the tip of her own blaster beneath The Guardman's barrel and flung it to the side.

"The hell with regulations," she blurted angrily, "I get the feeling we're going to need all the firepower we can get."

"Damn it, Leah, I understand your..." he began, pausing to look from one to the other several times while repositioning the blaster near Ben's midsection, "...the feelings you must be... *shit*...this is no time to cover...past loyalties. Somebody slaughtered my troops, and until I find out who's responsible, nobody is above suspicion, especially any and *all* escaped convicts."

After a moment's hesitation, Ben took a step back and placed his hands behind his back in a 'parade rest' posture.

"Much as I want to raise holy hell with such logic, I can't honestly say I'd be thinkin' any different if I were wearin' your shoes."

Marvella opened her mouth to argue, but fell silent once Ben raised a hand palms up in her direction.

"Save it, Leah. Luke's right as rain. I'm just as

343

much a convicted felon as whiskers or blockhead."

"Fucking A right," Shetah injected with a snicker.

A low, groaning sound originated from their far left as Anvil rolled over onto his back, massaging his jaw with one hand and his neck with the other.

"Sleep ugly awakes. Leah, you recharged enough to keep these three locked in separate fields 'til we get up top?" The Guardsman asked, secretly relieved to finally break eye contact with Ben.

A loud rumble that seemed to originate above their heads interrupted any possible response, causing the floor beneath their feet to shudder like mild aftershocks from a recent earthquake.

"Oh yeah, I was gonna mention *that*," Ben said, tilting his head to stare at the stone ceiling above.

The Guardsman continued to address Marvella, swallowing hard before replying with a shrug.

"Probably just some kind of seismic phenomenon caused by the dome's fragmentation."

Grunting loudly, Shetah sprang up on all fours and began sniffing the air as if to detect a nearby threat.

"Whatever makes you feel better, chief, but this specific seismic *phenom*was trailing our asses through the corridors just as we fell through the rabbit hole."

Donning a wry, doubtful expression, The Guardsman instantly turned back to Ben just as the ceiling above shook and trembled with increased power.

"The kitty-cat speaks gospel, G-Man. Less you folks have really, *really* shitty plumbing, somethin' big and extremely pissed off is comin' down the pipe." A third aftershock ensued, accompanied by an even louder roar.

With a loud sigh, The Guardsman swung the blaster's barrel towards the first of the three available elevators.

"Well, haul your asses toward the elevator then, while we've still got juice. Fair warning however..." he scolded with a forefinger pointed into the air, "...one false move and I won't hesitate lighting any of you up, regardless of the overall threat.

"Leah, bubble-up Anvil and drag him along. Let's get back up top and regroup."

"A born leader, that one," Ben said with a grin, joining Marvella in a quick sprint towards the nearest walkway, "a real take-charge guy."

Taking the lead, The Guardsman ran ahead, pausing to punch in a numerical code on a small keypad to the right of the elevator panel. As they crowded into the massive space, which had been built to safely hold up to two dozen staff personnel, a series of deafening shrieks engulfed the depot, like thick metal beams being bent to the breaking point.

Just before the panel door slid shut, essentially cutting off their view, it looked as though a far wall had indeed begun to collapse inward from some enormous outside pressure.

"Hate playing the role of pessimist, but that didn't look at all promising," Marvella blurted once the elevator had ascended several levels.

Despite the grimness of the overall mood, The Guardsman couldn't refrain from cracking the tiniest of smiles. Similarly, Ben began shaking his head from side to side, peering over at his former teammate and lover with a comically dismayed expression.

"Darlin', after all these years.... you're still sharp as a tack."

"Darn tootin', dozer-hands, and don't you ever forget it."

"Nooooow I remember why I went solo," The Guardsman retorted with a loud snort, sending all three into a fit of spastic hysterics while Shetah looked on in utter disgust.

Levitating several inches from the surface of the elevator floor in a transparent force-field, Anvil managed to balance himself upright after a brief struggle.

"Somebody mind letting me in on the joke?" he groaned as the transport ground to a halt.

Whipping his arms about like massive windmill sails, he began a gradual turn that left him hanging sideways.

"What the fuck...? Hey, let me out of here, damn it!" he scowled as the group turned as one to observe his hapless plight, "...at least poke an air-hole, will you? I just farted and it's curling my eyebrows!"

This time, even Shetah laughed

***

Part VI:

Missing Pieces

APPROXIMATELY FIVE MINUTES LATER/OUTSIDE THE COMMAND CENTER

ENTRANCE:

With a frustrated growl, The Guardsman hopped back several paces and fired three quick shots from the thermo-rifle. Although effectively dismembered upon impact fromthe first and second, the keypad was literally disintegrated by the third, which had also managed to remove a sizeable chunk of stone from the adjoining wall.

"Piece of shit!" he bellowed as the rest of the group seemed to reel back as one.

Remaining combat posed, his chest heaved in obvious rage.

"Damned mainframe computer locks up and we're forced to stand around with our thumbs up our asses."

"Believe ya killed 'er, Luke," Ben whispered after stepping forward and practically engulfing the other man's shoulder with the palm of one hand, "she can't hurt us no more."

Dipping the rifle, The Guardsman slumped and fell back a stride. "Don't sweat it, G-Man. Two to one we can pound our way inside."

"Let me out of this damn bodysuit and I'll head-butt my way right through that mo-fo," Anvil added, floating forward like the world's largest soap bubble.

"Forget it, pal," The Guardman barked, "keeping tabs on you is an extra hassle I definitely *do not* need right now."

Gently bumping the bubble with the edge of one elbow, Ben leaned in with a smirk, covering one side of his mouth with a spread palm.

"Yeah, just keep playin' Macys Thanksgivin' Day parade float, Blockhead. No doubt ya got the hot air to pull it off."

"Cram it, backhoe hands..." Anvil growled in reply, struggling to remain upright as the bubble titled hard to the left.

"Hello? Back here, fellas..." Marvella interrupted, waiving one hand like a school child requesting permission to speak, "...why do men always insist on doing things the hard way? Stand back and allow me."

"You got enough juice reserved? I sure wouldn't mind having you at full strength when the final act of this little drama plays out."

"Luke's right, Leah. We may well end up ridin' your coattails off this sinkin' burg, ya know? I know how these fields wear you out..."

"I've upgraded a bit in terms of firepower since we last walked the same grounds, Ben," she stated confidently, walking past each to face the double-paneled entrance. "Keep an eye on Anvil. His field might weaken once I divert the majority of my concentration."

The Guardsman nodded in acknowledgement while giving Anvil the once-over.

"Noted. You sure about this, Leah? I mean, Ben might be able to slug his way through..."

Shrugging wearily, Marvella reached up and began a quick series of finger stretches, as if prepping for a piano concerto.

"For the last time, I can handle it, *dad*."

"Yeah, you guys just tuck in your penises for a sec and let the girl do her thing," Shetah spat sourly, reaching forward to grasp the outer surface of the field encasing Anvil and pulling him slowly back.

Standing with her feet together and her head

tilted slightly to the left, Marvella lifted both arms shoulder level and straight out with each fist tightly clinched.

After a moment of utter stillness, she threw her head back while simultaneously thrusting both fists inward with the backsides facing up.

"Get a load of '*Jacqueline Chan*' over there. Gonna karate-chop her way in, I suppose," Anvil grunted, wriggling his colossal torso as to immediately test the field for any possible give.

The doors instantly began to expand outward with a loud metallic shriek, resembling over-inflated balloons on the verge of explosion.

"Damn…she *has* added an extra gear or two," Ben whispered in apparent awe, cocking an elbow on The Guardsman's shoulder.

"That's no Pepsi can either. We're talking titanium- based and almost a foot thick."

Two similar thrusts and the panel doors peeled apart like sliced orange wedges, creating a circular-shaped space at least four feet wide.

"Looks like I finally found the right key, boss," Marvella said, addressing The Guardsman with a nod.

"Ben, you accompany me inside," he replied, peering through the opening into the murky dimness beyond, "Leah, stay here with these two."

"Goddamn teacher's pet," Anvil grumbled as Ben stepped by to join The Guardsman at the newly formed entrance.

"Crock of shit," Shetah chimed in with a barely subdued hiss, "that just isn't right."

After watching first The Guardsman and then Ben vanish into the wide chasm, Marvell whirled

349

about in a complete circle without benefit of actually moving her feet.

"I wouldn't expect your kind to understand the words loyalty or teamwork, but those two fought back to back against the likes of you on many occasions, putting each other's lives on the line. Can either of you truthfully state you wouldn't gleefully fuck each other over for even the *tiniest* financial gain?"

Wearing similar expressions of wide-eyed bewilderment, Anvil and Shetah studied one another momentarily before turning back to Marvella as one to reply.

"Been there…done that," they spewed in almost perfect harmony.

"I rest my case," Marvella said, nodding grimly, "now cease the bitching before I seal your mouths shut."

Anvil's lips had barely parted in an attempted reply when The Guardsman shot from the darkened command center in a full gallop with Ben close on his heels. At almost that precise moment, the corridor shook from still another loud rumbling.

"Let's move, people. Nothing to see in there but more bodies. Leah, cut Anvil loose. From what I'm seeing, it's going to be a *fight to live* scenario once either we find the enemy or it finds us."

"About damn time, Chief," Anvil bellowed, pausing to literally pinch each forearm once the field had been lifted, "Time to settle a score."

"One false move, box head, and I'll cook your miserable hide," The Guardsman scowled, rotating glares from Anvil to Shetah, then back agai. "We've got a common foe to dispatch. Once that particular deed is done, you can hop aboard if you're still feeling froggy."

Donning a wry grin, Ben leaned in and tweaked the larger man with an elbow.

"Better watch your P's and Q's, big fella. I do believe the chief means bizzzz-nus."

Anvil shot him a menacing stare.

"You're first on the hit list, smart ass. Number one with an un-lubricated bullet."

Moments later, they sprinted down the curved corridor in single file with Ben and Marvella coming up the rear.

"Was it that bad, Ben?" Marvella asked, having slowed just enough to maintain a ten to twelve-foot distance between them and the rest of the group. "Remember the stash of bodies we found that vampire coven feedin' on down in Mexico a few years back?"

"Yeah, but it was Spain...I think. The *Fang Gang*, they called themselves. Teenaged gang-bangers with the gift of immortality."

"Well, makes that slaughterhouse look like romper-room. There were arms, legs and heads scattered about that com center like jigsaw pieces. Luke was pretty damn shaken...even tried to ID a few of the heads 'fore I pulled him outta there."

"No sign of the Warden or Director Willis?"

"Didn't see Terry among the ruins, but I ain't got a clueon this Willis dude."

"FBI deputy director...accompanied us on the trip over."

"Luke didn't mention 'im. Didn't see any bodies...or parts of bodies without a blue uniform hitched to 'em.

"By the way, 'fore I forget to mention it, did Luke say anything to you about a *Level X?*"

"First I've heard of it."

"Just checkin'. He told me I probably dreamed it. Gotta admit, the line between reality and fantasy in this funhouse is growin' mighty damn thin."

Carefully eyeing his former flame as they sped up a tad, Ben found himself cheerfully unable to force the smile from his lips.

"So…how you been? Ya look…fantastic…just…really great. I mean... hell, if anything, you're gettin' more gorgeous as the years pass."

She instantly shot him a questionable look, to which Ben raised a hand palms up in a 'swearing' gesture.

"Scouts honor, L. I ain't just shootin' you a line. I mean, we're beyond that, right? I never was one to lie to ya. Had my faults, for sure. Probably added a whole new list since I last saw ya, but dishonesty wasn't one of 'em."

"No…no, you never did," she replied softly and just a bit out of breath. "I'm…I've been all right I… guess. You know how it is in this business. One adapts to survive on an hourly basis."

As she paused to inhale, Ben started to interject but stopped just short. "I've…thought quite a bit…about you. Heard about…the trail and conviction. Had a hard time believing either. Then…what with coming here and finding you holed up…I, well…strange isn't the word, Ben. It's been…so damned surreal, you know?"

"I'm with ya, darling", he huffed, "came damn near peein' myself when I saw ya standin' there

352

next to Luke. Like a sledgehammer to the gut, it was, but…in a *good* way, if that makes any damn sense. Hell, make that a *great* way."

Watching the others round a sharp corner at least fifteen years ahead, Ben reached over and pulled Leah close, practically tripping them both up in the process.

"Darlin', would I be riskin' a punch in the kisser if I reached over and gave ya a big hug?" Ben whispered huskily, having leaned in until his lips were parked mere inches from Leah's left ear.

"Thrill me, big guy," she cooed seductively while placing her slim, toned arms around his thick, bulging neck.

Placing his shovel-sized hands on either side of her waist, he hoisted her airborne with shocking ease before lowering her and pulling her taunt to his bare chest.

Leah looked up and tilted her head slightly to the left, pursing her lips to allow easier access beneath the hard-edged cowl of her alter-ego.

The two locked eyes for the briefest of moments before their lips caressed. Though the longevity of the kiss was brief, the level of passion behind the gesture itself was immeasurable. Ben stepped back, keeping his hands balanced atop her narrow shoulders.

"Leah, this may sound cornball, so excuse me if I come off soundin' a little *wussy,*" Ben exclaimed in a surprisingly subdued whisper, his shoulders slightly slumped, "but I never dreamed…didn't dare let myself dream, that I'd ever lay eyes on you again. I gotta tell ya, this sad old heart got a full recharge the minute I realized it wasn't some kind'a cruel hallucination."

"Why, Benjamin Thomason," she replied, a slight hitch in her otherwise business-like tone, "in this girl's opinion, that didn't come off the slightest bit wussy. I've…missed you, too, ya big hairy lug."

"Same here, beautiful…big time."

They then shared a mutual smile, understanding without verbal confirmation that whatever had once been lost between them had remerged with a newfound fervor.

"We'll talk more later, Benji. Once we get off this cursed rock and back to safer climes," Leah concluded, stiffening her pose while reaching up to wipe away a fragmented tear drop that had somehow managed to breech the cowl's slim eyehole.

Pounding a fist against his own breastbone, Ben's expression was suddenly frighteningly intense.

"Babe, that's all the motivation I'll ever need. Let us now shag ass, my darlin'."

***

Having circled back, Shetah met them just as they'd turned the curve and shot them a curious glance.

"Let you two in on a little secret. Felines are noted for their unnatural hearing abilities," she whispered just loud enough to be heard in the short distance between them, "…and I've got to admit; these old heartstrings are on the very edge of snapping." Grinning mischievously and thus displaying a row of tiny, sharp teeth book-marked

354

by a pair of lengthy incisors, she then whipped back around and faced front, increasing her speed seemingly without effort.

"Mind your own bees-wax, Mittens," Ben replied between gasps, "or I'll make it my personal mission to piss in your milk bowl."

Partially winded, Leah still managed a hardy laugh, the tightly rolled pigtail at her back swinging back and forth like an uncoiled blacksnake.

Exchanging a final meaningful glance as the line began to slow in front of them, both Ben and Leah silently prayed there'd be time for one another once the imminent threat had passed.

As they neared a dead end at the far end of the hall, The Guardsman slowed to a trot, pulling what resembled a tiny remote device from his belt.

The others huddled closely behind as he pointed the device to a high point on the ceiling and the entire wall slid upward.

"Geez, place is one big-ass maze," Anvil blurted, having scooped up Shetah and placed her atop his left shoulder like a pet monkey.

"Secret compartments; endless hallways; underground walkways," Shetah countered, reaching down with her paw-like appendages to obtain a better handhold on Anvil's bulging shoulder. "They must've stole the Blueprint for this place from *Willy Wonka*."

"Crowd in, folks," The Guardsman ordered, posed at the back of elevator with his arms crossed atop his heaving chest. "This leads us to a supply warehouse that also serves as the emergency evac hanger. I can only figure the Warden and Director Willis are already on site. Damned storm is just minutes from swallowing this island whole. Command center monitor showed the dome field at sixty-five percent fragmented."

"Flight over *fight*, huh?" Anvil blurted once the panel door slid shut behind them, "Riddle me something, Mister Chief CO, is that per penal institution re-gu-la-tion or do I detect a bright *yellow streak* developing just below that spandex suit of yours?"

The Guardsman whirled about, pushing Ben to one side until he stood toe to toe with a man who outweighed him by at least a hundred pounds and stood a full foot taller.

"Tech manual is printed in simply layman's terms, pal. In the event of a *total loss* of communication coupled with full alert security breech, in this case meaning successful escape and/or liberation of all housed inmates, Eagle Island staff will be evacuated and the site nuked from air space. Pentagon written; congress approved; *presidential* seal intact.

That reg-u-la-tion enough for you, smart ass?"

For the next thirty seconds, nobody dared even breathe.

"Then again, nothing wrong with playing it safe," Anvil eventually muttered.

As they ascended at what felt like warp speed inside the dimly lit box, Shetah hopped from Anvil's back and directly in front of The Guardsman, who flinched back from her sudden intrusion.

"Dome field? Excuse my...*our* ignorance, Chief CO Sir, but if you don't mind, please *define*."

"The security force-field that blankets the

356

island is on the *fritz*, Fritz," Ben interrupted in a light, sarcastic tone. "Always heard you feline types ain't exactly fond of water. Well, darlin', ya might well learn to love it before this shit-storm concludes."

The fur on her arms, legs and torso suddenly standing out like quills, Shetah meowed seductively before responding.

"Then by all means, big boy, let's fly the hell off this burg before the first wave breaks."

"Almost there, people," The Guardsman announced sternly, "to state the obvious...be ready for anything."

Just as the elevator ground to a smooth, incident-free halt and the panel door swung open with a low hum, Marvella acted on pure instinct by shoving Anvil and Ben aside and shielding the group with a double-layered force-field. A brief instant later, to label such a decision as simply *wise* would be to downgrade its magnitude.

CHAPTER SEVEN

Desolation Day

"Welcome, gentlemen, *lady*, and assorted freaks. I must inquire, what took you so very long?"

Having crawled from what remained of the elevator's ravaged interior like cockroaches into the mid-day sun, the visibly shaken group instantly formed a straight line, shoulder-length apart.

"Man, this shit just keeps gettin' better and better," Benexclaimed wearily, "…gotta say, my shock meter's 'bout pegged the fuck out."

Floating several feet off the steel grid flooring, Mystic had his spindly arms crossed and his legs folded in his familiar 'Ali Baba' pose.

"What the hell's going on, Mystic?" The Guardsman inquiredirritably, shrugging jagged bits of stone and cement dust from his shoulders. "We've got about ten minutes before this place turns into *Atlantis'* sister city."

Just as the panel doors had slid open, the elevator had literally imploded from within, shattering brick and tearing steel into serrated strips and jagged shards, the majority of which had bounced harmlessly from the invisible barrier Marvella had placed with a flick of her wrists.

While The Guardsman and Shetah had managed to leap through the flying shrapnel and escape the confined space and Marvella had simply floated forward to safety inside a body cocoon of her own making, Ben and Anvil were left hanging onto a partially shredded elevator cable. Marvella

358

then levitated them from the smoking ruins of the shaft onto the hanger's steel grid while a welcoming committee of sorts had assembled at the center of the room near a clear glass dome. A dome that had emerged from a well-hidden trap door approximately the size of a greyhound bus, shoving several pieces of stacked furniture and long-discarded file cabinets aside upon its descent to the surface.

"Sorry to keep you in the dark for so long there, Chief Tight-Buns, but it was simply a matter of being on a 'need to know' basis. Afraid you're one of those stalwart, honest to a fault types who just couldn't have comprehended nor accepted the big picture. Afraid this is where we part ways, people. We win...you die."

"You guys recognize this Leprechaun faggot?" Anvil asked while sizing up the largest of the trio standing opposite of them.

Taking a single step forward as he wiped a thick layer of gravel from his bared chest, Ben took up position on Marvella's right just as The Guardsman fell back to her immediate left.

"Name's Mys-tic, emphasize the '*Miss*' part. Proud flag barrier of queer-eye worshipers everywhere. Most popular limp-wristed super-type on the World Wide Web to boot, I hear. Keeper of the magic flame or some similar horseshit. Also the murderin' rat bastard that knocked off *Crimson Condor* and framed yours truly for the killin'."

"Benjamin, Benjamin, Benjamin..." Mystic chortled cheerily, hovering directly over the glass dome launching pad with the tip of his day-glow shadedboot-tips just inches from the gleaming surface, "...I must admit that few can cop the 'sour grapes' attitude with more sincere conviction. You don't just hold a grudge, big boy, you grip that mother in a bear trap vice. And what a *pair* of vices...you know what they say about a man and the size of his feet. I wonder if that pertains to one's hands as well...Leah?   Sorry   if we've...um...covered this ground before."

"Turncoat son of a bitch," Marvella growled, floating several inches from the floor, "...have to admit, I'm not really asshocked as I ought to be. Never did quite trust you, *partner*."

Shetah bounded over until she sat crouched next to Anvil's massive left thigh.

"These other two seem vaguely familiar to you, Anvil?"

"Now that you mention it, yeah...*Screaming Eagle* and *Mass*, I...I think.

Not sure about-..."

"Big, stupid lookin' lummox is *Obliteration*," Ben chimed in, taking another half-step forward as his tightly muscled calves bulged from the building tension.

As if magically awakened by the mere mention of their names, the trio shambled forward to be formally introduced. All three were fully costumed; *Screaming Eagle* in his trademark black and crimson jumpsuit, calf-high maroon boots and talon-laden black gloves; *The Mass* in dark green spandex pants and 'raccoon eye' mask, and *Obliteration* in a faded blue-jeans, a dark blue spandex top with matching coil, spiked gloves and sharp-tipped combat boots.

"Somethin' ain't kosher here, Chief. Number

360

one, how in hell did they rate full regalia? Don't know 'bout anyone else, but my costume was left on the mainland."

"And number two?" The Guardsman queried, sizing up Screaming Eagle as they stood directly across from one another.

"You ever know *Obliteration* to keep that wind-tunnel flap'a his closed for this long a duration?"

"Ben's right. They even... they're not...moving quite right. Stiff, almost robotic..." Marvella added as Mystic glided directly into the air space across from her.

"So many questions, so little time..." Mystic sang, rotatinghis body in a tight circle until it was nothing more than a green blur, "...though what good are answers to those about to expire?

You see, folks...there be but a single, that's *one*, emergency transport with which to escape Paradise Lost, holding a grand total of eight warm bodies. Do the math, people...we've some serious subtractions to complete."

Rampaging forward like a wild bull elk in heat, Anvil's warrior cry pierced the air like a screamer alarm.

"Fuck all this jawing...let's *RUMMMM-BLLLLEEEE*!"

Reaching over to pat Marvella gently on one shoulder, Ben playfully cocked an eyebrow.

"Meet ya inside that dome, Leah."

She quickly returned the gesture before sailing off at warp speed.

"If not, I'll personally fly our ass out of here, Benji T. That's a promise."

"Got'cha. Just save me one of those luscious gams'a yoursto hang onto..." After brief deliberation, The Guardsman tossed the thermo-blaster aside like so much excess baggage before lunging forward with his arms locked in a blocking pose.

Similarly, Shetah pounced forward with a resounding hiss, slashing her retractable claws in a sweeping motion.

"Take 'em out quick, gang...then we find the Warden and Director Willis and book the hell off this dune..."

"By all means..." Mystic barked like a circus-tent ringmaster introducing the star attraction, "...let the game...BEGIN!!!"

As bodies sailed forward and the cumulative impact shook the surrounding walls, the hard-steel floor beneath their feet rocked and shimmed from an altogether different source. A source moving ever closer towards what would eventually become the ultimate showdown.

***

Part I:
Battle Royal (Round One)

Resembling a pay-per-view wrestling 'battle royal', the combatants had immediately paired off in separate brawls, a select few possessing personal histories to match the best-scripted drama ever created for just such a scenario.

The warehouse/secret hanger was littered with both metal and wooden shelves and filing cabinets

362

of various sizes, most of which were empty save a few dusty cardboard boxes, along with stacked office furniture, folded conference tables and a virtual blockade of ancient computer monitors with matching components. All had been scattered haphazardly, almost to the point of appearing too *inconspicuous*, as if to provide the perfect cover for the room's actual purpose. As a potential battleground, it contained just enough perfectly spaced obstacles to allow combatants a wide birth between skirmishes.

A blow-by-blow, panel-by-panel description of each (omitting the final outcome):

The Guardsman Vs Screaming Eagle:

The Guardsman soars airborne and tucks his legs, turning a mid-air summersault to avoid Eagle's flying clothesline.

Following a shaky but successful landing, The Guardsman times Eagle's next dive and executes a leaping sidekick that catches his fast-descending opponent just above the breastbone.

He follows this with a series of quick jabs to Screaming Eagle's forehead and chin before backing away a step and performing a windmill backhand that fractures his opponent's nose with a loud crunch.

Sailing back from the onslaught, Screaming Eagle manages to ascend airborne, cradling the bloodied mess at the center of his face. Using a far wall as a springboard, he then shoots forward with clinched fists leading the way.

The Guardsman sidesteps the assault to a

degree, but is still clipped on the right temple and sent sprawling back.

Twisting about and descending like a suicide bomber, Screaming Eagle nails The Guardsman with a solid knee to the chest, then rakes him across the back of the head with the talons of his left hand before again gliding out of range.

Posed on one knee with his head bowed (the back of his cowl essentially shredded as blood seeps onto his neck and between his shoulder blades), The Guardsman remains frozen as Screaming Eagle swoops overhead like a circling vulture.

Screaming Eagle spirals downward heels-first but finds nothing but hard metal surface as The Guardsman rolls forward out of harm's way. Whirling about and then diving forward, The Guardsman snatches each of Eagle's ankles just as he attempts still another liftoff from ground level.

Spinning about while using Eagle's body weight and momentum as added leverage, The Guardsman concludes two complete cycles and releases, sending Eagle careening headfirst into the first of a trio of wooden shelves and toppling them like a house of cards.

As Screaming Eagle struggles from the splintered wreckage, The Guardsman charges forward and plants a shoulder into his breastbone, then lands a solid right hook to the head for good measure.

Screaming Eagle's limp form flails back into a metal girder and bounces forward a full dozen feet before crumpling to the floor in a sprawled heap.

After narrowly dodging a streaking figure he barely recognized as Anvil sail by in a wind-milling blur, The Guardsman approaches the crumpled form with great trepidation, striking a defensive pose.

THE GUARDSMAN: "Let's call it a day, Eagle. Nobody's getting left behind. I give you my word…"

Screaming Eagle's right arm twitches suddenly to life and he proceeds to slash wildly from left to right with his talons fully extended…

Anvil & Shetah Vs The Mass:

ANVIL (bounding ahead in five to six-foot leaps): "Once I floor his fat ass, you shred 'im good, Shetah."

SHETAH (swiftly circling around their common foe): "Easier said than done, hammerhead…"

The Mass inflates his chest and midsection to twice their normal girth just seconds before Anvil makes initial contact with a flying shoulder-block.

Anvil literally sinks into the fleshly quagmire before being slung back out like a human cannonball.

Unable to halt his backward momentum, Anvil plays the part of a giant pinball, crashing into and through several wooden crates and eventually into an industrial-sized AC unit, leaving behind a deep dent in the precise shape of his bulky form.

The Mass spins his bloated mass towards Shetah, who had originally planned on playing stowaway atop his colossal upper back as Anvil pounded away from the front.

SHETAH (squatting on all fours): "Whoa, big boy. This shit isn't quite fair. Afraid I'm about nine-hundred pounds out of your weight class."

ANVIL (slowly jogging forward from the left, wiping wooden splinters and metal shards from his shoulders, chest, and arms): "Hang on, pussy 'n boots. Old dimple cheeks there didn't hurt nothing but this boy's pride."

Twisting his woefully undersized head (when compared to his bloated torso and matching appendages) back towards Anvil, The Mass swings his telephone-pole sized right arm around in a wide, looping arc, the attached fist visibly mutating; growing significantly as it trails behind like a giant medicine ball.

Unable to slide to a complete halt as the crane-sized arm makes impact, Anvil tucks into himself and is slammed like a Ping-Pong ball by an aluminum bat. Clearing a wide berth as he rips into and through everything in his path, Anvil is able to contort and twist in mid-air as to allow his skull to absorb the brunt of the continuous impact. The concrete wall that eventually halts his four-hundred-pound frame is minus several large chunks in the aftermath.

Pouncing forth in one fluid leap, Shetah extends the retractable claws of her hind feet and carves a series of deep groves across The Mass' multi-layered midsection before bouncing quickly out of striking range.

SHETAH (hissing): "Like trying to filet a goddamned sperm whale with a Boy Scout knife."

Resembling a horribly overweight toddler attempting his first steps, The Mass lumbers forward, leaving deep imprints in the steel flooring. Shetah easily dodges his wide, arcing punches,

366

though once his barrel shaped foot comes dangerously close to pinning her tail to the floor.

Climbing atop a three-tiered metal filing cabinet at least two dozen feet from the lumbering giant, Shetah spots Anvil barreling ahead from the opposite direction.

She notices the Mass, his head now resembling a peanut shell compared to the majority of his overstuffed torso, starts to turn in her partner's direction and begins hopping from one cabinet top to the other, waving her arms while yelling at the top of her lungs.

SHETAH: "Hey, *doughboy*! Over here! How does it feel to be getting your ass kicked by a ninety-pound housecat? Well, what you waiting for? Come get some more, butt-smack!"

Lurching forward as his midsection and chest continue to extend, the Mass is bent almost in half by Anvil's full-bore head butt into his lower waist.

The Mass topples headfirst onto the steel grids, his girth sliding forward in a blubbery tidal wave.

ANVIL (gesturing to Shetah): "Jump aboard, girl. Let's finish off this walking slush pile…"

Anvil leaps boots first onto the behemoths back, then proceeds to pound away at the back of his head and neck with a flurry of roundhouse punches that continuously slam The Mass's forehead into the floor.

Cautiously positioning herself between his mammoth thighs, Shetah slashes and tears at the soft meat behind each knee, effectively severing all connecting muscles, tendons, and ligaments as her furry coat is splattered in yellowish gore.

SHETAH: "He's a crip, hammerhead. Finish

'im off."

ANVIL (Sitting on The Mass's back with his boots parked on either side of the giant's bloodied skull. He has his hands curled beneath The Mass' triple-chin, and begins to slowly pull back as his arms bulge mightily from the increased strain) "My pleasure, Kitty-kins. Never did like this loud-mouthed pervert anyhow."

A sharp snap is heard as The Mass's neck bones give way and his spine instantly severs. Not yet satisfied, Anvil continues to tug away until the entire head pops free with a moist ripping sound. Shetah joins Anvil at the front end of the body, already in the process of licking herself clean.

ANVIL (cradling the detached skull in his left hand, which he cocks back playfully): "Hey, go deep and I'll spiral it to ya at the back of the end zone."

SHETAH (Shaking her head in disbelief, though unable to contain a sly grin): "You're one seriously sick pup, block-head."

-Tossing the head casually aside, Anvil watches it land with a muffled thump at the base of a large pile of stacked wooden pallets. Stepping toward Shetah, he starts to reply and watches the fur about her arms, shoulders and upper back snap to attention. Falling into a combat-ready crouch, Shetah hisses loudly and points back towards The Mass's limp form.

Anvil whips around just as the detached head slithers reptilian-like back towards the ruined stump it formerly called home…

Marvella Vs Mystic:

368

MYSTIC: "Sorry it had to go down this way, Leah. I truly am."

Mystic slowly circles Marvella as she ascends towards the eighteen to twenty-foot-high ceiling.

MARVELLA (waving a lifted forefinger from side to side): "Save it, girlfriend. You're gonna need all the hot air you can muster."

Increasing his speed in deliberate increments, he soon is nothing more than a green funnel cloud spinning a bleary web around her hovering frame.

MYSTIC (his voice a static-filled echo): "As hopelessly outmatched as you are, afraid you'll need more than just sassiness to prevail in this particular face-off, my dear dragon lady."

Bringing her hands together just beneath her chin, Marvella clinches them into fists and abruptly swings outward while tilting her head back with an expression of pure ecstasy.

The very air around her slim frame seems to visibly warp and contract, then explode outward, much like an underwater shock wave.

Mystic is blown from his spinning trajectory and sails towards the nearest wall with the speed of hollow point ammo fired from the barrel of a high-powered rifle.

Creating a bulbous pocket of air to serve as a cushion, Mystic is able to buffer the brunt of impact. Still, a man-sized chuck of stone is torn from the wall like paper machier.

MYSTIC (Whirling about in mid-air with the grace of a seasoned ballet dancer): "Immm-pressive. Very impressive. I see you bring more to the table than I'd have ever given you credit for."

Dropping lightly to the floor, Marvella looks quickly to her left and immediately levitates out of the path of a hard-charging mass she doesn't immediately recognize as Anvil, who has apparently been leveled from the opposite end of the warehouse.

MARVELLA (remaining airborne and raising a single finger in a sarcasm-laced 'cum hither' gesture): "You ain't seen nothing yet, fancy pants. Master of the Mystical Realm my *yellow ass*."

Curling his lithe form into a human cannonball-styled pose, Mystic pauses only briefly before barreling forward in a curvy, spinning roll. He abruptly straightens, gliding to a halt mere feet from where Marvella had held her ground. Striking a classic 'gunslingers' pose, he then points his right hand towards her with the forefinger acting as the invisible revolver's barrel and his thumb as the hammer.

MYSTIC (Grinning mischievously): "Bang!"

A squared pocket of air at least a dozen feet high and eight to ten feet wide blasts forward with the force of a high explosive. Despite the protective aura she'd put into place just seconds before, Marvella is sent spiraling back like a spec of confetti inside a wind tunnel.

Her downward trajectory forces her to ground level, where she cuts a wicked path through several oak hutches and a stack of folded conference tables, splintering them into jagged shards of kindling. Finally able to right herself at least somewhat, she skids to a halt less than two feet from the center of a two-foot wide metal strut.

MYSTIC (floating overhead, reaches and

thumps the strut with the same forefinger he used as a gun barrel): "Owww…that certainly would have left a bruise."

MARVELLA (remains grounded; using the brief respite to regain her battered senses): "That all you got, jackass? Not exactly doing your website justice."

MYSTIC (baring his highly glossed teeth, uses his left foot to spring from the strut): "*That,* my dear Leah, was the equivalent of a stale fart in a stout breeze. Trust me, you do not want to experience the extent of my talents. You and I are truly light worlds apart in that sense."

MARVELLA (her shoulders slumped, she falls to one knee and bows her head): "Though awed by the magnitude of your powers, my king, I seem to be unable to locate a white flag. In lieu of a formal surrender, let me instead say…"

Leaping to her feet, Marvella reaches over and grips the edge of the strut with her left hand. She then shuts her eyes, tilting her head slightly to the right as her lips part in an orgasmic moan.

MARVELLA: "…eat this, turncoat."

With a resounding shriek, the strut snaps like a brittle twig, the upper section sailing up and out like a colossal baseball bat ascending with a savage upper cut motion. The sharpened edge hits Mystic full force at chest level, swatting him from site in a yellowish/green smear that briefly hangs in the air like vapor trails from a passing jet.

A two-ton Raymond Forklift is battered airborne upon his meteoric fall, along with a half dozen metal cabinets and several stacks of skids that are tossed against a far wall and thereby reduced to instant toothpick status.

Marvella floats near the pile of smoking rubble and splintered wood chips where Mystic last vanished, keeping a reasonable safe distance while maintaining a 'body wrap' field in case of sudden retribution. Her powers badly drained by that last offensive maneuver, she fears the jig might well be up if her advisory is able to mount an assault similar to the last. She realizes, as does her worthy opponent, that he, indeed, is easily the more potent of the two. Worse yet, Mystic seems to possess an unlimited reservoir from which to feed requiring no 'down time' or 'rest periods' with which to recharge, as she most obviously does.

Flying just a bit closer as to better inspect the carnage, Marvella understands the gravity of the next few moments. If Mystic isn't down for the count, she has but one final chance to end it or not only be completely at his mercy, but leave Ben and the others in a similar quandary. Pressing her gloved hands gently together at the palms, she brings her arms aloft until her vision is effectively split on either side of her clasped fingers with the thumbs resting atop her chin.

Like a Phoenix rising from the ashes, Mystic explodes from the depths of the ruins as if propelled from twin rocket boosters, his aura bathed in blinding yellow flames. The Raymond Forklift, which had been previously overturned, goes sailing by her, while anything wood-based within a twenty-foot radius bursts into flames or is instantly singed to ash.

MYSTIC (voice is noticeably huskier): "Play times over, BITCH! I'm going to deep fry every

372

molecule in that tight little bod of yours."

Marvella refuses to budge nary an inch despite the sudden incendiary conditions slowly penetrating her protective shield; a shield growing thinner and less efficient by the second. Cocking her head back just slightly, the blazing nova blinding her temporarily vanishes beneath her cowl's nose piece. She hears Mystic's aggressive cries and feels his abrupt advance before actually visualizing it. Three seconds, perhaps less, she knows, before impact. As if lying in a cushioned drift of freshly fallen snow, Marvella spreads her arms and legs simultaneously as to create a perfectly sculpted 'snow angel'.

An agonizing scream follows; the originator as yet unknown.

Desolation Outlaw (FORCE) Vs Obliteration:

With a long-striding jog, Ben makes a b-line towards Obliteration, who stands unmoving with his head slightly bowed and his eyes lowered beneath his striped cowl.

Just as Ben narrows his stride and bounds to within two body lengths, Obliteration falls quickly to one knee and plants both fists into the metal flooring just past his boot tips.

Four rows of metal grids peel from the floor like warped wooden planks from a rotted sea vessel, their thick, sharpened edges leading the way.

Just able to crouch and lower his shoulder before impact, Ben barely avoids the razor-honed edges and instead plows into two of the grids at the mid-way point, bending them straight before being tossed back in whiplash fashion.

Flailing back in a running stumble, Ben barely avoids a viscous collision as Anvil sails by like a passing meteor.

Finally managing to halt his backward momentum by planting his heels into and thereby denting sections of the solid steel flooring, Ben then proceeds forward at a more deliberate pace.

BEN (snarling angrily): "Forgot about those shock-wave mitts'a yours, Hoss. Thinkin' back, ya never was one to stand toe to toe and fight like you owned a pair."

His stoic expression unchanged, Obliteration's only reply is a gentle wave of his left hand that serves to pull two of the four grids from their roots and twist them about until they snap free. Whipping the same glove forward with the fingers splayed, he sends the grids rocketing forward like oversized javelins.

With no time to perform a full duck and avoid, Ben manages to twist his upper body sideways just as the twin spears whiz by at chest-level. As one whooshes by, shaving the back of his neck but otherwise doing no damage, the other scrapes several layers of flesh from across his chest, left shoulder, and the entire length of his left arm.

BEN (shaking his head from side to side while ogling the shredded wounds, each of which bleeds profusely): "Now that's gonna leave one hell of a scab."

(Returns his gaze to Obliteration, whose casual pose remains strangely unaltered)

"Guess I can officially flush Plan A down the shitter. On to Plan B..." Sprinting over to his left,

Ben hoists an electric jack overhead by its wheeled forks and goes into a pitching-style windup, tossing the five-hundred-pound object across his torso with a nasty spin. He then breaks into a wild sprint while keeping in line with the lift's tumbling trajectory.

Obliteration calmly pauses until the lift is less than an arm's length away before raising both palms in a blocking gesture. The lift effectively splits neatly in half as if carved by laser beam, each section landing harmlessly in separate corners.

Ben had cocked his right arm just as the lift had halved, then gone airborne a split-second later. Having honed in on a precise target zone just as he'd leapt, Ben throws a roundhouse right landing with deadly accuracy just below Obliteration's left temple.

Staggered, Obliteration attempts to counter with a backhand left of his own which Ben easily blocks with a forearm. He then delivers a booming uppercut that impact's directly beneath Obliteration's exposed chin. Teeth gnash together in a sickening crunch as liftoff ensues. Clearing a row of stacked high-back chairs as he continues to ascend, Obliteration eventually lands atop a large combo box stocked full of shredded bond paper, approximately two dozen feet from initial takeoff.

BEN (posed in 'follow through' mode; his left fist still frozen at the point of impact): "Bingo. No *jawbreakers* for you for at least a month'a Sunday's, Mac."

Despite the fact he could clearly see the bottom of Obliteration's deeply grooved boots sticking from the top of the box, Ben approaches cautiously. He's learned from previous bouts with Obliteration

375

that craftiness is a major part of the man's arsenal.

As he gets to within reaching distance of the man's upturned boots, he leans down to retrieve one of the severed steel girds, then proceeds to rear it back over his right shoulder like a batsman awaiting an opposing pitcher's best fastball.

BEN (almost whispering): "Oblit, you so much as twitch a pubic hair and I'll swat ya like a horsefly. You know I ain't one for bluffin', either."

Ben barely has time to cock the grid before the cardboard box and all contents within blow apart in a virtual mushroom cloud that is eerily silent. After struggling to regain his balance in the aftermath, Ben swings blind; a looping cut grooves the twelve feet long, foot and a half wide solid steel bar forward through the glut of heavy print paper and thick cardboard. He feels a jarring sensation at his wrists as a sharp twanging sound follows, then peers up through the scattered confetti at the limp form sailing overhead in a high, curved arc. He sees one of Obliteration's boots fall loose from his foot just as he bounces off an upper section of wall and onto the hard floor some two to three stories below.

BEN (Between raucous howls): "Oh hell, *YES!* Goodbye Mister Spaulding! He got *ALL* of that one, folks! Som'bitch cleared the left field wall with fifty feet to spare!"

Pausing for a brief moment to scan the other three matches, Ben quickly dismisses all but one. Marvella levitates a good hundred yards to his right as Mystic circles a steel support beam just above her. He considers coming to her aid immediately, then decides to first ensure his own opponent's permanent demise.

Keeping the three hundred plus pound homemade 'bat' anchored over his shoulder, he fast walks the distance towards his fallen enemy in thirty quick strides. As he grows ever nearer, he can see the grotesquely warped condition of Obliteration's skull, which looks to be badly crushed on the right side and resembles a half-eaten melon. It's also obvious that either one or both of his legs is broken, and the neck, chest and abdomen of his formerly dark blue costume are soaked in crimson, which leaks from his mouth, nose, and eyes in thick streams.

BEN (again, practically whispering): "Ya can't say I didn't warn ya, son. Sometimes the best shots ya land are the lucky ones."

Turning away from his battered foe, Ben tosses the beam to the side and begins a slow jog to Marvella's location. He completes only a few short jaunts before skidding to a clumsy halt. Whirling about while instinctively falling onto one knee, his eyes grow huge just a mere two ticks before impact...

BEN (Bellowing in obvious disbelief): "Shit, just ain't possib-..."

***

Part II:

Battle Royal (The Not-So-Final Outcomes)

The Guardsman Vs Screaming Eagle:

Following a half-stumble, half-dance that

377

allows him to avoid Eagle's elongated talons, The Guardsman counters with a brutal series of front kicks to the side of the slumping figure's face and head. Stepping away from the battered still form to avoid yet another inexplicable awakening, he wears an expression of sincerest befuddlement as the prone body of Screaming Eagle starts to bubble and boil, then melt away as if constructed of half-settled pudding.

Anvil & Shetah Vs The Mass:

Having watched in comical shock as The Mass's previously decapitated head had magically reattached itself to its swollen torso, Anvil and Shetah pace the whale-sized body in an uneasy semi-circle. A thick, yellowish slug trail forms a horizontal line from where the severed skull had lain and the stump it had so loyally reunited with.

They witness as previously dead eyes glimmer with newfound life, and arms and legs begin to wriggle and spasm with ever-increasing vigor.

Pouncing as one, Anvil lands atop the back of The Mass's recently rejoined scalp with both of his size fifteen steel-heeled boots, while Shetah rips deep, strangely bloodless groves into his upper and lower back. Yelping in disgust, Anvil leaps to the side with gummy yellow blobs streaming from his boots like melted tar. He turns to see The Mass's head flattened like a deflated soccer ball, the same glutinous yellow liquid having spewed forth from each ear.

Shetah rejoins him on the sidelines as The Mass slowly dissolves into a pulsating pile of something

378

resembling pancake mix.

Marvella Vs Mystic:

Having effectively constricted Mystic's arms, chest and legs in steel banding she'd reshaped from the same strut previously used to disable him, Marvella nonetheless maintains a twenty to thirty-foot distance between them.

Lying face up like a man trapped in an anaconda's deadly squeeze, Mystic's eyes flutter continually between consciousness and an uneasy slumber.

Once he seems to regain at least a semblance of awareness, it takes him several moments to properly adjust. Marvella now stands directly to his left, leaning forward with her hands cupped over her knees. Huffing intermediately, her breathing is audibly strained, while thick beads of sweat drip from her upturned chin.

The Guardsman then takes up position to his immediate right, moments later to be followed by Shetah, Anvil, and Desolation Outlaw/Force.

As his enemies converses over what they mistakenly consider a dazed, hapless prisoner, Mystic temporarily appeases himself by envisioning the slaughter to come. Simultaneously, he cannot help but not only ponder the whereabouts of the man responsible for this day's festivities, but also the *true* motive behind them.

Desolation Outlaw (Force) Vs Obliteration:

After turning and essentially leaving the other

man for dead, Ben feels an overwhelming sense of impending danger that compels him to check over his shoulder one final time.

He has time to spout but a select few curse words before being pummeled thirty feet into the air and directly into the rusty shell of a long-discarded tow-motor, which subsequently executes a double-flip before smashing into a far wall.

Crawling from the wreckage with a trio of deep gashes carved into his forehead, Ben's mustache and beard are coated in fresh blood. Through bleary eyes, he can see the wavy outline of Obliteration trudging slowly his way. Reaching back into the ruins of the tow motor, he rips the tubular gas cylinder free from its binding and keeps it tucked tightly to his lower back.

Spitting out a mouthful of blackish blood, Ben feels his very bones are lit ablaze, and understands with dead certainty that another double-handful of Obliteration's *pulse-wave* punches might well meld his exo-skeleton, tendons and flesh into a mutated puree.

Strolling forward with a strangely mechanical gait, Obliteration seems utterly obliviousor uncaring in regard to a counter assault as he rears his fists straight back in a 'double-strike' pose. Having bent his knees just slightly, Ben uncoils as they reach striking distance, tossing forth a rather weak backhand that Obliteration successfully deflects with a forearm raise. Whipping the metal cylinder around like a battering ram, Ben drives its round end into Obliteration's exposed ribs, lifting him several feet from the floor. His body having already gone limp, Obliteration descends in a heap, only to be nailed flush in the face by a powerful follow-up that causes both himself and the cylinder to burst into flames. As Obliteration flails back, waving his arms madly in trying to somehow douse the blaze, Ben takes two quick steps back, then plows ahead and administers a savage front kick to the midsection. Resembling a flaming meteor, Obliteration leaves a burning trail of smoldering spandex and flaming body parts on his descent towards a wall lined with metal shelving. By the time what little remains spatters an upper shelf and backing wall like lava-based mudpies, a twenty to thirty-yard walkway of flaming goo is left in its wake.

***

Part III:

A Mystic-al Revelation

Despite a noted difficulty in breathing due to the tightly wound bands, Mystic can already feel the soothing replenishment cycle course through his veins in bombastic waves. Fueled by equal parts embarrassment and rage, he will need only a few short minutes of such recharging before snapping his bonds like wet tissue paper.

True, the extent of Marvella's power, as well as the grit and determination behind it had indeed caught him off-guard. Shockingly so, as a matter of fact. No matter, he deduced, such a bitter defeat would surely enhance the pleasure of impending victory.

"Just what we needed; another damn mystery that'll more than likely go unsolved," Anvil grumbled while scanning the nuclear wasteland the warehouse/secret hanger had become in the last four to five minutes.

Picking small fragments of fleshy slime from her otherwise fluffy coat, Shetah scrunched down onto her heels as her tail whipped back and forth like a pendulum in a Grandfather clock.

"Don't know what we were fighting there, chief, but it most definitely wasn't those portrayed."

"No shit, pussycat. All of 'em melted away like campfire marshmallows," Ben barked sarcastically, still giving the burning trail of gore his undivided attention, "That thing might'a had Oblit's powers, but it didn't even *move* like 'im.

'Sides the loudmouth, trash-talkin' Obliteration I knew and despised couldn't keep his trap door shut that long at gunpoint."

The Guardsman nodded in agreement, reaching down to retrieve the thermal rife he'd discarded earlier.

"*None* of them spoke, come to think of it."

Placing a foot firmly atop the steel binds holding Mystic at bay, Ben casually wiped away several clumps of dried ash from his bared chest.

"Well then, let's just see what ol' swishy-hips here has to say, 'bout this here mystery."

"Just…give me an additional moment or two, Force, and I'llbe… more than …accommodating."

With a grim laugh, The Guardsman glanced from Mystic to Marvella and then back again just as a fresh series of tremors shook the floor.

"Leah, you re-juiced enough to lock this lying

382

squirt into an air-pocket special?"

"Possibly, but I can't promise it'll hold him for very long," she shrugged wearily as a wave of aftershocks caused the group to brace around the fallen form, "especially if it comes down to saving some firepower to fly us off the island through hundred mile an hour winds."

Hopping over until Mystic's head lay at the tips of his massive boot-tips, Anvil grinned devilishly.

"In that case, how's about I dance a jig on his skull? Just to keep him nice and mellow, you understand."

"Forget it, Hoss. If anybody's roughin' up twinkle-toes, it's gonna be me," Ben growled, "and not while he's trussed up like a prize hog neither."

Stepping out of the circle and in the direction of the domed hanger, The Guardsman moaned loudly and checked his wristwatch.

"Drop it, you two...there's no time. We got less than eighteen minutes to find the Warden and cast off before the sea swallows us whole." ACTUALLY LUCAS, I'M AFRAID YOU HAVE WOEFULLY

OVERESTIMATED. IT'S MORE LIKE...TEN TO ELEVEN MINUTES AT THE OUTSET. AND BY THE WAY, I HAPPEN TO BE PRIVY TO THE FACT THAT BOTH WARDEN TERRY AND DEPUTY DIRECTOR WILLIS ARE IN GOOD HANDS.

Turning towards the others, The Guardsman wore a contorted expression as he shook his head from side to side as to shake water build-up from his ears.

"Did...anybody else...hear someth-"

"Welcome to the loony-vine, G-Man," Anvil cut in with a smirk.

Shetah whipped her tail about happily, hopping on Anvil's back piggy-back style.

"Now there's a voice I never thought I'd be so damn happy to hear pinging between my ears again!"

"Where ya at, Sweep?" Ben bellowed between cupped hands the size of dinner plates, "ya missed the party, dude. Curfew's closin' in fast."

AH, BUT THAT'S WHERE YOU'RE WRONG, BENJAMIN. THE PARTY, AS IT IS…HAS JUST BEGUN…

Without warning, the hanger's domed top exploded outward in a shower of glass slivers, fading like early morning mist once airborne.

With a low hum, the transport hovercraft arose to ground level atop a shiny tubular brace that protruded from its midsection like a probing antenna. The oval-shaped craft, pitch black in color and utterly without markings of any type, was shiny slick and without a visible visor or portal.

"It's one of those portable eggs like the Avengers use, only a hell of a lot more compact," Anvil remarked as the group took a cautious step forward, temporarily oblivious to their lone captive's very presence.

"Sure doesn't look sturdy enough to fend off hurricane conditions," Shetah added, sticking close to Anvil's thigh.

Instinctively taking the lead, The Guardsman walked ahead several paces, halting less than a dozen steps from where the craft had finally concluded its gradual ascent.

384

"Not to worry, group. That bad boy was scientifically designed, Marine built and Air Force tested to withstand the worst Mother Nature has to offer, not to mention whatever super-powered bad guys they had in mind at the time."

"Hey Sweep! Get your ass in tow, buddy…this here train's about to pull out of the station!" Anvil yelled as the ground shakes began anew.

"Start loading up while I initiate the entry code. Can't say I want to stick around to see what's causing *that*. Leah, can you…uh…" The Guardsman announced, gesturing towards Mystic, "…no way he'll fit with that steel anaconda pinning him down."

Posed with her hands on her hips, Marvella closed her eyes and sighed heavily while crossing her arms across her chest.

Seconds later, the thick steel banding began to uncurl itself from Mystic's lithe frame like a slowly uncoiling python.

Meanwhile, as still another series of aftershocks ensued, Ben stepped over and balanced his left boot heel less than six inches from the center of Mystic's face.

"Just gimme a reason, punk. Believe me, it won't take much of a shove." Just as the twisted metal was flung into a far corner, the sound of pressured air being released was heard, followed by a distinct electrical hum.

All but Marvella turned toward the hovercraft, whose lone entry hatch was in the process of peeling back in the form of two sliding panels located on its concave rooftop.

"You doing this, Guardsman?" Anvil queried,

backing away a half step. "Not on your life. Haven't even accessed the damn code yet."

"Just what we needed…more surprises," Shetah hissed, remaining partially bathed in Anvil's substantial shadow.

Having bound Mystic at the wrists and ankles with transparent 'cuffs' molded from forced pockets of air, Marvella left him lying on his side and joined the others to witness the latest mystery unfold.

Once the panels had slid completely ajar, there was a moment's pause wherein each member of the rag-tag group sucked in a mouthful of smoke-filled, tension-laden oxygen at almost precisely the same time.

As the figure slowly ascended until the full of his head, shoulders and upper torso were properly exposed to the fluorescent lighting, the tension instantly departed The Guardsman's bulging shoulders, though the others remained in separate combat-ready stances.

"Afternoon, ladies and gents. Someone here call for a cab?" the entity blurted through a wide, rather hideous grin, its robotic tone similar to answering machine auto-modes, the tone gravelly to the point of being incomprehensible.

Standing to The Guardsman's immediate left, Ben shuffled over and lightly nudged the other man without speaking, as if awaiting an answer to a question he hadn't yet bothered to ask.

"Well, you recognize this bird, Luke?" he finally grumbled as they watched the form prop itself onto the open hatch atop spread elbows.

"You probably know him better than I, Ben. Group, that there be the former *Ma Bell* of the

386

prison telepathic grapevine."

Bowing his head like a stage performer receiving a standing ovation, the entity's toothless grin never wavered.

"Sweep, as we live and barely breathe!" Anvil exclaimed, slapping his forehead with an open palm.

Shetah leaned from Anvil's cover just enough to give the new arrival a thorough once-over.

"Long time, *never* see, dude. Man, we figured you for toasted cheese by now."

"I have a penchant for survival, Shetah...among other things," Mind Sweep replied stiffly, the wily grin having faded into a pained scowl; the jocular tone he'd previously used having vanished as well.

As the floor began to rock and rumble with newfound ferocity, the group lunged forward towards the oil-slick edges of the tiny, circular launching pad.

Mystic brought up the rear as Marvella levitated his shackled form several inches from the surface and guided him forward like a marionette on a string.

The Guardsman was the first to discover the transparent field encircling the craft, impacting face-first and subsequently tumbling onto his backside with a pained huff, the thermal rifle windmilling from his grasp.

Anvil soon followed, stumbling back while cradling a bloodied nose, soon to be followed by Ben and Shetah, each of whom had been fortunate in leading with their shoulders in lieu of their faces.

More embarrassed than actually hurt, The

Guardsman leapt to his feet with balled fists clinched tightly at his sides just as Mind Sweep could be seen crawling from the hovercraft on his hands and elbows, resembled some mutated predatory insect escaping a test tube enclosure.

"Damn it, Mind Sweep...what the hell gives? This is no time for delays, mister."

"I'll say...fuckin' floor is about two ticks away from eatin' us whole," Ben chimed in while battering the transparent blockade with a flurry of left and right hooks.

"I do apologize for the lack of a suitable warning, but, to use the vernacular, Mister Chief Correctional Officer...do the math. The good warden and DD Willis are already taking up two of the eight available seatings. Far *too many* bodies present to safely accommodate, I sadly must report," came the raspy, robotic reply as the whole of the entity's lower body departed the craft with a soft plopping sound.

"Geez Louise..." Anvil blurted, staring through crimson-stained fingers as the hover's hatch resealed with a loud hiss.

"Ewwww shiiiiitttt..." Shetah purred, cringing back in obvious disgust. "Damn...ugly SOB must'a broke outta its vat on Sea World-*Mars*..." Ben whispered just loud enough to evoke a nervous giggle from The Guardsman, who somehow refrained from a verbal response of his own.

Settling onto the multiple tentacles that served as its lower appendages, Mind Sweep swayed back and forth as if somehow unable to gain the proper balance.

With its thickly scaled, football shaped noggin,

388

complete with equally pointed chin; pupil-less, maroon shaded eyes and lip-less, frog-like mouth strangely hollowed out, the possibility of an extraterrestrial origin was hardly in doubt.

All things considered, however, it was the slime-coated, squid-like appendages serving as its legs, along with a barrel-shaped torso coated in various sized growths that resembled mutated moles or polyps that ended all possible speculation. Raising one of its three arms airborne, it extended a single clawed digit while cocking its head dramatically to one side.

"I steadfastly refuse, however, to make apologies for my outward appearance Believe it or don't, I was sired from pure-blooded royalty."

"Can the speeches, Cone head," Ben blurted, giving the field a final kick before backing away with a wicked snarl, "...the math ain't hard at all. Answer is: leave the green fag over there lyin' on the dock to fend for himself."

Twisting about in order to shoot Marvella a lighthearted wink, he then proceeded to give Mystic the finger before turning back around.

"Ya see? Elementary. Like my dear old Pop used to spout...keep it *simple*, stupid."

"No way, Ben," The Guardsman replied sternly, "I said no one gets left behind, and I meant it. There has to be a way to-..."

Waiving him off with a frantic shake of a dark-green, elongated claw, Mind Sweep seemed to pause only long enough to briefly focus on Mystic, who had fallen uncharacteristically quiet while seemingly fighting back a case of the giggles.

"Ah, let me clarify what seems to be a rather

confusing issue. It isn't simply that there are too few spots and too many rear ends to fill them, people…" it bellowed in a foghorn tone that had seen the decibel level double since the last statement, "…it's just that…well, I'm afraid *all* flights from Eagle Island Detention Center have been canceled. No make-up flights, you understand. A more…*permanent* cancellation is the order of the day."

Like fractured shutters following monsoon winds, all mouths seemed to fall ajar at once.

"As for the earlier math quiz, Benjamin…afraid I was just, vernacular once more, *pulling your leg.*"

For the second time in less than three minutes, everyone froze.

***

Part V:

Swept Away

"Cut the bullshit and drop this damn wall, Sweep. The thought of attemptin' to back stroke through forty-foot waves ain't exactly givin' me a boner," Ben growled, angrily backhanding the force-field in-between front and side kicks equally ineffective.

"Don't…think he's kidding, shovel-hands," Anvil injected, balancing the palms of his hands against the invisible barricade.

With its tentacle-like appendages shuffling and swaying like algae in a fish tank, Mind Sweep held a single digit airborne as if to continue clarifying a vital point.

"So astute, Anvil. And here I never considered you the 'brainy' type. Not to worry, however, the protective screen will soon dissipate. At my discretion, you understand.

"I simply refuse to stoop to such borderline... *cowardly* tactics as the zero-minute approaches."

"You're...behind all this? *You?*" The Guardsman shrieked as the steel flooring at the far side of the warehouse began to visibly bulge from an enormous pressure beneath.

"Alas, as one of your greatest statesman once uttered...that much I cannot deny."

"Hell of a lot to go through just to scale the wall, assholes" Ben blurted while reaching to grasp a severed tow motor fork and cradling it like a warrior's spear, "ya could've at least let the rest of us in on the master plan."

"Scheming piece of shit was playing with our heads all this time," Shetah hissed.

Slinking forward like a mutated centipede, Mind Sweep held out both hands in a 'halting' gesture.

"Folks, folks, please...due to the constraints of time, I'm unable to stand here and explain each minute detail like some fictional movie villain. I can, however, provide a service that essentially covers the same ground in a more...shall we say, *cerebral* manner. Brace yourselves, gang, for a brief but rather bumpy ride. It's.... SHOWTIME!!"

With nothing more than a quick wink of an eye and tilting of its pointed skull, the group flinched back as one, instantaneously entranced; their eyes rolling back into their heads as their bodies grew

391

rigid and unmoving.

Blurred, frenzied images filled their collective minds, revealing:

A diamond shaped vessel streaking across darkened skies before crashing in a barren desert. A form crawls from the wreckage, led across the sandy dunes on multitudes of brightly glistening tentacles. Atop its broad, scaly chest hangs a talisman of sorts; shaped and sized like a masonry brick, its swirling colors are far too many to correctly identify. As the thickly armored entity glides purposely across the desolate landscape, it periodically reaches down to fondle the talisman, which seems to pulsate and gleam ever brighter in response.

A pack of horribly emaciated coyotes surround the entity in a wide clearing devoid of any living vegetation save the occasional cacti plant. As the beasts close in, each spitting froth as their growls intensify, the entity has but to gesture with one clawed hand while the other clasps the talisman in a steely vice. A series of pained yelps are overheard as the wild canines are instantly disintegrated into bubbling mush and pulsating piles of hair, bone and teeth. The entity lurches forward into the mix, absorbing the contents through quarter-sized pores that visibly inhale each drop until the bloat of its torso resembles an overfilled tick on the verge of popping. Within moments, the entity deflates back to its original size, pausing only briefly to rear its pointed head and howl at the full moon shining brightly overhead.

The same entity is shown standing atop a jagged cliff, battling an equally alien foe whose

392

shiny, silver form streaks by atop a flat board of the same color.

Lying dazed and battered at the bottom of a jagged ravine, the entity is stripped of the talisman as a silver hand clutches it tightly and pulls it free from the sinewy, cord-like appendages that had previously held it in place. A slick, squared grove, encased on all sides by scaly armor, is left inconspicuously bare in its place, as if a vital organ had been removed.

Within the confines of a blandly painted room with four squared walls bathed in some sort of laser light, the entity sits atop a cot with its tentacles tucked beneath it like an overgrown houseplant. The entity weeps quietly while stroking the empty space at its chest.

Standing at the center of the same room, the entity gestures with elongated fingers. It seems to either be talking to itself or possibly mediating a mental conference of sorts, as a bevy of voices can be heard prattling aloud in varied volumes.

Again within the same confined space, whipping its head violently from side to side, the entity at first seems enraged until the shaking subsides and its expression clears. It's gruesomely wide, lip-less maw is stretched in a horrible parody of a human smile; its black-pitted eyes upturned and seeping a thin, yellowish liquid from each corner.

A pair of pasty-white hands can be seen handing the entity an object wrapped in what appears to be burlap. The entity unwraps the object with great care, as if the contents are of some brittle, ancient relic. The talisman glows ever brighter within the entities loving embrace, finally illuminating to its peak once placed back into the waiting slot within the entity's chest.

Rapid, blurred images of grisly death ensue; limbs ripped from the hosts of victims whose faces are never made quite clear, a villainous giggle barely audible but consistently present as dozens upon dozens are mercilessly dispatched.

The final images are a montage of grotesque mutations; gore-drenched transformations wherein each victim is assaulted and immediately dismembered, the individual pieces disintegrated into foamy slush piles before being magically reassembled in the same fashion. Following each individual episode, the entity known as Mind Sweep sits at the center of its cell, shuddering in orgasmic delight as the shimmering talisman at his chest pulsates like a throbbing vein.

Snapping to as quickly as they'd gone under, the group stumble forward, each blinking rapidly as the effects gradually fade.

"Damn, talk about your head trips," Ben mumbled, thumping the left side of his skull with an open palm, "like watchin' a thousand video clips strung together."

Similarly, Anvil slapped himself across both sides of the face before attempting to refocus.

"Hope that wasn't supposed to explain this crazy shit. Didn't make a lick of sense to me."

After briefly rubbing his eyes through his mask's narrow slits, The Guardsman re-cocked the thermal rifle and pointed it directly at the entity's bared chest.

"I got the gist. That glowing brick brought onto the isle yesterday is your personal nine-volt battery.

The Silver Surfer took it from you but somehow couldn't manage to destroy it.

"That damn rock provides all the extra kick you needed to not only fly the coup, but essentially torch the son of a bitch and everyone in her as you go. Those...things we fought back there were clones you created; zombies forged from the same rough clay."

Sliding forward until it stood less than a dozen feet from the field's demarcation line, Mind Sweep reached up with clawed hands to fondle the object's smooth, marble-like edges.

"Impressive on at least two counts, Mister Chief CO. True, I was woefully incomplete without my *Dundrio*...or talisman, as you earth-people ignorantly label such objects. Once it was again within my palms, I do believe my fellow inmates were subjected to quite the temporary 'rush' during the initial 'power-up' phase."

"That explains that minute long 'acid' trip a while back, anyhow," Shetah injected as both Anvil and Ben nodded their acknowledgement. Mind Sweep briefly eyed her with sincere disdain before continuing.

"Regardless, to be endowed with its magical presence is not preordained for my kind, you see. This is not a trinket, but *earned* through eons of strife. It isn't as if I couldn't exist without it, but 'tis a *woeful* existence indeed, as these last several earth years have proven.

"Ditto, your 'clone' theory is only partially flawed. I like to think of them more as... crude *extensions* of my inner aggression. Re-obtaining my *Dundrio*...um... my talisman allowed for the

395

extermination and regurgitation of our fellow inmates. The altering of tissue and subsequent reproduction of same is child's play, as is playing the role of puppet master. Such games might seem cruel and unjustified to the uninformed eye, but they were indeed vital to replenishing my power for the battle to come. Some went quite peacefully...others not so. *Black Plague, The Mass* and *Shemeleon* in particular insisted on...*doing it the hard way*, as your kind is so apt to say. I believe *Black Plague* even attempted a telepathic warning or two before expiring via a rather nasty overdose. I found it poetically ironic that a being such as he could be so easily dispatched by simply rearranging the poisons within his very own system.

"As for my motivation and intentions, neither is as complex as one might think. It's nothing personal, Mister Chief, difficult as that might be to believe."

"You murdered my staff, you piece of shit," The Guardsman spat angrily, the rifle visibly shaking in his steely grip.

"Alas, like yourselves...victims of circumstance."

The first to completely shake off the cobwebs, Marvella instinctively floated several feet above the gyrating floor while ensuring Mystic stayed within striking range.

"Luke...we've...we've got to move. The floor...something's coming...and I don't think it's just salt water."

"Your female intuition is...as you people like to say...right on the money, Marvella," Mind Sweep injected in a in a deep, guttural tone, "... ah, you people have taught me so much about the slang of your language through the years. Honestly, I've cherished each nugget of knowledge you've provided."

The steel flooring began to crack and split like an arid desert surface, seemingly making a b-line directly towards the hovercraft pad.

Whirling about on his heels, The Guardsman reached up and grasped Marvella's left ankle and pulled her gently to the surface. "Tell me you can crack this barrier."

"Why, these next few minutes should make for some interesting viewing, to say the least..." Mind Sweep continued to cackle in a voice that grew increasingly alien with every syllable, "...a final ...exam that I alone am privy to both witness and critique before the final bout of the evening."

Marvella stared past The Guardsman and at the slithering entity that seemed to be in the middle of a political speech only it could truly comprehend.

"I can...give it my best shot, but I'll have to release Mystic. I'm way too drained to pull double-duty."

"Do it. Ben...Anvil...stand on either side of Mystic," The Guardsman commanded while administering a gentle pat to Marvella's left shoulder.

"If the scrawny bastard so much as twitches, break him in half."

Both men did as ordered, each wearing equally demented grins as Mystic slid slowly back down to the surface directly between them.

"I always did like your kinda leadership, G-man," Ben quipped, cocking back his left arm as his manhole-sized fist curled inward with a low crunch.

"And I'm gaining new respect by the minute," Anvil added, his right arm similarly positioned.

Mystic briefly regarded each with a sour grimace. "Brutish, bloodthirsty barbarians."

Glancing back and forth from Mystic to the gradually approaching seam in the warehouse floor, The Guardsman then locked in on Marvella and nodded.

"Give it a go, Leah."

As Marvella stepped up and raised a single hand towards the invisible barricade, three distinct actions transpired within the same exact instant.

Mystic's previously bound wrists fell to his sides and he took off like a heat-seeking missile towards the ceiling, leaving Anvil and Force swinging through dead air and narrowly avoiding each other's punch trajectory.

The flooring near the warehouse's entry point peeled away like a soda can punctured from the inside, a greenish fog seeping upward in thick, billowy waves.

Like a mighty sequoia taking root, a veritable army of new tentacles sprang from Mind Sweep's underbelly and spread the width of the hover pad as to effectively block any possible passage.

"Awww, shit…looks like our uninvited guest has officially arrived," Shetah exclaimed, hopping aboard Anvil's back as the big man trailed Mystic's flight pattern from ground level.

Ben reared back and tossed the forklift blade like a javelin, then cursed under his breath as it missed Mystic's streaking form by a wide margin.

"Gimme a priority target, G-Man," he scowled,

alternating his focus from Mystic's circling flight pattern to Mind Sweep's plant-like mutation, "...I got no special preference on who or what gets pounded first."

The Guardsman kept his aim steady even as Mind Sweep sprouted upward like a blooming flower petal, pushed skyward by several elongated tentacles serving solely as lift rods. Less than a dozen feet away, Marvella struggled in vain to pierce a seemingly impenetrable field with powers that had long since peaked, her entire frame bathed in streams of cool sweat.

"You three stay with Mystic, Ben. Leah and I will stay locked on Mind-squid over here."

Glancing momentarily towards the cloud of green hue filling the room from their west, the Chief CO paused, just a hint of indecisiveness in his normally authoritative tone.

"We'll worry about the new kid on the block once it steps out of that damn fog and shows itself."

As if in acknowledgement of those very words, a series of rumbling growls could be heard from somewhere deep within the swirling green mist.

***

Part VI:

Lambs to the Slaughter

"I must...apologize for this, MS," Mystic blurted, gradually building speed as he flew in a tight circle above Anvil, who was in the process of lifting the remains of a battered Cherry Picker from

399

a pile of smoldering steel, "...no excuses for allowing these...*cretins* to survive for this long."

"No apologies necessary, my boy," Mind Sweep replied with a slightlyrobotic tilt of its head, "I never tire of such sport. Besides, one can never receive too much training when preparing for a major bout."

"Major bout? Why do you insist on keeping up this *charade,* Mind Sweep? Let's just dispatch of this rather...insignificant trash and be on our way."

"Hey, asshole...DOWN HERE!" Ben bellowed from Mystic's right, standing atop a crumbled pile of mashed shelving.

"This here...insignificant piece of trash is waitin' for the garbage man to pick up..." he continued, gesturing with the forefingers of both hands, "...I ain't getting any younger, swishy-pants!"

Winding his arms as if shadow boxing, Mystic then whipped out his left arm in a hacking motion just as Anvil had hurled the cab of the cherry picker from directly below.

The cab split neatly in half and sailed off in opposite directions.

"Amateurs. You actually believe one such as I could be fooled by a simple misdirection ploy? Reeeallllly now..."

Standing less than twenty yards away, The Guardsman backed up a step while maintaining a steady aim at Mind Sweep's chest, the center of which had turned a shade of pure ivory as its glow continued to intensify.

"Any luck at all, Leah? I really hate to be a *pest*, but according to my timepiece we've got less than six minutes before this island is one big coral reef."

"Whatever...it is...I can't even penetrate...its outer layer..." she replied through unblinking eyes drenched in perspiration, both her tightly clinched hands shaking uncontrollably.

"Gonna...have to...give it up soon...Luke, or I'll...be riding waves with...the rest...of you..."

"Shit...let it go."

Releasing a hand from the thermal rifle, he reached over and firmly clamped her left shoulder.

"Leah...let it go..."

"Now what...Chief?" she huffed, bending down with her hands atop her knees.

"Leah, grab Ben and fly out of here."

"Fly...what about...no way," she barked angrily, wiping fresh tears from the corners of each eye, "...seems to me you'll need us both against tha-..."

"We're not *all* gonna make it, Leah, but *somebody* has to."

"I'm not leaving you here, Luke," she replied with renewed vigor, gesturing with a thumb towards Anvil and Shetah, "or even them, for that matter. Don't even ask m-"

Visibly stiffening, he inadvertently swung the barrel of the rifle around and narrowly missed tweaking her left thigh. From the corner of his eye, he watched Mystic use a simple hand gesture to rip up the flooring beneath Anvil's feet, sending the large man sprawling headfirst into a steel girder.

"Damn it, Leah, it isn't as if I'm sending you out on a picnic...you'll have to navigate through hurricane winds! We can't get to the shuttle...there

401

is no other choice, unless you think you can carry *all* of us. If so, hell…I'm game."

"Not…possible. I'd need a day's downtime to pull that off."

The Guardsman shrugged, forcing a tight smile. Less than ten yards away, Mystic seemed to be playing air guitar while bombarding Ben with two tons of shattered rubble. Curling into a tight ball, Ben was able to avoid the majority, with his forearms, shoulders and back taking the brunt.

"End of discussion. Snag Ben by the gonads and get going then. Fly due East. It's a hell of a trek, but you'll spot solid ground eventually."

"Due…east. Right. Damn…" she moaned wearily, "…might end up backstroking the majority of the…" then paused, her mouth standing agape as her widening eyes threatened to pop from the cowl's narrow slits, "…oh shit… heads *UP!*"

Lurching hard to the right, Marvella placed both hands on The Guardsman's chest and shoved, just as the tree-trunk sized tentacle plowed a crater into the spot they'd just inhabited.

"Flight my ass, Luke…looks like we're in this 'til the bitter end," Marvella yelped, having landed atop his broad chest and instantly covering them both in a thinly veiled field.

Directly above them, posed on scaly stilts that resembled the spread legs of a giant, mutated spider, stood an entity barely recognizable from its earlier incarnation. While its rotund torso was swollen to four times its original size, resembling a scaly, bloated roach, the squared talisman had remained the same, though it shone brighter than ever. Its arms had grown taunt and wiry, each elongated to a

402

length of at least fifteen feet.

"Enough of this useless folly. My challenger...the only one present worthy of such a prestigious title, is mere moments from arrival. Time and circumstance dictates an end to this foolishness."

Pausing in mid-flight, Mystic raised a single hand palms up to easily deflect the jagged metal girder Ben had tossed end over end from ground level.

"Aw, come now, MS. I need another three to four minutes tops to wipe the floor with these amateurish clowns."

"We don't *have* three to four minutes, Mystic," Mind Sweep cackled gleefully while pointing to the left with an extended claw, "witness the rebirth of the most powerful creature this pathetic planet has to offer in terms of pure, primal *malevolence.*"

"Ohhhhh...sh--" Anvil managed as the floor between his boots split apart like tenderized meat beneath a razor sharp clever. Landing ten yards from where he'd been so unceremoniously dumped, he hopped to his feet after a single bounce. Shetah stood to his right just moments later as the floor continued to ascend in serrated waves of shredded steel.

The creature that spewed forth did so in gradual increments purposely executed, as if to shock its impending opponents.

"Behold, a God is *REBORN!!*" Mind Sweep screamed like some extraterrestrial circus barker, waiving its spindly arms like the outstretched feelers of some gargantuan insect.

"Looks to me like a *maggot* is reborn. Shit, and

here I thought ol'

Mind-Scrape was the ugliest SOB present," Ben quipped, taking up a blocking position to the left of The Guardsman and directly in front of Marvella.

Within moments, the entire eastern end of the warehouse was filled by its slimy bulk, the entire floor having opened up like an outer shell to a recent birthing. Easily the size of three Greyhound buses parked back to back, it wobbled forth without benefit of legs, like a colossal slug. Its outer layer was infested with scaly growths similar to overgrown polyps, each seeping a greenish fluid that instantly evaporated into a foggy smokescreen upon entering airspace. Its bowling ball shaped head bulled forth atop a surprisingly spindly neck no thicker than one of Anvil's thighs, though the skull remained stable and utterly without movement.

At the center of its skull probed a single eye; a constantly rotating, bright orange orb the shape of a perfectly cut diamond and as large as an SUV. Mere inches below that sat what logically served as its mouth; encased by tubular lips the shape and texture of radial tires, its wide, drooling maw opened and closed at what seemed like timed intervals, revealing a triple-layered set of perfectly squared teeth. As large as rail spikes, each layer appeared a bit shorter than the last to allow an evenly executed bite. As it quivered forward in ten to twenty-foot lunges, a wide netting of flesh would periodically protrude from between the flattened teeth like a serpent's tongue.

"Oh, this is going to be glorious...simply glorious. Truly once in a millennium," Mystic beamed, having sailed just beyond the spot Mind Sweep had chosen to dig into for a final stand, "...battle of the *titans,* indeed. I'll be sure to emphasize the high points to both media and civilians alike, MS. My website will, of course, sing your praises. That is, after you've departed for your home planet and your clone safely put away behind bars, courtesy everyone's friendly neighborhood *Mystical*-man.

I simply adore playing the part of eye-witness reporter *slash* World Savior."

"Well, that explains a lot," Marvella snapped angrily, "egotistical jackass." Twisting its diminutive head completely around despite its bloated body still facing front, Mind Sweep donned a pained scowl while studying Mystic like one would a pesky fly.

As its lips parted and subsequently spat forth a thin, purplish mist, Mystic could have sworn he'd seen Mind Sweep shoot him the briefest of winks. Caught completely off-guard and thus unable to either dodge or create a suitable blockade of anykind, Mystic's face and eyes were coated in warm, slimy goo. Using his gloved hands in an attempt to wipe the substance from his eyes, his flight pattern became wildly erratic, barely avoiding sailing blindly into a cluster of hanging lead pipes.

"Wha...wha...the... fuck? *Gaaawwdd...*"

"Change in plans. Actually, more like...a *slight* amendment," Mind Sweep mumbled, turning about with casual aplomb, "...to *delete* a rather annoying side note."

Back at ground zero, Anvil and Shetah held their ground even as The Guardsman, Marvella and

Ben turned about and sprinted towards the suddenly accessible hovercraft.

"Anvil...Shetah! Get your asses in gear...we're leaving...NOW!!" The Guardsman bellowed, skidding to a halt in front of a tiny keypad to the left of the hover and frantically pecked in a six-digit code.

Above them and slightly to the left, Mystic ricocheted from the wall to the ceiling, his muffled screams growing increasingly muffled and weak. As his mask and the flesh beneath sizzled and smoked, small tatters of each fell free and floated to the surface like wind-blown ash.

"He's...he's melting...almost like the others," Marvella said, looking up as The Guardsman continued to fiddle with the keypad.

Consciously playing the part of bodyguard for his former mates, Ben glanced up and grinned, catching a snippet of scorched spandex on one of his front teeth.

"Burnt fag on the half-shell. Couldn't happen to a nicer guy."

Digging smoldering, skeletal fingers deep into the melted ruin of his face, Mystic whirled about in a frantic loop-t-loop before finally sailing headfirst into a dark chasm that had been the warehouse floor.

"Anvil! Shetah! Get over here, Damn it!" The Guardsman yelled once more, hopping atop the hover as the hatch began its tedious slide inward.

The trio crouched down defensively as the hover shook and shimmed from the creatures progression.

"Don't wait for me, Chief," Anvil replied,

stepping towards the mammoth blob with both fists pumping his chest, "I'm in this one 'til the end, man. You with me, cat-girl?"

"Aw, why the hell not? Never planned on leaving this burg alive anyhow," Shetah replied sassily, glancing back and forth from both mammoth entities book-ending them.

Backing from the opened hatch, The Guardsman gripped Marvella by the left wrist to push her inside.

"Damned fools. *Now* they want to play hero. Hop in, Leah...their choice. Nothing we can do t-"

"SHIT! Whazat?" Marvella shrieked, jerking her boot clear from the hatch opening and almost knocking The Guardsman from the roof in the aftermath.

"About time, I must say. Very difficult to guess what's going on out there, you know," barked a vaguely familiar voice from within.

"Jesus, Doc..." The Guardsman gasped, having already cocked his right arm.

Poking his head from the hatch, Doctor James began vigorously rubbing both eyes as if emerging from a dark catacomb. He was horribly pale, and looked as though someone had torn a sizeable chunk of hair from the tip of his skull.

"Oh my...ohhhh yes," he exclaimed happily, his eyes bugging wildly as the creature lurched into clear view, "...magnificent. I never truly believed...Mind Sweep is quite the unpredictable character you know. When he mentioned the possibility of such a being, the scientist in me was naturally skeptical..."

Placing a firm grip on the frail man's left

shoulder, The Guardsman turned only briefly and saw the lumbering form was less than twenty yards to their west and closing ever so slowly.

"Back in the hover, Doc. We've got less than two minutes to clear the roof." Balanced on the balls of his feet, Ben grasped Marvella's waist to prevent slipping off the slick metal hull.

"Goddamn, G-Man, let's go if we're goin…the earthworm from hell is eyeballin' us like a breakfast buffet."

Slapping the larger man's hand away with a surprisingly stout swipe of his left forearm, the doctor slid from the hover and rolled roughly onto the pad some fifteen feet below.

Struggling to regain his balance as a vicious series of tremors shook the pad, he then stumbled directly towards the creature in a wobbly gait, the white smock he wore coated in dried blood.

"Crazy som'bitch wants to takes its temperature," Ben blurted, pushing Marvella forward as The Guardsman sidestepped over.

"I get the feeling Sweep's had the poor bastard entranced since they arrived. Probably killed his cronies and brought the talisman to him. Conspiracy's all around me and I never had a single damn clue. Hop aboard, Leah…we've got to motivate."

Ben glanced over a final time before following his comrades inside, shaking his head in comical disbelief as the doctor wobbled forward and directly into the thing's wide, destructive path.

Anvil and Shetah had taken up positions on opposite sides even as Mind Sweep lumbered forward, cackling madly with its spindly forelegs leading the way. "Freak show city, Hoss. A real live nightmare come to life."

The hover had indeed held eight separate seats, though each had been installed in true 'space capsule' design, built to accommodate what NASA deemed an average-sized male.

It wasn't until he'd finished monitoring the hatch to ensure closure that Ben turned about and directly into The Guardsman's upper back.

"Damn, Luke...what gives?"

Peering over the other man's shoulder, Ben saw Marvella leaning over a fallen form whose face remained a mystery until seconds later, when The Guardsman also fell to one knee.

"Hey, it's the Warden. We figured you for worm dirt eons ago, pal." The Guardsman turned and shot Ben a bothersome glance before refocusing on the thick leather straps binding Warden Terry's ankles. "He's unconscious, Benji."

"Lucky bastard. Wish I was him."

Marvella had already removed a strip of duct tape from his mouth, and was working diligently at tearing away a pair of plastic cuffs securing his wrists when the craft was suddenly joggled hard from the left and tipped at a thirty-degree angle before collapsing back into place.

Placing a hand on The Guardsman's shoulder, Ben leaned down and popped the leather strap with the simple flick of his right forefinger.

"I'll take it from here, G-man. How's about you concentrate on gettin' us airborne 'fore the worm turns...literally speakin'."

"You got it. Strap him in and then yourselves. This is apt to be one seriously bumpy ride."

Approximately forty-five seconds and three increasingly violent jolts later, The Guardsman sat in the lone pilot's chair, cautiously navigating the tiny craft from atop its flexible metal base via a series of three and four code unlock sequences executed from a tiny PC unit built into the dash. Ben had strapped the Warden's limp frame into the middle of three back row seats, then joined Marvella in the two chairs provided just behind the cockpit and pilot's seat.

"And away…we go…I hope," he murmured, utilizing a joystick-type control to swing the craft around at a ninety-degree angle before ascension.

The craft hovered barely a dozen feet from the surface and had yet to levitate towards the retractable roof when the pad below them practically imploded, swallowed base and all as the floor collapsed like a sink hole in a mud slide.

"No sweat. Leah could'a flown us outta there with a couple a twitches of her nose, right sweet-thang?" Ben queried nervously, looking up from the smoke-filled chasm below to Marvella, who nodded solemnly.

"Like I said, it's all about timin'. Luke, if this bucket of bolts has a warp-speed button, punch that mother."

"Can't put the petal to the metal until the roof retracts, Benji, or we'll all be stuck to that titanium ceiling like mashed flies."

As the craft began to slowly levitate upward toward the highest portion of the ceiling, Marvella stuck out a shaky hand and pointed straight out from the narrow, rectangle-shaped windshield.

"Check it out. Battle of the century has

begun…"

Within the next three minutes, and while rising at a snail's pace, they were able to witness the aforementioned clash in its entirety as what remained of the Eagle Island Detention Center was essentially laid to waste like an ancient structure tagged for demolition.

***

Part VII:

Isle of The *Damned*

"Get a load'a that…Mind-scrape is swellin' up like a blowfish," Ben blurted, joining Marvella as they both pointed in the same general direction.

The creature had slithered forward until it had drawn to within twenty yards of Mind Sweep's position, while Anvil and Shetah had taken up defensive poses on either side and a drooling Doctor James stood at ground zero, holding his arms wide as if to greet a long-lost child.

"That what Sweep does best, Ben. He…*it* absorbs the powers of those it kills," The Guardsman injected, his eyes darting from the cockpit panel to the drama being played out thirty yards below them, "…since he... *it* killed off practically the entire D-Wing, it must be overflowing with a variety of powers. Must be how he creates those damn clones. Mind Sweep wasn't complete until he reclaimed that damned talisman."

"So those must be The Mass's powers he's imitating. The power to increase bulk," Marvella

411

practically whispered.

Ben nodded, his mouth hanging ajar in dumbstruck awe.

"Yeah…and that flesh-eatin' acid he spewed at Mystic must'a been from *Black Plague's* arsenal. That's major league shit, man. But just where in blazes did the giant tapeworm come from anyhow?"

"*Level X*," The Guardsman mumbled, clearing his throat and purposely avoiding the intrusive stares from both his ex-teammates, "… it's… a long story. I'll fill in the blanks once we get this puppy through the storm."

"Damn straight you will, Luke," Ben growled good-naturedly, "…I'm developin' a healthy boner just thinkin' about it."

"Oh god…look!" Marvella yelled, leaning forward until the strap over her shoulder and chest was pulled taunt.

Both Anvil and Shetah had lept into action at precisely the same moment; Anvil heaving a jagged metal slab roughly the size of an MTA bus towards the worm creature's head, while Shetah had jumped from a support beam atop Mind Sweep's back.

"Shit, this is liable to get messy…" Ben replied, tilting forward until the binding strap practically cut into his bared chest.

Once the slab had bounced harmlessly from just below its multi-layered chin, the creature seemed to eye Anvil with a curious glance, much like an exterminator might a bothersome insect.

Quickly refocusing on the larger of visible opponents, the creature then leaned its bulbous head back just a tad as a duo of stringy appendages shot from its throat like twin lasers.

412

The first penetrated Anvil's broad chest just below the breastbone, exiting out a softball-sized hole directly between his shoulder blades, while the second plunged into his lower abdomen and through his heavily muscled thigh. The ends of the thorny appendages instantly mutated upon exit, curling into a grisly facsimile of a fisherman's hook.

The big man's limp frame hung like a gutted fish as he was jerked airborne and directly into the creature's open maw. The cavern-like opening slammed shut like a shattered shutter, spewing forth a tidal wave of crimson, along with a pair of prison-issued steel-toed boots with the accompanying ankles and lower calves still attached.

At almost the exact time of Anvil's skewering and devoured demise, Shetah had busied herself tearing into the soft tissue at the back of Mind Sweep's upper back with bared claws and teeth in an attempt to dig into a major artery near the entities throat.

With little or no visible evidence it had ever bothered to acknowledge her presence, Mind Sweep's stoic expression remained unchanged even as a rash of bubble-shaped blisters the size of basketballs welled up on both shoulders.

Meanwhile, the creature had used the brief sabbatical to whip its phone pole-sized tail around and essentially transform one Doctor James, highly respected, well-known scholar within the world-wide scientific community, into a quivering pile of fleshy oatmeal.

Pausing her assault as an even larger welt appeared at the base of the entity's neck, Shetah's nostrils began to flare wildly and her eyes grew wide. Her tail whipping madly from side to side, she fell into an instant crouch as if prepping to leap away, the hair atop her back and tail puffed from a healthy dose of static electricity.

Her ill-fated jump was only partially executed when the mammoth blister erupted in a violent gush, spewing a thick, blackish liquid that coated her entire frame.

Squealing in anguish, the majority of Shetah's fur had burned away midway to the floor. By the time of impact some three seconds later, the floor was coated by a mishmash of sizzling meat and charred bone, only the tip of her pointed ears spared for identification purposes.

"Jesus. Those...blisters. Black Plague strikes again, I'd wager," The Guardsman sighed, pulling back ever harder on the steering joystick as to speed their departure.

Leaning back with a resounding moan, Ben's face had grown frighteningly pale.

"Hell's *bells*. That was...quick. That Anvil was one roughneck mo-fo, too.

Strong as a hundred bulls. Kinda paints a sad picture on how long I would'a lasted."

"Let's just go before one of them figures out we're here and decides to eliminate *all* witnesses," Marvella injected, wringing her hands nervously.

The creature paused, having twisted its massive bulk slightly to the left just as Mind Sweep reared back its horribly engorged head like a cobra readying a preemptive strike.

"So many planets I've traveled within countless solar systems, dreaming of such a monumental clash," it proclaimed in a banshee-like wail easily

414

drowning out the humanity surrounding it, "...To find you here...within this *damned* isle...buried practically right below the rancid cell I was forced to inhabit...was beyond my wildest expectations. My kind exists only for this, you understand. Now we can truly discover who indeed is the elite warrior between the races! *Ancient one* versus the *future king*...let the final struggle...*BEGIN!!*"

Whipping its heavily scaled tail forward with a speed that belied its gargantuan bulk, the creature twisted its torso like a sidewinder snake, ripping a large section of wall into metal shavings while peeling away a thirty-foot section of flooring.

Standing at least ten yards from his intended target, Mind Sweep leaned back and threw a series of straight jabs that emitted what at first resembled heat or thermal waves.

With each punch thrown, the creature's heavily scaled torso visibly shook from impact, though no visible damage resulted.

"Hey, ya see those vapor trails shootin' from Sweep's fists? He's usin' Obliteration's shock waves," Ben said as The Guardsman had tilted the front end of the ship just enough to allow a continuous view of the action.

"Doesn't look like they even so much as raised a knot either."

"My god, Luke," Marvella shrieked, slapping the seats narrow arm rests with both hands, "...how long does that damn roof take to open? I thought this was supposed to be an emergency exit for *shit's* sake..."

"It must be the power drain that's causing the delay. Back-up generator must be damned close to

415

fried."

Ben reached over with a baseball mitt sized hand and gently stroked her own.

"Steady, babe, *steady*. Those two ain't worried about the likes of us.

They're into their very own *War of the Worlds.*"

As the hover neared the crest of the high ceiling, the opening of the hatch was approximately ninety percent complete. A thin watery mist spattered the windshield even as a gray/brownish sky loomed through the contracted space.

"Almost there, gang," The Guardsman sighed, slowing the vessel to a virtual halt while eyeing the sliding panels above, "storms still raging, looks like."

"You're gonna miss round two, Luke," Ben said, his face practically pressed to the glass.

"I can live with that. Just give me the highlights."

"Color commentary ain't usually my game, pal, but here she goes...the giant leech seems to be slitherin' back a tad as Mind-scrape holds his ground..."

As the length of its vast torso seemed to roll back in a defensive posture, the creature's head remained utterly unmoved, almost as if that particular part were totally independent and not at all effected by the enormous baggage it controlled.

"Enough of this annoying foreplay then!' Mind Sweep bellowed, the decibel level of its voice the equivalent of a thousand synchronized bullhorns, the shock-waves it created actually causing the hovercraft to shimmy in mid-air, "...I require but a

416

single cell of your DNA to effectively absorb the massive power you possess!"

As to acknowledge the request, a multitude of ropy arms emerged from the creature's upturned torso like taser wire, each finding its mark within Mind Sweep's woefully exposed chest and abdomen.

"Sweep was in the middle of another campaign speech and got speared but good," Ben chimed in, clapping his hands as if attending a paid sporting event, "...arrogant som'bitch just keeps flappin' his gums. Looks like a prize catfish hooked on a trout-line."

Peering down at the half-dozen puncture wounds, one of which protruded from the side of his neck like an oversized IV tube, Mind Sweep howled in sarcastic approval.

"I truly appreciate your kind assistance, oh ancient one. After all, it didn't matter *how* I obtained the needed sample!"

"So there's your master plan," The Guardsman said as the hover remained in a holding pattern less than ten feet from the now completely cleared hatch.

"Can you imagine the power that lunatic's gonna carry back to the mainland with a butt-load of that giant slug's DNA?" Ben replied.

"We...can't allow it, Luke," Marvella chimed in wearily, "...we have to stop ...it...them. Otherwise, what are we even escaping *to*?"

Turning back to meet her searing gaze, The Guardsman flashed a mischievous smile.

"Not to worry, Leah. Once we reach a safe distance, this burg is going up in mushroom shaped flames, remember?"

"You can...? From inside this hover you can...nuke the isle?"

The Guardsman nodded, reaching with a free hand to pull a tiny remote device from his utility belt.

"Punch in a six-digit code and press the tiny red button. Simple as that. Only the Warden and I are privy to the code. The ultimate security measure, but oneI never gave serious thought to ever actually utilizing."

Leaning up and over until his grinning, unshaven mug covered Marvella's completely, Ben tilted his head and gave a quick wink.

"Whoa big fella, let's just make damn sure ya keep the *'safe distance'* part of that particular mental checklist listed as pri-or-ity list numero uno."

The trio leaned down and gave the tattered battlefield a final look before the hover rose even with and then through the opened hatch. Of what little undamaged floor space remained, less than half wasn't already under several feet of water.

"Can't lie. A part of me wants to hang around and see who wins."

"There is the curiosity factor present, Ben. I'm with you there. Irrefutably enigmatic, yet morbidly so."

"Um...yeah. Got'cha Luke...whatever ya said. For what it's worth, my cash was on the earthworm."

The Guardsman smirked. "Mind Sweep in a TKO."

After a moment's pause, wherein the hover

418

cleared the roof and flew into a murky cloudbank accompanied by swirling winds instantly causing a dramatic tilt that was quickly corrected, Marvella groaned aloud.

"Sick puppies, both of you. Incurably warped."

"No denial here, darling," Ben replied with a grin.

A heavy mist bombarded both entities from the open hatch, which apparently had ran out of sufficient juice to re-secure itself in the wake of the craft's departure.

Mind Sweep gave the circular chasm a quick glance, but quickly dismissed its very existence as insignificant. Flexing its armored torso much like a body-builder on some faraway 'Muscle Beach', it watched in bemused glee as the worm creature's hook-like arms were cleanly severed at both the entry and exit points, falling away like slashed puppet strings and seeping a thick, yellowish fluid from the frayed tips of each.

"It's all about molecular control, oh great one. I could just have easily liquefied each cell, thus melding with this rancid seawater and escaping without fanfare with the *golden fleece* of Earth DNA's tucked away within my inner housing."

The creature reclaimed its severed attachments, essentially sucking them back into its bulk while rolling away a short distance to recoup before mounting a fresh attack.

"But I digress..." Mind Sweep's rant continued as its hollowed eye sockets began to glimmer a light shade of green, "...that would be...such a universal cheat. My kind are deemed the elite interms of combat skill; fearless, unwavering, unmerciful, not

419

to mention the savviest of hunters. To pass up the opportunity to best such a legendary warrior; a dark god whose own kind long since labeled as mythological tripe, would truly be an unforgivable sin not easily lived with. Just owning your power isn't enough, oh ancient one. I must take it, yes, for in future battles it will no doubt prove invaluable. But I must take it as your centuries old existence ebbs away at my own hands. For that is the way of the warrior. The way…of *our* kind."

Hobbling forward like some giant, interstellar crab, Mind Sweep fired a quick succession of jade-colored lasers from each eye while simultaneously shadow boxing a combination of straight jabs with each clinched fist.

The creature appeared unfazed even as the searing lasers blew baseball-sized holes through its armor-protected flesh and sonic waves pounded deep dents into its blubbery trunk.

Splashing through what would have been waist high water on an average- sized man, Mind Sweep used its multitude of elongated back legs as springboards to accelerate into close range of the creature's massive cranium while maintaining the laser beam barrage.

Using its lengthiest front appendage like a pole vault, Mind Sweep ascended from the water once the creature was within physical striking range, hoping to get a handhold on either its neck or cranium.

Descending within reaching distance, Mind Sweep had curled its hands into claws and shrieked a warrior's howl just before being bludgeoned in mid-air by a single, vicious blow from the creature's spiked tail, which had whipped forth at turbo speed.

Landing with a loud crunch, Mind Sweep's head and upper body penetrated the wall like bazooka fire, ripping away a large section that provided instant access to literally thousands of gallons of ocean water to come spewing forth in gigantic swells.

Driven back into the fray by crashing waves that had effectively collapsed the remaining section of wall on the West side of the warehouse, Mind Sweep managed to keep its head above water while attempting to gauge its enemies exact whereabouts.

Using several of its rear tentacles to wrap around one of the few remaining metal struts still standing upright, Mind Sweep scanned the room over the ruins rushing by but was unable to spot the creature within the swirling wreckage. Bowing its octagon-shaped dome, a radiant aura instantly covered the whole of its shape like a transparent body cast. The rushing water and floating debris bounced harmlessly from the energy field as Mind Sweep levitated from the water until only the lower portion of its tentacles remained submerged.

"Where are you hiding, oh great one? Surely cowardice is not to answer for such reluctance to continue this historic melee. I'll confess all the waterworks are a bit annoying, but come now...let's finish this in the honorable tradition of our creators...our...mentors. For the ones who came before...and the ones that will...follow our lea-

...follow our...l-lead..."

Its shoulders visibly sagging as it seemed to fall into a hypnotic state, the entity known as Mind Sweep rested its pointed chin atop its chest and peered downward.

Slowly, a bemused grin stretched across its purplish maw, its pupil-less eyes wide and inexplicably awestruck even as it drifted slowly downward back into the churning murk.

"Well, I'll be. Never... would have thought such a thing possible. Looks like...the joke is indeed...on me."

Pulsating like timed beacons, the trio of circular wounds previously opened by the creature's thorny spears gradually reopened as the tissue around them began to decompose eas though filled with toxic waste.

Feeling its hold on the energy field ebb away even as its internal and external organs began to fall victim to a slow, agonizing paralysis, Mind Sweep was hapless to do anything save admit defeat with as much grace as one born of warrior heritage could possibly muster.

As its face grew numb and the mass of tentacles holding it upright in the crashing waves began to peel and fall away like rotted chum, Mind Sweep raised its rapidly shriveling arms airborne in a final salute.

"Even with...the power of Black Plague... it is you who manages to...infect me. Oh my...this is truly...the equivalent of a *viral nuclear meltdown*. Blinding me now...no longer...able to...feel...any...anything. Bravo...oh ancient one...bravo indeed...your greatness was...not...overstated..."

The water to Mind Sweep's immediate left built to titanic proportions a scant second before the creature shot from the swirling froth like a meteor erupting from the ocean's core. The worm creature was roughly the size of a seven-forty-seven, its maw stretched wide to feed as it descended upon its quivering prey.

"Oh yes...you are indeed...the *one*..." Mind Sweep whimpered in maniacal glee as the massive jaws clamped shut, essentially swallowing whole the remaining remnants of Eagle Island Detention Center, and thereby closing the book on its relatively short but eventful existence.

***

"How much farther, Luke?"

"We'll be at safe minimum distance in approximately...one minute, eighteen seconds, Leah."

"This tub moves pretty swift once she hits open air. Cut through those typhoon winds with a minimum of turbulence."

"Um, G-Man?"

"Yeah, Ben?"

"That's cause Leah's been blanketin' us ever since we flew outta that collapsin' roof back there on Pigeon-Toe Isle."

Twisting about, The Guardsman briefly studied Marvella's pale, sweat-moistened face and strained expression before again facing front with a resounding sigh. Though the ocean waves below were still far from calm, the sporadic cloudbanks they'd encountered were no longer as dark or nearly as ominous.

"Should've known. I just never figured you'd have the juice to maintain a protective field after that firefight."

"Had just enough in reserve to get us past the worst," she replied wearily, "... dropped it about two minutes ago. Seriously thought my eyes were gonna stay permanently crossed there for a sec."

Ben leaned over and gently propped his bearded chin atop her right shoulder.

"Dragon lady, you'd still be a babe with wall-eyes, chipped teeth, and Dumbo ears."

"Same old Ben," she snickered, "six feet, two-and one-half inches of walking, talking horse manure. So, how goes the countdown to extinction?"

"Just under…twenty ticks to safe distance. We've covered nearly forty miles already," The Guardsman replied while reaching up to access a small sliding panel just above the cockpit controls. Once he'd slid his laminated security badge through a narrow slit just to the panel's right, a squared keypad was ejected. Cocking his head slightly to the right, he then reached with a gloved finger and pecked in a six-digit code. The panel slid open, revealing a single black button encircled in a tiny glass dome.

"Shatterproof glass," he whispered primarily to himself.

"*VOICE ACTIVATION PLEASE,*" hummed a robotic voice "Chief Correctional Officer, Eagle Island Detention Center."

A short pause ensued, wherein The Guardsman's shoulders grew visibly taunt

"*ACTIVATION COMPLETE.*"

Another short respite ensued before the glass dome slid upward to leave the quarter-sized black

424

button fully exposed.

Checking the cockpit PC one final time, The Guardsman then turned back to his comrades wearing a rather sad smile.

"Hang onto your hats, gang. We're liable to get a hell of a jolt about thirty seconds after I activate this bad boy."

"We're thoroughly braced," Ben quipped, "by all means, stick the flame to the fuse, brother."

Marvella simply nodded without speaking.

As he extended an arm and firmly pressed with the forefinger of his right hand, The Guardsman bowed his head in silent memoriam.

***

Part VIII:

Identity Sweep

"*YEEEEE-HAAAAAAAAA*! That's what I'm talkin' about! Deep-fried Alien bad-ass on the half shell! Fuckin' A!" Ben screamed, hanging tight to the armrest on his right with one arm while gripping the back portion of Marvella's seat in a steely vice with the other. Within moments, the sudden and violent bout with turbulence gave way to a tranquil serenity marked by calm seas and relatively cloudless skies.

A series of thundering shock waves had arrived less than twenty seconds after the nuclear device was detonated, and subsided in less than half that time.

"Seems the...deed is done, guys," The

425

Guardsman remarked in a somewhat subdued tone, checking a rear camera that revealed a horizon split into two distinct layers; the inner resembling a thick cloud of whitish mist and the outer shaded in bright yellow like a colossal rainbow.

Releasing her safety strap, Marvella leaned up and gave him a gentle pat on the shoulder.

"I'm sorry, Luke. I...know you lost a lot back there. You...you were following orders, after all. It wasn't as if it wasn't justified."

"Damn straight, partner," Ben chimed in, "...you did what ya had to do...*period.* The powers that be have to understand that. Don't lose no shuteye over it. Your track record speaks for itself, man."

Having removed both his cowl and gloves, The Guardsman set the hover on autopilot with a few simple keystrokes before leaning back with his hands propped at either side of his head.

"It's...just...the troops I lost, you know? They were a great group of men and women. Dedicated to a fault. None better. Men and women with...families. Families that won't...*can't* understand why something like this could happen. Just wish I could've seen this shit coming...somehow. Maybe I could've spared some of their parents, wives and children a lifetime of grief."

"Comes with the territory, Hoss. They all know that when they sign whatever dotted line officially qualifies 'em for the job. Military rules."

"Ben's right, Luke," Marvella added, removing her own cowl with shaky hands, "such people aren't far removed from our own kind, except they don't

426

even have the added security blanket of special endowments.

"Besides, nobody present had the telekinetic abilities to see this coming. That was Mind Sweep's biggest advantage other than the raping and absorption of superpowers...the complete element of surprise."

"Simple...but always effec-...effective," replied the raspy voice behind them in a barely audible whisper.

They whirled about as one, The Guardsman practically leaping from the pilot's chair.

"Warden! Welcome back, sir," he grinned, kneeling to loosen the chest strap holding the man upright. The Warden blinked rapidly while attempting tofocus, a thin trail of drool hanging from his lower lip like morning dew from a flower petal.

"H-hey... hey, chief. Sight...for sore eyes, you...a-are."

"How you feeling, boss?"

"H-hammered...crap," he replied, smiling weakly, "...and you?"

"I've seen better days, but not many worse."

"Ya missed one hell of a party, Warden," Ben said, hopping into the vacated pilot's chair and giving the cockpit PC a bemused once-over.

"What...what did ...happen? I don't recall much after the...the Director...h-he..."

"Take it slow, Warden. We're in the clear now," Marvella said reassuringly, kneeling on the opposite side of the man's seat.

"In...the clear? We're...off site, you mean?" he asked his Chief CO a bit more coherently, though

427

his visage maintained its pasty, dazed look.

The Guardsman bowed his head, temporarily breaking eye contact with his long-time superior.

"Checklist Def-One, Sir. I…there was no other call."

His shoulders slumping anew, the Warden leaned back with a heavy, labored sigh.

"From what I'd seen before…blacking out…I'm not at all surprised. Horrified yes, but… not surprised."

Ben swiveled the chair around, his massive thighs barely fitting within the confined space.

"In Luke's defense, it was a goat-rope of the highest order, Warden. I'm talkin' *FUBAR* City. Mind Sweep and some intergalactic worm were goin' at it for top of the food chain status, and everybody else involved was basically meat on a platter. I ain't big on fight over flight, ya understand, but this was the exception to the rule."

Vigorously rubbing his face with both hands, the Warden then ran them through the tuffs of tangled hair behind his ears.

"My god…I just never thought such a…cataclysmic measure would ever be…necessary."

"The D-One checklist had been breached to hell and back, boss…" The Guardsman stated firmly, rising to his feet and falling into the first available seat. Following a brief moment of subdued silence, a rather heated exchange ensued:

The Warden: "A two-billion-dollar facility blown into dust fragments. The boys in Washington aren't exactly going to be tinkled pink over this…"

The Guardsman: "…I mean, first off we had

428

zero percent in terms of inmate control..."

The Warden: "...no way they'll fund to rebuild. Many feel the taxpayers were raped on the first go round..."

The Guardsman: "...secondly, the permanent power outages under hurricane conditions..."

The Warden: "...Personal credibility shot to *shit*. I'll be lucky if I can get a job overseeing a county lock-up in Toe-Cheese, Wisconsin..."

The Guardsman: "...the entire CO staff had been systematically slaughtered like livestock..."

The Warden: "...there simply *had* to be other, more viable options..."

The Guardsman: "...somehow, Mind Sweep and that damned talisman had managed to reanimate that skeletal fossil cubed in *Level X*...and it awoke at an extremely high *level* of pissed off..."

The Warden: "...even with com capability shot, the internal alarm beacons are there for a reason..."

The Guardsman: "...leaving two mutated aliens fighting over the spoils...either one capable of reaching populated areas within a matter of hours..."

The Warden: "...you might as well have left my rear parked atop that burnt rock back there, Luke...because as of now I'm *completely, irrevocably*..."

The Guardsman: "...the threat was just too great to take chances on either surviving to fight...and kill another day..."

The Warden: "...*FUCKED*!"

The Guardsman: "...I followed proper procedures, Warden *Sir*...to the FUCKING TEE!"

As the exchange had commenced and grown

increasingly heated, Ben had slipped from the pilot's chair and took up a rather awkward position between the two men while Marvella had turned completely away and faced front as to ignore them altogether.

"Whoa...ease up, Warden. The man ain't exaggeratin' the shitstorm we just waded throu-" Ben said calmly, cut off by the Warden's raised right hand, which was clinched in a tight ball and wracked with tremors of rage.

"When I want the opinion of a convicted felon, which isn't likely, I'll most certainly *ask*."

Following a perfectly executed double take in which he glanced from The Guardsman to the Warden and then back again, Ben leaned in while stepping by his former teammate.

"Afraid he's alllll yours, bud."

Marvella moaned aloud as Ben stood behind her seat and began gently massaging the tension from her shoulders.

"Relax darlin'...just let it go. Ain't nothin' but blue skies ahead as far as these baby-blues can see."

"Listen, Chuck...," The Guardsman pleaded in a mild, composed tone one might normally associate with an adult lecturing a young child, "...you're obviously fatigued. We'll have plenty of time to bounce this around once we're docked."

"Not to mention the congressional hearing where my balls will no doubt be impaled, sliced off and put on display."

"You want some water...maybe an aspirin? Leah, hand me that canteen from that first aid kit under the pilot's seat..."

"What I need, you incompetent *fuck*..." the

430

Warden scowled, leaping from seat and wrapping both hands around the larger man's exposed throat, "...is a right-hand man who can be trusted *not* toblow the entire engine when a new *spark plug* would've sufficed!"

Clamping his own hands around each of his superior's wrists, The Guardsman pulled and tugged with increased fervor, even as he was hoisted airborne until the top of his scalp brushed the surface of the hover's roof.

"Let...l-let...go, Charles...d-damn it...turn l-loose..."

Twisting about with the speed of a startled feline, Ben gripped the Warden's right arm and began to squeeze, attempting to apply just enough pressure to force release but not in excess as to unnecessarily snap bones in the process.

"Damn, Warden..." he strained through gritted teeth, "I take it ya still work out. Shiiiiit...this old man's stout as a boulder..."

The Warden's focus turned gradually from his subordinate to the newest attacker, his lips slowly curling into a wide, toothy smile of pure malevolence.

"To paraphrase a popular slang expression from years past...you ain't seen n*othing* yet."

With a single thrust of his upper body, the Warden slung The Guardsman's body around like a foam-filled rag doll, driving the two men's heads together with a resounding thud and essentially battering Ben into the side of the hover like a swatted insect.

Marvella swung around just as the Warden began repeatedly banging The Guardsman's head

431

against the roof with what looked like a simple flick of his right wrist even as his left arm hung limply at the side.

"Warden, what the hell are you-"

"Patience, *honey* pie. Get to you momentarily…" Warden Terry replied gleefully, white froth coating his lips in thick, bubbly strands.

While being slowly choked and beaten to the edge of unconsciousness, The Guardsman managed to land several solid rabbit punches to the sides of the smaller man's head and ears while also planting his knees and boots to the man's exposed midsection. Each blow was met with casual indifference as The Warden continued unabated, pounding a hole the size and shape of the larger man's skull in the hover's combination fiberglass/metal inner ceiling.

Marvella had pushed herself forward on visibly wobbly legs just as Ben lurched forward to intervene.

"Back off, babe," he growled, spitting out a mouthful of fresh blood, "…ya just ain't up to it. I got 'im…"

"Sorry, Warden," he continued, cocking his right fist while using the left to scope the trajectory, "…but this is definitely gonna hurt *you* more than it does me."

The swooping, overhead right landed flush on the Warden's chin with a sharp snapping sound, like dried leaves crunched beneath heavy work boots. Though he'd originally had every intention of pulling the punch, the final execution of said blow had definitely been more along the lines of 'terminate' than 'stun'.

Standing flat-footed, Ben blinked in disbelief as the Warden's body remained unmoved even as his head twisted about in a complete three-sixty, his skull now woefully misshapen, like a partially deflated soccer ball.

"Whoa…Exorcist shit…" Ben mumbled, tossing a short but forceful left jab towards the center of the warden's warped mug while shuffling back a step.

Without allowing The Guardsman's now limp form to descend nary an inch, The Warden's left arm shot up in a streaky blur to resume the combination choking/ bludgeoning even as his right effortlessly halted Ben's punch in mid-stroke with an upraised palm.

"Now, *now* Force…generally, I only allow one free shot per opponent," the Warden spat harshly, spewing forth several shattered teeth in the process, "…I'll admit, yours was quite the head-turner indeed. I do believe you not only fractured my skull *and* jawbone, but also severed my spine to boot."

"Lousy son… of… a …bitch…" Ben growled, trying in vain to pull his oversized fist free from the comparatively small fingers grasping it like the steely jaws of a bear trap.

Tossing The Guardsman aside like bagged trash, the Warden then swung an upturned forearm just below Ben's left elbow, which instantly fractured at the crook and bent backwards into a V-shape.

Ben's follow-up right hook bounced harmlessly from the Warden's wobbly noggin just before he fell to one knee, his left arm dangling in at a decidedly grisly angle.

Taking a single step back, the Warden then shot forward and planted his right foot dead center at Ben's breastbone, essentially punting him into the cockpit where his head nailed the hover's windshield, splintering the supposedly 'unbreakable' glass from end to end.

As The Guardsman rolled over onto his back just to her right and Ben lay frighteningly still on the opposite side, Marvella's eyes locked with the Warden's as she backed into the cramped cockpit with her arms spread wide. "Told you I'd get to you eventually, Sweet cheeks."

"I don't want to hurt you, Warden. Don't force my hand…"

"Not to fret, my dear Marvella," the Warden screeched in a gravelly, alien tone, piercing her eardrums like ultra-sonic waves from a silent dog whistle, "the chances of such a happenstance are, sadly in your case, *slim* to *none*."

"Oh…shit…" she murmured, crossing her arms across her chest in an 'X' shape.

The Warden/Thing's smile creased the center of its face like a gaping wound, the corners of its trembling lips stretched to beneath each ear lobe even as the pupils of its eyes vanished in lieu of a red shading streaked in pitch-black bolts "Oh shit…*indeed*."

It lunged forward with outstretched arms, the sound of crushed bone and torn cartilage filling the tiny enclosure as Marvella's weak but serviceable force field sent it sprawling back into the hover's back wall with an echoing crash.

Tossing splintered sections of seat aside with its grotesquely mangled arms, The Warden/Thing's

434

dementia-laced grin never wavered.

"I am duly impressed, young lady. I took it for granted you were much too drained to perform such fancy feats. My mistake for underestimating what you humans refer to as 'the weaker sex'. Believe me, it won't happen again."

Standing stiffly, the Warden/Thing raised both arms chest high while cocking its head slightly to the left.

A series of sharp snapping noises ensued, followed by a raw tearing sound as flesh andtendon initially torn asunder began to instantaneously straighten and reconstruct.

Marvella noticed both of her fallen allies were slowly stirring from either side of her, noting their continued vulnerability and realizing the desperate need to keep the creature held at bay if for no other reason.

"I take it the warden was your little insurance policy then? That is, in case that giant piece of fish bait kicked your ass?"

The Warden/Thing gyrated as if performing some type of eternal emissions check, allowing its arms to drop back to its sides even as its head seemed to lean and fall slightly out of kilter.

"As it turns out, my dear Marvella, it didn't really matter who triumphed in the clash of the titans, now does it? True, I needed an out just in case. While Director Willis was my first choice of hosts, he'd...now what is that term again? ...*gone off the deep end* by then, much like the good doctor. The talisman had that effect on the human psyche, as you well know, I'm certain.

"I will say this for the Warden...the man was a

scrapper. Strong as a bull also…for a mortal."

Seemingly focused on her alone, the Warden/Thing stepped casually past the fallen men, both of whom had managed to crawl onto all fours and position themselves like gridiron warriors awaiting the quarterback's snap count.

"Afraid I can't allow you to make the mainland, Mind Sweep," she blurted for want of a lengthier diversion as the force field grew ever weaker as moments ticked by, "for two varied but distinct reasons."

"And those would be, my dear?" the Warden/Mind Sweep hybrid growled, pausing to reach up with both hands and snap its warped skull back into proper position.

Marvella removed her clinched fists from across her chest and thrust them violently outward.

"Number one, you pose quite the threat to my species as a whole. Number two, being born of one race, I never could stomach half-breeds, or in your case, *multiple* breeds. Particularly those of alien origin. Call me racist…it's simply a matter of semantics."

The hybrid being grinned ever wider, its tongue whipping back and forth like a live wire. Covering the twelve to fifteen-foot distance between them in a single, lightning quick bound, it slammed into the field with open palms, visibly bending the invisible plain and jarring Marvella back, essentially pinning her to the cockpit windshield.

"Let it go, Sweetie," the being shrieked, shoving its clawed hands through until the fingernails of each hand sat but a few inches from Marvella's exposed throat, "at least in death you'll

436

have the satisfaction of knowing you'll soon be a vital part of a much *greater* whole."

Forging ahead, the thing's index fingers scraped the tender flesh just below Marvella's chin. Straining to maintain what little remained of the fast-fading barrier, she twisted her head to the right to briefly avoid further contact with the clutching claws.

"Parasitic…piece of…shit…" she whispered, on the verge of passing out just as a blur of frantic movement from behind the entity caught her fading attention.

The Warden/Thing twisted its wobbly head as its hands and upper body remained frozen in a 'sleepwalkers' pose.

Punch number one, executed with pinpoint expertise by The Guardsman, impacted squarely on the being's chin, cracking its lower jaw until the bottom plate collapsed like a shattered hinge. Punch number two, thrown at nearly twice the velocity and overall force by the man more recently dubbed '*Desolation Outlaw*', landed at the center of the beings expanded chest, splintering ribs like dried kindling while leaving a concave outline of the mammoth fist responsible.

Thecreature was instantly catapulted from the elasticity of the protective field back into the rear of the craft, leaving a sizeable dent in the back wall as it impacted headfirst. Meanwhile, Ben raised his damaged left arm with the right and then allowed it to drop like dead weight before snapping the dislocated elbow back into place with a savage horse-whip motion.

"Ya really should learn to follow up, Sweep.

When ya got a man down, you damn well better make sure he stays that way," Ben said with a wink, fronting Marvella as she'd collapsed onto one knee.

Hoisting a tiny thermal revolver no larger than a cell phone from his utility belt, The Guardsman cocked its hammer before setting its miniscule sights directly between the fallen being's pupil-less eyes.

"Should've went down with the island, asshole."

"Yawww…canzzz beee serhious…" the hybrid grumbled almost incoherently before reaching up to reset his shattered jaw with a violent jerk, "the only thing you'll accomplish with that… popgun is possibly open up a rather useless suck-hole in this flying tin-can of yours."

The Guardsman smiled grimly, shrugging his shoulders while lowering the revolver's site several inches.

"Just call me a reckless daredevil, but as we all know, nothing is ever *accomplished* without experimentation..."

A bright flash filled the chamber, accompanied by a low, barely audible hum.

The Warden/Mind Sweep hybrid stared down through thick plumes of smoke at the grapefruit-sized chasm at its lower abdomen, then peered slowly upward, having donned the same cheesy grin as just moments before.

"Um…am I supposed to say…ouch?"

The trio unconsciously huddled shoulder to shoulder, watching in dumbfounded frustration as a bubbly, greenish ooze refilled the gash like hot tar poured in a paved pothole.

Groaning aloud, Ben turned to The Guardsman with a cocked eyebrow. "Guess it's on to plan B, huh? Or is that C?"

As if experiencing a life-altering epiphany, The Guardsman's expression slowly transformed from grim desperation to joyous enlightenment.

"Impressive, Sweep...reeeeallly impressive how you can survive and thrive on the bastardized DNA of your victims. Then again, I don't recall Warden Terry being this...resilient or downright cock strong."

Crouching slightly as to lunge, the hybrid entity abruptly paused; its forehead creased as if in deep thought.

"Give credit where credit is due, Chief. A *portion* of the physical strength is your former superior's, true, but the systematic and molecular controls are all my own, thanks in large part to the talisman, of course. Once I'm through here...my one and *only* mission is to retrieve it from the smoking ruin of what was Eagle Island."

Backing away a step, The Guardsman whispered to Ben from the right side of his mouth while maintaining eye contact with the entity.

"Give me thirty good seconds, Ben."

"My pleasure, G-Man," Ben replied with a mischievous wink, "but whatever your plannin', make it quick."

Tilting its severely misshapen head to one side, The Warden/Mind Sweep/Thing stared each of them down one at a time, as if purposely taking in their images a final time for sentimental reasons. Relaxing its aggressive pose, it stood in a slightly off-kilter 'parade rest' stance with both hands pinned behind its back and its feet spread shoulder length apart.

"Time to expire, kiddies. I so tire of this dance. Not to worry, I have no plans for domination of your pathetic planet, as the *Ancient One* would have so effectively done, or bathe myself in waves of worldwide publicity, as was *Mystic's* hidden agenda."

"So what was your master plan, pumpkin head, openin' a corndog stand on Hollywood an' Vine?" Ben snapped, stepping up to take point as The Guardsman wriggled past Marvella and kneeled down next to a tiny control box positioned just under the cockpit's PC controls.

"You can have your rancid World in all its self-destructive glory, Benjamin. I arrived here as a warrior in search of the ultimate challenge. I depart with my thirst for combat duly quenched. I have considered searching out the being responsible for my forced indenture here, but alas, the time it would take to locate the Silver Surfer is time I simply cannot spare.

"I have, in fact, activated an inner beacon that will precede the arrival of a rescue patrol that will transport me back to the home planet."

Ben flashed a wide, devilish grin.

"I'll make sure to tell 'em ya couldn't make it, Hoss."

"I so admire your spirit, Benjamin," the entity replied a split-second before leaping, "if *not* your sublime ignorance…"

Bulling forward headfirst, the entity was slowed only somewhat by a paper-thin energy field Marvella managed to finagle from a sadly weakened

440

arsenal. The Mind Sweep/Warden/Thing slammed into Ben chest-level with the majority of its momentum in tow, and the two barreled into the narrow space above the cockpit amid dented hardware, a spattering of electrical sparks and a windshield now completely engulfed in spider-web cracks. Marvella was tossed roughly to the side as they had pummeled forward, bouncing from a side wall into a splintered pile of seating before landing hard on her left side at the rear of the craft. The Guardsman, meanwhile, had ducked away just as the pair rocketed forward, having pulled a small plastic box from the control box panel. He subsequently rolled back into the clear as the combatants had sailed into the cockpit at full force. As eternal circuits popped and the hovercraft fell into a slow but steady dive, he struggled to balance himself against a badly bent armrest while removing the box's contents with great care.

With his back pinned firmly against the flaming cockpit panel, Ben delivered a trio of brutal head-butts to the entity's forehead, warping the thing's already deformed skull into pureed mush. He followed this with a short right jab and a wide, looping left hook, effectively sending the creature bouncing from wall to wall like a ricocheting bullet and leaving behind a slimy trail of greenish skid marks.

Standing on badly fractured ankles, the Mind Sweep/Warden/Thing swayed drunkenly as the hover continued its gradual descent. His hair, mustache and beard drenched in blood from a dozen seeping wounds, Ben crawled forward on all fours and pulled Marvella's sprawled form into a far corner before turning back towards the creature with an enraged scowl.

"Damn, Sweep…looks to me like you're gettin' your ass handed to ya twice in the same one-hour time frame. See, the word we humans use to describe assholes like you is…*overrated.*"

The entity reared its mangled head back and roared while submerging its clawed hands deep into its own chest cavity.

With three quick tugs, it ripped away its outer flesh like peeled fruit, any resemblance to Warden Charles V. Terry expunged and subsequently discarded like a hollowed-out shell.

What was left intact was a man-sized version of the same entity they'd faced down a half hour earlier in the warehouse/hover pad; a scaled down but still lethal clone of a creature with a cone shaped head; a hollow, toothless maw and cold, pupil-less eyes floating about on squid-like tentacles.

"Afraid you…pushed the wrong button, human," it growled, shaking off a thick gel coating that stuck to the surrounding walls in foamy clumps. "I will not be…mocked, Benjamin Thomason."

Cocking an eyebrow in defiance, Ben unclenched his right fist and gestured towards the creature in a 'come hither' motion with all the fingers curling in toward the palm before flipping it the bird with the middle finger only.

"Big *talk*, shit-heel. Now *walk the walk…*"

Lumbering towards Ben in a downward slope as the hover continued in freefall, Mind Sweep had spread both its arms wide as to block any possible escape.

Having resolved to go on the defensive as to avoid leaving Marvella unprotected, Ben sprang from his crouch and prepped a spinning front kick he'd hoped would at least slow the creature's charge.

Diving from Ben's right, The Guardsman nailed the creature at the center of the chest with a flying backhand that did little to slow its forward momentum. With a grunting smirk, Mind Sweep swatted him aside just as Ben's left boot landed with a sharp crunching sound at almost the exact same spot, just below what served as the alien's breastbone.

Wrapping the elongated fingers of its left hand securely around Ben's neck, itflung him back with a fierce jerk, then turned about to watch him sail thelength of the craft and bash a deep dent into the rear inner hull.

Whirling its head about in vengeful glee, Mind Sweep then focused on Marvella, whose eyes fluttered sporadically as she lay in an awkward, semi-fetal position.

"Don't fret, sweet one, you'll be glad to know I've decided to spare your precious existence, although admittedly for experimental reasons only. I normally don't collect specimens from the planets I've inhabited, but your powers have...intrigued me. Come now...we must eject before this tin box submerges into the swirling waves below. I must re-claim my birthright before departure."

Having initially reached down for her left arm, the entity froze momentarily as the hover's frontward tilt became more dramatic. It was then it first noticed a trio of shattered plastic shards

443

protruding from its upper chest like jagged rail spikes. Pausing to gently stroke the broken ends with an outstretched digit, what served as the creature's lips curled into a weak smile that would soon transform into an agonizing grimace.

"Wha-…some kind of…trickery?"

Its moistened tentacles began to twitch and gyrate out of sequence, resembling a heaping pile of throbbing maggots battling for feeding position on some unseen carcass.

"This…is…quite unpleasant, I must say…"

Asthe spastic tentacles essentially forced its attached host up the slime-coated grade toward the middle of the craft, Mind Sweep's arms collapsed as if all shoulder tendons and connecting tissue had suddenly been severed from the inside.

Rubbing his blood-soaked, knot ravaged noggin as he lay flat on his stomach at the rear of the craft, Ben studied the strange happenings through rapidly blinking eyes.

"What's happenin' to 'im, Luke? Looks like he's shrivelin' up like an orange peel in desert heat."

Laying on his right side just a few feet away, The Guardsman frowned while pulling a metal shard from his right thigh.

"You pretty much nailed it, Benji. Son of a bitch is doing just that. He's just too damn arrogant to comprehend it…yet."

As its torso and skull began to contort and slowly deflate, seeping what literally seemed like gallons of foamy yellow gore from its dime-sized pores, Mind Sweep managed to twist about on a neck no larger than a number five pencil and eye the

444

two men with a comically exaggerated expression of pure horror.

"Wha----wha…di- did yew…dew tew meeee?"

"Elementary, Mind-shit," The Guardsman replied with a sardonic wink, "My friend the Warden had only one weakness. A very safe-guarded one, at that. Charlie Terry was diabetic. The hover's first aid kit included a healthy supply of insulin…just in case. You just received a quadruple dose, buddy boy. Guess you should've picked a healthier DNA to pilfer, Sweep. Looks like it isn't exactly agreeing with you, either."

"Butttt…diabe? Diabat? …di-disease…sim-simple…disease…howwww …coul…could…some…something…so…simpli-simplistic…beeeee so fat-tal…to…one…such…as…I?" it rambled as its nose fell away like moist putty and its left arm shrank like a weathered vine.

Resting his chin on a propped fist, Ben shook his head and grinned.

"Hey, butt-munch, welcome to the human race. It's those *simple* things that always seem to kick our asses in the end."

Releasing a final, drawn-out groan, Mind Sweep's face imploded with a wet slurping sound one might associate with sucking Jell-O through a straw, its dried, flaking tentacles collapsing into scaly mounds of grayish dust as its torso flayed apart like torn sections of rotted fruit.

"Phew-weee," Ben quipped, scrunching his face in disgust, "poor bastard's scrambled like a three-minute egg."

The Guardsman slid past the bubbling mass and

445

toward the smoking, scorched remains of the cockpit.

"Leah, you with us?"

A moment later, Ben tumbled over the melting scraps and rolled shoulder first into the dented panel next to Marvella, who studied him woozily.

"She's dazed, but okay. Right darlin'?"

Flashing a weak smile, Marvella managed the slightest of nods.

"Good deal," The Guardsman said before huffing in obvious frustration, "...damn. Internal controls are shot to hell and back, Benji. Which means..."

"Don't tell me...we're back-strokin' to the mainland after all."

"Very astute, old buddy. Let's prep to eject. I'd say we're less than three minutes to impact with Mother Ocean. Since Leah can't fly us out, break out the chutes."

Moments later, The Guardsman reached up to disengage the hatch's airlock handle while Ben stood behind with Marvella cradled to his chest, all three having donned separate chutes.

"Almost...there," he groaned, pulling the handle in a counterclockwise motion. "You jumping with Leah in tow or what?"

"Yeah. She's beyond pullin' any cord, much less timin' such a maneuver," Ben replied, side-stepping over to avoid a steaming pile of pulsating goo that had flowed to within inches of his left boot. "I tore off a strap from an extra chute and tied it around both of us."

"Well, here she blows. Brace yourself, Ben. Electrical system is shot, so I'm gonna pull her open manually. Going to experience some heavy suction once these panels part."

"Ready Freddy, let's hit it while we still got enough airspace."

Grunting loudly, The Guardsman cranked the handle one final time, then grabbed the outer edges of the opening once the panel slid ajar. Seconds later, he was sucked from the hatchway with a resounding 'whoosh'.

As he pulled himself through the narrow opening, Ben reached for a handhold with his left arm while securing Marvella with the other.

"Hang on, darlin'. We're about to go air surfin'," he yelled as the craft's interior was instantly transformed into a mini-wind tunnel.

Marvella nodded weakly, peering down into the craft's demolished interior a final time before tucking her head against Ben's upper chest and neck. Amid the blowing debris and flying glass, she could have sworn she spotted a single dislodged eyeball bounding about like a Ping Pong ball; a maroon-shaded eye that was utterly pupil-less.

Each watched the hover pierce a low-laying cloudbank, then reappear seconds later as it continued to descend at a forty-five-degree angle.

The Guardsman engaged his chute less than thirty seconds after whisked into the open air like tumbleweed from a funnel cloud. Ben and Marvella followed suit just moments later, the pair resembling a set of conjoined twins fused at the chest.

It took less than five minutes for The Guardsman to be the first to touch water, plowing feet first into relatively calm seas and subsequently canvassed by the billowy chute.

Ben and Marvella touched down a minute or so later, with Ben twisting about just before impact to absorb the brunt of the landing with his upper back.

Swimming in an Easterly direction, The Guardsman quickly covered the two to three-hundred-foot distance between them in a looping backstroke.

"*Aquaman* ain't got nothin' to worry 'bout, G-man," Ben blurted with a toothy smile, floating on his back with Marvella serving as passenger following a brief struggle to disconnect them from the chute.

"And you, *skip-loader* mitts, resemble a hairy inner-tube," he replied with a wide grin. "Leah, you doing okay?"

Her words slurred by pure exhaustion, Marvella managed a slight nod. "Own one humdinger…of a headache. Other than that…tiptop, Luke. Just happy…to be here."

"Yeah, wherever *here* is. Any notion how far we are from terra firma, G-man? I wasn't exactly built for treadin' water ya know."

"Not to worry, Benji. Once I detonated that warhead, a search and rescue team should've been immediately dispatched from the stati-…um, from home base."

"Jeez, let's hope so," Ben replied, spitting out a thin spray of sea water, "…'fore a school of Great Whites saunter on by for a quick snack…"

"Mister *Optimism*…strikes…yet again," Marvella grumbled, triggering a snorting guffaw from The Guardsman that sent all three into various stages of uncontrollable hysterics.

Once a semblance of self-control had been reclaimed, all fell silent for several moments as if savoring the unabashed serenity. As the bright rays warmed their moistened flesh and the tiny swells pushed them along like leaves in a brisk fall breeze, they each silently ran the gamut of emotions. From stark fear (rarely if *ever* confessed to within the tiny minority of those labeled 'superhero') to pure, primal rage to unbridled relief, the obstacle course of human emotions had rarely seen such a vigorous workout within such a limited time span. Covering her face with a bare forearm as to ward off the sunlight's glaring intrusion, Marvella's eyes momentarily brimmed with warm tears even as her midsection was briefly racked with tremors. With a gentle stroke of her scalp with the massive palm of his right hand, Ben was able to console without verbal acknowledgement, and felt her hug him ever tighter in response.

Similarly, The Guardsman felt a hollow chasm near his midsection grow ever wider as thoughts turned to either those many stalwart individuals lost while under his charge, or to the man he'd called both boss and friend.

Meanwhile, Benjamin *'Desolation Outlaw'* Thomason pondered an uncertain future. In the final outcome, would the powers that be view him through redemptive eyes or simply as a convicted felon who had assisted in Mind Sweep's demise merely to survive?

Coughing up a mouthful of clear, blue sea water, it was Ben who eventually broke the silence.

"Ya know, I know it's been awhile since myself and Mother Ocean have exchanged tastes, but this is

449

the non-saltiest mix I've ever come across. It's almost like…hell, like *tap* water."

The Guardsman started to respond but paused, instead pointing into the sky with one hand while shielding his eyes with the other.

"Incoming, troops. The Calvary has arrived."

Pumping both his huge fists airborne, Ben wailed like a hyena on helium, inadvertently waking Marvella from a fatigue-induced catnap.

"Hot DAMN! Now that's what I call service! Hot…*DOUBLE-DAMN*!" Thetwin hovercrafts were carbon copies of the one they'd been forced to discard, their oval shapes, shiny slick surfaces and color schemes almost identical, though these were equipped with clear markings ('E. I. ERT') and were at least a size larger in scope.

As one continued to levitate several hundred feet overhead, a set of narrow pontoons emerged from the lower end of the second as it descended to the surface a few dozen yards to the trio's right.

They were then pulled aboard by a two-man crew donned in dark visors and full body coveralls with bright yellow patches that read 'ERT-1' above their left breasts.

"Chief, your presence is requested in the cockpit," the larger of the two men said once they'd been loaded into the rear compartment and each had been handed a cotton towel and matching blanket.

Briskly wiping his face and tossing the towel aside, The Guardsman nodded without speaking as the guard stepped back through the tiny portal leading to the cockpit.

"Back in sec, guys."

"Outta one shit-storm, into another, right G?"

450

Ben asked wearily while pulling a blanket over Marvella's shoulders.

"We all have our burdens, Ben. Can't say I didn't volunteer for the majority of mine."

Once the portal panel shut behind him, The Guardsman reset his cowl and stormed into the cockpit wearing an angry scowl.

"Is this really necessary, Captain? Those people just went through hell on earth, mister. I think the time for keeping secrets is well past."

"Just following regulations, chief," the pilot replied without ever turning from the cockpit controls, "Sergeant Maxwell, initiate operation sleepover."

"Government regulated horseshit..." The Guardsman grumbled as the trooper to his left flicked a series of switches on a separate keypad to the left of the main control panel.

"Initiated, Cap. Compartment locked down and canisters released."

"Affirmative, Max. Give it the required five clicks for the gas to dissipate, then mask up and check the cargo. I'll contact home base to have a med team prepped at the dock."

"Yes, sir," the sergeant replied, sliding his visor up while leaning opposite The Guardsman, whom he regarded with a stern glare. After a moment's silence, the larger man matched the searing gaze with one of his own.

"Something on your mind, Sergeant?"

"Just pondering, Chief."

"Well, don't hold back, son. Ponder aloud if you feel the need."

The troop shuffled his feet from side to side,

though his unblinking stare never wavered.

"I had some good friends on that island, Chief."

"As did I, Sergeant. I lost friends, subordinates, co-workers, and one hell of a boss. Your point?"

"I dunno…seems damned strange that out of over thirty staff personnel, the only salvage is one convicted felon and an outsider with visitor's clearance only…"

The Guardsman leaned up, uncrossing his bulging arms while flashing a pained smile.

"One shouldn't speak of things they have no knowledge of, trooper. I don't answer to correctional CO's…only to a President."

Shrugging, the trooper finally broke eye contact. "But to detonate a goddamn nuke when their mi-"

"Might want to reel in your pet monkey, Captain. To say the very least, I'm *not* in the mood for amateur critiques," The Guardsman interrupted, addressing the pilot while continuing to stare holes into the Sergeant's darting eyes.

"Drop it, Max. You know better. A congressional board will investigate such matters. It isn't our place."

Laughing sarcastically, The Guardsman re-crossed his arms and took a seat behind the empty co-pilot's chair, then leaned back and closed his badly bloodshot eyes.

"Forget it, Cap. The man is justifiably bummed out over the loss of some fine comrades."

Opening his eyes briefly to scan the slumping troop a final time, The Guardsman calmly nodded before re-shutting his eyes.

"Comrades I would've willingly sold my soul

to spare. It…just wasn't…possible. Lord knows, it just wasn't meant to be."

Within minutes, as the twin hovercrafts practically skimmed the sea's surface at jet speed in an easterly direction, the former Chief Correctional Officer of Eagle Island Detention Center fell into a deep, exhaustive slumber. Within the foggy recesses of his tattered mind resided an endless array of frenzied snapshots, like the pages of a photo album turned at warped speed. Snapshots displaying the smiling faces of many of those left behind.

Upon awakening some forty-five minutes later, Lucas T. Bradley, AKA The Guardsman, resigned himself to the cold hard fact that this particular photo album, however haunting, would no doubt remain lodged within his subconscious for the rest of his natural born life.

***

Part IX:

The Edge of Nowhere

"He's fully revived, sir."

"Coherent?"

"Well, he's having no problems cussing the staff, and he's broken two tray tables and put his fist through a metal locker if that's any indica-"

The man hung his head and smiled, pushing his chair back from the wide oak desk he'd been stationed behind.

"Yep, he's awake. I'm on my way."

Moments later, after departing a glass elevator,

the man strolled purposely down a narrow, domed hallway, inhaling and exhaling nervously as if preparing for a rather unpleasant encounter.

He nodded at the armed guard stationed in front of a double-paneled metal door, flashing a badge he'd unhooked from his shirt collar. The guard returned the nod and sidestepped to the left to provide the man clear access.

Pausing to enter a four-digit code into a nearby entry pad, the man sucked in a final deep breath as the panels separated with a low hum.

The man he'd come to see sat on the edge of a king-sized bed, wearing only a pair of boxer briefs and brown sandals; his hair, mustache and beard matted to his flesh like seaweed to a ship's hull. The confined space smelled stoutly of antiseptic and alcohol, and sat in comical disarray, with pieces of broken furniture and chunks of dry wall scattered about like confetti from a street dance.

"Well, I'll be damned," Ben bellowed, hopping from the bed with energetic zest only to swagger drunkenly upon landing, "the prodigal son...*of a bitch* returns! Now maybe I can get some answers, like... who turned the lights out in that hover... where the hell am *I* and where the hell is Leah, in no particular order."

"Whoa, Ben. Inhale, big fella. Take a breath. That sedative is a real corker to shake, I hear. You'll get answers, just take a quick inventory of your faculties, because I flat refuse to perform CPR on your ugly mug."

Stepping forward with a wobbly gait, Ben slapped the other man on the right shoulder, almost tipping over in the aftermath.

"I'm hunky-dory, pal. Rates about a six on the buzz scale. I've had fifths of JB rev me up a hell of a lot higher. So what gives, Luke? Ya look like a fuckin' criminal lawyer or somethin'. Don't tell me you're my court appointed attorney. Aw shit, I'll be hammerin' boulders into pebbles for the rest of my days..."

"Ben," The Guardsman replied coolly, placing his left hand on the larger man's shoulder while his right clutched a clipboard to the button-up dress shirt and tie he wore, "... do me a favor. Sit down and *clam up*. I want to make this as short and sweet as humanly possible. To quote somebody important...time is of the essence."

Reaching to rub the haze from his blurred sight, Ben backed until his rear end rediscovered the edge of the bed and sat down with a huffed moan.

"Shoot, G-Man. I get the feelin' from your tone that I'm fixin' to be handed a shit sandwich with a glass of *federally regulated* piss for a chaser."

"Settle down, Benji. It isn't as bad as all that."

Taking a seat on the opposite end of the bed, The Guardsman gave his former colleague the once over, shaking his head from side to side and unable to conceal a wry smile.

"Damn, you're a mess."

"No arguments. How long I been out, Luke? Feel like Rip Van Wrinkles."

"Just under seventy-four hours. A lifetime in my terms, pal. This has easily been the hardest three days I've managed to survive with my sanity at least partially intact."

"Three days? Why keep me doped for three-"

"Allow me the opportunity to divulge the

Readers Digest version, Ben," the smaller man injected, flashing a bare palm.

"Divulge away, Lucas. Damn, ya even sound like an ambulance chaser."

"Number one…Leah's fine and is on site. She's been paged to meet us here in about ten minutes."

"Whew," Ben sighed, wiping a fresh coating of perspiration from his forehead with a bared forearm. "Great. Thought I'd lost that woman again. Was havin' nightmares about it, man."

"Number two…you're on home base. Safe, sound, and duly secured. More on that later. Now to the true meat of the matter, as Warden Charles V. Terry was apt to say on a semi-regular basis…"

The Guardsman stood, having laid the clipboard on the far corner of the bed, and began pacing the twenty by twenty-five room like an expectant father in a hospital maternity ward.

"If I get ahead of myself, just chuck a shoe at me, old buddy. I've slept all of three, four hours since we escaped Eagle Isle."

Ben cocked an eyebrow while raising a bare foot airborne.

"Smart ass," The Guardsman groaned, halting momentarily before again resuming his circular pacing.

"Educate me, Hoss. Lord knows it won't take much."

"All right then, here she goes…"

"Less than three hours after we arrived here, I was subjected to a hearing…actually more like a grilling, from…assigned government representatives concerning the events that led to the destruction of Eagle Island Detention Center.

456

Approximately ten hours later, the verdict came down."

Backing against the room's lone undamaged metal locker, he sighed deeply before continuing.

"Hit me with it, Luke. What's the worst they could do, *double* my life sentence?"

"It was ruled the destruction of Eagle Island was justifiable under set security guidelines. Wasn't a landslide by any means, though. I was later told the vote was only three-two. The panel voted that a lack of viable security was to blame."

"No shit," Ben replied with a wink. "Mind Sweep pretty much had a free run of the place."

"That, and I informed the panel the creature housed on *Level X* was deemed a non-security risk long before construction on Eagle Island was even complete."

"That's another thing, hoss. Ya never got back with me on that. What the hell was that thing anyhow?"

The Guardsman shrugged and massaged his temples with outstretched fingers.

"As I understand it, the site was built *around* that thing. Only Charles, um, Warden Terry was privy to the details. Legend and scuttlebutt had it that the thing had been dug up on some mid-eastern expedition back in the mid-nineteen twenties and labeled a fossilized hunk of DNA from one of the ancient ones of *Cthulhu Mythos* fame. Only thing I could figure is that Mind Sweep was able to awaken it somehow…draw it out for what he called the 'ultimate' battle. Crazy bastard fed it energy and allowed it to nurture until it ate his alien rear end for lunch.

457

"The panel also cited Mystic, Director Willis and Doctor James as criminal accomplices, although it's unknown if they were somehow controlled or entranced by the power of that damned talisman. There's even an FBI investigation underway concerning a string of sadistic murders they think Willis might've been responsible for before you guys left Wyoming."

"*Bullshit*, Luke," Ben bellowed angrily, "don't know about Willis or the doc, but the green fairy knew exactly what he was doin'. He was in it for the fame, straight up. Remember what he told us just before Sweep waxed his queer ass in that warehouse? Sweep had promised him fame and fortune, which is all the enticement that little shit ever needed to turn to the dark side. Hell, he offed Crimson Condor and framed me for nothin' more than a pat on the back and a bolded headline on his fuckin' website."

"Speaking of which, Ben. In light of what both Leah and I divulged about Mystic's character, or lack thereof, the panel agreed… to grant you a full pardon in that particular conviction."

Ben clapped his massive palms together, causing the other man to involuntarily flinch back.

"Justice is only partially blind after all!"

"That said, there is the matter of the second conviction."

"Yep, there is that," Ben mumbled, his chin dipping onto his upper chest in apparent defeat.

"You've been assigned to me as a trustee of the newly formed *World Corrections Alliance*, a United Nations backed agency spearheaded by the Pentagon."

458

Cocking an eyebrow, Ben's head tilted dramatically to the left.

"Trustee? *World* Corrections…? Okay-dokie, spill the beans, Mac. Spell it out in layman's terms for idiots."

Smiling as he strolled over, The Guardsman crossed his arms over his chest and propped his chin atop a curled fist.

"Going to take a truckload of effort on your part, Ben, but I wouldn't have proposed it if I didn't think you were up to the task."

"Hell's Bell's, Luke…" the larger man spat, rolling his eyes impatiently. "They're rebuilding the site, Ben. The United Nations already has nine separate construction crews from five countries working on the blueprint, not to mention three teams of handpicked eggheads to handle the particulars of making damn certain what happened with Mind Sweep cannot and *will not* transpire again.

"Believe it or not, they hope to have it built and completely functional in ninety days.

"Once she's operational, you're looking at the newly assigned warden." Beaming, Ben reached up and slapped the smaller man across the shoulder.

"Damn, congrats G-Man. They picked the right hard-ass, that's for sure."

"Going to need a kick-butt, take no sass, hard as nails Chief Correctional Officer by my side, Benji."

The big man's lower jaw dropped like a shattered hinge as his eyes widened to coffee saucer capacity.

"Aw shit, ya gotta be…"

459

"You're the one individual I didn't even hesitate to recommend, old buddy." Ben's lips parted to respond, a single hand frozen in mid-air. After several swallows and a deep breath, he managed to regain the power of speech. "Me, the head screw? Damn, Luke...Uh...I'm...um...shit, I ain't accustomed to bein' struck speechless, man. Ya mean it? They...you're willin' to take that big of a chance on my gnarly ass?"

"Well, me and the United Nations Penal board, yes..." Throwing his arms up in jest, Ben scowled playfully. "Aw, is that all? No pressure there."

"Well, at least you won't be facing such a monumental task alone."

"Meanin'?"

"Now Ben, I know that besides your work with the Revenge Squad you've always been the loner type, but I do believe this new partnership will be to your lik-"

The paneled entrance slid apart with a whooshing sound, effectively cutting off whatever had remained of The Guardsman's reply.

"Officially reporting for duty, Mister Warden in Training Sir!" announced the newest visitor, essentially marching into the room like a goose-stepping infantryman, "I take it this is the clown you've assigned as my new partner?"

His face having turned from pasty white to glowing maroon and back again, Ben practically floated from the bed with his arms spread wide.

"Leah! You're my...your gonna be..."he rambled, turning towards The Guardsman even as he scooped Marvella into his arms and lifted her from the tiled floor as if hoisting a cardboard cutout,

460

"ya mean,Leah and me…partners…the *three* of us in charge…"

"It's your unique style with the English language that swayed me, big guy," The Guardsman said with a smile, easily the most sincere, *with feeling* gesture he'd displayed in weeks.

"Put me down, ya big ape," Marvella spewed between giggles, the dark blue uniform shirt she adorned being pulled loose from a similarly shaded pair of creased khaki pants. Unmasked with her hair twisted into a tightly wound pigtail that ran the length of her back, she more resembled a state trooper sans the required insignia.

He spun her around twice more before complying, leaning forward with pursed lips to administer a quick smack on her left cheek before backing away in an impromptu 'curly' dance.

"This is a dream, right babe? Shit like this just don't happen to Ben Thomason without dire consequences creepin' over the horizon."

"I won't lie to you, Benji. Like I've discussed with Leah, whose title is Female CO in charge by the way, you'll both be required to learn at least four languages. Spanish, Russian, French and Chinese, and that's only the beginning."

Halting his wild jig in mid-step, Ben whirled about with a warped grin. "Man, I ain't never officially been certified in English."

"I'm serious, Benji. The new site will be the first *Global* Penitentiary, thus we'll be charged to house specially 'endowed' inmates from several countries. Plus which, you two will be in charge of training the correctional staff, who will all be required to possess at least one serviceable

461

superpower of their own. Leah has no qualms whatsoever. You?"

The big man shrugged, smiling ever wider while stepping forward with an extended hand.

"Not real sure what a qualm is, Hoss, but I guess I ain't got none either. Count me in, Luke. I won't disappoint ya."

"Well then, welcome aboard…Hoss," The Guardsman replied, reaching around to slap the larger man's exposed palm in a 'low-five' gesture.

"The Revenge Squad reformed," Marvella beamed, "no doubt the World has been waiting with bated breath for this historic moment."

The trio stood back and laughed as one, then came together in a spontaneous group 'hug' that best resembled a mini football huddle.

***

"Apologize for the temporary wardrobe, Ben. Home base laundry isn't used to fitting folks with fifty-something inch chests and thirty-inch waists."

Peering down at himself, Ben couldn't help but snicker along with Marvella, who stood directly behind him once they'd entered the relatively small, circular room which was utterly void of furniture of any type.

"Don't sweat it, pal. Gotta admit though, this robe would make me right at home at Hefner Mansion. Looks like Walt Disney heaved all over it…several times."

"I'll get with you about uniforms later. You'll need to decide on a design. Meanwhile, as to your earlier question concerning our present location…"

The Guardsman pointed him towards a paneled wall that took up the majority of the room.

"Allow me to solve that little mystery."

Stepping over to the wall, he pushed an octagon shaped button from just beneath the panel's lower edge.

As the panel slid gradually to the left, essentially revealing the entire room as nothing more than a specially designed 'observation tower' of sorts, Ben's throat hitched noisily.

"Well, ain't that a kick in the gonads."

"Sure caught me off guard," Marvella said, resting an elbow on Ben's shoulder, "makes perfect sense if you really think about it."

"Over two decades in the making it was," The Guardsman added, "station took almost fifteen, counting the planning phase. The isle itself was another five or six in the blue book stage before the first brick was lain or the first force-field set."

Ben stood glassy eyed, nodding in a surreal mix of dumbstruck awe and comical bemusement.

"Yeah, but…what about that damned hurricane we flew through? Ya tellin' me that was man-made?"

"Not at all, Benji. See about three or four of those a year, much like the East and Southern coasts of the good ol' US of A. Scientists simply couldn't find a way to control or alter the atmospheric conditions that spawn 'em…thus the dome field had a separate use other than being the last line of security on the isle."

Shuffling forward as if entranced, Ben practically stuck his nose to the glass window while slapping both palms to the cool, slick surface.

"Far out, man…the final frontier…"

Marvella grinned mischievously, now massaging her lover's shoulders with both hands.

"Literally."

The nearest of what appeared to be an infinite number of stars blinked and sparkled like a Christmas tree light, blanketed in a bluish haze that dominated the vast horizon as far as their limited visibility allowed. The occasional meteorite particle floated by, as did patches of whitish fog in various shapes and sizes.

"They're already working on a new title for home base," The Guardsman concluded, "somehow *Eagle Island Space Station* just isn't appropriate any longer."

"Where's home?" Ben whispered, reaching back to pull Marvella close. "Eight million or so miles, give or take. Most assigned to the station are on one to two-year tours. Station has limited family housing. We all take our weekends here. Has all the amenities. Leah's assignment is still being ironed out. Ben, the board wants you assigned for at least five years. It's…part of the trustee slash employee deal I hashed out with them. Hope you don't mind. You won't be seeing Mother Earth for quite a spell, old pal."

"G-Man, considerin' the alternative I just left back on that sand dune, ya ain't likely to hear complaint one from this here boy," Ben replied in a uncharacteristically subdued tone, reaching back with both of his huge hands to practically engulf Marvella's lower back.

"Come on then," The Guardsman said with a tilt of his head towards the entrance, "grand tour

464

time...ready?"

Forming a single line, they headed for the exit with the newly assigned Warden of a yet-to-be constructed penal colony leading the way.

"Neh, neh," Ben blurted, causing both his ex and future comrades to execute textbook double-takes.

"That's Korean for *yes*, right, Leah?" he asked after a short pause. "Uh...huh...so?" she responded with guarded caution.

"Might as well get started on the language thing. Could be one mean mofo from the far east waitin' in the wings," he blurted proudly while lightly nudging her with an elbow, "thought I only knew the *cuss* words, didn't ya, sweet-thang?"

"Dear Lord help us," Marvella groaned, and all three entered the tubular-shaped corridor wearing wide, toothy smiles.

EPILOGUE

Exactly one-hundred twelve days later:

They stood at attention in four horizontal rows of five to a line, staring straight ahead at a bare stonewall within a tiny, square room engulfed in silence save the sounds of their own breathing.

A door slung open nosily behind him, then slammed shut with a resounding bang, followed by the echoes of hard-soled boots thumping atop a tiled floor.

"Check out what the trash detail dragged in," bellowed a husky male voice. "Pitiful. Looks like twenty separate bags of civilian excrement," replied another, obviously female, and with just a hint of an Asia-based accent.

The male groaned in apparent disgust.

"Yeah, looks like it's up to you an' me to find five po-ten-tial CO's out of twenty walkin' turds. About face, boneheads...NOW!"

The formation, consisting of sixteen males and four females, swung around in almost perfect unison and without a single stumble.

"Listen up, people. I'll make the intros quick and painless before the real agony begins," the female announced. Donned in a red cowl, bright yellow gloves with matching knee-high boots and a skintight black body suit that extenuated her shapely curves, she stepped forward and pointed at the light green patch above her left breast.

"My name is *Marvella*. I am the Assistant Chief Correctional Officer for all assigned CO's and inmates. You can refer to me as either Marvella or

Chief Marvella."

Backing a step, she cocked her head to the left without turning.

"The man standing behind me goes by the name of *Force*. You will refer to him only as Chief. For all assigned CO's to this burg, he is the man in charge."

Stepping up and beside her, the man called Force quietly cleared his throat as the room again fell silent. He wore a similar body suit, only shaded bright red with streaks of dark blue in the shape of barbed wire wrapped around the biceps and wrists. His cowl was light gray, and a thick Fu Manchu styled mustache ran the length of his jaws and off the edges of his squared chin. A silver, chain-linked utility belt wrapped around his slim waist, a large circular buckle with the letter 'F' at its shiny center. The boots he wore were pitch black and meticulously shined.

"Salutations, ladies and gentlemen,' he began calmly, his bulging arms crossed over his barrel-shaped chest, "let's get the formalities out of the way post haste. The Warden will be callin' on us in less than a half-hour to look you over, so this ain't the time for group masturbation, mental or otherwise."

Pacing the front row of the formation, Force paused briefly to look each candidate directly in the eye before moving to the next while displaying an occasional smirk.

"Chief Marvella and I will alone decide who makes the cut here, folks. I'll give it to ya straight, 'cause BS ain't part of the trainin' agenda on this burg. Only three outta the last class cut the mustard.

467

Three outta twenty. Shitty odds, folks. Survival of the fittest kind of scenario. Cut and dry. See, there is a problem here. A quandary, if ya prefer. Not really difficult in terms of solutions. Hell, it ain't complicated at all. There's twenty of ya standin' here. We only need five more. Do the math."

Swinging about abruptly, Force pounded his left fist against his chest, causing several trainees in the front row to flinch back as if physically slapped.

"Ten of ya won't last a week. Another three or four will wash out in week two," he ranted, pacing between the first and second rows while staring down each body he passed, "and by week three it'll be dog eat dog, assholes. Ya might consider yourselves blood kin about now, but come final cut day you'd gladly slash the throat of the man, or woman, next to ya.

"Final construction is set to wrap in four weeks, people. We've got twenty-six inmates from nine different countries landin' here in five.

Nothin' but the elite will be here to greet 'em and help keep 'em in check on a day to day basis.

Now I know all of ya were chosen for your...*special* talents...some great power that separates ya from the civilian populace. Cocky superhero wanna-be's, right? Shiiiitttt..."

He paused after pacing the last row, continuing only once he'd again taken up position beside the female Chief.

"Well, me and the Chief here have seen many the rugged veteran of the hero biz get turned into flesh 'n bone puree by the likes of some of the same creatures you're gonna be tasked to guard. Saw several rough and tumble SOB's bite the big one

468

right here on this very site less than four short months ago. So don't bother tryin' to sell us with *words alone* just how powerful or resilient ya are. Won't...wash. You confer, Chief Marvella?"

"Abso-tively, Chief. It's all about temperament, professionalism, bravery, and other intangibles that one either possesses or doesn't for this kind of work."

Force peered over at his partner and recently announced fiancé and nodded, their secret signal that the initial in-processing brief for recruit CO's was nearing an end. Executing a textbook about-face maneuver of her own, Chief Marvella turned and headed towards the exit.

"To sum up, if ya make the cut, ya sure as hell earned it. A lot of good people died during the last incarnation of this unit. A repeat performance ain't gonna happen on my watch, folks. That's a promise. A select few of ya are gonna help myself and Chief Marvella keep that particular vow."

Force half-turned before halting in his tracks and then resumed an 'at ease' pose at the center of the formation. "Oh yeah, almost forgot...

.... welcome to *Desolation Island*, troops."

www.ingramcontent.com/pod-product-compliance
Lightning Source LLC
Chambersburg PA
CBHW011737010726
47496CB00010B/2972